Street Life

Peter Harrison

ISBN No: 978.1.906542.05.4

Publishers: Barny Books
                Hough on the Hill
                Grantham
                Lincolnshire
                NG32 2BB

                Tel: 01400 250246
                www.barnybooks.biz

Other books written by the same author:

Hovis Brown   978.1.903172.91.9
The Hillbillies   978.1.903172.89.6

Prologue

"Gilbert," whispered the girl, "Gilbert, are you all right?"

The old man opened his eyes and stared through weary eyes at the young nurse. *Fine, nurse,* he mused, *I appreciate being disturbed. I've been sleeping. The same awful dream, younger then and powerful, someone to be reckoned with. The nightmare's always there.*

"Gilbert," said the pretty nurse, "it's such a lovely day I thought we'd walk in the garden, the grounds are beautiful at this time of year. Shall we, Gilbert?" she patted his white mop of hair as if he were a favourite puppy-dog and she waved the leash, "I know you'll like it outside." She was kneeling close to him; her fragrance was exquisite and stirred passions and memories from another era, smelled her breath and gazed at her red, pouting lips. Caressing his thigh she said, "Gilbert, would you like that, a stroll around the grounds?... Talk to me, Gilbert."

I don't want to go outside; I don't like the autumn. Leave me next to the big windows and let the sun warm me, please! His words more frantic now as the short journey commenced and he was wheeled quickly through long corridors. *Don't leave my blankets, nurse, I'm so cold. My feet hurt, my fingers are cold!*

The old man was talking rapidly in his head, telling her to wrap a blanket around his legs and midriff and to put his hands inside the bedspread and not outside on his exposed lap. Gilbert hated the cold, detested the winter, only time he really slept was when the sun scorched his wizened, ancient features. *Why can't anyone hear me any more? Why am I trapped inside this tomb? My mind is working, I have emotions. Can't they see? Don't they understand? I'm alive! I'm alive! Listen to me, I don't want to go outside!*

The wheel-chair slowed as the fellow approached. The nurse greeted the man warmly, chatted pleasantly for some minutes, both occasionally glancing and touching the pensioner. He could hear the gossip, frivolous and light-hearted and all about him as if he were some inanimate object, some alien being, without receptors or antennae, a mannequin, devoid of feelings and emotion.

'How is he today, Nurse Hardy, still nothing? He's still eating well, that's a blessing in itself.' The young man touched and toyed with his father's shoulder, kneading it as if it were human dough, caressed and stroked his neck, 'Still no response, Nurse? No, it's not really important. As long as he's alive, that's all that matters.'

They were lies of course. Gilbert knew that, could see through the ruse; his son, Simon, going through the motion of the loving dutiful son, calling to see his invalid father, his infirm, innate father, a living, breathing vegetable … That's what they thought, unseeing and unfeeling, that's what they imagined. *I can hear every word, do you hear me, Simon. I don't want you here; I don't wish to see you! It was you that caused all of this. Leave me alone, I don't want to go outside in the cold, please!*

The nurse moved aside and allowed the young man to take over the controls of the invalid carriage, a moment's pleasantries followed,

'You are the exception, I'm afraid, and it's usually wives or daughters, and not sons,' she murmured, 'still calling after so long. So few like you these days, so unusual, Doctor. Lots of visitors initially, and then especially if the patient is in need of long-term care they gradually peter out, then it's left to the immediate family.' She nodded with sad resignation, 'Then usually it's birthdays and Christmas. Sad but true.'

The old man was livid, the bile spitting from his thoughts. *Guilty conscience, nurse, that's why the bounder*

4

of a son is visiting, full of remorse because of his despicable act.

"I'll take father for a walk, nurse," said the man earnestly, "the fresh air will do him good."

At the bottom of the ramp, the man stopped and engaged the hand-brake, walked to the front of the wheelchair, 'It's fresh, don't you think, father... invigorating, blow the old cobwebs?' He eased forward and adjusted the blankets, carefully wrapping the material around his father's legs, carefully placed the cripple's hands under the warmth of the blankets, 'There, that's better, don't want you getting cold, do we, father?' The journey continued through the expansive and well-manicured gardens of the nursing-home. They reached a bench close to the ornate pond and the carriage was positioned so that the silent figure had a view of the picturesque setting, and of his dutiful son.

Take me inside, you hear me,' Gilbert mused, *'I don't want to be with you, I can't forgive you ... I'm cold and hungry!*

'I took flowers to mother's grave today, father,' he said softly, reached out and touched the invalid, leaned close and gazed at the dead eyes, 'can you hear me, father? First anniversary for Simone? Remember Simone, father ... your wife?' stared intently into the unseeing orbs, hoping for some movement, some spark of humanity, patted the stiff frame of his father, glanced across at the tree-filled patio, at the dying flowers, the still dark pond. His voice now a whisper, 'Five years, father, you've been here, five years, can you believe that?' He looked at the seated figure, 'and not a word from you. Nothing. You might as well be... dead, like mother.'

I want to die, I don't want this nightmare!

'Mother was so loved,' he gushed, staring at the ground, 'her funeral so perfect. All of her friends called and paid their respects. Didn't know she knew so many famous people. Show business. I know you didn't approve of her friends, father, she told me so often. I remember the arguments, when I was a child, so many arguments. Were you always so controlling, father, did it have to be your way or no way? Mother had dreams, father, and when her health deteriorated she unselfishly thought of me, knew I had talent, pushed me, guided me. Fought you! Remember, father, fought and lost, my life already mapped out by you, had to follow in your footsteps. Always succeeded, didn't you, father? Never gave up on your beliefs. Well, you were the stronger one after all, cared little for mother's feelings, or my talent, wanted me to attend medical school. You won, father but what a price you paid. Lost mum, lost me, but it didn't matter, did it?'

The son stood and slowly walked away from the invalid-carriage and the bench and stood staring at the splendid gardens. 'Mother's dead,' he whispered, 'and all her old friends called and spoke to me. They loved her, said she could have been a star; wrong timing, poor direction ... awful scripts. They told me!' He sighed long and loud. 'Mother was so unlucky. Show-business, they all agreed. Important, powerful people called and paid their respects, Donald Wolfit was one, Johnny Mills another. Roger Livesey phoned personally, Max Wall too; remember him, father, the comedian with the fez and the silly sand-walk, he cried, father, Max Wall, cried for mother, can you believe that?' Simon glanced back and stared for long moments at the living corpse that was his father. He looked so frail and small and vulnerable, difficult to comprehend. He'd been one of the most powerful figures in the community, a man to be reckoned with, a respectable eminent figure of the establishment. *If only they knew the truth about him,* he mused, *the amoral, despicable ogre that was my father.*

Is the guilt making you stare at me, Simon? After so long do the demons still haunt you; can you believe what you have done to me? My failings were never intentional, never pre-planned, I tried to be a good father and protect my only son from destroying his life. I'm not evil, life took me and changed me forever, I never purposely meant to destroy your marriage. It was never premeditated, on the contrary, it was your wife who opened Pandora's Box when she begged for help, when she pleaded for me to approach your lover. It all happened so fast and I was deeply ashamed. I never imagined, especially after so long, that she would tell you about that night, that eventful night.

Simon wandered aimlessly back to the seated, silent figure, 'Come on, father, I'll take you back inside,' he grasped the carriage and walked slowly back towards the main building.

Blame her, Simon, for loving you. She suffered your rebuffs and coldness and still loved you deeply, unconditionally. But really, it was your fault, son, after so long, your gaffe for trying to rekindle the flame of lost love. That's what finally made Elizabeth snap, your unquenchable thirst for that one unreachable person. When she discovered your awful treason after so many years she couldn't take any more pain, decided to inflict torture on you, told you about your precious father and his unforgivable sin, told you all about his awful crime. It worked, didn't it? Destroyed you ... made you fester and plot and plan. Always the coward, son, couldn't face me or confront me, had to bide your time and seize the moment ... behind me, top of the staircase and the explosion of emotion inside your head as you yelled obscenities and pushed!

'There we are father,' he whispered, locking the contraption close to the bed, eased forward and manipulated the small screen, 'safe and warm inside. Few hours watching the television, eh?'

Look at me, Simon! Can't you look at me? I'm talking to you. Remember when you tried to help me, when I was so

7

hurt after your cowardly action and you were crying for me, calling for your mother, realising what you had done? Simon, listen...I put it right, do you hear? I had finally stopped your lover from ever coming back on to the scene. I was trying to tell you that I had avenged Elizabeth. I had evened the score, taken revenge, I thought Elizabeth would realise the sacrifice I had made for her and ultimately for you. Elizabeth misread my actions totally, ridiculed and physically attacked me, said I was evil. I thought I would save your marriage, planned it that way, how could Elizabeth think anything else? I loved my wife, I didn't want to do what I knew I had to do; I loved you, Simon, always have, perhaps too much. My indiscretion, my momentous error all those years ago, but Elizabeth was saying how you didn't love her, believed the marriage was over, I wasn't thinking straight, Simon, I was exhausted after a heavy day at the hospital. Then I was following instructions from Elizabeth, your wife, doing what I thought was right and ... stopping you from making a fool of yourself. I'd had too much to drink, an excuse, perhaps. Simone, your mother, was in the middle of one of her periodic depressions, I felt lonely, isolated. I was vulnerable, son. My fault it happened but I never imagined the grief or pain it would cause. I am so sorry, please believe me, Simon. I should have stayed out of the argument, allowed fate to take its course and then it would have all been so different.

'Father, can you hear me?' whispered the man, leaning across the wheelchair, kissed his distant father tenderly on the cheek, 'I'm going now, father, I'll call next week, okay?'

I told Elizabeth about Mildred... such a monumental mistake but I had to tell her, thought she would be thrilled. It was my way of putting things right between you and Elizabeth, imagined you would stay away from your love, thought it would knock sense into you and make you realise your error. As soon as I told Elizabeth I realised my miscalculation, should have said nothing and allowed your imagination to run riot, because it surely would have ended the affair forever. The outcome you know. Elizabeth not only told you of my awful lapse years ago, dead and buried I thought, but dug the knife deep, twisted and cut me, left nothing to the imagination, and as if that wasn't enough, she told you about my affair with Mildred... said it as I enjoyed destroying someone, withheld the truth. Simon, listen, it was for you. It was all for you and Elizabeth, I wasn't saving one marriage, I was saving two. Simon, don't go. Simon, don't walk away, I'm talking to you!

A male nurse breezed into view, reached the corpse-like figure, said jovially, 'Gilbert, how are you?' fondled the shock of white unkempt hair, 'no one been to see you again, eh?' He moved aside and released the hand-brake, 'Come on then, I'll take you for a slow walk around the gardens. You'd like that, wouldn't you, Gilbert?'

Leave me alone! Please leave me be, I don't want to go outside, I'm so cold.

**

CHAPTER ONE

Jack and Joseph Connelly were brothers; Jack, five years old, fair and slight and Joe, dark-hared and stocky, almost eleven, in his final year before the transfer to the Secondary at the nearby Waterworks. They lived with their mother, Vera and their grandmother, Annie Goodrich, in Easington Village, Durham. Jack's recollection of his absent father was dimming by the day and he had to rely on his brother to fit the jigsaw together. Fact was Jack relied on big brother for most things, more like a father than an older brother, a mentor and teacher. Something special was Joe Connelly.

"Tell me a story, Joe," said the kid, close enough to feel the body heat, "you promised."

The brothers shared a double bed in the biggest bedroom in their grandmother's council semi. In one corner stood their mother's single bed, *'Cramped,'* said Joe, *'Cosy,'* said the kid, close enough to hear Ma's breathing at night. Comforting for both.

Joe was tired, hadn't long been back from the cinema. Good show too, *Gunga Din,* twenty years old and still powerful enough to pull a few midweek punters. "Close your eyes then, Jack," he said, knew it was guaranteed to send him to sleep.

Joseph started telling his baby brother about the adventure story, special effects thrown in for free, reached the part where the water-carrier was shot and fell from the Golden Temple, made a little sound mimicking *Gunga Din's* stirring bugle call, sounded exactly the same, even perfected the dying man's final blows, out-of-key and desperate, sounded so good he repeated it twice. Glanced at Jack and smiled, his kid brother was fast asleep.

Joe had spent the evening at the *Rialto* Picture House with new friends, Davy Duckworth and Sammy

McAndrew, wanted to tell his kid brother about the incident at the cinema. He was still unnerved and upset, wanted to share the burden with Jack. If he'd been a bit older, Jack would have heard about the pervert who sat next to them. Bold as brass he was, an old man but big and powerful-looking. It was Sammy who gave Joe the nod, who then nudged Davy, and all three watched the stranger slowly change his seat time and time again, each move brought him closer to the boys until he was sitting next to Davy. The trio were stupefied with fear and stared hopelessly at the big screen. The actor pretending to be Rudyard Kipling, expelled the virtues of *Gunga Gin,* ex-water-carrier and now honoured as a brave soldier and the schoolboys feigning wonder at the golden screen, hearts aching, wondering when the pervert was going to act, the night's entertainment going rapidly down the plug-hole as their minds raced with fearful expectation. Davy not able to wait for the rolling credits, said loudly, *'Going to the toilet,'* and moved along the crowded aisles for the lavatories, Joe breathless now that the stranger was so close to him. Then the clatter of the upturned seat as the man, Morris Buckingham, a known homosexual and predator, hurried to the toilets after Davy Duckworth, wrongly thinking the boy wanted to play. Sammy whispering anxiously, *'Shall we go, Joe?'* not waiting for an answer as he made his way to the exit door, Joe Connelly following slowly, looking for his pal, seeing him running up the central isle, waving frantically at him, *'Joe, come on!'* The usher, torch splattering and searching like a deranged, gung-ho air-craft beacon, calling for order, *'Settle down, you lot or you'll be barred!'*

The boys, now safely outside and already scampering away from the colliery cinema, headed for Easington Village and home, ran comfortably, periodically glancing over their shoulders. Joe recognised the big frame and the shock of white hair hurrying from the building. *'I see him!'*

he gasped, and the race became more urgent, more frantic now. Joe still the bravest of the bunch, strong enough to turn and yell, *'Pervert! Pervert!'*

Tomorrow was the start of a brand-new school-term and Joe wasn't looking forward to it, apprehensive, even scared. The Head teacher and he didn't see eye to eye. The six-week school holiday had scorched past, thought it would never end. Passed in a flash and now it was Mr Albright again. It was a small school and the Head was teaching full-time, concentrating on the final-year pupils. Joe Connelly hated the fat man to distraction, maybe the feeling was mutual because they tended to rub each other the wrong way. Corporal punishment was dished out daily, second nature to Mr Albright, used to buzz about the school-yard with stick or strap in his hand like some demented sergeant-major and Joe felt his wrath more than most. Wanted to tell his Ma, knew he couldn't, not the way she was acting lately. Told his nana who told him to behave himself or he'd get the same off her. Joe closed his eyes and started to drift, back in the *North-West Frontier,* pictured Victor Mclaglen and thought he looked a lot like his Uncle Mick who lived across the road and had pneumoconiosis so bad he could hardly walk. Pictured *Gunga Din,* who looked like a white man covered with brown dye and thought Sabu would have played the part better. Fell asleep playing that tuneless bugle.

Downstairs in the sitting-room the mother and daughter sat either side of the sizzling, spitting coal-fire. After a while, the oldest woman, Annie Goodrich, stout, bottled-blonde and bespectacled, removed the *Woodbine*, threw it into the flames and looked directly at her daughter.

"Made your mind up, Vera?" heart bouncing twelve to the dozen knowing how volatile her daughter was, had to ask, knew she was probably wasting her time.

Five months had past since Vera Connelly had thrown her no-good husband George out of their colliery house, caught him once too often gallivanting where he had no right, which, in hindsight, was a big mistake because after the last shebang he had stayed away. Trouble with Vera was she loved George too much, wore her heart on her sleeve. Years ago, George charmed and romanced her and swept her off her feet. Vera chose to ignore the gossip from all those close to her, the all depressing tittle-tattle, and managed to get herself pregnant with Joe, married almost immediately and settled down to suffer the consequences. '*Wandering eyes,*' said her mother. Never a truer word said, anything in a skirt. The man was without conscience, cared little about his wife or his son but Vera persevered hoping he would settle down, even gave him a second son, absolute double of him, fair-hared, blue-eyed. George didn't stop for air. The final straw came when she found out that George wasn't spending his weekends away from home with the Territorial Army. Away from home, yes, but on a different set of manoeuvres, some little hussy living in Yorkshire. Vera lost it good and proper, smashed dinner-plates over his head, which she immediately regretted. They were a wedding-present and part of a set. George Connelly bolted, fearful of his life. Vera imagined her husband would eventually return as he had in the past but, months later, Vera had to bite the bullet and vacate her colliery house and move in with her widowed mother; wouldn't give up on her philandering husband, wanted to confront him face to face, only then would she know her marriage was over.

"Tomorrow," she said sternly, "Uncle Mick is taking me."

"It's a hell of a drive," said the mother, reaching for another cigarette. Fifty four years old, smoked fifty a day and never ailed, not so much as a bad cough. Her late husband, Bart, never touched a cigarette in his life, dead at thirty with lung cancer. *'Swings and roundabouts,'* Annie used to say; *'when He points the finger your number is up.'*

"Uncle Mick says he doesn't mind."

Married to Mary Jane, thought Annie unkindly, *who could blame him if he wanted a few hours peace away from the woman.*

"What did Mary Jane say about that?"

"The usual, warned Micky off, worried about his chest."

Michael Green, Annie's brother had the symptoms of *Miner's Lung,* pneumoconiosis, fifty-three years old and wheezing like a bellows, been for tests and was waiting for the results. He still worked at the colliery but had been transferred to light work.

"Pontefract, hell of a journey," regurgitated Annie Goodrich, added, "still, can't get lost, turn off the A1 when you see chimney-stacks, follow the signs." Probably would have gone herself if she didn't have to watch the kids, could have made a day of it, stop in a café, bit of a chat, maybe a Guinness or two, forecast was for sun and showers. *Never mind,* she thought, *there'll be other days.*

"Be worth it just to see the look on his face."

"Maybe you should have let George know," *Give him time to run and hide,* "still can't believe Geordie's mother gave you his address."

"Told Dolly Connelly I was there for the duration, wasn't leaving her house until she told me!" Vera's tone angry and resolute, "There's two boys never had a penny-piece in maintenance. Adam put his mother straight about his little brother, *'Ma, you gotta tell Vera, for the boys sake....'* I should have married Adam."

"Not satisfied with one from the Connelly brood?"

"Different kettle of fish is Adam."

Annie Goodrich shook her head, said, "Six and two threes, you ask my opinion." *All the same, never known a man pass on an invitation to a good time, even the*

14

*respectable ones. Roll your eyes, tease and torment and they all fall into the honey-trap. G*lanced at her stubborn daughter, started cleaning her spectacles on her blouse. "About time you put your head on straight, girl."

"Whatever, Ma, I'm going tomorrow and that's a fact!"

Annie said absently, "Have you told Alvin Brown?"

Alvin Brown was under-manager at the co-op store in the village, Alvin had been instrumental in getting her hired as a part-time counter-assistant a month ago, same age, shared schooldays together. He was single and a sucker for a sad story, a lovely, vulnerable and lonely man, had agreed her leave of absence. Easy for Vera to persuade the under-manager, putty in her hands, always was kind and considerate since she'd known him; the couple close friends once, a long time ago. The two used to share secrets. A lifetime ago Alvin Brown had been her rock when she was confused and concerned about her relationship with the scallywag, George Connelly. Alvin fought her corner. He was the only one who cared enough about her to understand the depths of love she had for the collier from Horden, only one to tell her to follow her heart.

"Sorted," she said, her head in Yorkshire wondering what lay in store for her, missed the rascal so much she felt pain in her stomach.

"Nice man is Alvin Brown," said Annie, "been a better bet for you, Vera."

The younger woman shook her head but didn't answer, didn't suffer fools gladly, *Good old Ma, thinking of discounts from Alvin Brown.*

"Alvin Brown is a friend," she replied harshly, "you know that, Ma. He's always been a friend."

Annie Goodrich said, "Friendships have a habit of growing, Vera,"

"Ma, we're friends, nothing more!"

"Hell of a job he's got, old man Mix kicks the bucket and Alvin will be first in line!"

The younger woman tried diplomacy, didn't want to say too much about the under-manager, "He's not my type, Ma, give it a rest!"

Annie shrugged her shoulders, adjusted her spectacles and said, "Man lived alone in *Hall Walk,* opposite the big church, best part of the village, parents long gone, all I'm sayin'...."

"Shut up, Ma!"

"I'll make a cup of tea, Vera," said Annie Goodrich, eased her heavy frame out of the arm-chair and shuffled towards the kitchen. *No respect,* she mused bitterly, *no wonder she can't keep a man.* Thought about her grandchild, said carefully, "Jack's first day at school tomorrow, pet, not fancy taking him yourself?"

"He'll be fine. Joe will look after him," said Vera, stretching for one of her mother's cigarettes, "school's no big deal, Ma."

"Joe always looks after him," replied Annie Goodrich, "more and more ... that's the trouble.

**

It was almost closing time and the chief librarian, Mildred Mix, strutted and strode about the few rooms as if it were her private domain, "Roxanne," she said acidly, as she spied her young assistant tittle-tattling with the teenagers, "a moment, please!" and proceeded to walk elegantly to the main desk.

Roxanne Harper, frumpish and forlorn, huge spectacles hiding most of her moon face, hair sodden with liberal layers of lacquer that allowed her auburn locks to defy gravity and logic, gawked and waited for the rebuff.

"Well, young lady?" demanded the chief librarian, "what have I told you *not* to do?"

"Don't know, Miss," whispered Roxanne, toying with her outsize glasses, glancing nervously at the youths.

16

"Idle gossip, Roxanne," reprimanded the supervisor, "that's what!"

"Miss," responded the girl, "those boys were enquiring about a book. I was only trying to help them find it ... I was confused."

Mildred Mix said sardonically, "Surely you understand the logic of the Dewey-Decimal System by now?"

"I think so, Miss."

"Well?"

"Well, what, Miss?"

"The book, Roxanne, fiction or non-fiction?" said an exasperated chief librarian, puffing with impatience, irritated at her employee. *Fools at work,* she thought, *and fools waiting for me at home!*

"A novel, Miss Mix," whispered the assistant, glanced again at the two youths who smirked and giggled at her.

"Literature," boasted the older woman, "numbers 800 to 899. British or American?"

"D. H. Lawrence, Miss," said Roxanne.

"English ... Nottingham," replied the chief librarian snootily and heard the sniggering from the youths which sent alarm bells off in her head. Staring coldly at the immature boys she croaked, "And the name of this novel, Roxanne?"

"Lady Chatterley's Lover."

Like a storm-trooper Mildred Mix strode angrily towards the shocked youths who, at the last moment, faltered in the face of such a monumental foe and bolted for the exit doors, "How dare you!" barked an incensed Mildred Mix, "how dare you come into my library and inquire about such filth!" The woman stomped back to the desk, glowered at her cowering assistant, *'Stupid Girl!'* she seethed under her breath, glanced at her wrist-watch, minutes to go before lights-out, muttered wearily, "Get your coat, Roxanne, I think we'll call it a night."

Minutes later and Mildred Mix stood alone in the colliery library so tranquil, so peaceful without staff or customers. She wandered up and down the aisles, smiling at the rows of books, proud as punch at her pristine branch, at her status and standing in the neighbourhood. She was the only *female* chief librarian in the immediate locality. Twelve years she'd been top of the tree, still made her feel ecstatic, only *female* chief librarian in the North-East and that was quite an achievement.

Mildred paused momentarily, checked the numbers, 300 – 399 … *Religion,* and moved a few steps forward. *Philosophy and Psychology,* numbers 100 – 199, looked along the long lines of books and spotted the three volumes, ordered by her … well, friendly persuasion, gentle barracking and little white lies about visitors to the library asking her to order texts by the noted Durham psychiatrist, Dr. G. S. Stoker: *Alzheimer's: The Forgotten Few. Living with Alzheimer's Disease. The Scourge of the Aged: The Sad Truth about Alzheimer's.* Mildred Mix could picture him still, a colossus, a gentle compassionate man who broke her heart; beautiful and affectionate, a man who swept her off her feet, loyal to his family, put his wife and sons before himself, sacrificed everything out of a misguided sense of loyalty: missed him then, missed him still.

Mildred Mix sighed long and loud and stared morosely at the text, thinking of the irony of it all, a lifetime of study and for what? *Life's bitter satire,* she thought, so much empathy and soul-searching into the horrid disease, and the quirk of fate mocking his life's work. 'Poor Gilbert,' she mused solemnly, 'my poor, sad Gilbert!'

Tears fell down her face as she remembered his long and lonely demise. She called once to see the physician, near the end, made an excuse about spending a day in Durham, more lies to Delwin, who cared less what she did, made excuses about a conference held in County Hall, *The future of libraries in County Durham*, went to the expense of preparing and photocopying a leaflet for the benefit of her husband, wasted her time and effort. Del Mix lived in a world of his own, lived every day like it was the last day on this earth, heart-scare years ago, a minor angina attack that had forever shaped her husband's morbid and bleak future and now he waited patiently, resigned, for the big-one ... the big-bang! Del Mix was a pathetic creature who lacked gumption and grit and old age only heightened the expectation of his so-called spectacular exit from this world. Of course it never came, the man was a hypochondriac, the slightest pain was enough to scatter him to the local surgery. There wasn't a day past when Mildred Mix did not regret marrying the fool. *'I'll be gone all day,'* she'd warned him, stuffed the photo-copy under his nose and he never gave it a glance. Visited the nursing-home, shaking with trepidation and fear, knew she was taking chances, even informed the nurses she was related, had to see him, if only to say goodbye to Gilbert Stoker. He didn't recognise her, not a glimmer, not a spark, didn't stop her talking to him, told him everything, everything important, kissed him when she finally took her leave. He never once acknowledged her, his old face set in stone, lost in his own private hell, kissed him again and bade a tearful farewell.

The telephone buzzed and brought Mildred back to the present, she hurried from the aisles and picked up the receiver, "Yes, son," she said calmly, "I'm coming home now, Albert. Is your father there, Albert? He's asleep on the couch .... no, leave him, I'll sort it out, Mummy will sort it out!"

Her youngest, Albert Gilbert Mix, her own pride and joy. Some-day, she promised, she would tell her boy everything.

**

CHAPTER TWO

"Don't leave me, Joe," begged the kid.

Joe said, "Stand by that door, Jack, that's your classroom. It's Mrs Wainwright's. She's nice." He was anxious to get on the small playing field to play marbles with Henry Mitchell.

"I'm scared Joe," whined the boy.

It was almost nine-o-clock and the start of lessons and the few marbles Joe possessed were jangling loud in his trouser pocket, knew he could beat snotty-nosed Henry seven days a week, muttered under his breath, "Come on, our kid, I'll show you round the place." The game could be played later, break-time, lunch-time. Stopped in his tracks when he spotted the mooching adult, "That's Albright over there," he said, "let's go," led his brother to the safety of the first-year classroom, out of sight of the headmaster.

"Is that the nasty one, Joe?"

Joe said, "Horrible! Normally he carries a stick. We'll wait …."

Albright loomed out of nowhere, roly-poly, moustachioed, sour-faced. He interrupted, snapped, "Well, Connelly, what's going on?"

"My brother, sir," quaked Joe, "it's his first day!"

"Another headache for me, no doubt," grunted the man, glowered like a walrus as he glanced at the fearful newcomer. "Name?"

Jack instinctively grasped his brother's hand for comfort, pouted and dithered.

"Jack, sir," offered Joe, "his name is Jack Connelly."

"No manners, boy, cat got your tongue? Not like your brother are you, has an opinion on everything!" Beady eyes darted towards the oldest boy, "Isn't that right, sonny?"

A mother strode into view, pulling at her distraught and tearful daughter and stopped the discussion dead. The demeanour of the teacher immediately altered, his face cracked into something resembling a smile, focused on the woman and her sniffling child, gave the adult the usual spiel, calmed the girl enough for her to relinquish her grip on her mother, "Be okay, dear," soothed the teacher, "leave her with little Jack, he's another starter, let them talk some. Come along with me, Missus," turned to the anguished girl and pointed an official finger at her. "Be a good girl now," he said, "whistle's going to sound any moment … stand with Jack." He led the mother out of sight leaving the perturbed trio in a quandary.

Moments passed before Joe said, "Jack, do as the teacher says and watch the girl," and slapped him playfully on the head, still buzzing to take booty off Henry Mitchell. "Don't move, right?" he ordered, then ran away to find his friends.

Jack Connelly suddenly felt better. He wasn't crying which was more than could be said for the girl whose palms were lifted and wrapped over her distressed and sniffling features.

"Don't cry," he said, trying to put on a brave face, realised he did not know her name. "I'm Jack," he said, "what's yours?"

The sobbing stopped and the girl's face lifted into view, "Alice."

"Alice what?"

"Alice Raine," she answered bravely, wiped a sleeve over her face.

"Be alright," he said, "I'll look after you."

"Ma promised me she'd not leave until the teacher came," stammered the tot, "I don't know where to go or what to do."

Jack gestured to the classroom, "That's where we go, think we've got to wait until some teacher blows a whistle or rings a bell." He remembered Joe's instructions.

"Aren't you scared?"

"Of course not," he lied, stuck out his hand, "give me your hand, Alice, I'll look after you," felt her fingers intertwine with his, lifted his spirits and his strength soared, knew he could get through the day.

An adult voice screamed in the distance, *'Line up! Line up!'* and a hand-bell started clanking noisily. The girl visibly jumped, squeezed his hand tight and snuggled up close to her protector. Somehow Jack was able to hide his terror, told her matter of fact they would look for their class-line.

"Don't leave me, Jack," pleaded the girl and followed the boy towards the central area.

Alice Raine didn't leave go of his hand until the female teacher persuaded her to do so.

**

Vera Connelly left her Uncle in the car next to the shops. Micky didn't complain, hated confrontation and was already starting to regret his decision to get involved with Vera's private life, saw everything through rose-tinted spectacles, imagined a leisurely drive with his niece, maybe a draught of ale in one of the Pontefract pubs, a welcome break from the humdrum life of the colliery. He thought of George Connelly, quite liked the young man, nothing really to dislike about him, apart from his dalliances. He was happy, funny, and considerate, the few times they'd drank together. George was generous, shame really, it was only the one flaw that buggered everything well and proper. He was a charmer, couldn't stop himself, thought Micky Green. He'd even made a play for Mary Jane, his wife of twenty five years and in front of him! Mary Jane, eighteen stone and growing, thought his wife would be immune from the lothario, God, even he didn't fancy panky-panky with Mary Jane any more. Only married her because he wanted a quiet life, seen the trouble a woman could inflict

22

when they wandered, go no further than his own sister, Annie, married Barty Goodrich and tortured him for years with her loose ways. Wasn't cancer that finished old Barty, it was grief. He remembered the effect that George's magnetism had on his overweight, frumpy wife, one month later and she still struggled with her diet, only stopped when George Connelly focused on someone else and ignored her. *Patent what George had and I'd be rich,* he sniggered to himself. Hell, it wasn't George's fault he was so popular, see a mile off what kind of man he was, loved himself did George, the mirror fixed to his shoulder was a dead giveaway, his smooth patter told the same story, not his fault women were so naïve and gullible. Told Vera same as he told his own Mary Jane, *Man's got the gift of the gab, fool if you don't know it, blind if you can't see it.*

Like talking to a wall, talking to a woman smitten.

Windows and the front door were spotless and Vera didn't know whether to be pleased or not. *So she's clean,* thought the visitor, then cast such thoughts aside, *means nothing at all, could be all show for the neighbours,* fooling herself, knocked quietly, wanted to surprise the hussy, maybe slap sense into her, bawl at George enough to get him to return. Hell, it had been months, George had to be sick of her by now. No one answered so Vera seized the steel door-knob and rapped hard enough to wake the dead.

A small girl answered the door, so small that she struggled to reach the handle, blonde ringlets danced about her cherub features as she smiled at the stranger. *Two, three years old,* thought Vera Connelly, *good enough for Miss Pears.*

"Honey," said the woman, feeding the poppet with a smile, knew it wasn't the kid's fault her mother was a whore, not the kid's fault her mother couldn't keep a husband, "tell your Ma, will you?"

The small girl said innocently, "Mummy is at the shop with our George, I'll tell daddy," the smile a permanent fixture as she nodded and disappeared.

"Who is it, Samantha?" said the man, then his words froze as he pushed his whiskered head into view.

"George?" spluttered Vera, gawking at her husband who stood stiff and dumbstruck, looked silly in white vest, trousers loose about his hips, threadbare slippers on his feet, like he *belonged* there.

"Vera!" his tone pitched high with the unexpected shock of confrontation.

The little girl struggled between the man and the door, glanced up and said, "Daddy?"

"Daddy," gasped Vera Connelly, eyes riveted on the girl who stretched her arms in the air and demanded attention from the man, looked at him with tears in her eyes, "she's your daughter?"

There was commotion behind. Vera turned and saw a female close by, heavily pregnant, carrier-bag in one hand, and standing next to her, grimacing, features grey with apprehension, was a five year old boy who glowered at the stranger. The woman was small and dumpy, shape like an Easter egg, face the same, round and fleshy, pan-shaped and puffy. Vera was in denial.

"This is her," she gasped at George, "this is the one you left me for?" A manic smile cracked over pained features; eyes rolled with disbelief as she focussed on the other woman. "The state of you," she spat venomously, "no wonder your husband binned you."

"George is my husband," the woman stammered; still holding the shopping and the boy, voice faltering as she waited for the explosion, "common-law."

"Been busy, have we?" grunted Vera, glaring at the silent boy, before nodding at the woman's pendulous stomach.

24

"They're my kids, Vera," stuttered George Connelly, picked up his daughter and cuddled her, more for protection than a sense of love. Knew all about her temper, felt her tongue and her fists more than once, "All three," he whispered, unconsciously back-tracking into the home.

Something happened inside Vera's head. She felt a deep rush of anger, screamed to the heavens then hurled herself forward after her retreating husband, attacking him savagely. Didn't care that he held the girl, *The bastard,* like the son and the child in the womb, *bastards all,* threw a punch so hard and so fast it caught the man flush on the nose. Blood erupted like a geyser and covered George Connelly and his demented daughter and both collapsed back into the house; the fellow moaning, the daughter screaming. The pregnant female dropped her shopping, abandoned her son and bolted along the terraced street. The boy, crying and gesticulating frantically, ran after his mother.

Vera Connelly felt a mist covering her, slowing and calming her. Stepped into the stranger's home, plucked the girl from the flailing arms of the man and placed her absently to one side like an unwanted parcel. She straddled her husband, "George," she whispered pathetically, her temper disappearing, reason and sanity returning like a switch clicking on, "talk to me George, tell me it's not true?" He turned on his stomach, holding his bloodied hand over the wound, vainly trying to stem the flow, shielding his face from further attacks. "One more chance, George," she gasped at the squirming figure, "please George, give me one more chance, for the boys sake. Joe misses you so much, cries every night for you."

"Let me alone, Vera," said the prostrate man, "it's over between me and you."

"Don't believe it, George," whispered the female, *She's so ugly, George.* Thought she was dreaming, any minute and she'd wake up from the nightmare, remembered his lame excuses from way back when. Used to reassure her when they rowed about his flirtatious ways, *'Couldn't fuck fat, Vera,'* he once said. In the Colliery Club at the time, caught him chatting up Linda Bellingham, hand on her fat arse, slapped him then, slapped him all the way home. Next day he had almost convinced her about his loathing for blubber. *'Run a mile from big girls!'* Gave him another chance. She always gave George another chance.

"Please, George," she begged, "come home, promise I'll not say a thing. Come on, love, pack your bags and let's go. Uncle Mick is waiting in the next street, got the car, George." *Don't you love me any more, George. I love you, George, always have…said I was pretty, George, said I was the prettiest girl in Easington, George. Look at me one last time, George. I'm beautiful, you told me!*

Vera couldn't remember leaving George, vaguely recalled climbing into Uncle Mick's Ford *Popular* and causing a scene, shouting at her poor Uncle until she could shout no more. The return journey became a nightmare as the reality slowly hit her, Micky the scapegoat as she unburdened her sorrow.

Vera, sobbing, upset, wailed at her relation, "Uncle Mick, what can I do? I'm thirty years old with two kids to support. No maintenance from their father. Who'll want me, Uncle Mick?"

"Be all right, pet," answered Micky Green, thought about the long journey home, *Fool for getting involved,* he thought, had enough troubles of his own, "can't say you haven't tried, Vera."

"George has been leading a double-life, Uncle Mick!"

"The bastard," muttered the man, pushed his foot hard on the gas pedal, thinking ruefully, *Christ, another two hours of this!*

"Hate him, Uncle Mick," sobbed a distraught Vera Connelly, "hope I've broke his bloody nose!"

Should have broken something else while you were at it, thought the man, scorching along the motorway, body slouched, chest heaving with discomfort, *maybe snap something in half!*

Vera Connelly cried all the way home. By the time the journey ended in Durham, Uncle Micky was weeping too.

**

The queue of customers made him irritable. Two old dears in front of him were like excited hens, never stopped for breath, their turn at the counter and they were so engrossed with the petty gossip that Morris Buckingham intervened. "Missus", he snapped impatiently at the taller of the pair, headscarf tied so tight could have caused a headache, "some of us have work to do, haven't got all day to chat!" A blatant lie of course, hadn't worked for ages but the old woman didn't know that. The short dumpling next to the witch with the headscarf wasn't shy with her acerbic comment, "How dare you talk to us like that?" she barked, loud enough for all to hear, "ought to tell my husband... never been so insulted!"

Morris Buckingham grimaced and snarled, glowered at one, then the other, made his point perfectly clear without uttering a word.

The slim, well-dressed assistant behind the counter interjected, attempting to take the heat out of the confrontation. Smiled genuinely and said, "Ladies, I'll serve you now!"

Felicity Bellows turned away from the obnoxious stranger, forced a smile, said, "Staff missing again, Mr Brown... managers don't normally serve?"

Alvin Brown, under-manager, grinned infectiously. He answered warmly, "One of the girls needed time off, Mrs Bellows."

"So it's temporary then," asked Norah Chapman, fiddling nervously with her headscarf, focussing on the assistant, wanting to be served quickly and out of the store. The old man breathing down her neck made her anxious, could feel her heart flutter.

Mr Brown nodded, asked politely, "Right, ladies, what would you like today?"

"Best butter, about half a pound in weight, Mr Brown, bit more if the cut is generous."

Alvin Brown pulled an enormous block of butter into view, took the wire-cutter and began expertly slicing off a chunky bar, weighed it, crunched his featured and said, "It's a bit on the heavy side, will I cut some off, Mrs Bellows?"

"That'll do fine, young man," said the pensioner, adding, "small bag of sugar, pet, couple of slices of side-bacon … on the heavy side." Handed over the list, glanced determinedly at the glowering stranger, "and these, Mr Brown!"

Ten minutes later the women sauntered towards the double-door of the co-op store. As she opened the door her companion glared at the white-haired stranger, stepped out into the cold September day, her companion dutifully followed, swivelled and made as if to close the door, stared sullenly for some moments at the ill-mannered, uncouth man who was finally being served. She slammed the door loudly.

Morris Buckingham handed over his note, eyed the under-manager, got the feeling he was in the presence of some like-minded chap. Shopped at the store once maybe twice a week, always felt the young man's gaze on him, took a chance at intimacy, said casually, "Mr Brown is it, didn't know you were a manager, thought Mr Mix was in charge of the place?"

"Mr Mix is manager," answered the young assistant, pushing his thinning locks unconsciously over his balding pate. "I'm the under-manager," stared a little too long, felt the man was a kindred soul, assessed the situation, thought he was too old to be of real interest.

"Mr Mix is absent again," asked Morris Buckingham, "never seem to see him anymore."

"Upstairs," said Alvin Brown scanning the hand-written note, impressed with the style and fluency and the lack of errors, fellow wasn't only a pretty face. *Too old* he thought, *much too old!* "You know Mr Mix, do you?"

"Very well, known him all my life," said Morris Buckingham, a wry smile on his wizened face. *Brother-in-law,* he thought wistfully, *one of the few decent men he'd ever met, a lovely man who always followed his heart,* sighed, could never understand the attraction of his arrogant, snooty, pain-in-the-arse sister. *Always followed his heart... his only flaw!*

"The main office is on the first floor," said Alvin Brown, "Mr Mix works there, occasionally graces us with his presence. He runs a tight ship!"

Morris Buckingham said impulsively, "Is he in now, maybe I could call and see him?"

Ever the loyal under-manager, Alvin Brown answered, "I'm afraid he's running late today... doctor's appointment."

"Always liked doctors," said the older man, thinking, *could be kind and say he was a hypochondriac.*

"Pardon me?"

"Suffered for years," offered Morris Buckingham, "ill health."

"Yes," agreed the under-manager, "how right you are. Poor Mr Mix has been struggling for some time!"

A little after five-o-clock and Alvin Brown locked up the double-doors to the store, shivered involuntary at the coolness of the evening, stood moments as he fastened his overcoat, gathered his shopping-bag and set off for his home at the western boundary of the village. A stiff breeze suddenly buffeted him as he set off from the co-op building towards the steep incline that led to the church, the highest vantage point of the village. He could always find his way home when he was a child thanks to the imposing Norman edifice, couldn't ever lose his way ...the church, the primary school then home situated in the private cul-de-sac of *Hall Walk*.

Alvin walked nimbly, reckoned he could reach home in under ten minutes if he didn't saunter or see familiar faces. He had lived all of his life in Easington Village, knew every nook and cranny, loved the place, the people, the camaraderie, never ever wanted to leave the area. Hadn't the slightest inkling to see new places, felt comfortable, felt a part of the place. He checked his watch, almost five-thirty, walked and imagined his night, liked to keep busy, on the go, active, didn't want the stench of loneliness scratching him, only made him susceptible and open to weakness and vulnerability. Only drawback living in a goldfish-bowl, folks tended to know your business and Alvin had secrets that he could not share with too many people. He was gay, a queer. Once, years ago, and still struggling through the rough and tumble of secondary school in the killing-fields of the nearby colliery, he had been called a faggot by Henry Houseman, one of the local riff-raff bullies who dominated the school, called a faggot because he refused to play football, and got a bloody nose from the horrid boy. Alvin Brown made the fateful mistake of telling his mother, first and last time, saw the initial look on her face that said it all, as if she'd been waiting all her life for confirmation, recovered quickly enough to say, *Meatball... bundle of sticks,* but Alvin knew when his mother was covering her tracks. First and last time for Alvin to confide in his mother.

Fourteen years of age and he started accepting the fact that he was different. He liked girls, always preferred their company to the macho homophobic bedlam of his male counterparts, his best friend, until she eventually married, was Vera Goodrich, loved Vera, shared everything with her, even told her about his sexuality, in his bedroom at the time, sipping from a stolen bottle of sherry and a little tipsy with the effects of the alcohol, blurting it all out, weeping softly because he was at a loss as to what to do. Vera was a good person, didn't poke fun at him, laugh at him, or even try and change him, told him Jesus made us all different and he had to follow his heart.

Now he was thirty and a bachelor who lived a lie and told no one about his penchant and his inclinations, only Vera Goodrich or Vera Connelly as she was now known, knew about his dark secret. Thirty years old and lonely, aching for someone to come into his life, knowing his chances at finding such a person was close to zero. He rarely socialised, didn't frequent the pubs and Workingmen's Clubs that dotted the area, tried it over the years but always came away feeling more lonely and desperate than before. Alvin was a home-bird longing for companionship and love, resigned to the fact that fate had dealt him a cruel blow. Knowing, deep down, a move to another location, maybe a big city with its myriad facades and faces would suit him better, heard so much about the seedier places … Soho, London, but lacked the guile or the resolve to make the move. In a rut, loved Easington and its people but wished it were different, wished it would cater for more of his type.

Alvin Brown thought again of the stranger who had shopped in his store that very day. Tall, craggy-looking, maybe in his fifties or early sixties, tried to remember his name. Alvin could tell the man was like-minded, a homosexual, looked in his eyes and held his gaze, could have sworn the fellow was keen; it was as if Alvin had a sixth-sense, because electricity tingled through his body. Not the first time either, the man had shopped occasionally and always stared too long at the under-manager, actually

31

started a conversation today, well-spoken too. *Too old,* thought Alvin ruefully, *old enough to be my father,* wished now he had talked more to the chap, should have taken a chance. He was so lonely, desperate for company, any company, old or young. Thirty years old and never had he tasted an affair, always ran a mile when fate intervened and thrust some titbit his way, fearful of rejection, terrified of the consequences. Small town gossip could destroy him; take away his career and his standing in the community. Alvin Brown had respect from those close to him, his boss, his work-mates and he did not want to jeopardise a lifetime's work.

He reached the apex of the incline and the exertions made him perspire, kept his punishing stride going, hurried past the pub, *The Seven Sisters,* still in darkness, another hour and the lights would shine out like a beacon to the thirsty moths. The road levelled and then slowly dipped, the home-stretch now and he could taste the hot sweet tea, checked his wrist-watch again, decided to visit the library later that evening, maybe spend an hour perusing and wondered if the obnoxious Chief Librarian, Mrs Mix - his boss's horrid wife - had ordered the A. J. Cronin book, *The Citadel,* tried for the past two weeks to obtain the novel, approached the unapproachable female and was rebuffed each time with flimsy excuses, *'I'll send you a card, Mr Brown, now please, let me do my work!'* Alvin Brown could not see what attracted Delwin Mix to such an arrogant, obnoxious creature.

"Hello again," came the voice. "Twice in one day, this is a surprise."

Alvin Brown almost dropped his shopping-bag, never heard the fellow approach, stopped him in his tracks. It was the man who had shopped that very morning, the tall, confident chap with the thatch of unruly white hair, striding quickly across the road.

Alvin could only gawk, too nervous and tongue-tied to open his mouth.

Morris Buckingham said, "Just finished?"

"Yes," stammered Alvin Brown, "on the way home."

"Thought you lived around here," said Morris, big winning smile to calm the dithering under-manager, "seen you a few times walking from work."

"Hall Walk," replied the younger man, his thoughts spiralling to the stratosphere, "I live in *Hall Walk.*"

"Nice!"

"Comfortable," agreed Morris Brown, nodding his head earnestly.

"Lived there long?"

"All my life," retorted the man, added, "about five years on my own since my parents died."

Morris Buckingham gestured towards the distant houses, threw out a line, said casually, "I'm walking that way. Shall we walk together?"

"Walk together?"

Morris Buckingham smiled like a leech and said softly, "That would be nice, don't you think, Alvin?"

A sudden gnawing fear enveloped Alvin Brown, imagined the fellow was one of those predators who stalked, harassed or harangued their victims. He hesitated, stuttered, "No... no I'd rather not if you don't mind," and turned away from his companion and hurried away.

Perplexed and confused at the rebuke, Morris could only call after the scurrying figure, "Only wanted to talk, Alvin, nothing more!"

A furtive glance from the fleeing under-manager, a look of anguish and indecision oozed from his troubled face as Alvin Brown hurried to the sanctuary of his home.

"Shall I call and see you tomorrow?" shouted a desperate Morris Buckingham.

The under-manager started to run along the deserted roadway, never once looking back until he had reached the safety of his home.

"Fuck you!" muttered a despondent Morris Buckingham, decided to make a wide detour of the area, maybe saunter towards the old quarry or try Little Thorpe, see if any kiddies were still out playing. It was too early to go home, too early to throw in the towel for the evening.

Alvin Brown forgot all about his tea or his proposed library visit, he stood on the landing-stairs and gazed anxiously out of the side-window, the only window that allowed access to the main road. Stood an age, unsure, uncertain, expecting the tall stranger to appear at any moment, his head bombarded with an emotional display that made him dizzy with anticipation, didn't know if he was happy or sad at the obvious flirtation. Wasn't sure if he would chase the scoundrel or welcome him into his home. He stood for ages in a sorry state of flux.

CHAPTER THREE

Monday evening and Joe had joined his mates near the abandoned gravel quarry, close to Little Thorpe. Top-Enders they were, aptly named, as they lived close to the apex of the village, didn't bother with the Bottom-Enders, threw stones at them, chased them when the gang had enough members to muscle their way against rivals, rarely went further than name-calling and youthful bravado: blagging and shamming, the real stuff reserved for their later teenage years. The September night was warm and dry, ideal conditions for collecting bonfire, buying fireworks, harum-scarum around the houses for two months before the big night.

Joe Connelly loved the autumn nights when the days shortened and allowed the fun and games to commence more easily with the anonymous mask of darkness. Hated being stuck in the home at any time, especially now that they boarded at his nana's house. It took Joe weeks and weeks to become accepted in the village, the atmosphere frightening, not only the awful departure from the colliery but the agony of starting the village school, intense and almost too much to bear. Wept buckets to stay at his beloved colliery school, *'One year, Ma,'* he'd pleaded, *'one year and then I'm transferred to the Secondary. I know everyone, all my friends live in the colliery. I know the school, the teachers, back lanes, recreation ground, beaches... please, Ma'* like talking to a brick-wall when his mother made her mind up. Bags packed they moved out of their colliery house, one mile inland and west of the coastal colliery, past the council houses at the Waterworks to Easington Village. The mile seemed like a thousand to Joe.

New house with Nana Goodrich who was out more than she was in, booze or bingo, his grandmother enjoyed herself. New home and brand new school; first day and Albert Mix, the school bully, made his move on Joe.

Whacked him from behind, knocked him to the ground and laughed at the new kid spread-eagled between the waste-bins. Picked on the wrong one did Albert, goading and kicking at the fallen figure, not knowing the smaller, slighter boy had a temper like his mother. Struggling to his feet and looking up at the thick-set, bloated opponent, reached for the metal-lid from one of the waste-bins and flattened the bully with one roundhouse swipe. Albert Mix cried like a baby, blabbed all the way to Mr Albright's classroom, whined and lied. First day at the school and Joe was beaten soundly, three straps on each hand; pain made him flinch but he didn't complain. Tried to explain that it wasn't his fault, told Mr Albright about the bully but was called a liar and slapped across the face by the headmaster.

Every cloud has a silver lining, thought Joe later. The mishap with Albert Mix brought him instant friendship with half a dozen local boys, Top-Enders they called themselves and allowed Joe membership to the club, made his new life so much easier. Summer holidays and the gang had enjoyed the warm weather to explore the local dene that stretched from Little Thorpe to nearby Horden colliery. Frolicking in the dene, thinking of his Dad, Horden born and bred, remembered visiting his nana Connelly, *'Call me Dolly, nana sounds so old,'* hadn't been there for ages, last time was with his mother and his baby brother, Ma bawling and shouting at his nana. Never been back since, tried not to think about his dad anymore, made him sad, made him cry. Summer break saw Joe and the gang enjoying the mayhem of the dene, making rope swings across streams that meandered the entire width of the woodland. Other times they would buy *London Lights,* giant matches, start a camp-fire and throw potatoes in the flames, pretending they were the *James Gang* or *Quantrill's Raiders* hiding out from the posse of lawmen. Three days ago and Joe, full of devilment, started a fire deliberately which eventually destroyed half the dene, heard the fire-engines clanging the bells as they raced towards the woods and the gang scampered. Closer to his dad's relations in Horden than to Easington, Joe still took the long haul home, wasn't so much bothered about his grandmother's reaction to his appearance after so long, more concerned about how his Ma would react. Taboo subject nowadays, liable to skittle you, slap you black and blue if Dad's name was mentioned.

The gang were reconnoitring in the farmer's field midway between the hamlet of Little Thorpe and Thorpe farm and their homes, knew for a fact that the Bottom-Enders had started building a bonfire near the open land between the village and the council houses at the Waterworks and Ernie Bracken had an Uncle in the Waterworks who said the a second bonfire was being built in the allotments and was enormous. Joe had pinched matches from his mother's bag, prayed the night would stay dry as the gang had arson in mind, wanted their bonfire to be the only bonfire in the district.

"Ready, men," asked Joe Connelly, self-appointed leader of the small band of guerrillas, "all got balaclavas?"

Sammy McAndrew said they should call themselves the Balaclava Gang instead of the Top-Enders. *'Come the summer,'* said Joe, *'we'd sweat too much.'* The suggestion was shelved.

The boys dutifully pulled the knitted head-gear down over their faces.

Davy Duckworth, whose dad owned a ramshackle garage near the big road at the top of the village shouted encouragingly, "I've got a tin of petrol, Joe, just like you asked."

Joe moved off towards the distant smudge of council dwellings, the rest followed single-file, acting the part, "Keep the noise down, men, don't want anyone to hear us."

Sammy McAndrew, who shared a big paper-round with Joe Connelly, said, "Brought some newspapers; Northern Echo and Sunderland Echo ... a batch of them!"

Ernie Bracken quipped, "Shh, pretend we're in Burma and it's Japs and English! Shh," felt in his pockets, touched the fireworks ... *toyed with the grenades, couldn't wait to see the Japanese stronghold!*

Davy closed on Joe, "Look what I've borrowed from the garage," switched on the powerful torch and the probe of brilliant light sprayed a path for them across the darkening ground.

Joe said, "On the ground, Dave, shine it on the ground, less the Bottom-Enders will see it for sure!"

"Shh!" hissed Ernie Bracken thinking he was Errol Flynn and this was his version of *Objective Burma.*

Only took minutes before they reached the waste land that separated the village from the Waterworks. In the distance the gang observed the antics of several youths as they danced and jigged around the large mound of debris and wood. Big boys, older by years, the bonfire definitely out of reach.

Joe whispered, "Bottom-Enders must have their big brothers with them tonight," acted tough, "we wait, or move to the allotments?"

The decision was unanimous and the journey continued towards the perimeter of council houses and bonfire number two.

Ernie Bracken moved to Joe's side, whispered, "People at the second bonfire, Joe, maybe we scare them away?"

"How do we do that?"

"With these," pulled the fireworks from his pockets, turned to Davy Duckworth, said, "Shine your torch on me, Dave," twisted his body so that the beam of light highlighted the booty, leaned down and plucked three skyrockets out of his Wellington boots, "and these as well. Frighten the pants off them, eh?"

They reached the rough walkway that separated scrubland from allotments, silent as a graveyard as they moved single-file in the moonlight, reached the southern perimeter of the gardens and hadn't passed a solitary soul in any of the allotments. There was no one about. The path widened into open fields and before them was the blur of nature's canopy, the bonfire big as a single-storey building, 'Shine your torch, Davy,' said Joe Connelly and the probe blazed brilliantly at the mound of tree and posts and household remnants. 'Look,' muttered Joe, 'a settee!'

From the other side of the bonfire a lone voice called out hesitantly, "Who's that?"

Ernie Bracken forgot he was Errol and almost wet his pants, whined desperately; "Let's go!" turned and started moving away from the danger.

Joe said, "There's only one voice! Come on men, we'll charge him, see what happens," turned and looked at the grim and fearful faces. Said again, "There's only one guarding the bonfire, the rest will be down the dene cutting trees!" His tone remained strong and resolute, "Ready?"

There were mutterings of faint approval from the gang as they waited for inspiration from their leader.

"Charge!" Joe bellowed and hurtled across the open land followed by a motley crew of half-hearted desperadoes.

**

"Come out with me, Vera," said the mother, "we'll go to the *Southside,* bit o' chat, cheer yourself up no end, pet. No point sitting in and moping."

Conniving Annie Goodrich wanting company, *Southside Social* was always good for a laugh, even on a Monday night, and Evelyn Stoker would be there, dentist at

Peterlee, so much money he needed help spending it, didn't care he had a stammer like an incessant hammer that halted all serious conversation. A lovely man, according to Annie, insisted on buying her drinks every time he saw her. A proper gentleman too, never as much laid a hand on her which bothered her a little, wondered if he was one of those homosexuals. He certainly didn't look like one, didn't look at all like Morris Buckingham who lived a few streets away; shifty and sly, stood out a mile did Morris. No one bothered the man. Evelyn Stoker looked normal enough, impeccable manners too, maybe that was it, a gentleman, not too many about. The fellow was probably shy around women; stammer like that who could blame him.

The woman looked in the big mirror overhanging the fire, didn't look fifty-three, didn't look forty; Jane Mansfield had nothing on her, that's what Evelyn had said last week, Jayne Mansfield or Jane Eyre, whatever ... Jane or Joan something or other, bullshit of course, but she enjoyed it nevertheless. Took him three attempts to finish the compliment but it was worth it. If he said the same tonight, she might let him kiss her, might let him do a lot more, if he was in the mood. That was another troubling attribute about the little dentist, never acted like other men she'd known, wasn't a gob-shite, a braggart or a rogue. Evelyn Stoker didn't make snide remarks about women in general, no gossip of ever having a girl-friend or a wife, no history on that score. Annie Goodrich concluded that it was all about the infirmity, the stutter. She recalled their first meeting at the pub, her pushing and playing, flirting madly. *'Should have been an optician not a dentist, Evelyn,'* she'd said, *'could have got my spectacles on discount,'* didn't want to tell him she wore dentures, didn't want to give away all her secrets, put a lot of men off, gave them ample opportunity to wisecrack and embarrass a woman, *'Where do you keep them, Annie, glass at the side of the bed? Annie, fancy a blow-job, you gonna take out your teeth?'*

Evelyn taking all the teasing and toying with a nervous smile, nodding at her feeble jokes, pushed her luck did Annie Goodrich, followed the doctrine of *squeaking doors getting oiled* with a subtle hint for a drink, "You drinking stout, Evelyn? Horrible stuff, piles the weight on you, gin and tonic girl myself, that's if you're buying," subtle as throwing a brick but the dinky dentist, ever the gentleman, took the bait and bought Annie a double.

Men could be so cruel when they wanted, not Evelyn Stoker. He was a gentleman, not like his young brother. That was the only trouble with Evelyn, his young, arrogant brother. Such a handful, a wiseacre, full of his own importance, loved himself. Evelyn's very own Achilles heel, stuck together like proverbial glue, chalk and cheese, she thought, been a mix-up at the maternity, Evelyn so short, her size in fact, tubby, balding, rich, Elmore Stoker, and baby brother, six feet tall, thick black hair and unemployed, ex-social worker until he was caught with one of his clients, wasn't caught as such, client made a formal complaint. Elmore was a fool making a play for the girl; girl was a fool for flirting and spilling the beans when the game ended. If Annie could palm Elmore on to her grieving daughter it would kill two birds, give something for Vera to moan about, get her head away from her no-account husband. Sometimes Annie wanted to tell her Vera about George Connelly, things he'd said to her, suggestions he made when Vera was out of sight. Man like George needed castrating like a eunuch, doubted it would stop his wicked ways. No damn good for anyone.

"And the boys, Ma?" Vera glanced at Jack, straddled across the big sofa, lost in the *Eagle* comic-book, mild-mannered, docile, reminded her of Martin Goodrich, her late father; meek, submissive, loveable. Shout at Jack and he folded, not like big brother, Joe gave as good as he got, met fire with fire, Joe cloned from Vera's breast, a firebrand and a rebel. Joe could have watched his kid brother, allow Vera an hour out of the house but Joe was out, mischief-making.

"Plenty of time, pet," said Annie, "couple of hours and Joe might be back to baby-sit his brother."

There was a loud knocking at the front door, 'Ready-money knock,' said Annie, 'can't be Provident, that's tomorrow,' glanced at her daughter, 'Answer the door, pet, I've got my curlers in.'

Shemp Douglas was filling the door-space like a goliath, looked angry, features twisted in an arthritic grimace, held on tight to the protesting child who squirmed and struggled under the giant's vice-like grip on his collar. Stuck his free hand towards the startled mother, palm open, showing the burn-out remains of fireworks.

"Shemp?" said Vera, trying to smile and pacify the grim-faced collier, one year older and a brood of his own, Shemp Douglas lived in *Paradise Lane* at the nearby Waterworks. Big as a bear but soft and gentle, took an explosion to fire the man. Shemp could hardly put a sentence together his emotions so screwed and jerked.

"This little bugger and his gang," gasped the miner, "tied a boatload of bangers to my letterbox, lit the bloody fuses and knocked on my door!"

Vera leaned forward, faced her ashen-faced son, read him like a book, glanced up at Shemp Douglas, "Have you called the police, Shemp," one hurdle at time for the young mother, "well?"

"Know me better than that, Vera," grunted the man, "got six lads of my own, know what they're capable of!"

Vera looked at Joe, said, "You little bastard!"

"Thought I'd leave it to you, Vera."

Vera said with disbelief, "You haven't hit him, Shemp?"

It sounded incredulous to her. A year ago and living in the colliery, she caught a kid who'd broken her kitchen window, only meant to reprimand him but when he started bad-mouthing, Vera kicked him all the way to his parent's home, told them what she'd do next time it happened, slapped him black and blue before leaving.

"Not my job, Vera," said the man, calming some, "leave it up to you."

"You've got my blessing, Shemp," said Vera, "kick his arse round the garden!"

"Ma!" pleaded Joe.

Shemp Douglas hoisted the boy from the step and manoeuvred the flaying body into the kitchen, said, "Leave it to you to sort out, Vera?"

His words had barely left his mouth when the woman took a swipe at her son's unprotected head, sent him reeling into the house, Annie Goodrich was waiting like a hungry vulture, a myriad of yellow curlers festooning her scalp, both arms raised, slapping and chastising her grandson who bolted for the stairs, watched by an amazed and alarmed little brother.

"Hope you don't mind, Vera," said Shemp Douglas, "could have blinded someone with his daftness, bad enough he scorched the door, I can mend that. Someone had opened the door when the fireworks went off, could have been killed."

"Appreciate you not calling the police, Shemp," said a chastised and embarrassed female.

"Goodnight, then," said the collier, he turned and strode away.

Vera stormed into the living-room, face creased with anger, livid with her oldest son. Glanced at Jack, hands over his trembling mouth, eyes wide with fear, stopped her in her tracks, "It's okay, Jack, nothing to worry about. Joe's been in trouble again, been a naughty boy!" Jack's eyes burrowed into her, full of apprehension and anxiety, calmed her enough to say, "I'm fine, Jack, lost my temper again," eased on to the settee, cuddled her frightened little boy, "Joe should be more like you, eh?"

43

"Don't hit him, Ma," begged Jack, held on to his mother like a scared rabbit.

Vera kissed him, said, "Go and get him, tell him to come downstairs, I want a word with Joe."

"Can I say you won't hit him, Ma?" Jack struggled out of her arms wanting to be with his brother, give him the good news.

"Promise, son," said Vera, watched him disappear, turned to her mother, "looks like you've got company for tonight, mother."

"You'll enjoy the *Southside Social,* our Vera," answered Annie Goodrich, "put today behind you, eh?"

'First day of the rest of my life,' thought Vera Connelly, full of resolve, walked to the bottom of the stairs, shouted for her eldest, "Come on, Joe, come down here, I'm not going to hit you!"

There was movement at the top landing, Jack's worried features eased into view, stared morosely at her.

"Jack, pet, tell your brother."

"He's not coming down. Ma, says you'll kill him again!"

Vera smiled, "Tell him if he doesn't come down this very minute, I'll come up!"

A second head loomed above the first.

Joe asked carefully, "What?"

"I'm going for a drink with nana, you can baby-sit your brother!"

"You're not going to hit me?"

"No."

Joe sneered, took a gamble, said "How much, Ma, how much for baby-sitting?"

Vera launched herself up the staircase, "You cheeky little bastard!" she screamed.

**

44

Across the cul-de-sac from the Goodrich house in Passfield Square was North Crescent. Micky Green squatted uncomfortably at the kitchen table, elbows rested on the table-top, fag-end hanging lethargically from the corner of his mouth, empty dinner-plate, licked dry, in front of him. Opposite and still chomping noisily at the steak and chips was his wife Mary Jane. '*Manners of a porky-pig,*' thought Micky, counted her chins, three big ones, looked more like a fleshy cravat than a neck these days, '*manners of a pig and looks like a pig,*' nodded at his observations.

The woman must have sensed movement, said, "What, Micky, what are you noddin' at?" eyes still focussed on the meal, as an afterthought muttered longingly, "meat's so tender."

'*A three-eyed Cyclops,*' thought the man, peering at her thinning scalp looking for the eye-socket, said, "Vera's in a right state, hope she'll be okay, cried all the way from Yorkshire!"

"Mmm," she whispered, chewing slowly on the meat, "done to perfection."

"You hear me, Mary Jane?"

"Heard you the first time," retorted the woman, burped loudly, "pardon me," said smugly, "told you not to go, told you sparks would fly, as usual you wouldn't be told!"

"It's our Annie's lass, how could I refuse?"

Just say no! "Whatever, Micky," said Mary Jane, "you always do what you want!"

Mick Green stubbed out the cigarette-stub in the tea-cup, grabbed at the packet of *Players,* found the *Swan Vestas* and lit up, inhaled long and loud. Grunted disapprovingly and said, "Bloody rubbish, not a patch on Woodbines."

"Thought you were givin' up the shite?"

"More or less have."

"Dr. Brown told you they were cancer sticks!"

"You call these cigarettes?" he replied, tapping ash into the cup, "*Barratt's* candy cigarettes are stronger!"

Mary Jane pushed aside the empty plate, "Lovely that," smacked her lips, "delicious in fact," said like she was on a *Spam* commercial for Tyne-Tees Television.

The kitchen door cranked open and the two boys stumbled into view, oldest grinning like a hyena, youngest shielding himself behind his big brother, worried look on his angelic face.

"Now youngun," said Micky, "how's tricks?" acting like Robert Mitchum, cigarette stuck precariously in the corner of his mouth. Glanced at the kid brother and said cheerfully, "Now then, Talky-Tom," nodding as he spoke, "cat got your tongue?"

Jack Connelly bit his lip with nerves and glanced at his brother for help, his hand gripping at his brother's coat-tails. Looked sheepishly at his uncle and aunt and never uttered a word.

"Uncle Mick," said Joe, bursting with confidence, "Ma sent me..."

Mary Jane interjected, sniffed the air like a hound-dog, pouted and said, "What the hell is that smell?"

"Petrol, Aunt Mary," confessed the boy, pride in his voice, "spilt a bit when we lit a bonfire."

"Honey, you got your dates wrong, November not September for Guy Fawkes," looked at her husband for approval, "that right, Mick?"

"Depends whose bonfire," smiled when he said it, some things you never forgot. Glancing at the kid he said, "Fun and games, Joe?"

Joe smiled then asked again, "Ma sent me, Uncle Mick."

"Heard the first time, son," answered the man solemnly, stuck his hands in his trouser-pockets.

"Ma says can she borrow some money, pay you back Friday pay-day," stuck his hand out in anticipation, palms open like a beggar.

Money was handed over with a warning, "Tell your Ma she hasn't paid me for last week. Want it all Friday mind, or it stops!"

"I'll tell her, Uncle Mick," said Joe, pushed his kid brother out of the open door, stopped, played a fast one, knew his uncle was all bark. "Uncle Mick," smiling as he spoke, "any errands you want me to do? Andy Croft is doorman all week at the Club, you want to give me some dosh, I'll ask him to wrap a bottle for you ... or some supper, I'll run to Trotter's fish-shop for you and Aunt Mary." Ran errands sometimes twice, three times a week, knew the order backwards, 'Light on the salt, soaked with vinegar.'

The man shook his head, the kid had brass balls for sure, flipped a silver coin at him, "Don't spend it all at once, eh?"

"Thanks, Uncle Mick," grinning infectiously he bolted out of sight.

CHAPTER FOUR

The *Southside Social* was a quaint, quiet pub, quiz a few times a week, darts and dominoes for the regulars; the place was a throw-back to the forties. No acts ventured into the pub, occasional sing-a-long when some daring soul stood on the ancient stage, no jigging or jiving, only background music to soothe and calm; the public-house an old fashioned watering-hole with a well-behaved crowd of punters. Vera had a vague recollection of childhood days, weekends mainly, hurrying into an empty house, knew where to find her parents, ran all the way to the village-green, into the murky dingy atmosphere of the pub, talked to Mr Divine, the door-man, *'Your folks are in the bar, love, finishing off their drinks, tell them it's closing-time.'*

The woman sat in the lounge next to her mother and gazed at the room, hardly changed in years, same décor, lulling background music. Tonight, Al Martino was singing about his heart.

Vera said, "Ask the man to change the record, Ma, see if they'll play Dickie Vantentine or Malcolm Vaughan."

"I'll have a Guinness, pet," said Annie Goodrich ignoring her daughter's request, "make it a pint, save you goin' back."

"Ma," protested Vera, "don't think I'm buying your drinks all night!" Waved the solitary note at her parent, "Uncle Mick wants this back Friday, plus I still owe him!"

Annie, skin thick as a rhinoceros, glanced at her *Timex* wrist-watch, said indifferently, "It's almost nine-o-clock, Evelyn will be calling in soon. Like clockwork; in at nine, out by ten-thirty, by the book. Tells me he goes to bed eleven-thirty, reads for thirty minutes then it's light-out." Took a breath, "Bloody sad really."

"Evelyn, kind of name is that?" said Vera. "You seeing him, Ma?"

"Don't be silly! There'd no hanky-panky at all," fussed Annie, "buys me a drink now and then, no harm in that is there?"

Two men strolled into the room, mid-thirties, one built like a film star, the other, a short, balding, bespectacled heavyweight. The squat figure waved towards the women while the taller, younger brother glanced at Vera, eyed her up and down and stripped her with a lingering stare.

"That's Evelyn," Annie said, "and before you say anything, looks are skin deep, right!" Waved a warm welcome at the dumpy figure, mimed her order, *'Gin and tonic,'* used her finger to point at her daughter, *'gin and tonic twice, Evelyn.'* Glanced at her daughter and saw the look of disapproval so big it didn't need capital letters. She elaborated, "He's loaded, our Vera, lives in Stockton Road, top of the village, big detached house next to the co-op boss, Mr Mix. Evelyn's father was a doctor, or something clever; Evelyn is a dentist, works in Peterlee, never been married, you'll see why when he brings over the drinks."

"Did his dad want a girl?" asked Vera, never was one for schoolwork, nearest to a book would have been *Reader's Digest* or the *Weekend Mail*, mention *Decline and Fall* and she'd think alcoholic poisoning, or maybe George, soon to be ex-husband George, every weekend legless with the booze.

"It's a boy's name," said Annie, knew the story, first time she heard the name she was as confused as her daughter. Wasn't going to give her the satisfaction of admitting her ignorance, "One of those names, either or."

"It's a girl's name!"

Annie Goodrich said, "It's like Lesley, call a boy Lesley, call a girl Lesley...either....or!"

"Evelyn?"

"Stop acting stupid, Vera!"

"But Evelyn!" chortled Vera, "why not Tracy...bloody stupid!"

Annie said resolutely, "Tracy is a boy's name in America!" Remembered her late husband, Barty, telling her about the Hollywood Star, nudged her daughter and said, "Marion is a boy's name too...Marion Morrison was John Wayne's name!"

"Evelyn, eh," whispered Vera, watched the dumpling struggle towards them with the drinks, "some anchor to carry around!"

Annie Goodrich was reminiscing. A lifetime ago her Barty was the double of the cowboy star, once, could walk like him, especially after a bellyful of drink, thought he could mimic the man too, *'I'll be seein' ya,'* he would drawl, *'the hell I will,'* sounded more like Bob Hope, didn't have the heart to tell him.

"Drinks," said the diminutive stranger.

"Thanks, Evelyn," said Annie, smiled so wide her dentures shone like stars. "This is my daughter, Vera," glanced at the companion, "Vera, this is Mr Stoker, the dentist I was telling you about."

Evelyn Stoker said, "Hi," said it like he was in a rush.

Vera acknowledged the man and thanked him for the drink.

The man nodded profusely, looked like a confused horse at a water-trough, said, "Fine," turned like a dancer and tapped his way back to the counter, "bye, bye."

"Ignorant bastard," muttered Vera Connelly.

"Can't talk properly, our Vera!" reprimanded Annie Goodrich, could imagine a whole night's drink being lost because of her daughter's tactless outbursts.

Vera said sarcastically, "Sounded fine to me!"

"Stammers!"

"He stutters?" said Vera.

Annie became a mimic, saved time explaining, hiccupped, "Hel, hel ... hello," shrugged her shoulders, sipped at the drink and licked her lips, said, "One word answers easy-peasy, but string a sentence together and you'd think Evelyn was taking the piss!"

"And he's a dentist ... qualified?"

"The man has his own dentistry in Peterlee, senior partner!"

"So how does he manage to discuss his patient's problems without getting into a twist?"

"Can we leave it, our Vera?" said Annie, seething. Gulped greedily at her drink and saw the men weaving their way towards them, offered an explanation, "Maybe the patient finishes the sentences for him, somethin' like that," shrugged her shoulders, "who gives a damn anyway? He's a very nice man."

"Hello, girls," said Elmore Stoker, "now which one is the mother?"

Made Annie Goodrich feel like a million dollars; made Vera Connelly moan and wince.

Evelyn spoke, staccato quick, gestured, "Anne. Vera," grinned wildly, not a trance of the impediment, glanced again at the youngest of the women, could have sworn someone groaned.

The handsome man made a bee-line for Vera, found a stool and scraped it close to her, sat and smiled infectiously, "Not seen you before," glanced and nodded at Annie Goodrich who was fumbling for cigarettes, "Annie practically lives here but this must be your first time?" Picked up his pint glass and drained it expertly, smacked his lips with pleasure, added, "Al Martino, hell of a singer. American you know, prefer Sinatra myself, and you, who do you like?"

Vera said, "You ... what?"

"Singers, you must have favourites?"

Nodded as she took her first sip, said, "Ronnie Carroll, Ronnie Hilton."

"So anyone with the forename *Ronnie*," chortled and nodded wickedly, "I'll have to remember that."

Vera said, "Cheeky bugger," and returned the smile. Thought she might actually enjoy the night.

**

"Joe," whispered the kid, eyes still clamped, hated the darkness, nudged at his brother, "you still awake?"

"Shh!"

"Joe, I'm frightened!"

"What for?"

"The dark!"

"There's nothing to be frightened of Jack," said a sympathetic brother, "keep your eyes closed."

"Eyes closed and I'm still scared!"

"I'm here!"

"What if someone breaks in?"

"No one can break in, the door's locked!"

"What if they find a key, Joe… and they have a knife like Jim Bowie!"

"Shall I tell you a story, Jack? It's got Jim Bowie in it but it's really about Davy Crockett fighting the Mexicans."

"Is it a cowboy picture, Joe?"

"Sort of, but instead of Indians there's Mexicans."

"What's a Mexican, Joe?"

Joe Connelly didn't answer immediately, said eventually, "Another kind of cowboy."

"So it's cowboys versus cowboys?"

"Sort of."

"Is John Wayne in it, Joe?"

"Fess Parker is like John Wayne."

"What's a Fess Parker?"

"Fess Parker, that's his name!" Joe irritated and annoyed, half-asleep and thinking about seeing his Uncle Mick about borrowing his bow-saw, wanted to cut down some big trees for the bonfire.

52

"Joe," asked the kid, elbow tapping into the back of his brother, "you ever think of our Dad?"

"Sometimes."

"Why for?"

"Because!"

"Ernie Johnson in my class said he had a new dad, liked him better than his real one!"

"So?"

"Will we get a new Dad?"

"It's up to Ma."

"Why did our Dad leave, Joe?"

"Because he did!"

"Joe, will our Dad not miss us?"

"Don't know."

"Do you miss our Dad?"

"Sometimes."

"Dad forgot my birthday, Joe."

"Mine too."

"When Christmas comes, will our Dad buy us some presents? Ernie Johnson's new dad is always buying him stuff. Last week Ernie's new dad bought him a *Hopalong Cassidy* six-gun and a holster with real plastic bullets and five *Dinky* cars - a *Brooke Bond Tea* van, a *Cadillac Eldorado* and a *Vauxhall Cresta* - d'you think our Dad will buy us lots of Christmas presents, Joe?"

"Probably buy us the same as last year!"

"Joe, what did he buy us?"

"Nowt! Ma always gets our presents. She's in a savings club at Davison's and she's in Daniels's shop at the colliery."

"What's a savings club. Joe?"

"Give the shop money every week until it's Christmas time and then the shop gives you it back but you have to spend it in their shop."

"Joe?"

"What?"

"Why did you tell me there's no Santa Claus?"

"Because there's not!"

"But I thought there was, Ma said you were nasty."

"Told you the truth, Jack. Think about it. If there was a Santa Claus, we'd all get the same. How come some kids get loads of presents and people like Anthony Jenkins gets nothing?"

"I don't know, Joe."

"Because Anthony has no dad and his mother spends all her money on beer!"

"Ernie Johnson said there was a Father Christmas and when I told him the truth he told his mother and she called me a wicked boy, said if I went to their house Christmas Eve I'd see Santa climbing down the chimney!"

Joe Connelly turned on his side, said, "Go to sleep, Jack."

"Joe, tell me that cowboy story, will you?"

"And will you promise to go to sleep?"

"If you don't frighten me. Sometimes you tell a story and you make it scary and I can't sleep!"

"It's about cowboys. It's not scary!"

"Will you start with, *Once upon a time,* that's what I like?"

"If that's what you want."

"I do, Joe."

"Once upon a time, Davy Crockett was lost in a big forest ....."

Jack waited several seconds before asking, "What happened next, Joe?"

Joe continued, his voice deep and unnatural, "Davy Crockett was lost in the forest and a ghost slowly crept up behind him......" Joe started howling and growling.

"Ma! Ma!" screamed the kid, hiding under the blankets, snuggling into his brother.

**

54

CHAPTER FIVE

Alice Raine seemed more confident the second day at school. It was raining buckets outside so the class were allowed indoors. Most suffered the rain and played in the yard, but six kids loitered about the classroom and two hovered next to the teacher's desk. Mrs Wainwright, had long ago given up trying to work through a lesson plan, the tots vying for attention were too distracting.

"Joe's brother, eh?" said Mrs Wainwright. Remembered the lad joining the school during the last few weeks of the term, remembered the scuffle with Albert Mix, pleased Albert had finally met his match. George Albright, headmaster, had told her the reason for Joe Connelly's transfer from the colliery school, knew the pain of loss, sympathised with Joe's mother, never met her but still understood.

"Yes, Miss, he's ten and a half, next year he's at the Secondary," Jack Connelly ecstatic with his life, loved school and Alice and the teacher.

"The Secondary, Jack?"

Confused he said, "Don't know what it means, Miss but he goes next year."

"It's a school for big boys, Jack," interjected Alice Raine, "my sister Mary went last year."

"Very good, Alice," said the teacher, nodded and smiled.

"My Dad ran away, Miss," said the boy matter-of-fact. Turned to Alice Raine, "Told you yesterday, didn't I?"

Alice said, "Yes," turned to the tutor, seeking attention, "I only see my dad at weekends, Miss, bit like Jack."

Jack answered sullenly, "Not like me, I don't ever see mine!"

"Almost the same," pouted the girl, "because he sleeps all day Saturday and he goes out for a drink Sunday afternoon...." Glanced at the teacher, "Drives a truck, Miss, all over the country and the world and sleeps at the weekend."

"Ma says my Dad lives on another planet because he's got a tile loose in his head," said Jack Connelly.

"A tile in his head," laughed Alice, "like a flower-pot man?"

"Ma says he's like a Mongol with two wives," retorted the boy, "or Mormon." Wasn't sure about the name.

Alice asked, "What's one of them, Jack?"

"Not sure," said Jack "but Ma says Dad is definitely one!"

The bell sounded the end of the morning-break; the door was almost wrenched off its hinges as the hordes trooped into the room. Jack and Alice sauntered back to their seats, sat side by side and waited contentedly for the lesson to begin. Denise Wainwright walked to the blackboard, looked at the twenty six letters of the alphabet. Picked up the cane, bedlam behind her as children scrapped and pushed at chairs and found their allocated places, absently pointed the marker at three letters, t. o. m. She thought about her ex-husband Tom Wainwright, married one year and he'd found another love, understood the pain suffered by Jack's mother, losing someone, missing someone, Denise didn't have the comfort of a family, didn't know whether that was a good thing or a bad thing, pleased to be working, took away some of the misery.

At the other end of the school building, the older children were filing into Albright's classroom single-file and subdued. The tutor, stick stuffed under his arm like a sergeant drilling his men, stood parade-ground stiff, ready to squash any mutiny or unrest in his disciplined regime. He closed the door and noticed there were absent pupils, grimaced and cursed, Connelly and McAndrew, *'Late again,'* he thought, walked briskly back to his desk and replaced the cane with the strap, started filling out information in the punishment-book when the door bust open and the two miscreants hurried towards their desks, soaked to the skin, hair flattened with the rain, heads downcast, praying for a reprieve.

"You two," barked the tutor, "come here!"

McAndrew meandered, allowing Connelly to reach the teacher's desk first, both looking like two rejects from the workhouse. Samuel McAndrew visibly cringing, Joseph Connelly's chin sticking out, arrogance written all over his face. The heat of the room made steam rise from the wet clothing of the pupils.

"Well," asked the tutor, holding on to the leather strap, "anything to say before I punish you two?"

Sammy McAndrew quaked, muttered humbly, "Sorry, Sir," stared at the wooden floor, wiping at his wet nose on his coat-sleeve, sniffling incessantly, "never heard the bell."

"Connelly?"

"Playing marbles, Mr Albright," eyes locked on the stout tutor's moustache, so trim and cut to perfection, looked like a spiked pencil under his nose.

"You didn't hear the bell? All the school hears the bell apart from you miscreants, well? Answer me before I strap you!"

Albright detested the newcomer, landed at the end of the summer term and immediately started disrupting the place, fighting and brawling and causing trouble. First day at school he was involved in a fight with Albert Mix. The very first day! Albright had to phone Mrs Mix at the library, who phoned her husband, manager at the Co-op store, who had to leave work and drive Albert to the hospital to have his face stitched. *Why couldn't the misfit have stayed at the colliery along with all the other ruffians,* thought the tutor, *another year and he'd be at the Secondary Modern. Why bother transferring?* Joseph Connelly esquire, was a cocky troublemaker and it was his misfortune to have him for a full year. He thought about the first lesson that morning, told them all about the Space Race between Russia and America, thought the lesson would be interesting, read all about satellite technology the previous week in *The Times,* wanted to blind the pupils with science, show them what a clever-clogs he was, lesson went belly-up when Connelly embarrassed him with his knowledge. *'Sir,'* corrected the little monster, grinning with pleasure, *'Sputnik 2 had the dog, Sputnik 1 was unmanned!'* George Albright found out Connelly had a newspaper-round, read all the papers avidly before he delivered, then the double-whammy that made the tutor take the horrors and halt the instruction immediately, *'Sir, the Americans launched Explorer after Sputnik 2, read that in the Telegraph, Sir!'* The little bastard trying his best to disrupt his lesson and embarrass him totally, Albright insisting the Russians had launched three artificial satellites before the Americans could counter. *'Not so, Sir!'* The little bastard!

"I'm waiting, boy," demanded the incensed tutor, "you deaf as well as stupid?"

"Truth is, Sir," said the pupil, "we heard the bell, but we were drawn, last game won."

"So you deliberately ignored the school-bell?"

"Only late by a minute, Sir!"

"Shut up," hissed Sammy McAndrew, head still bowed in subservience, prodding at his companion, terrified of the coming punishment, last time he was strapped he wept openly, wanted no more of that heartache, even the girls chided him for weeks afterwards.

"Three minutes, Connelly!"

"Sir," persisted the boy, "the monitors hadn't even started handing out the books!"

Albright lost his patience and slapped his hand across the pupil's startled face. The noise of the blow echoed around the classroom, and Joe, caught unawares and off-balance, stumbled backwards into Sammy McAndrew who inadvertently yelped with fear. One of the girls in the front desk, Elsie Bowers, began to sob softly. *'Sit down, the pair of you!'* yelled the anxious tutor, praying that Connelly wouldn't bolt for the door, hoping his bluff might carry the day. *'Next time I'll strap you good and proper!'* McAndrew hurried to his seat, Connelly glowered at the man for some moments before slowly and deliberately finding his seat.

Mr Albright recovered his composure, kept staring at Joseph Connelly, the welt marks on his face already subsiding, told himself he had nothing to worry about, announced to the class, "Class, I've checked reference books about this morning's lesson, must apologise about the numerical order of the artificial satellites. Connelly was correct, Sputnik 1 and 2 were indeed followed by the American Explorer." He tried his best to smile at Joseph Connelly, "We do have our differences, as you are all aware," shook his head in mock annoyance, "but Joseph was correct about the satellites." Glanced at the stiff features of the boy and brazened out the sham, "If you would like to come to my desk, Connelly, I'll give you a Gold Star to stick in your science exercise book and you can get a gold nib for your pen." Albright waited and prayed.

Joe took a deep breath, pleased he had not cried or shirked away from the punishment, stood and walked to the front of the class, saw all eyes on him, could read their minds, made him feel good. "While I'm giving Connelly a star-sticker," said Albright in a loud clear voice, "I want you to open your maths-books on a clean page, title and date please. Title is 'Long Division' and I want you to try the ten sums on the blackboard," shot a cursory glance at the hovering figure of the pupil, noticed the red weal still evident, hoped they would disappear before lunchtime, muttered a grudging, "Well done, Connelly," stuck a Gold Star on the relevant page in his exercise-book, handed back the book and a brand-new gold ink-nib, "there we go." He gestured towards the blackboard and kept the momentum going, "I want all of the sums finishing before lunch, son."

"Yes Sir," said the boy, "thanks Sir", and moved back to his desk, smiling broadly at Sammy McAndrew, parading the open page and the award.

George Albright said a silent prayer of thanks to his maker, calmed enough to make further concessions, bawled out, "Connelly!"

"Sir," said Joe Connelly, stopped, turned and faced his tormentor.

"You can be the ink-monitor today," barked Albright, smiling like a weasel, "fill all the ink-wells and don't spill a drop, you hear?"

**

Alvin Brown, thirty, gaunt with wispy thinning hair, stood in the upstairs office, the manager's office, perspiration visibly oozing over his blanched features. Hated confrontation, run a mile from trouble, done it all his life, all through school and his brief stint at the colliery, hated all the rough and tumble of pit life, pleased when he left and more pleased when he landed a job at the Co-op. Took ten years of obedience and deference and he had almost made it to the top of the pile, thirty years old and he was under-manager at the Sherburn Hill Cooperative Society, Easington Village Branch. Delwin Mix was general manager, sixty years old, bloated and world-weary, mainly due to his unexpected and astonished late entry into fatherhood, forty-nine and easing down into early retirement and his perplexed and embarrassed wife announcing the news that she was expecting their third child. Almost fifty years old, and Del Mix with a son and a daughter in their thirties, the news brought on the first angina attack, his mortified and frumpy wife inflaming the situation with her stupid remarks about middle-aged people still active sexually. *'We'll be the laughing-stock of the place!'* Separate beds for a decade, the man soaked in alcohol most nights, unconscious most nights, *'Laughing-stock'*, thought, Delwin Mix, *'more like a bloody miracle.'* If Delwin Mix had known the trouble his new son would cause him he would have drowned him at birth. Albert Mix, almost eleven, built like a swollen giant and always in bother, was a cross he had to carry for the rest of his miserable life.

"Mr Mix," said Alvin Brown for the second time in as many seconds, "you did say you wanted to see me?"

"The new girl, Connelly," said Delwin Mix, "you sure the right choice was made?"

"On one month's probation, Sir," answered the nervous under-manager, "part-time position, never missed a shift until this week. Personal trouble, Mr Mix, had to visit her estranged husband yesterday, Yorkshire I believe...."

Delwin Mix asked, "Was there something stopping her from travelling over the weekend, Mr Brown?" Before Alvin Brown could answer the general manager said, "This morning she walked in with me at nine-thirty. The branch opens at eight-thirty, an hour late, Mr Brown!"

What's good for the goose, thought the younger man, kept his mouth clamped and gazed apologetically at his boss, nodded slowly, "I'll have a word with Mrs Connelly. She told me she stayed overnight attempting to salvage the marriage, Sir, promised me it won't happen again."

"First and last warning, Mr Brown!"

A chastened, sheepish under-manager hurried away from the office and an exhausted Delwin Mix eased his weary head on to the surface of the desk, closed his eyes and cat-napped for some minutes, only way the man could survive the day. The desk-phone shocked him awake, it was an outside-line, had to be his wife, no one else ever called.

"Hello, dear," said the weary general manager, closed his eyes and waited patiently for the barrage of abuse.

His wife of forty years was irritated, yapping incessantly into his earpiece, "Well," whined Mildred Mix, chief librarian at the Easington Colliery Branch, "did you manage to persuade him?"

"Albert said he didn't feel well enough to go to school today," replied the man, wondering if it were too late to have his young son adopted. "I did try, Milly, made me late for work, managed to drag him to the car then he started crying again!"

"Never been the same since that horrid boy from the colliery hit him with that weapon. First day of term yesterday and he refused to attend and now today! This can't continue Delwin, you'll have to do something, it's our boy who is suffering at the hands of that bully!"

Joseph Connelly used a dust-bin lid on Albert. There had been times in the past when his father was tempted to do the same. Mildred had spoilt the boy rotten, guilty conscience perhaps, compensation because she didn't love him enough to relinquish her position at the library. *I've only just been promoted, Delwin, I couldn't possible give it up. We'll hire child-minders.'* Bought her son's love, drowned him with silly presents, catered to his every whim, and turned him into an obnoxious and arrogant bully.

"I'm doing all I can, Milly!"

"Of course you are," her tone echoed disrespect and dismay. "Hell, Delwin, you've even given his awful mother a job at the store, what could be better?"

"Stop that, Milly, you know fine well I was having tests in Ryhope Hospital when the recruiting took place!"

"There's nothing wrong with your heart, Del, not now, not when Albert was born. The angina attack happened because you're overweight!"

"Of course you'd know!"

"We're getting away from the subject," said the enraged spouse, "have you sacked her?"

"Mrs Connelly has been given a reprimand, next time she steps out of line and I'll dismiss her."

"She's on a month's probation, you don't need a reason!"

"Completed her four weeks probationary period last week. Mr Brown, the under-manager agreed her leave of absence for personal reasons, everything is above board, Milly."

"Sack her, she only works three damn days a week," insisted the irate woman, "she might move back to the bloody colliery and the riff-raff she left. Her son is the only reason Albert refuses to go to school. You've got to have the courage of your convictions, Delwin, you've got to sack the woman!"

"I have to go, Milly," said the fellow, grovelling now, the ache in his chest matching the pain in his head, "I promise you, next time Mrs Connelly ….."

The line went dead.

Delwin Mix shook his head morosely, too old for daily grief, searched the top drawer of his desk for the tablets, swallowed them dry, pulled out the ledgers and started transferring invoices into his books of account. Told himself, *'Next time she steps out of line, Mrs Connelly will be sacked, promise you Mildred, a minute late, one complaint from a customer and she goes the journey!'* The manager felt unwell, breathless, thought he would show his presence about the lower floor, maybe first visit the lavatory.

Alvin Brown found it difficult to act the part of under-manager when he was around Vera. Truth was, he found it almost impossible to treat her as one of his staff. They'd gone through school together and, for months after school, especially when Alvin had to mix with uncouth colliery youths at the mine, Vera had been his anchor, his friend, the couple were close friends. Family imagined something deeper. Nothing could have been further from the truth, Alvin had no interest sexually in the beautiful Vera Goodrich, loved her as a friend, confided in her, told her about his deepest feelings, loved her more when she sympathised and accepted his preferences. The friendship was not one-sided; Alvin Brown held council and told the girl she should follow her heart and marry George Connelly, told her true love came only once in a lifetime. Alvin, ever the romantic. More than a decade later and he still regarded her as someone special.

"Hi," he said, closing on her, smiling as she cut the bacon expertly using the mechanical slicing machine, watching as she chattered to the pensioner, like she was born for the job. Who could be angry with Vera Goodrich?

Vera said, turning her pretty head, "Hello, Alvin, checking on me again?" smiled sweetly at the man.

The pensioner was handed the purchase, money accepted, nodded her goodbyes and walked stiffly towards the exit-door, the walking-stick a necessity for the arthritic old lady.

"Don't ever want to get old, Alvin," she mused as the pensioner left the shop and disappeared into the downpour.

"Can we talk, Vera?" trying to play the part of under-manager, already beads of perspiration dotting his worried face, his heart not in the job, especially when he found no justification in what appeared like a personal vendetta against her.

"I said I was sorry about being late, Alvin, won't happen again."

Alvin Brown tried to keep a straight face, said solemnly, sympathetically, "It's not me, Vera. Old Mr Mix seems to be after your blood, always quizzing me about your progress," sighed and glanced at the floor, couldn't look Vera in the eyes, stammered, "I have to tell you it's your first and last warning. Late again and he'll give you notice to quit," took a deep breath, thankful that the worst part was over.

Vera Connelly said softly, "You know why, Alvin?"

"I haven't a clue," said Alvin, shook his head, perplexed, added, "never know him be like this towards any of the staff, full or part-time. If anything he's more lenient than me."

"You don't know about his son," said the woman.

Alvin Brown said, "Mr Mix's son, you mean young Albert?"

"Albert Mix, yes!"

"He is something of a handful for Mr Mix. It is embarrassing having to bar your own son from the store. He is so impertinent and rude to the staff. The manager had no alternative after he stole confectionery and cursed Mary Whitehead in sales." Alvin Brown nodded sincerely, added, "I had no idea young Albert had upset you....."

Vera interrupted, "Wrong end of the stick, Alvin, Albert Mix was bullying my eldest son, Joe, happened last term, at school."

"Yes I've heard he's a bully," sighed with consternation, folded his arms across his thin chest, shook his head and pursed his lips, "well, he's such a size!"

"Joe put him in hospital."

Alvin Brown gasped, "Goodness me!"

Vera Connelly pouted and sneered with contempt, "Now you know why Mr Mix doesn't want me employed at the store."

"It has to be his wife, Mildred," offered Alvin, knew all the stores' gossip, brightened up the long boring days in the shop. "Between you and me," glanced around quickly, didn't want to give bullets for staff to fire against him, no one near so he continued, "he is totally under her thumb, hen-pecked to death. If it's not his wife shouting orders down the phone to him, it's his horrible son embarrassing him in front of the staff. Last few years I've seen deterioration in Mr Mix and it's not work that's the culprit, it's his home life. Bit of a hypochondriac you know, if it's not the doctor it's the hospital, poor man is looking for sympathy, in my opinion of course, Vera."

"My job is on the line, Alvin?"

Alvin Briggs, loyal friend, stroked her shoulder, "Don't you worry, Vera, I've known Mr Mix for years," continued caressing and comforting, "he'll have me to contend with me if this goes any further. He's all bark, you know, puts the store first, always looks after his staff. I'm not frightened of him," shook his anxious head without conviction. "I mean, when we had bother with young Albert, his son, I actually confronted Mr Mix myself, *'Mr Mix,'* I said firmly, *'we can't have your son being impertinent to members of staff, not good for staff morale,'* and he listened, Vera, he actually listened!"

Vera thought, *Pull the other one, Alvin,* knew him that well.

**

The telephone was picked up immediately. Dolly Connelly still afraid of the technology shouted, "Hello, who's there?"

George, her absent son, answered, "Ma, you don't have to shout!"

"George," still in overdrive and revving, "what took you so long?"

"Busy, Ma, you know how it is!"

"Had any visitors, son?" knowing the response, wanting the gossip.

"Ma, you tell Vera where I live and you think she's gonna pass up the opportunity?"

"George, I had no choice, you know what she's like."

"You seen her since?"

"No, son," sucked in a lungful of air and started barking like a dog, muttered, "bloody fags'll be the death of me! Called over the weekend, wouldn't budge an eyelid 'till I told her your address. Never been back, don't suppose I'll see her for a while."

"Well she called all right, full of fire and piss as usual! Didn't give me the lickin's of a dog!"

"It's not just you, son, it's the money. She mentioned Joe and young Jack... maintenance?"

"Ma, she bloody attacked me!"

"That's Vera!"

"Drew blood, Ma," whined George Connelly, "in front of the kids and Joyce!"

"End of the day, son, she's your wife, legal and all."

"Ma, she ever come again, you'll let me know beforehand ... gimme chance to sort something out?"

Dolly grimaced, thought, *Hide from Vera? Chance'd be a fine thing!*

"Ma, you still there?"

"Sure son, Vera tells me she's on a mission, I'll phone, let you know."

"Any gossip, Ma?" asked George Connelly, wondered if anyone missed him, homesick for his cronies at the Club, wondered if any women had asked about his whereabouts.

"Yesterday's news, son, no one is interested," she pondered awhile, asked, "you havin' second thoughts, our George?"

George playing the tough guy, "About what, Ma?"

"About comin' back home, Vera is missin' you... kids too."

"I'm okay down here, Ma. Joyce is a different kettle of fish than Vera, peace it's own self, she is, quiet as a mouse, do what I want."

Dolly asked, "You want to speak to Adam, he's here?"

"Big brother not at work?"

67

The telephone was handed over and there was muted conversation between Adam Connelly and his mother.

"George," said Adam, "On the way out the door, night-shift.... "

"Can't keep a good man down, eh?"

"And you?"

George chortled, glad to hear familiar voices, "Day-shift, well, I should be... thought I'd take a week or two off, keep my benefits right, don't want to look too healthy, you know?"

Adam pinched his face, some days he thought he was talking to a stranger, stuck him with the gentlest of reprimands, "George, you oughta be at work, idle hands and all that shite?"

George ignored the jibe, "Hey, Adam, when you gonna come and visit? We got three bedrooms and Joyce says you're welcome any time." Any excuse for a booze-up.

"George, man," shrugged his shoulders, holding the phone, "it's awkward. You're still married to Vera. She was here at the weekend, wasn't too happy, tell you for nothin'."

"Too much like hard work was Vera. Hell, she was out with the stop-watch if I was a bit late!"

"George," muttered the brother in disbelief, "some nights you didn't go home!"

"Whatever, you gonna come and see me sometime, or what?"

"Sure, George," glanced at the clock, "got to go, brother, late for the pit, you take care?"

George replaced the telephone, looked glumly at Joyce, his common-law, "Nothin' changes, pet, nothin' changes."

CHAPTER SIX

"Elmore called," said Annie, standing next to the kitchen sink, big silly grin on her wrinkled face.

"Not tonight, Ma," answered Vera, pulling off her long coat, shivering with the cold, thinking about the previous night……..

Persuaded by Elmore, they left the pub at 11.05pm, Evelyn's body-clock already askew, strode the short distance to the big detached house owned by the dentist, Elmore acting like an enjoined twin with Vera, carrier-bag full of booze clanking noisily by his side, singing into the night like a love-sick teenager, crooning like Como, *Magic Moments,* too loud and feckless for Vera Connelly who tried to silence him, and stop his too-familiar hands from roaming and touching. She chastised him endlessly. The older couple, Annie and Evelyn, way ahead, walking and talking like two old and dear friends, at ease with one another.

Still full of the little barber, Elmore said, "Have you heard Perry's new release, *Delaware,* clever tune, a pun on words, plays with the names of all the American states so that…."

"Let's change that record, Elmore," said Vera, steering the conversation towards something more personal. "Your brother Evelyn, I've noticed, the more he drinks the less he stammers."

"Rarely stammers with me," answered the big man, "hardly a stutter when he's happy." Paused for a moment, asked, "You like Andy Williams… heard, *Butterfly?"*

Vera asked, "You always so sociable, Elmore, what's with the singing and dancing malarkey? Ma was telling me she couldn't remember the last time anyone had climbed on the stage and sang unaccompanied. Is this the real you, or does Guinness turn your senses?"

Elmore grinned, said stoically, "One life, Vera!"

"You enjoy socialising, then?"

"Always," replied the man jovially. "Singing, dancing, why not?"

"Not a home bird, Elmore?" Vera quizzing and probing.

"Twenty questions, Vera," chortled the inebriated man, "where's this leading?" Squeezed her shoulders gently and said, "I don't hurt anyone, don't harm anyone, always found being housebound was like being in a cage, inside looking out, with the world passing you by."

"Better out than in?"

"Bad memories when I was a kid, Vera." Reminiscing now, his features furrowed, "Atmosphere at home was, how can I say this, awkward, stressful even, always pleased when I could disappear with friends. Got to be a habit, rarely stayed around the house much."

"And Evelyn?"

"If I was from the Orient I'd mimic *Charlie Chan* and say, '*Evelyn Number One Son.*'"

Vera sighed loudly, "Right," she said softly, sardonically.

"Long story!"

"I can wait," she said sympathetically, "sounds interesting."

Elmore said, "It's the way life takes you, Vera. Got to go with the flow, can see why I've always loved a good time, always enjoyed a busy social life."

"And it didn't interfere with your job, you being a professional?" remembering the gossip from her mother about Elmore's dismissal, fishing for information, wanting to know all about him.

Earlier that evening they had drank and chattered, helped by the continuous draughts of alcohol supplied, observed Vera, by the elder brother, not one round of drinks bought by Elmore. Ten-o-clock and Vera, tied up with a heavy conscience, walked alone to the counter and ordered drinks, hoping Elmore would take the subtle hint. Water off a duck's back, left his chair, strode to the small stage, stooping over the ancient piano, tinkled with the keys to gain attention, few bars of *Side-Saddle,* before he left the instrument and started singing full throttle, not a care in the world, better than Bobby Darin. *Mack the Knife,* loud and clear, sang until closing time, one song after another, heard the rapturous applause, accepted the occasional drink, and continued. Vera counted five freebies from the crowd, finished a song, and finished a pint.

"Are you saying that professional folk shouldn't enjoy themselves, Vera, you think the possession of a degree should be an entry to a profession but a bar on happiness, doctors, lawyers and social workers should all be staid and miserable? I'm hurting no one. You think I should stop having fun? Time flies, Vera, tomorrow I'll wake up in a nursing-home, old, decrepit and incontinent, like my old grandfather. I want the memories!"

"Hey, I'm curious is all."

The group passed the *Half Moon* pub, walked along the plush residential Stockton Road for a few minutes before reaching the private driveway that snaked between overhanging trees to the imposing property, Vera watched as Evelyn and her mother strode out of sight, *How the other half live,* she thought enviously.

"Your brother lives alone?" she asked.

"Left in the will, got the house, Evelyn always was the favourite." Elmore sighed, "Told you, *Number One Son."*

"And you?"

"Me," irony cloaking his reply, "got the short straw, sweet FA!"

"Why was that?"

Elmore Stoker stopped the groping and placed an arm on her shoulder, hugged her, said, "You want the life story," he said, smiled to himself, never got tired of telling

71

the hard-luck story, better than a magnet for pulling gullible females, cared less.

Vera said, "Any way you want to play it."

"Evelyn and I are half-brothers, same mother different father." He paused momentarily, sighing, a slight shrug of the broad shoulders, "Mother apparently was having a mid-life crisis, had an affair. I was the result."

They stopped walking, Vera like an anchor, pulling the man to a stop, looked up at the man, "You having me on, Elmore?"

He was telling the truth, smiling still but the eyes could not mask the reality and the hurt.

He said quietly, "Shit happens, eh?"

"Elmore, I didn't know!"

"Not the kind of news one broadcasts." Shrugged his shoulders, "Still, had a decent life, could have been a lot worse. Mother was forgiven; I was accepted, grudgingly, brought up as part of the Stoker family. Twelve years ago mother died and I was told the truth by the man I thought was my father."

The journey continued, "And your father, your real father?"

Elmore Stoker shook his head bewilderedly, "I think my mother would have told me had I confronted her when she was alive, but my father, sorry, Evelyn's father, would never talk about it, always sent him into a rage, said he didn't know, only knew mother was unfaithful because she confessed to an affair. I'd just left university, accepted a position at Hartlepool, Social Services... rented in the town. Everything fine and dandy, still visited, mainly to see Evelyn, then father died, Evelyn's father actually, bit of a recluse for years, not a full shilling, a regular Howard Hughes. Then I had a bit of a calamity a few months ago and Evelyn offered me shelter until things were resolved. That's it in a nutshell."

"Ma said you'd lost your job."

Elmore said, "Not quite true. Suspension on full pay, the enquiry is ongoing," reached the open front door, "enough for tonight, eh, let's enjoy ourselves, Vera." He eased towards her face, kissed her gently and laughed awkwardly.

"Hey, why not," she replied coyly, flirting and teasing, a little too much alcohol and the barriers were falling.....................

Vera," reminded Annie Goodrich, "Elmore says they'll be in the *Half Moon* tonight about nine-o-clock, wants to know if we'll join them for the quiz?"

Vera said, "Ma, you can't be serious? We were drinking and dancing until three in the morning, late for work, had to lie to Alvin Brown, almost lost my job, Ma, I'm on a final warning.... you making a cup of tea, I'm bushed!"

"Vera, I don't want to go out on my own, pet."

"Then stay in for once," said with sarcasm, walked into the room and saw her boys squatting in front of the red-hot fire engrossed in making a matchstick-gun, Joe the teacher, Jack absorbed, as big brother explained the complexities of the task.

Jack glanced quickly at his mother and smiled warmly, nodded and said proudly, "Matchstick-gun!"

"Pay attention, Jack," said Joe, plucked a slim piece of wood from the floor, the length of a long pencil, twice as thick, looked at his mother, said, "Nana said I could use firewood, okay Ma?"

"There's plenty left," said Vera, knowing there was a boxful under the kitchen sink, courtesy of Uncle Mick's thieving from the colliery coffers.

Joe turned to his brother, said, "Choose a hairclip then," gestured at the marble fireplace and the half a dozen borrowed clips lying there, large and small, placed in a neat row by Joe and dwarfed either side by two large, empty, *Lowcocks's* pop bottles.

Jack picked up one of the smallest, smiled weakly at big brother.

"Try another, Jack," head shaking, rejecting and grinning.

A second attempt was successful, the large hair-clip handed over.

"Good," said Joe, "what next?"

Jack studying, Vera absorbed.

Joe grasped the single piece of kindling in one hand and one of the bottles in the other, said, "Stick. Bottle. Clip."

Jack shook his head, remembered and grinned mischievously, "Rubber band," grasped the bottle unscrewed the stopper, planted the bottle on the carpet and pulled and prised at the rubber gasket that was fixed on to the bottle-lid, took minutes before the rubber band was pulled free. Joe handed the small wooden stick to his brother who screwed and forced the rubber stopper midway on to the stick, then paused, out of ideas.

"Right, that's good," said Joe encouragingly, "you've got a stick with a rubber-band on it," showed his gawking brother the large hair-clip, "what shall we do with this?"

"Push it under the rubber-band?"

"It'll come out of the other side, Jack... how can we hold it firm so that it grips the rubber?"

Jack shook his head, said apologetically, "Forgot, Joe."

Joe held the large hair-clip and with a deft twist bent both ends of the clip, pushed the body of the clip between the wood and the rubber-band until the protruding ends of the metal clip were gripped on the rubber ring. The young teacher held the stick in one hand and with the other eased the body of the clip away from the surface of the wood and back over the rubber-band like a trigger.

"Watch!" he said, and released the clip.

Whack! The spring-loaded trigger slapped forward on to the stick. He repeated the exercise, *Whack!*

"Ma," said Joe, smugly, "give me a match."

Jack watched spellbound as a single spent match was accepted and the hair-clip was hoisted back like a trigger and the matchstick fed into the clip. 'Ready. Aim. Fire,' said Joe, released the clip and the match shot across the room.

"Brilliant," shouted Jack ecstatically, "do it again, Joe!"

Joe handed the weapon to his kid brother, "Your turn, Jack."

Annie Goodrich trudged into the room carrying the single cup of tea, muttered sourly, "One bloody hour he's been showing Jack how to do that... talk about slow!"

Jack smiled, immune to the discontent of his grandmother, happy to possess his very own matchstick-gun.

"Nana," protested Joe, "he's only five, I couldn't make one until I was eight, remember. Dad kept slapping me, calling me stupid!"

"Good at clouting kids and women was George Connelly," grunted the disillusioned grandmother, pining already for her little dentist, said again, desperation in her voice, "what about an hour at the *Half Moon*, our Vera, back by ten?"

"Tired, Ma," answered the young mother, "you have a drink," sipped at the tea, said, "maybe I'll have a look out Saturday."

Ten-o-clock and all three were fast asleep. Vera sprawled comfortably in the huge arm-chair, the two boys, top and tailed, on the sofa. Someone knocked gently at the door, third time and the woman jumped to her feet, dazed and confused with the heavy drag of slumber still gripping her, stumbled to the rear door, jerked it open and the big grinning winning smile melting her.

"Hi," said Elmore Stoker, "had to see you, I'm sorry," nodded apologetically, "brought my own," shoved a bottle of whiskey at her, stolen from his brother's vast collection a short time ago.

She said, "Elmore, what time is it?" stepped aside to allow him to pass, adding, "the kids are fast asleep ..." wasn't allowed to finish.

Elmore Stoker interrupted, "That's good,"

Vera said, "They're both on the sofa!"

"That's not so good," joking with her, "suppose I'll have to carry them to bed for you?"

"Shh," said Vera, "make yourself useful, Elmore, stay in the kitchen, find some glasses, make a sandwich, stay out of sight until I take them to bed."

"One condition!"

Vera said, "Anything, you big lump!"

"Gimme a kiss!"

A child's voice interjected, cut the romance dead in the water, Joe, struggling upright on the settee, rubbing sleep from his eyes.

"Ma, who's in the house?" peering into the kitchen, Joe's eyes wide with a mix of curiosity and apprehension.

Vera strode into view, "Come on," she said softly, "time for bed. You lead the way, I'll carry Jack."

Joe waited, stiff, eyes focussed on the kitchen, not interested as his mother struggled and hoisted baby brother aloft, pushed and prodded towards the stairs.

"Ma, who's the man, what does he want?"

"Climb the stairs and I'll tell you," a carrot rather than the stick.

Joe clomped noisily up the staircase.

"Man from the council," soothed the woman, a gnawing panic taking her, "called a social worker," half a truth better than none, "council checking on us, Joe, see if we can manage on our own."

"Because dad left us," asked the boy, "is that why, Ma?"

More mistruths as Vera said, "Man has to write a report about us, Joe, give it to the council, told you about your father not sending money for you and Jack… man downstairs checking on us."

Joe said, "So we might get help, Ma?"

"Chance would be a fine thing," the mother said softly, "but fingers crossed, we might get some money off the council."

Joe admitted, shamefully, "Ma, council man asks, I didn't fasten those fireworks to Douglas's door, it was Sammy McAndrew, he even lit them but they went out, I went with some more matches, the rest of the gang had a head start Ma, that's why he caught me. And the bonfire, Ma that was a pure accident, Ernie Bracken….."

Vera said, "Shut up, Joe, it's nothing to do with you, now sleep!"

Jack opened his eyes, whispered hoarsely, "Is my matchstick-gun safe?"

"In your toy-box, Jack, shh."

Joe admitted gravely, "Didn't mean to set fire to the quarry-side, Ma, fire got out of hand, honest."

"When the hell was that?"

"Saturday dinnertime. Man chased us with his dog, said he knew who I was and was reporting me!"

"Sleep!" chided the young mother.

**

CHAPTER SEVEN

The boys overslept, Jack prodded Joe, anxious about his matchstick-gun. Joe jumped out of bed and hurried down the stairs. Clock said 8.40, twenty minutes to dress and run to the top of the village, looked at the crumpled snoring figure that littered the big arm-chair and bolted back up the stairs, "Get dressed, our Jack, quick as you can, we'll leave by the front door, Ma still has that council man here, checkin' on us!"

"What's a council-man, Joe?" said the kid, pulling on shorts and shirt, "shoes, where are my *Tuf* shoes?"

"Under the bed. Man downstairs is here to see if we can stay with nana. The council own this house and we've been reported. Ma says we might have to move or get more money. She said I'll definitely have extra pocket-money!" Dressed now apart from his coat, "Hurry Jack or we'll be late and Albright will strap me!"

"Want a pee," demanded the kid, "want some breakfast, Joe." He finished fastening his shoes, "Where's Ma?"

Made Joe study, he rubbed at his dry mouth, dying for tea and jam and bread. "Wait there," he said, and moved to the other bedroom, came back a minute later. "Ma's asleep!"

"Wake her, Joe!"

"Tried. Can't, think she's drunk again. Come on!" He left the room and hurried down the stairs, grabbed the two coats and eased open the front-door, "Come on Jack, I'll call over Uncle Mick's and borrow some money!"

"Want Ma," gasped Jack, slowly, reluctantly, descending the stairs.

Joe wasn't listening, his gaze on the strangers' overcoat on the floor which must have fallen when he grabbed at their coats. His head plotting and planning as he contemplated action.

Jack asked, "What's the matter?"

"Shh!" Dropping to his knees, fingers darting through the pockets, Joe became a modern-day Artful Dodger. He found a handful of coins, "Here, some for you, Jack," offering the bribe.

Jack, fearful of the repercussions, shook his head and refused the offer, "Don't do that Joe!" Pulled on his jacket and waited with bated breath for something awful to happen.

"Shh!" Joe took control and attempted to calm his little brother.

Jack pleaded, "Want Ma!"

Joe responded by grabbing and hoisting his kid brother clear of the door-step. He carefully closed the door, "Ma is drunk! If I can't wake her you won't be able to, come on or we'll be late for school." Bolted like a gazelle for the gate with Jack like the protesting calf trying to catch its disappearing mother.

"Joe," called the kid, "you said we were going to Uncle Mick's?"

"No need, we've plenty," running and laughing despite the drabness and dampness of the early morning. "We'll call in Davison's shop, gimme your order, Jack!"

"Vimto," gasped an out-of-breath youngster. "Candy cigarettes, gobstopper …. packet of spangles too!"

Joe Connelly burst through the school-gate like Jesse Owens howling past the finishing line. One minute to commencement of the lesson and Albright on the prowl like Herman Goering, baton replaced by stick, ready to squash any rebellion in the ranks. Joe almost collided with a hesitant Albert Mix, in a quandary contemplating whether or not to venture further into the school. Blanched white when he saw Joe Connelly, amazed when the smaller boy smiled a welcome.

"Is Albright about, Albert?" the summer fracas long ago forgotten, Joe couldn't hold a grudge if he were paid.

Albert Mix recovered quickly enough to say, "Never seen him, Joe," pleasantly surprised that the diminutive terror wasn't spoiling for a return fight.

Joe said, "New bike, Albert," suddenly remembering that the giant had been missing for days, "you better then, been sick?"

"Sniffles, but Ma fusses too much, wouldn't let me come to school 'till I was better." Ate humble pie when he said casually, "You want to ride it to the bike-shed, Joe, it's a *Raleigh Lenton Sports...4-speed!*"

"It's brand-new, you don't mind?"

"Joe," chortled the chubby leviathan, "we're still mates, aren't we? It was just a daft fight we had, come on, try it for size!" Smiled warmly and added, "Special chrome-green, brilliant, eh, Joe?"

Joe jumped on to the sparkling bicycle, said, apologetically, "Shouldn't have used that bin-lid on you, Albert, you know that?"

"Would have done the same," answered Albert, starting to enjoy the moment, plotting and planning for any possible wisecracks from fellow-pupils, *Joe said he was sorry, said that was the only way he could have beaten me... you got a problem with that?* Yes, it was going to be a joyful day, pleased he was back.

A first-year kid ran into the yard and sidled up to Joe, shouted angrily, "You said you'd wait for me," saw the beautiful bike and his brother sitting astride. "Joe, give me a piggy-back!"

Albert Mix laughed, said, "Never your kid brother, Joe?" bent down and lifted him on to the seat, "give him a ride, Joe, and keep the bairn happy!"

The bell sounded, someone sounding like a Field Marshal bawling frantically, *'Line up! Line up!'* Herman Albright on a mission.

Albert Mix put his formidable strength behind the bicycle and pushed, shouted, "See you in class, Joe!"

Joe Connelly laughing hysterically, Jack frantic as he clung on to his brothers clothing, "Slow down, our Joe," he called, "slow down!"

Albert Mix pulled out the absence-note, read again the contents, needed to know why he'd been away from school, *Diarrhoea and sickness,* looked again at the spelling, confused, thinking *Ma said she would write I had the shits, what the hell does that mean?* saw the chunky tutor striding towards him, smile on his moustachioed smarmy face, nodded acknowledgement. Wasn't frightened of the head-teacher, not when his dad was a general manager and his mother was a chief librarian. Seen Albright quake too many times when his mother took one of her turns, shake in his tiny shoes when his mother had barracked him in the past.

**

The nausea pulled her from sleep, knew instantly she'd overslept and probably lost her job. Absent Monday, and two late starts, straddled her mother's bed feeling wretched, knowing her Co-op days were down the proverbial spout, tried to think but her head ached so much, too much whiskey, too late at night. *The boys,* forgot all about her sons, *Jesus Christ,* managed to haul herself upright but the swimming, unrelenting sickness made her double-up and she began retching violently. Bile and stench filling her mouth as she struggled to her bedroom. The boys were gone, nodded at the image of Joe taking charge of the situation, dressing both of them and leaving for school, *Good old Joe,* she thought, *one in a million.*

One unsteady step at a time Vera manipulated the steep swaying staircase, saw the crumpled coat at the foot of the stairs and knew the man was still in the house, couldn't think straight anymore, didn't know what to do next. Took a deep breath, then another, and opened the living-room door. Elmore Stoker was draped like a broken mannequin over the arm-chair and snorting like an excited pig. He was fast asleep. Vera moved out of the room, through the kitchen and into the lavatory, couldn't believe the image gawking back from the mirror, waxen, red-eyed and miserable, wearing last-night's clothing, creased and stained, felt so ashamed of herself. Blamed Elmore, her mother, blamed George Connelly most of all for destroying her life. Sat on the toilet and wept bitter tears, wanted her life back, wanted her husband back, knew deep down he was never returning. It was all her fault, short-fuse all of her life, hindsight and she might have calmed enough to write a letter to George, tell him how she really felt. Hell it was a leg-over, a bit on the side, played her cards right and waited until the hot steam of passion blew cold then George would have been home again with his tail between his legs.

**

Delwin Mix said with authority, *'Chief librarian!'* waited minutes before his wife Mildred picked up the phone, smiled as he listened to her best telephone-voice, lardy-dar, lardy-dar, Lady Muck with a twang to equal the Queen, soon as she recognised the caller she relaxed and her natural guttural tones returned.

"What... I'm really busy!" Mildred was full of impatience as she glanced at the sweet face of the borrower, miming, *'One moment, please.'*

The husband was enjoying himself, exaggerating as usual, playing the strict, no-nonsense disciplinarian, "One minute late, Mildred, young Mrs Connelly was one minute late and I sent her home, sacked her, Milly, thought you'd like to know."

"That's wonderful news," smiled genuinely at the pouting customer, in heaven with the news, "everything is working out at last." She hesitated and checked her wrist-watch, "Albert's okay, isn't he, he hasn't returned from school?"

"I think the *Raleigh* bike was the answer all along."

"You're so generous with our boy, Delwin; it must have cost a fortune."

Delwin Mix said, "It was worth it to see the look on his face." The 20% discount was an added sweetener.

"I know we spoil him," whispered the woman, "but he hasn't had it easy since he was child, you know baby-sitters, childminders. Albert's had it rough at times, hasn't he?"

"He's happy, you're happy, that's all that matters, Mildred," said Delwin Mix, "and he's actually gone to school with a smile on his face." He sighed loudly then said, "Have to go, Milly, busy busy," replaced the receiver and took a mouthful of painkillers.

Alvin Brown, under-manager, walked into the cluttered office, face chiselled with deep groves of annoyance, pouting and sulking like an overgrown child, handed over the stock-lists from the food section, wanting to say so much, dumbstruck with the deep weight of subservience, *'Will there be anything else, Mr Mix?'* fought a brief losing battle with the general manager about the dismissal of Vera Connelly. The store was open only one minute when Mix announced adamantly, "If she shows her face, Mr Brown, show her the door and send her home! Woman is taking liberties!"

"Could be ill, Mr Mix," but the protest was half-hearted, knew what the manager would say.

"She could phone and at least explain her absence, Mr Brown."

Alvin Brown found the gumption to try one last time, "An accident, Mr Mix, perhaps she's had an accident or one of her sons. Mrs Connelly might be in a hospital emergency-room this very minute. Are we not being too hasty?"

"An accident?" he said sarcastically.

"Yes, yes sir," he said, stammering, stood his ground, blanched with trepidation.

"Go stack some shelves, Mr Brown," the words said quietly, venomously, effectively. "This matter is closed!" Looked at the fidgeting fellow, a cursory glance at the stock to be ordered, toyed with the page, said absently, "Mrs Connelly turn up for work yet?"

Mr Brown shook his miserable head, regretting his impulsiveness, angry at himself for defending the absentee assistant, wondering how to mend bridges with the manager, muttered almost inaudibly, "I'm sorry, Sir, you were right and I was out of order. I do apologise for questioning your good judgement."

"Don't worry about it," said Mix gruffly, thinking, '*Arse-licker*,' "we all make mistakes, takes a man to admit it, Mr Brown."

Delwin Mix watched his under-manager stride away, head downcast, arms pumping, imaginary feathers flying off embarrassed wings. Smiled at the vacillating fool that was Alvin Brown, didn't know what mistakes were, probably ruined his day because of harsh words from his manager, kind of man who fretted if he wore the wrong tie or missed a doctor's appointment. Mistakes, blunders, life-changing experiences, Del Mix knew all about such things. Held a degree in calamity and mayhem, paid the price in full. He wandered to the side-window and stared absently into the large concrete yard, watched as the large wagon manoeuvred supplies towards the loading-bay, observed the uniformed driver leaning out from the cab, laughing and talking to one of his female staff as if he didn't have a care in the world. Delwin Mix felt a stab of jealousy as he stood morosely and stiff, observing the antics below, the driver flirting outrageously, the young girl reciprocating. Thought again of his lost love, his beautiful lost love and his horrendous stupendous error all those years ago, shook his head glumly as the proud face loomed before him, closed his eyes and shivered involuntary as he smelled the fragrant skin and touched the auburn hair, kissed luscious lips. Sell his soul to see his love again.

**

Annie Goodrich said, "You should be at work!" Embarrassment written all over her face, caught out, no hiding the fact that she'd stayed overnight with Evelyn Stoker, separate beds but who'd believe her. Evelyn not responsive or amenable to her advances.

"Had you slept in your own bed, I wouldn't have overslept again!" Tit for tat, from Vera.

"How the hell could you have overslept," grunted the mother, "you've got my alarm-clock."

Vera was sheepish with her answer, "Elmore called, didn't he, brought a bottle." Waited for the flack as she eased to the sink, "Tea, Ma?"

"Elmore Stoker called at my house?" feigning annoyance, didn't want to explain her sleepover to her own daughter, wouldn't have minded if she'd scored with the diminutive dentist.

"That's what I said, mother," turned on the cold tap and filled the kettle, "you eaten yet?"

"What's that supposed to mean, our Vera," quick glance at her watch, almost noon, gulped with guilt, "I've done nothing wrong."

Vera eased, "Elmore just left, couldn't wake him earlier."

"I only hope he hasn't been sleeping in my bed, Vera?"

The younger woman smiled for the first time that day, "Bit of a tight squeeze in my bed and with the boys in the same room," digging holes for herself, added, "I don't think so, Ma!"

"So where did *he* sleep?" like she was reading *The Three Bears*.

"Arm-chair, all night." Wondered why she had slept in her mother's bed and not her own, had no recollection of any passion or play from Elmore. Vera pondered, *Brewer's Droop?*

Annie Goodrich said, "If the boys are at school, Vera, how come you didn't go to work?"

Sucked in air, muttered grudgingly, "Took themselves, I never heard a thing, Ma."

"You gonna get yourself a bad name, pet, you know what people are like."

"Elmore was easy listening, Ma," she admitted, "had one drink, listened to his patter, had another… you know how it is," glanced at her parent, trying to read the signs, wanting some kind of approval or understanding. "Mother, I've been on my own for months, you know what it's like. Lonely, Ma, that's all, my head is full of shite, I'm lonely," wandered lethargically into the sitting-room followed by the mother.

"Marty's been dead for years, our Vera! Sometimes you have to grasp the nettle and get on with your life."

"Ma, better if George was dead, at least then I'd know it was over… finished. Him down Yorkshire with that woman and her kids, well, you know, I keep thinking George might ….."

Annie Goodrich interrupted angrily, "Hell's teeth, girl, have you not had enough of George Connelly? When you gonna learn he's no damn good?"

Vera slumped on the arm-chair, Elmore's body heat still present, said glumly, "You think I want to be this way Ma, you think I enjoy fretting for George? Can't help it, give anything to stop thinking about him. He's a bastard, Ma, I'm under no illusion, trouble is…." Her voice trailed away, knew she was wasting her time talking about George Connelly, no one was bothered that she still had deep feelings for the man. Who could replace him? Oozed charm by the bucket-load, made you feel a million dollars when the mood took him, made you forget all about the bad times. She thought about Elmore Stoker, tall and film-star handsome, Easington's answer to *Rock Hudson,* made her laugh, easy listening too, wanted so much to like someone enough to start a relationship. Thought about last night, Elmore on a roll, glass in hand, spouting tall tales............

"If your mother told you that, then all I can say is bunk!" sipped at the whiskey like it was nectar, smiled and shrugged his wide shoulders.

Vera lifted her glass, "Cheers," drained in one, the alcohol warming and lifting her spirits, sat opposite him, close enough to the coal-fire to feel the heat on her bare legs. "Only repeating what she said, Elmore."

"Why would my brother fabricate. He knows for a fact about my suspension," lifted his glass and drank the fiery contents. "The family in question were drunkards, mother and father, barred out of every pub in Hartlepool, systematically abusing their children, only recently reunited with their two girls with a weekly visit from my department to supervise and observe. I was one of the case officers, called three times in one week and was given flimsy excuses why I couldn't see the children .... dentists, doctors, the kids were never present. On the third visit I went against procedure and entered the home, had a gut feeling and I was proved right, both girls were watching television dressed in a deplorable condition, one of the tots, eight years old, was bruised about the face. I was right and I don't regret anything."

Vera asked, "So why the suspension?"

"I should have waited for back-up, a female officer, maybe phoned the police. The trouble was the mother, out of her head on Valium and booze, made accusations against me, said I was too familiar with her, accused me of being intoxicated, even had the audacity of suggestion I made a pass at her!"

Vera said, "I'm sorry, Elmore, Ma must have heard wrong. It's awful what's happened to you."

"Part and parcel of the job I suppose," reached for the bottle, said "can I refill your glass?" started filling his tumbler to the rim.

She joined him, sat at his feet, wedged her back against him, felt his warmth, lifted her glass and forced her head away from George Connelly, seemed every time she sipped at the whiskey Vera could feel the attraction growing, told herself there were more fish in the sea. She had a life, a future waiting ... maybe with Elmore Stoker.

Elmore said casually, as if he were checking out all the options, "I might resign, Vera, six months and nothing has happened, feel in limbo, you understand what I'm saying?"

Always spoke from the heart, said matter-of-fact, "That would be giving in to those horrid people, Elmore. Ask me and I'd have to say you should stick to your principles, can't be much longer."

"Didn't help my case when someone commented that they could smell drink on my breath," paused momentarily as he gulped whiskey as if it were water, "honest Vera, as I live and breathe, I'd had a pint with my lunch, same every day; a pub sandwich and a pint of *Nimmo's Best.* One pint!"

Vera sympathised, "Never mind, Elmore."

"Trouble was, if I'm being totally honest, I was a high flier in the department, only the boss and myself had degrees. You can imagine the jealousy, Vera, people above me with a few certificates to their name, bloody clerks really, any excuse to block my path, stop my promotion!" Another long guzzle, a smack of lips as he felt the fire in his belly, said poignantly, "You can see my problem, Vera, too many staff trying to block progress in the department, any excuse to keep me shackled to mediocre routine work. I don't want to be doing the same hum-drum knocking on doors and file-filling for the next few years. If anything I want to run the bloody place. Chance would be a fine thing; I know it isn't going to happen. Time, I think, to seek pastures new."

Her head was spinning, more used to beers or lagers, never one for spirits, too potent, too strong, said dreamily, "It must be awful, Elmore, you're probably right, pastures new." Took another sip, thinking she could get used to the gentle lull of alcohol coursing through her veins, hadn't finished her second glass and already she felt wonderful. Started to enjoy the man's company, reminded her of the way she used to be with George when they first married, when the world was their oyster. Opposite ends of the candle for looks, George small and petite, Elmore so tall and powerful; George a compulsive liar and womaniser, Elmore educated and seemingly focused on her. She thought he could be the special one, if she could only allow it to happen. Finishing her drink she said, "Can you fill my glass, Elmore?" felt him kiss the top of her head, so like George it scared her, added, "you've always liked music, Elmore, you like Dicky Valentine, Michael Holliday?" leading him on.............

"They're not brothers, Ma," said Vera, pushing aside the reminiscences, the hot tea taking away the intensity of the headache. Watched her mother light up two cigarettes and hand one to her, "Thanks Ma."

Annie Goodrich eased on to the sofa, grasped the crumpled edition of the *Northern Echo* and started absently flipping pages, "Evelyn said they were brothers, I was laughing at how they were so different, tall, small, fat, thin, you know. Said they were brothers, Vera, maybe he regards him as a brother, brought up together?"

"Elmore mentioned he was suspended, not sacked."

"Not according to Evelyn," Annie said, sucking at the fag, reading her horoscope, smiling at the good news, *Your love life will take a new turn.* Chuckling quietly she said, "How many turns can you have, I've tried them all!"

"Ma?"

Annie said, "Elmore was given his notice because he was drunk at work, second warning. I believe Evelyn is telling the truth." glanced at her morose daughter, "He's bad news, our Vera. You want my advice, stay away from him. Out of the frying-pan and into the fire! My advice, and you're free to piss on it, is to play the field. Someone decent will come along; don't be in too much of a hurry to settle down with anyone just yet."

"I didn't call on Elmore," insisted the younger woman, "he called on me."

"You make arrangements to see him again?"

"Maybe, maybe not," she said, "I'm not sure what to do, Ma, man's looking for somewhere to rent, wants me to help."

CHAPTER EIGHT

Jack shared a double-desk with Alice Raine, the class of first-year kiddies had listened for half an hour as Mrs Wainwright talked about the Roman Empire, supplementing her lesson with pictures of soldiers and slaves, maps and diagrams; the whole works. After the first lesson of the day, mathematics, the infants had wearied and needed a pleasant change so the tutor wisely introduced the class to ancient history. Jack listened enthralled as Mrs Wainwright described the rise of the empire, the defeat of Cathage, better than a fairy tale, especially when she mentioned Hannibal and elephants, confusion set in when Mrs Wainwright, pointing at a huge map of the Mediterranean, started prodding at a section of the map and talking about a place called Italy which really was a big foot! Jack had jerked his head back to the lesson as Mrs Wainwright was starting to talk in nursery rhymes, "You see class, big-footed Italy kicked off Sicily," said it again to reinforce the map reference, "Big-footed Italy kicked off Sicily!" Jack's head was a jumble of elephants and giant's legs, glanced at Alice Raine who appeared as confused as he, shrugged his shoulders and tried to concentrate.

Towards the end of the lesson, when the pupils were attempting to use crayons to colour in worksheets provided by the teacher, Alice whispered, "I once saw an elephant at Billy Smarts Circus, Jack." She carefully finished colouring her elephant's trunk, nudged her companion, said, "Look, Jack," proud as punch at her attempt.

Jack grimaced, said, "Elephants are brown Alice; don't have yellow trunks and yellow ears!"

Alice paled, "It's supposed to be a fairy-tale, isn't it?" pouted like a spoilt princess.

"Don't know!" another shrug of his shoulders, looked at his efforts with a Roman soldier, remembered the teachers advice, *'When you've finished colouring in the tunic, try and imagine all the weapons used by a typical soldier, try and enhance your drawing with all the weapons at his disposal,'* couldn't understand some of the big words used by Mrs Wainwright, knew all about weapons though, tried his best to please her.

Alice was staring at Jack's attempts, whispered, "Soldiers didn't have guns in those days, Jack, only swords," pondered a while then added, "I think."

Jack was adamant, "It's only pretend, Alice, didn't the teacher say that the giants had big catapults... there's no such thing as big catapults, our Joe has a catapult and it fits in his pocket!" He leaned forward defensively so that his torso hid his picture from the mocking eyes of the girl, remembered something relevant to his argument. "And another thing," he added firmly, "if it was real then how come the giant in the map has only one leg, and why is he wearing women's high-heels?"

Alice pouted, wanted to stay friends with Jack Connelly, pet-lip and wet eyes, learning the game already, said, "I'm sorry, Jack, your picture is better than mine, can I see it again?"

Reluctantly he eased back into his chair, stared proudly at his soldier, sword in one hand and a rifle in the other, knew he was right, Mrs Wainwright said the Romans had pinched some gunpowder from the Indians or Chinese who lived on the island next to the giant's foot. He wasn't stupid, knew for a fact that gunpowder made guns work, Joe had told him that.

"It's lovely, Jack," gushed the girl.

"I know that," raised his hand, wanted Mrs Wainwright to see it.

**

It was Albert Mix who put the idea into Joe's head, never had any idea that the first storey in the co-op building

92

was for anything other than offices and food storage. Albert, who made it absolutely sure to anyone listening that his father was *General Manager* of the entire store, told Joe all about the electrical and general goods that were sold on the first floor, "There's only three people who work upstairs, Joe, sell furniture, televisions, cookers, everything!"

"And that's where you got your bike, Albert?" said Joe Connelly.

They were playing football during the long lunch-break. Joe was Preston North-End, Albert was Everton, their first tussle, when Joe was Sunderland and Albert was Newcastle had ended twenty-three to four, Joe the clear winner; the rough ground was a factor in the high score, plus the tennis ball used instead of a football was guaranteed to result in high scores. Two on the field, Albert and Joe plus two in either goal: Sammy McAndrew paired with Joe Connelly, Ernie Bracken in goal for Albert, and Joe like a greyhound running circles around big cumbersome Albert Mix, the new score already in double figures for the smaller boy and the all-new non-aggressive Albert Briggs seemingly enjoying the thrashing.

"*Raleigh Sports,* Joe," the pair of them taking a breather, sweat pouring down their faces, clothes warm and damp with the physical exertions, Ernie and Sammy content to throw the ball at one another while the big guns talked, "Should get your Ma to buy you one for Christmas, money off when you work there!"

Joe Connelly nodded, couldn't say he tended to get hand-me-downs and second-hand, "Okay, I'll tell her that," remembered the colliery co-op, same layout, maybe even bigger, never knew there was so much stuff on the upper decks, his young head in overdrive, needed to talk with someone, said casually, "Going to the bogs, Albert, it's almost bell-time."

Albert Mix never missed a trick, "Games forfeited if you walk away?"

"Okay, Albert."

Albert Mix bellowed at his team mate, "Ernie… Joe's had enough, so we win the second game, one game each, it's a draw!" Proud as punch as he faced Sammy McAndrew, "We'll have one in goal, Ernie, and you and me will have a game, eh?"

"Need a piss, Albert," whined Sammy, knew for a fact the bully would resort to his usual horrible ways once Joe was out of sight. He scampered after Joe Connelly.

Albert mouthed to the disappearing Sammy, "I'll let you be Nat Lofthouse and I'll be John Charles?"

Sammy kept running. Cursing silently, Albert turned to his quaking goalkeeper, "Ernie, we're playing penalties, okay?"

"Can I swap," begged the nervous boy, "and you be in goal?"

"Why?" grunted the young tyrant, leering as he neared his companion. "What's the problem?" added, "pass the tennis-ball."

"Not hard, Albert," begged Ernie Bracken, "take your time."

Albert Mix grinned mischievously, threw the missile hard towards the goalkeeper. The ball struck Ernie's head, "How's that, Ernie," watched as the boy flinched with pain, "soft enough?"

"Wait on, Joe," shouted Sammy McAndrew, reaching his friend, they walked together into the outside lavatory, open-roofed and exposed to all the elements, stood beside the troughs, "what's up?"

"Fancy a dare, Sam?" looking at the powerful stream of urine, stepped back a pace, didn't want to be covered in droplets of piss from the splash-back.

Sammy misread the challenge and immediately nipped his foreskin shut, watched it fill like a small balloon, aimed skywards and then pressed at the bulge in his penis, shouting gleefully as the stream of putrid liquid shot over the walls of the urinal, "Beat that!" waited for the shouts and protests from the school-yard.

"Naw, not a pissin' contest," muttered Joe, "proper dare. Tonight, do you fancy……"

The wooden door of the lavatory was almost pulled off its hinges by a hysterical head-master, "Out! Out! You filthy creature," Mr Albright bright crimson with anger interjected, "get to my room now, you dirty animals!"

"Done nowt, Sir!" protested Sammy McAndrew, knowing he was in for a beating, not the first time he'd been caught peeing over the walls of the toilet wall, nervously buttoning up his trousers, wiping wet fingers over his pants.

Albright grabbed the first boy by his ears, yanked him from the toilet and proceeded to drag him across the school-yard, "You too, Connelly" bellowed the angry tutor never bothering to look back at the second lad, "follow me!"

Joe Connelly sighed, fastened up his trousers and walked out of the lavatories, past the milling fretful crowds and grimaced as Mr Albright manhandled his pal towards the main building with Sammy McAndrew howling that his ear was hurting. The Headmaster released his grip and started slapping at the head of the wailing boy and pushed him bodily through the entrance-door with an enormous clatter and out of sight. Joe Connelly knew it was pointless protesting his innocence, saw his kid brother gawking at him, standing in the middle of the yard with the girl, winked and smiled courageously, didn't want to show fear.

Joe chortled at his sibling, winked at Alice Raine and stuck his thumb in the air, "It's all right, Jack," he said bravely, "Sammy pissed on Albright."

"Will you get the strap, Joe?" said the morose younger brother.

"Naw, he'll probably shout at me."

"Connelly!" screamed a distant voice from within the confines of the nearby classroom.

Alice Raine's eyes moistened with horror, glanced fretfully at her best friend, "Shall we go, Jack?"

Joe intervened to calm the situation, "Jack," he asked, "have you shown Alice how to walk like Douglas Bader?"

"Who's he?" asked Alice, never heard of Kenneth Moore or the film about the legless flying ace.

"*Reach for the Sky,*" said Jack proudly, turned and stuck his arms out spectacularly from his body, legs became wooden and rickety as the boy lumbered across the playground like some miniature Frankenstein monster, "Lost his legs in a plane crash!"

"Connelly," howled the demented head teacher from within the school building, "now!"

Joe Connelly hurried towards the building, spitting liberally on his hands, heard that moisture softened the pain, head down concentrating on the task and ran straight into the incensed, puffing peacock called Albright.

"Dirty boy," shrieked the tutor, "vile boy!" and hoisted Joe from the ground and flung him into the room.

"Please sir!" protested Joe Connelly, cute as a cucumber, "my hands were dirty, sir … only trying to wash off the muck."

"One urinating, the other spitting!" grunted a livid Albright. "Why on earth are they looking for the Missing Link?"

"Don't understand about the missing link, Mr Albright?"

The tutor side-swiped the boy and sent him sprawling, "Monkeys! You and bloody McAndrew! Put you pair in a zoo and you could urinate and spit on the visitors to your heart's content!"

"Sir?" said Joe, straight-face, masking the pain of the beating, acting like a dumb chimpanzee.

A further slap and he stumbled into the master's classroom, made his way slowly to Sammy McAndrew's side.

Nearby, in the playground, Jack had a crowd of eager beavers wanting to do the *Bader Walk*, Jack Connelly in his element as he explained the movie to the onlookers, vague on details about the latest bedtime story courtesy of his big brother. Few cared.

"Fell out of his plane, didn't he!" said an adamant Jack Connelly, sure his brother had said something along those lines.

"How can you fall out of a plane?" asked Nathan Brooks.

"Easy," interjected Alice Raine, defending her flustered friend, "if the plane turns upside-down!"

"But if you fall out," said Timmy Brownlee, "won't the parachute work?" waited patiently for an answer, one finger stuck up his nose, raking with an undiluted pleasure.

Jack Connelly shrugged thin shoulders, "I think the Germans or the Japs pinched them!"

"Why didn't he float to earth, twist his body so that he landed legs first?" asked Nathan Brooks. Adjusting thick spectacles, he said innocently, "You know, just before the plane crashed, step away from it and be safe?"

Too young to comprehend the laws of physics, Jack pouted, "Got caught on one of the wings didn't he ... sliced his legs clean off!"

"We should be like worms," said Timmy Brownlee to a bemused Alice, "should be able to grow our legs back again!"

"Stupid!" said Alice, turned again to her best friend, "Jack, show us again how he learned to walk with tin legs!"

"Get behind me!" shouted Jack Connelly resolutely.

Five youngsters dutifully stood in a snake-line behind the diminutive instructor.

"Ready," asked Jack, sticking out his arms for balance, prizing apart his legs, Kenneth Moore would have been proud, "go!"

The untidy line of human mannequins started the slow manic walk across the school yard, forgot all about McAndrew and Connelly.

**

Michael Green didn't bother to knock at his sister's door, opened it up and strolled in. "Anyone in, then," he said, wheezing like a consumptive, troubled for hours, wanting information about the stranger who had strolled from the place a few hours earlier, tall and striking, if a bit dishevelled, could have been a detective or a tally-man. Curiosity got the better of him hence the visit, wanted the juicy gossip.

Vera said, "Uncle Micky, what brings you over?" Remembered the debt, "If it's about the money, Uncle Mick, I said I'd pay you back Friday."

Annie Goodrich, Mick's sister, popped her head into view, "Now Mick," she greeted him warmly, loved her brother, and tolerated Mary Jane, his ignorant, overbearing wife. Gestured at Vera, "Put kettle on, pet," and walked into the living-room.

Michael went for the jugular, straight to the point as he asked, "Saw the stranger leave earlier, Annie, no bother is there?" Saw the startled look on his sister's face and elaborated, "Tall with black hair, not your average working-class fella, well-dressed … wore one of those daft, long over-coats?"

Vera appeared, "Can't fart around here without people sniffing where they shouldn't!"

Annie smiled painfully, "Wrong end of the stick, Mick, man's interested in our Vera is all, looks like she's got an admirer."

"Ma!" chided the younger woman

Michael Green grinned at his niece, "Didn't take you long to leave the wake?"

Vera Connelly folded arms over chest and pouted furiously.

Michael tried again, taunting, "I thought I recognised him," nodded at the women, teasing an answer.

Annie took the bait, "Go on then, how do you know him?"

"I only drink in two places, well three if you count the Club. The *Shoulder of Mutton* and the *Southside Social Club,* and he's not your average working man so we'll discount the *Club.*"

"Carry on," said a quizzical Annie Goodrich.

"So he's not really a stranger, Uncle Mick?" whined Vera.

"Hell of a singin' voice, he has," said Michael Green, "heard him often enough. Sometimes sings for his supper, sings better drunk than sober. Tell you somethin' else too, he used to be a dentist, according to the crack!"

"That's his brother," corrected Annie, glancing at her daughter, "his brother is a dentist."

"Oh, got my facts wrong," muttered the man, "so he didn't used to be a dentist?" Shook his head, "Well that's the chat, anyhow"

"No, Uncle Mick," said Vera, "he didn't used to be a dentist!"

"So what did he used to be then?" commented the man.

"He's a Social Worker," said Vera Connelly.

"Used to be!" corrected the mother, smirking.

"He still works for the Council!" said Vera angrily.

"Social worker be buggered," said Michael Green, "you'll be getting' a rent increase Annie!"

"On a Widow's Pension, pull the other one!"

Michael kept digging for clues. Looked at his niece, "Checkin' on the bairns was he? Noticed they were late for school this mornin' Vera. Little one was chasin' after Joe with his shirt adrift and no vest on, damp as hell too!"

"Uncle Mick," said Vera, a cloud of anger starting to show in her face, the man overstepping the mark, "one more word and I'll forget I like you!"

The man's shoulders lifted in mock compliance. Smiling weakly he said, "Nothin' meant love, just curious about the big fella. Your life if you want to mix with the likes of him." He'd said enough, moved further into the room, squatted comfortably on the sofa and asked, "tea is a long time comin'."

Like a dog after a bone, Vera growled, "Finish your story, what do you mean, *the likes of him,* what about Elmore?"

"Elmore," asked the man, "that his stage name?" said it with a genuine surprise.

"Cheeky bastard," muttered Vera, moved to the fire and faced her uncle. Her tone poisoned, said, "Call him Elmore Stoker!"

"Hey, Vera, don't take offence. All I'm sayin' is it's a strange name, Elmore. Heard of Fenimore, Fenimore Cooper, man wrote about *Hawk-eye, Last of the Mohicans,* but Elmore, that's a new one on me."

"So tell me about him, I don't like half a story, Uncle Mick."

"It's nothin' to get your knickers in a twist, Vera. All I'm sayin' is, well, man seems to enjoy himself," Michael Green, big as a house-end, squirmed like a snake struggling for shade, observed the grimace starting to creep over the face of his niece. He added, "What, it's no big thing Vera, man wants to drink too much, thinks he's Rudy Vallee, not a problem." Glanced again at Vera, knew how George Connelly felt after confessing his affairs and waiting for the fireworks. "How can I say this ... seems as if he's always busy around women," his voice a whisper, nodding the facts, a pained, dyspeptic looks over his pan face.

100

Annie stomped into the room carrying the tea for her brother. A welcome relief when she said, "Could be worse, I suppose, Mick," offering a lifeline, "at least the man is single, not like he's playin' the field?"

"Never thought of that," sighed the grateful brother. "I always imagined he was a married man. Live and learn, eh?"

The disagreement was kicked thankfully into touch. Michael could have mentioned he'd seen the fellow with the occasional married woman, even watched as he flirted outrageously in the pub with married couples. Watched more than once as an incensed husband had barracked his act, could have said a lot more but he valued his life. Some things better left unsaid.

"Put my foot in it, haven't I?" said an apologetic Michael Green.

"Up to your neck," hissed Vera Connelly.

**

"Hello, Elizabeth," he said warmly as he entered the house, quickly closed the door as a flurry of snow invaded the landing. Dusted himself down and moved into the large lounge.

"Let me take your hat, overcoat," she replied. "Please, warm yourself next to the fire."

The young mother placed the garments over the nearest chair, excused herself, hurried to the kitchen and found the tray, timed to perfection. Returned to the room, "Tea, Gilbert," she asked, and prayed the news was good, began pouring tea.

The tall figure fumbled in his pocket and pulled out the small cigar, struck the match and for some moments enjoyed the deep throaty aroma of the smoke. He said smugly, "I think I've managed to dissuade a certain someone from continuing with the charade," glanced at the girl busy with refreshments, stole a glimpse of her bare thigh, trim figure, pouting exquisite porcelain features, sighed with envy at the buffoon he called his son.

Elizabeth said, "I appreciate all of your help, Gilbert."

Gilbert asked, "Is he here?"

"Simon's out with friends," replied the young mother, handing over the tea. Stammered as she admitted, "I'm sorry, I told him you'd be calling, he made some excuse and left."

"Always was a moral coward," grunted the man, sucked deeply on the cigar, blew translucent circles into the cool room. Pondered a while before adding nonchalantly, "Takes after his fool of a mother, and I don't only mean height or looks. He won't face reality, head in the old sand."

"How is Simone, well I hope?"

"Ever the actress, always some malady ailing her." Tasting the refreshment he said, "Delightful tea, Elizabeth," thought momentarily of his wife and said, "Simone is visiting friends in Bournemouth, recuperating from a cold, well, if I'm to believe Simone... pneumonia. Warmer weather on the south coast, apparently."

"You're welcome to stay here, Gilbert, I'm sure Simon won't mind," thinking of herself and her sham of a marriage. "In fact it might calm things."

Gilbert's weary head in overdrive, misreading her kindness for something more, 'You're welcome to stay here, Gilbert,' leading him on, flirting with him, and not for the first time.

Gilbert said, "I've been an idiot, Elizabeth, always knew there was something lacking with that boy of mine. Damn and blast, my fault of course, always busy at work you see, earning the old bread and butter, left Simone to bring up baby. Not the best of role-models, having an amateur dramatist as a mother, what do you say, eh? Pretty enough in her prime but rather shallow, I always was a sucker for a pretty face." He gave a nervous guffaw, "There you go, no fool like an old fool, eh." The man paused reflectively, added, "When one thinks about it, one could say Simone was trying to live her sad life through the boy, always dressing him up and smothering him with damn cosmetics, face-paint and all that rubbish, encouraging him, 'He'll be a star someday, Gilbert,' she'd insist, 'he could be on the stage, I've written to Charles Bartholomew, he's keeping in touch!' Old girl wasn't in touch with reality!"

"Charles Bartholomew?"

The man said, "Shady character, runs a flea-pit of a theatre in Brighton. Bounder will do anything but earn an honest crust, one of Simone's cronies from her days as a starlet."

"Simone was a starlet?"

"Her description not mine, Simone was nothing more than an under-study, decoration for a set, until illness took its toll. Spent her days auditioning, gave her a purpose I suppose, until she realised her singularly lack of talent. Always name-dropping, so bloody insecure you know... 'I was with Margaret Rutherford all morning, Gilbert, elocution lessons, such a good teacher, I told her she should give the acting-bug a try, no confidence... poor woman looks like a bull-dog, you know. 'Margaret,' I said, 'Look at Charlie Laughton, does he care?' Simone was so unsure of herself, poor girl, couldn't stop, 'Had a coffee with Rex the other day, what a devil he is with the ladies.' I told her so many times, 'Bloody actors should try some honest labour for a change; all got their heads in the clouds.' I think that was why Simone focussed so much on the damn boy, trying to continue with the fantasy through him, almost turned his head away from his studies...nearly lost Simon through bloody amateur dramatics! He was at medical school and, unknown to me, continued with the *stage nonsense. One wasn't told, you understand, always closer to his mother."*

"I have all of his photographs and cuttings, Gilbert."

"Waste of damn time, Elizabeth, feet on the ground, I say, thought when he qualified he'd knock all that nonsense on the head."

"He has, Gilbert."

The man stammered, "Head in the damn clouds, you know, full of his own importance, thinks he has carte blanche to do anything!"

Elizabeth asked, "What do you mean, Gilbert?"

The man visibly squirmed, "The other nonsense!"

"His transgression?"

"Yes, all that foolish baloney, you know," he fidgeted uncomfortably as if he struggled with the reality of his son's proclivity.

"I couldn't believe it," she said stoically, "the meetings, the flirtation took place before we were married. I didn't have any idea... thought he loved me."

Gilbert countered, "He does, old girl! Simon is acting like an imbecile, bloody temporary madness, you understand?"

Elizabeth said stiffly, "You're being very kind, Gilbert." She paused, took a deep breath and added sorrowfully, "Perhaps I'm old-fashioned; I always thought you could only love one person. I thought that person would have been me."

"Damn fool of a son is confused, Elizabeth!"

"I don't think so," she answered morosely, "Simon has admitted he had deep feelings for...."

"Bloody nonsense," Gilbert interjected bitterly, writhing in anger, "matter of discipline, you know, man gets silly notions he has to be given firm direction, can't cater to such whims."

Elizabeth said, "He said he loves me, I'm so confused, Gilbert, how can he love me and yet won't sleep with me anymore, I don't understand."

Gilbert sighed and admitted ruefully, "I know my son better than most, Elizabeth. If he had made up his mind about leaving you, the marriage would be well and truly dead. We must be patient, my dear, mustn't do anything on impulse. Separate beds might simply mean Simon has a warped sense of conscience. It'll pass, I'm convinced, he'll not wish to jeopardise his career and bring disgrace to the family or himself."

"Gilbert," she put down her tea and looked intently at him, "I think Simon was confused when he married me, he treats me more like a friend than a wife."

"No, my dear, that can't be so, after all, you've got a beautiful baby boy. It's a phase he's going through, we must persevere."

"He told me he's besotted!" Elizabeth started weeping, "He is so cruel."

Gilbert stubbed out his cigar, placed the cup on the carpet, leaned forward in the chair and said acerbically, "I've visited the home, had a quiet word," self-satisfied tone to his voice, "too much to lose, too much at stake." He added as an afterthought, "The woman is career-minded, if any of this sordid business is made known!"

Elizabeth was incredulous, "She works? ...I didn't know!"

Gilbert grimaced, said with a gritty determination, "The partner hasn't been told, no one else knows about the affair," muttered the man, "apart from you and me... and Simon."

Elizabeth said hopefully, "Can't be too sure about Simon then?"

"My thoughts entirely!"

Elizabeth's head was spinning with utter confusion, knowing her husband's lover vacillated about their affair.

105

Gilbert was adamant; "I've put my cards on the table, no point beating about the damn bush. I won't be returning. The one warning will suffice. Mentioned I have influence and money and enough contacts to cause ruination."

"What was said?" Elizabeth was reeling, imagined her marriage over then suddenly to be impassioned with the expectation of success she started to believe again. Thought she had lost Simon forever to her rival, now there was a glimmer of hope.

"Windbag! All bluff, told me to do whatever but when I asked if I could wait in the house until the family returned the ruse collapsed! Bloody creature flustered and flapped until I took my leave, left my name and number, mentioned my influence in the community."

"Chief psychiatrist, Gilbert, I'd say that's influence."

"Whatever. I think that's the last of it, Elizabeth. When Simon realises that his new love is fickle and false, when Simon sees that he was being used as a plaything, he'll have a change of heart. Simon loves you, Elizabeth, he simply needs firm direction, stiff upper lip."

"Gilbert," said Elizabeth Stoker compassionately, "I will always be in you debt."

The man found himself saying, "He's been a bloody fool, Elizabeth!" Stood suddenly, erect and proud, "Prettiest girl in the world and my son can't see it,' he blurted out unashamedly. "There we are, said it and meant every word!"

The woman closed on her father-in-law, touched his arms, reached up and kissed him on the lips, said sincerely, "I can't thank you enough, Gilbert."

"It's been my pleasure, Elizabeth." Words came in a rush, his emotions dictating, unable to stop himself, "Damn son of mine needs his head examining," leaned towards her stunned, open face and returned the kiss with a passion belying his age. He whispered tenderly, "If I'd been twenty years younger!"

106

His words, deep and provocative, caught her unawares; she glanced at Gilbert as if expecting some apology or punch-line, anything to lessen the impact of the implications but the man smiled benevolently, nodded politely but his eyes could not mask his feelings or his intentions.

Moments past as Elizabeth gently, carefully pushed and prised her way from her father-in-law, her face showing growing alarm. Tried to smile as she pleaded, "I think perhaps you should leave, Gilbert. I'm grateful..."

Gilbert Stoker said hoarsely, "Elizabeth, darling," placed his hands on her voluptuous body, whispered, "I've always admired you as a person, always loved you."

She could detect the faint aroma of whiskey on his breath, and reacted with a nervous fumbling as she tried to stop the man from fondling her. Panicking and placating, Elizabeth begged, "Please, Gilbert, don't touch me ......"

CHAPTER NINE

Joe Connelly sat upstairs in Sammy McAndrew's house trying to persuade his pal to rob the colliery co-op store. It was like pulling teeth with pliers.

"Honest, Sam," said a confident Joe, "I've lived all my life in the colliery, used to shop with Ma at the store. Next down from the co-op is the public urinal, flat-roof, climbed on it a thousand times; just need a leg-up."

"And how do we get in the co-op?" Sammy was flapping quickly through the *Beezer* comic, threw it across the bed and studied his freckle-faced friend.

"They're joined together like one building, all on the main road!"

"So it'll be busy," hesitated a moment, added, "too dangerous."

"The colliery is like a morgue some nights. Listen, we climb on to the roof of the bogs then climb in through the open window, it's that easy!"

"You telling me the co-op always leaves a window open?"

"Only a little bit, but yes, open. Hard to see from the street, looks closed when you stand on the footpath."

"So why now, why haven't you done it before?"

He didn't have a ready answer, too frightened before, too young; knew that if they could reach the flat roof of the public lavatory Sammy could give him a leg up to the small side window. Didn't know that the manager of the store, Amos Spellman, had an infestation of mice in the upper decks of the festering, pre-war building and had borrowed one of his mother's three cats, on a semi-permanent basis, to rid the place of rodents. The open window allowed the cat access to and from the store.

"Never thought about robbing the place until today, not until Albert Mix said all the co-op stores have loads of stuff upstairs, bikes and things. Thought we could get a *Raleigh* each?"

Never a thought in his young head as to how they would manipulate bicycles out of the small window, all he could visualise was riding a brand-new bike.

"Me and you?"

Joe Connelly said, "I haven't told a soul," crossed his fingers, "shall we have a go?"

"And if I change my mind when we reach the colliery you won't lose your rag?"

"Cross my heart and hope to die!"

"Even if we climb on top of the urinal and I bottle, you won't call me 'chicken'?"

"On my word, Sammy!"

"Hand and spit?"

Joe Connelly spat on to the palm of his hand, watched Sammy follow suit, shook hands like grown-ups.

"Done deal."

They reached the cooperative building a little after six. Took their time walking the ten minutes from the village to the colliery, the streets empty of people and traffic. The weather was on their side; damp hanging curtains of mist and light rain covered the place, perfect conditions for the boys, the talk however not on the imminent robbery of the store but on the stranger meandering past the pair as they left Sammy McAndrew's house in Thorpe Road. Didn't register at first, Joe laughing about the school day and the thrashing by the headmaster, Albright, because of Sammy's Olympian display of urine squirting, *'Wet his shoes with piss,* said Joe, chortling, *nearly choked on his moustache,"* then it struck him, recognised the tall, well-dressed stranger, overcoat down to his heels, cigarette in one hand and a bottle in the other. *The Council-Care man,* he mused, nudged Sammy and whispered, *'He's on the prowl again,'* thinking his companion knew his mother's friend, *'checking on folk,'* then watched as Elmore Stoker knocked and entered the house adjoining Sammy's.

Sammy McAndrew said, "Ma's made a complaint about him!"

Joe gazed at Sammy's neighbour's home, said, "Is there overcrowding, is that why he's checking ... making a report?"

"What are you talking about, Joe?"

"That big fella."

Sammy, perplexed, said, "Who do you think he is, Joe?"

"It's the Council-Man. People report stuff and he has to investigate, give you a bigger house or sometimes you get money from the council-offices. Did you not know that?"

"Joe, you can't half talk bollocks," then he told him about the man who called most nights on divorcee, Agnes Lincoln.

**

Delwin Mix felt awful, blamed his obnoxious son, Albert, and his whining windbag of a wife Mildred. Albert because he had apparently made friends with his nemesis and occasional arch-enemy, Joseph Connelly, Mildred because of her back-tracking illogical ways, the pair of them facing him across the dining-table, not allowing him to enjoy his steak dinner, prepared, Delwin imagined, as some kind of reward by his scheming spouse to thank him for scuppering the Connelly woman. Albert had started the ball rolling midway through the meal, more interested in devouring his meal in record time, grunting like a proverbial hog, face forward so his open mouth was almost touching the plate of food, the utensils like miniature shovels and the glutton in ecstasy when suddenly his bat-like ears twitched.

"Ma," he said, lifting his head from the trough, "what about Joe Connelly's mother?"

Mildred was joyful as she explained the events leading to the dismissal of Vera Connelly from the Easington Village Co-op, grinning like a Cheshire cat, patting her proud husband's hand, "All for you, son," she gloated majestically, "no one will hurt you, Albert. That horrible woman has lost her job so the family might move back to the colliery and you'll have no more trouble at the school from that delinquent son of hers."

The shit hit the fan.

An hour later and Delwin Mix escaped, took to his *Hillman Minx* and drove away from Stockton Road, needing solitude and sanctuary from his fractious wife and son, wasn't bothered about the mist and the clinging dampness of sea fret that cloaked the whole district in wet gloom, anything for some peace and quiet. Depression was scratching at him again, as it had for a lifetime. Thirty years ago he imagined his world over, never thought he'd recover from the pain, in the doldrums for years as he survived the break-up, existing really, then slowly dragging himself from the mire and finding some kind of peace again. Then the horror, the absolute horror of Mildred's unexpected pregnancy, called it *the virgin birth,* followed weeks later by the tragic death of his neighbour Elizabeth Stoker. Fifty years old and the double nightmare too great a burden, too much to bear, his health deteriorated, had a seizure, an angina attack and spent worrying days in hospital, and that only the beginning of the trauma. His son, Albert, was born, and he was never so exhausted with the gargantuan task of late fatherhood, the sleepless nights, a new baby, and a demented middle-aged wife who, like he, was buckled and broken by the new arrival ... and the awful, heart-breaking loss of his only true love. Until then his life was slowly easing into second gear, imagined his last decade of working would have been a gentle decline into semi-retirement, unofficial, of course, delegating more and more to his workaholic and conscientious under-manager, Alvin Brown, remembered thinking about taking up membership at the prestigious Castle Eden Golf Club, long weekends on the greens followed by relaxing hours in the bar. Gone in an instant, dreams dashed forever by the nightmare pregnancy, the hysterical wife and the child from hell.

He drove the car in a daydream, images of his wife and son loomed, demented and hysterical as both of them pleaded and begged, *'You've got to reinstate Mrs Connelly,'* whined Mildred, *'for Albert's sake!'* Didn't matter that he'd sacked the woman for Albert's sake. His son crying like a baby too, fuelling the situation, *'Joe's my friend now dad, if he finds out you've sacked his mother he'll be after me again! Please dad!'* How on earth could he reinstate Vera Connelly without making a complete fool of himself, hated his overbearing wife, detested his spoilt son and wished he were stronger. Delwin Mix reached the outskirts of Shotton and had calmed sufficiently enough to attempt a U turn at the first junction, his head clear enough to assess the situation; he would have to visit the home of Mrs Connelly. Still remembered the address in the council estate, Passfield Square, payroll records and dismissal notice still on his desk, yes, Passfield Square, Easington Village, the number of the property unimportant, he would knock on doors until he found the woman. What to say to his under-manager, didn't want to appear weak or vacillating, *'Called with her P45, wanted to see Mrs Connelly, tell her what I thought of her. Damn woman started crying, told me about her no-good husband, begged for another chance. You were right, Mr Brown, she had to take her youngest son to out-patients, didn't get back until early afternoon, knew she'd lost her job.'* Sounded plausible enough, he could reprimand the Connelly woman, give her one more chance to prove herself, then he would mention about the face-saving suggestion, the hospital outpatients. She'd go along with him, hell she'd say black was white to get her job back, only had to remind her about what to say to the staff in the store so as not to embarrass him.

Minutes later and he had reached the lonely streets of the village, drove the car slowly, had to stop several times to check street signs and ask directions from scurrying pedestrians, "Passfield Square," said the old man, blowing like a whale, resting heavily on his walking-sticks, "next street, fella, you got a name, maybe I know the family?" The pensioner knew Vera and her mother, got the life story for free, "No luck has young Vera Goodrich, that's her maiden-name, dad was Marty, died years ago, collier like me, worked at Easington Colliery...." Had to be firm with the old man otherwise Delwin Mix would have stood all night in the clinging mists, "Aye, Vera is number 3 Passfield," pointed an arthritic finger at the nearby house, "that one, youngun, curtains open, lights on. Annie, her mother, lives there, Vera and the lads live with her since George done a runner."

Delwin Mix took a deep breath to steady his nerves, knocked on the door and waited with bated breath.

A woman answered, fifty plus, done up like a dog's dinner, smiled cautiously at the stranger, straining to see his face "Can I help you, pet?" asked Annie Goodrich, glanced through the gloom at the tall stocky man, her age too, wondered if he were married, knew Evelyn Stoker, was a temporary affair and needed to keep her options open, stuck out her sagging chest, lifted her chin, pulled the door wide open, realised who it was and the grovelling and fawning began, "Mr Mix, this is a surprise. Please, come in."

"Hello," he said authoritatively, not recognising the woman, "I wonder if I could speak to Mrs Connelly."

He was led through the poky kitchen into a large sitting-room, television playing to itself; two figures

113

sprawled across the ancient threadbare carpet close to the roaring coal-fire, mother and child, engrossed in their task, not realising the stranger was watching with genuine interest.

"Vera," barked the mother, "company!"

The young woman glanced at the man and visibly jerked as if a switch had tripped and electricity had surged through her. Up in a second, dusting herself down, stammering with anxiety in front of her employer, "Mr Mix!" her hand rubbing frantically at her mouth, gulping, lost for words, gesturing blindly at her son and mother, "you've met my mother… this is my son, Jack, we're trying to learn the alphabet," pulling at her boy, glancing sheepishly at the man. "He's shy, Mr Mix, not like his brother."

Delwin Mix smiled warmly, could feel the tangible bond between the young mother and the boy, wondered what it was like, never had deep feelings for his own son, Albert … only regret.

**

A quick glance up and down the street, not a soul in sight as Joe squatted, leaned his back firmly against the wall of the public toilet, inter-locked fingers, palms up and gestured to his pal to place his boot into the fleshy stirrup. With all of his strength Joe straightened his protesting body and hoisted Sammy McAndrew towards the low, flat roof of the urinal, watched as his scrawny pal grasped at the metal spouting and heaved upwards, Joe pushing frantically at the kicking feet, goading him, "Don't stop now, Sam, lift yourself!" Sammy disappeared from sight. A lone vehicle neared, the driver's head blossoming close to the windscreen, desperate to see past the smudge of muck and cloud, wipers working overtime, the sea-fret smothering the colliery in a grey gloom. There wasn't a soul about to spoil the adventure. "Joe," hissed Sammy McAndrew, leaning over the edge of the roof, arm reaching down towards his friend, "grab hold!" The grip vice-like as he strained and pulled Joe slowly upwards, grunting and wheezing all the while. The pair sat on the roof resting for minutes, puffing and blowing like steam trains. "Ready?" asked Joe, stood below the co-op window, repeated his earlier stance, body low and back against the wet wall, fingers wedged into a cup, Sammy grasping Joe's shoulders, foot stuck safely into palms, Joe lifting, Sammy reaching for the window-ledge, like a spider as he squeezed into the gap of window. A final, desperate lunge and he disappeared inside the store in an almighty crash.

"Bloody hell, Sammy," whispered Joe, straining against the gloom to see his friend, "you okay?"

The young burglar's tousled head appeared, "Tripped," he muttered ruefully, "it's pitch black inside," reached down and gripped the outstretched fingers. "Heave, heave," he moaned, pulled at the human cargo and helped him inside.

They stood statuesque, unsure of their next move, the huge three-storey building was a shadowy mine-field, couldn't see a hand in front of their face. "Must be like this at the pit," said Joe, "if your helmet-light is broken," stuck his hands out in front of him, and stepped gingerly away from the window. "Follow me," he whispered, felt Sammy's fingers grasping his coat-tails, closed his eyes and used his outstretched arms like a blind man, "this way."

Laurel and Hardy in the desert, blinded by the sandstorm, the blind leading the blind, walking towards the steep sand-dune.

Connelly and McAndrew in *Flying Deuces,* Joe's foot touching and tripping over an abandoned foot-stool, screaming like a banshee as he stumbled forwards, careered into a wooden chair, followed by the hysterical Sammy who clung desperately to his falling friend, limbs flaying as the pair screamed in unison; the inept burglars sprawling and squirming like fish out of water before struggling to uncertain feet, clinging together like lovers as the store cat, returning from its nocturnal meandering, loomed at the open window then jumped on to a nearby counter. "What was that?" gasped Sammy, about to soil his best jeans. The cat stayed motionless and stared at the intruders. Moments passed before Joe stammered, "Never heard anything," stuck a solitary hand out and felt the counter, "found the counter, Sam, come on, feel your way along it, we might find a till!" Sammy McAndrew hissed, "You lead, I'll follow, Joe," wouldn't let go of his pal, not for all the tea in China.

The cash register was eventually found. Joe unsure at first, eyes not functioning other than seeing different shades of darkness, felt and caressed the device, still at a loss until his hand absently touched the release-catch and the cash-draw sprung open, fingers poking and prodding at the plastic compartments. "Sammy," he gasped, "we've struck gold," moved along so that the pair stood either side of the register. "Help yourself to the cash, Sam, fill your pockets!"

With the coins bulging in their coat-pockets, the boys found the confidence to explore, Sammy whispering, "Downstairs, Joe, let's go downstairs, there'll be another cash-register," all thoughts of stealing bicycles on the back-burner as they decided to search for more money. So dim inside the store that the pair, Joe bravely leading Sammy gripping him from behind, inched their way towards the wide landing. Joe gesticulating wildly into the inky unknown, eased past the staircase and headed for the staff lavatories, unlucky Sammy meandering blindly stepped into empty space as one foot left the safety of the floor and dropped towards a lower step. With a howl to wake the dead, Sammy McAndrew pitched sideways, released his grip on his companion and fell headlong down the stairs, screamed every step of the way, coins cascading from his pockets as he continued his downwards plunge. The noise was deafening and only ceased when the lad lay spread-eagled at the foot of the stairwell, moaning softly now, coins still rolling freely across the downstairs floor.

Joe Connelly fingers holding frantically on to the stair-rail for balance slowly loomed into view. "I'm here, Sammy," he said, and walked into the prostrate, protesting body. Joe striking perfectly with is toe-cap into the belly of his fallen comrade. "Is that you, Sam?" reached down and felt for his friend, dragged him to his protesting feet. "You okay, Sammy, no broken bones?"

"I've had enough, Joe," whined a bruised Sam McAndrew, "let's go home, I've lost all my money!"

"What about the till, I know where it is, come on, follow me!"

Joe had not visited the store since his family moved to the village, didn't know about the internal changes. Shifting and sliding into the black interior like human penguins, holding hands for comfort. They hadn't walked a dozen paces before Sammy stepped into a mobile clothes-rack. Another ungodly shriek as the boy was suddenly festooned in dresses and fell headlong through the clothing-rack. Propelled by his own frantic forward motion Sammy McAndrew shot across the floor as the rack became a sleigh scattering everything in his path. Didn't stop yelling until Joe almost shook him senseless, "Shh! Shh!" begged Joe.

The store cat decided to investigate the noise, shot down the staircase like a miniature black panther and moved across the floor, didn't stop until it climbed on to Sammy's outstretched legs, dug its claws into the boys flesh and meowed and hissed menacingly. Loyalty gone in an instant as Joe abandoned his pal and scrambled in the direction of the stairs, Sammy crying hysterically followed on all fours, the cat followed passively. All three hurried up the staircase, Joe gasping at Sammy, "There, the window, straight ahead, come on!" The animal followed, started spitting and growling as it sensed fear from the intruders. Joe like a trapeze-artiste, scrambled expertly through the small window and landed feet-first on the urinal roof, Sammy, whimpering for his life as he struggled for freedom, lost his balance and fell heavily at the feet of his accomplice. Joe dragged and pulled him to the edge of the flat roof. "Give me your hand," demanded Joe, and eased his friend over the side of the building, lowered him carefully, then released his grip and watched Sammy slip effortlessly to the wet ground. Joe heaved his frame over the edge of the building and fell silently to the ground.

"You okay, Sammy?" asked Joe Connelly as he hoisted his friend to his feet.

"Never again!" protested Sammy McAndrew, rubbing his aching ankle, "bloody cat scared the shit out of me!"

Joe said, "I'll share my money, Sam!"

"Lost a fortune when I fell down the stairs," looked forlornly at the open window, "could have broken my neck, Joe!"

"Here," offered Joe, scooped a handful of coins from one of his pockets, "down the middle," then glanced in disbelief at the pile of bronze. "They've only left coppers in the till... don't believe it!"

"We should have brought a torch," moaned Sammy, "we'll know next time," bravado replacing the stench of fear now that he was out of the building.

"Not for me, Sam!"

"Probably right."

"You need a hand or can you walk?" asked Joe Connelly.

"Sprained my ankle," said Sammy, "might be worse, Joe!" He stood ostrich-like with one leg lifted off the ground, "Might be broken!"

"Put your arm round my shoulder, I'll take the weight."

Slowly, hesitantly, the pair struggled towards the distant village.

**

Elmore said, "A few quid, come on," his voice hushed, didn't want too many people knowing his business, glanced around, nodded reassuringly at Agnes propping up the bar. "You know I'm good for it, Evelyn."

He folded, always did, pulled a few notes from his pocket and slipped them under the table for his brother, "Th....that's the last, Elmore. I can't g...g...go, go, go, on subsidising y... y.. your, your lifestyle!" The stammers always full throttle when Evelyn was stressed or nervous.

Cocky now that he had drinking money for the rest of the night, Elmore ignored his older sibling, "Chill out, Evelyn, you might be getting your own way. Agnes wants me to move in with her, I'll tell you all about it later, maybe tomorrow." Didn't like his half-brother at the best of times, but always imagined Evelyn kept things close to his chest, never realised he was such a gossip. "Tell me, Evelyn, what else did you tell the old hen, eh? You know how it feels when your own brother confides in some whore! Come on, brother, what else did you say to Annie Goodrich? Don't you dare deny it or I'll have to get physical again. I told her dumb specimen of a daughter that I was suspended not sacked, made me feel an utter chump, Evelyn!"

"Please s... s... st...st... stop, stop....."

Evelyn blushed, hurt and saddened by the outburst. Should have been used to the aggression and the embarrassment metered out by his brother, took it all his adult life, accepted it as part and parcel of Elmore's damaged state of mind, understood his pain and anger at the way life had dealt him a cruel set of cards. Years ago, and the younger brother broke down and wept bitter tears, bewildered, confused and damaged by his father's revelations, *'Evelyn, this is not true, my mother could not have done such a cruel thing,'* Weeping and wailing hysterically, *'Thought we were brothers, thought my dad was my dad!* First time Evelyn had witnessed his brother fold and break, *'All those years! I knew something was wrong! I knew! Dad was always cold towards me, no matter what I did he couldn't show any emotion, cold and aloof! Thought it was me, thought I was doing something wrong! All these years and I wasn't his son. Why did he wait until mother died, why wait until then, it was so cruel of him to wait until mother's funeral!* Evelyn saw the torture in his eyes, *'He never touched me, Evelyn, never held my hand, not once! When I was a child I told mother time and time again and she brushed me aside with excuses, 'All in your head, Elmore, dad loves you, can't show his emotions, can't show his emotions to anyone.' I didn't believe her, I thought it was me. Deep down, I thought it was me.'*

Evelyn understood the misery, the rebellion scratching incessantly at his brother's head, would have felt the same if it had happened to him, but he was exhausted, humiliated and running out of funds shoring up his brother's life. Had reservations about opening his home to him but felt obligated, the least he could do for Elmore. It had been a costly error and he had immediately felt the wrath from his brother, *'Nice house, Evelyn, but really, if you say you care for me ... and I'm your brother, shouldn't I have half of the place? Shouldn't you sell the house and split the proceeds down the middle ... if you really meant what you say about me.'*

"Hope you, you, you will be, be, hap hap....."

"I'll be happy enough, Evelyn," grunted Elmore Stoker, standing and gazing down at his pathetic brother, "no thanks to you!"

**

120

Annie Goodrich was upstairs dressing. 6.20pm and she was preparing for her usual jaunt with Jenny Flowers to the Regal in Hartlepool, Wednesday and Saturday was Bingo for the girls, back in time to catch last orders at the Workingman's Club in the village. Downstairs, Vera was fighting fatigue, sprawled on the arm-chair next to the roasting fire, trying to concentrate on a Catherine Cookson novel. Once she'd finished the chapter she had promised to escort Jack's friend, Alice Raine, to her home minutes away in North Crescent. Jack and Alice filled the floor-space, shoulders touching, both engrossed in their own special worlds; Jack patiently filling in the second page of a Littlewoods Football Coupon, expertly marking stars inside every square on the page, head resting on one arm, the other manipulating the pen expertly, never stopping. Alice, drawing-book open, crayons at the ready, shading gaudy colours on to the cartoon images, nudging her friend, wanting approval from Jack, the boy glancing, nodding agreement, then back to his endless task of criss-cross.

Vera put aside the book, stared at the tots and smiled. It had been an eventful day, in the doldrums before lunch, embarrassed with the previous evening, compounded by the snide comments from both her mother and uncle, knowing she had acted irresponsibly in front of her boys, believing she had forfeited her job and then suddenly a lifeline from none other than Mr Mix himself. An hour later and she was still in shock, reinstated by the general manager of the store, dumbfounded and dazed as she tried to find escape in the novel. Couldn't stop thinking about Alvin Brown, the under-manager, knew he had been responsible in persuading Mr Mix to keep her position at the shop, determined to make it up to him. Thought of Elmore Stoker, grinned at the image of Elmore, big lovable Elmore, full of life, wanting to cram as much as he could into every day. Maybe he was the one, had one or two doubts niggling at her, wasn't keen on his busy social life, especially when he told her he couldn't stay at home for a single night. *'It's because you're living with your brother,'* assured Vera, *'only natural you want your own space. Maybe Saturday you'll find suitable rented accommodation, bet you stay home at nights then, Elmore?'* Wondered too if he was a liar and a braggart, couldn't decide if he was telling the truth about his suspension. Time would tell. Mixed up emotionally, the woman was in a quandary, thinking about Elmore, Alvin, Mr Mix, her boys, her future.

"Well, you two," she said softly, "time to walk Alice home."

Jack said, half-heartedly, "Five more minutes, Ma."

Alice Raine carefully collected her crayons, closed her book and yawned infectiously, soon Jack and his mother followed. Minutes later and the trio walked from the house, Vera holding the children's hands, Jack enjoying the girl's company. "Ma, can Alice come tomorrow night?" and the adult nodding agreeably, but Alice pulling at her, demanding sweetly, "Mrs Connelly, can Jack come to mine please, he's going to show me how to make a matchstick-gun." Leaned across and gestured at her friend, "Aren't you, Jack?"

"He's a clever boy is Jack," offered the woman, "making things and he's only five years old." She squeezed his fingers playfully, added cautiously, "I don't think Alice's mother will be too pleased."

"Oh, yes," said the girl excitedly, "I've already told my mum about Jack. She says he can do what he wants as long as he's quiet!"

Vera Connelly grinned and chuckled, happy despite the clag of mist and fog that covered her, crossed over the road and into the cul-de-sac and Alice Raine's home.

"Home early for a change?" said Vera Connelly to Joe.

"Anything to eat, Ma?" replied her oldest, who started rummaging around in the pantry, grumbling under his breath at the lack of food.

Vera said, "If you want, Joe, you can run to the fish-shop I fancy something from Trotter's."

He didn't need a reminder, bounced into the sitting-room and stuck out his hand, asked, "Where's Jack?"

"Bath, told him to leave the water in for you." She handed over the money, placed the order and watched him bolt for the door.

Joe Connelly ran all the way to the fish-shop, smiled when he saw Bobby Muncaster behind the counter. Bobby, nineteen, married with two kids, worked for the council as a refuse-collector, and supplemented his income working part-time for Bradley Trotter week-days. Joe knew he could get away with murder when Bobby worked the tills.

"Bobby," said Joe apologetically, "Ma says will you take pay for the suppers with these ... skint she is." and placed a huge mound of copper coins on the counter and smiled at the acne-scared teenager.

"Jesus, I'm not sure about that," groaned the youth. "What was the order?"

"Fish-cake and chips three times, salt and vinegar, bottle of lemonade."

Bobby glanced through the preparation-area which led to the property. Shrugging his shoulders he said, "Suppose it'll be okay, Joe. You want to count it into piles for me? Easier to count that way."

"You can keep the change Bobby," soothed the kid.

Joe thinking that threepence wasn't a fortune to lose, especially since he was pocketing his mother's money, watched the youth wrap and parcel the food, then the door banged open and the big man and his female friend stepped into the shop. Joe Connelly could hardly believe it, the Council Officer, twice in one night, then he recalled Sammy's words of wisdom, *'He's a drunk, Joe, He don't work for no council and that's a fact, Ma has reported him and his girl-friend to the council because of the noise every night.'* Laughed at Joe's explanation, *'He's a drunk, Joe, even told Ma he was a policeman but that was a lie.'*

The man said loudly, "We'll share, Agnes, need the shekels for *The Half Moon.*" He looked dazed and bewildered, his clothing dishevelled and stained, saw the boy watching him, said angrily, "What you looking at, boy?"

"Shh, Elmore," interjected the woman, "he's just a child," her words blurred with drink. Smiling at Joe she said, "Take no notice lad, it's the drink talking," gestured at Bobby Muncaster, "big bag of chips, son, don't scrimp, old Trotter can afford it!"

Joe Connelly hurried from the premises, the confrontation frightening. He'd forgotten all about the earlier sighting of the man but the debacle in the fast-food shop jogged his memory, ran all the way home, anxious to tell his mother, needing to know why his mother had lied. Kept repeating the names in his head so that his mother would know who he was talking about, *Elmore and Agnes. Elmore and Agnes..........*

Vera said, "Say again, Joe, from the beginning."

His mother sat in the middle of the large settee, her sons either side of her, their laps blossoming with old newspaper, the supper heaped, steaming and delicious, Joe and the mother discussing. Jack, fork in one hand, matchstick-gun in the other wondering if he could reassemble the device for Alice, not hearing a word from his brother or mother, head concentrating, *Stick, rubber, clip! No, bend clip, insert match! No, first bend the clip back over the rubber-band, put match in clip, fire!* Easy, didn't need to ask Joe for help.

Joe said, "Sammy McAndrew lives next door to a woman called Agnes and she has a boyfriend who told

Sammy's mother he was a cop but he's really a liar and he's the same man who came here …the man from the council, you said." Stuffed his mouth with chips and washed them down with lemonade, stole a glance at his mother, recognised the look on her face. "Ma, you told a lie," more hot food and chomping before he added sarcastically, "even know his name because he just walked in the fish-shop with a woman, he called her Agnes and she called him Elmore, like Elmore Fudge in the cartoons. Oh, and Sammy's mother says he's a drunk!"

Vera Connelly wasn't hungry anymore, tried to be honest with her son, while her head was bombarded with Elmore's deceit and mistruths. "Thorpe Road, that'll be Agnes Lincoln. My age, common as muck, can't keep a husband." Soon as she said the words Vera grimaced at the reality of the statement. "I'm sorry, Joe, I was in a muddle, honestly didn't know he was calling on me, then you woke up and I panicked and told a lie, then another, but he did actually once work for social services, honest. I'm so sorry Joe, I thought he cared about me!"

"Were you gonna marry him, Ma?"

"Don't be daft, Joe!"

Joe asked, "Why can't Dad come home like before, Ma, didn't he like Jack or me…didn't like you?"

"Silly. Your Dad found someone else, love, I tried to persuade him to come back but he wouldn't … couldn't." Vera was digging a hole and didn't know how to stop the spadework, shrugged her shoulders, didn't know whether to tell her boy about George Connelly's other life. Thought about the complications and bit her tongue, "Your dad wasn't happy, pet, I don't think he ever was…" her voice trailed off and she toyed with her fork.

"Ma," asked Joe, "if the man comes back here, what will you do, would you let him in again, would you let him sleep in the chair? Does nana know about him because we live in her house and he stayed all night? Ma, why can't we go back to the colliery, it was better when we lived at the colliery, even without dad?"

"Elmore Fudge will not get across the door, son, I promise." She looked at Joe and smiled warmly, spoke from the heart, "Never meant to hurt you, Joe, you believe me?"

Joe nodded, felt better, loved his mother, didn't want her hurt, especially by a man like Elmore Fudge. He asked, "Ma, shall I turn the channel? Hate talking programmes."

"What's on the other side?"

"Emergency Ward Ten, about doctors and nurses, shall I?"

**

"Joe," said his mother, "make up your mind, are you coming or not, we're not waiting all day!"

Joe had fever, aches and pains and had missed the last three days of school. *Flu,* insisted his mother. *Cold,* said his nana, and Jack didn't have an opinion, missed his older brother and wanted him back to normal. Two long days in bed was enough for Joe, mooched all day Friday and generally got in the way of the routine in the Goodrich house, pleased it was Saturday and the weekend, planned on having a good time but awoke feeling wretched and stayed close to the coal-fire all morning.

"Joe," said Annie Goodrich, putting on the act of temporary matriarch while daughter Vera was powdering her face, "we're all going to Sunderland, *Hardy's Furniture* has to be paid whether you come or not..... make up your mind!"

Jack, holding on to his nana's wrinkled hand, wearing his Sunday-best, smiling hopefully, said, "Ma's taking us all to the ice-cream shop, and Alice is coming too. We're gonna ride on the moving stairs in the big shop!"

Annie corrected her grandson, "Escalators, Jack, they're called escalators!"

Joe finally spoke, "What about after dinner, might feel a bit better then?" Truth was he felt ill. His head ached, his throat was sore and he lacked energy, "No hurry is there, nana?"

The lavatory flushed and Vera hurried into the living-room still adjusting her dress, glanced at her oldest, then at the clock perched on the mantelpiece. "Well, Joe," she said, "what's it to be?"

"Leave him, our Vera, still twisty as hell," said Annie as she struggled to fit into her decade-old slim line jacket, bought when her figure was more svelte-like, still fitted like a glove, as long as she wore her *Spirella* corset and the coat-buttons weren't fastened. Turned to the boy and said sternly, "And no mischief my lad or you'll feel the back of my hand, no mistake!"

"Come on, Joe," said Vera selfishly, knowing Jack and Alice Raines would be a handful in the town bustle, bills to pay, mother to watch, this and that, "I'll drop you off at *Louis's i*ce cream shop?"

"And me and Alice, Ma!" said a worried kid brother.

Joe shrugged his shoulders, wanted to go, and knew the old ones were generous with their money when they shopped in the town but he couldn't be bothered. He shook his head lethargically.

Vera handed over a pound note, told him to pay half at Monk's shop, Christmas club account, small nick-knacks for the boys, *Eagle Annual, Billy the Kid Annual, Games Compendium, Superman* outfit for Jack, small stuff, main account still at Daniels's shop at the colliery. "If you feel better, call in Trotter's for your dinner," pondered a moment then added dryly, "and I want to see all the change when I get back, you hear, Joe?"

There was a slight, almost indistinct knock at the door; a faint voice echoed through the house, "Jack, are you coming out?" Alice Raine, five years old and dressed to kill, looked forward to a day out with her best friend, Jack Connelly, double-decker, top-deck all the way to Sunderland. Christmas had come early for the tot, "Jack, I'm ready," Alice was on a mission.

"Well?" asked Vera, one last time and watched as Joe shook his head and closed his eyes.

"Leave him," grunted the old woman, "awkward little bugger!"

One-o-clock and Joe finally stirred and opened his eyes, he felt better, hungry too, saw the money on the mantelpiece and smiled. He'd pay Monk's bill and pocket the rest, shuffled towards the pantry, saw the *Fray Bentos* corned beef, *Stork* margarine, *Hovis* loaf, "Dinner," he muttered, "and money for fireworks," grabbed the gingersnaps and the *Lowcocks* ginger-beer and meandered to the kitchen-sink. The sun burned a warm gentle of white curtain over him as he worked, glanced up and saw the next door neighbours, Miriam and Roy Roche, twins and two years older than Joe. He smiled. Twins, and yet the girl was head and shoulders bigger than her brother. Siblings, and the pair had a mutual hatred for one another. Joe watched as the fracas heightened; the brother demanding the bicycle and his stubborn sister brushing him aside like he was a piece of fluff in the wind. There was a final, defiant bellow from Roy Roche before he stormed into the house leaving his sister triumphant and smirking.

Joe Connolly shuffled to the back door, opened it and squatted on the steps and plonked the picnic of biscuits and pop either side of him. He acknowledged the girl with a cheeky grin. "Now, Miriam," he called, "how's tricks?"

"You been watching me again, Joe Connelly?" asked the flirtatious female. Almost thirteen and hormones on the front-burner, sexual carburettor tuned to perfection as she throttled up to the small decrepit garden fence beaming a mouthful of perfect teeth in his direction. Saw the food and asked coyly, "Been abandoned, then?"

"Want a gingersnap, Miriam," asked the boy, "some ginger beer?" Felt heady again but in a strange and beautiful way, his mind suddenly emptying of aches and pains and replaced with more lurid, complicated thoughts. He'd heard all the stories and gossip about girls from his friends, wondered if they were all true.

Took the lithe female seconds to vault the fence, Joe watched incredulously as she parachuted expertly into his garden, saw the thin expanse of white stocking and the long slender thighs as the skirt ballooned in the warm autumn breeze. The nymphet grinned infectiously as she read his mind.

"Sunderland," said Joe.

Miriam said, "What's that?"

"Mother, and everyone, all gone to the town to pay bills."

"You been a bad boy again, Joe?" inquired Miriam, couldn't help hearing the occasional outbursts from the Goodrich house, mainly directed at the oldest boy. Council-houses had paper walls, break wind and the neighbours made comment.

"Been poorly, off school few days. Back on Monday though."

"Secondary next year, Joe?"

"Yeah, wish I was there now, can't stand Albright!"

"Still a pain in the arse?"

"Worse!"

Miriam said, whimsically, "It's a lovely day, Joe."

Miriam testing the water, putting out feelers. She liked Joe, always had, wasn't bothered she was a year older. Joe always seemed so grown-up, old for his age, older than her brother, Roy, even though he wasn't. Miriam was sick of her whining brother; nothing seemed to satisfy him these days, used to let him play with her while she touched his *thing,* been doing it to each other for well over a year and now Roy wanted to *do* her! Miriam was steadfast in her refusal, knew for a fact that horrible things could happen if a brother and a sister had sex together. Janice Longfellow, her best friend who lived at the Waterworks, told her. She'd read one of her mother's books and it said that if a girl got pregnant by her brother or father then the baby would be born a freak, with three arms or two heads, things like that. She knew her father wouldn't play with her because she could hear her mother most nights cursing her dad because he was *important,* or some word like that. That was why her mother had to employ a *dodo* to help her. Miriam could never understand how her mother had found an extinct bird that somehow helped her enjoy sex again. Janice Longfellow didn't have a clue either.

"It's warm, Miriam," answered Joe, through a mouthful of corned-dog.

Miriam played a blinder, said casually, "Thought I might go for a walk, Joe," looked up at the big blue sky and closed her eyes, thinking she might let Joe play with her, even let him *do* her properly. Wondered what it would be like, would be better than Roy's rough hands, thought about her brother's pathetic excuse of a *thing.* She'd called it a *tiddler* and made Roy shriek with anger and squeeze her little breast, well, clamp his finger and thumb on her nipple. Breasts would definitely sprout soon, Janice Longfellow told her that when she confided in her best friend and showed her flat chest. *'Next year,'* said Janice, who had balloons since she was ten, *'definitely next year.'* Trouble was, she'd said the same last year too… whatever. She focussed again on Joe Connelly, eyes shut, feeling the hot sun on her face, wondered if Joe's *thing* was bigger than Roy's *tiddler.*

"You fancy a walk, Joe?" asked the tease.

"I'm easy, Miriam," answered Joe casually, playing hard to get, "if you want."

130

Fifteen minutes later, washed and brushed, Joe was ready for the off , even cleaned his teeth with toothpaste, normally a Monday morning preserve, the rest of the week limited to toothbrush and tap-water, shouted over the fence for Miriam and the two set off walking through the village. They reached the private row of houses called Craig View, meandered along the quiet street until they reached the open wound of the old gravel quarry, skirted the infested area, and headed for the hamlet of Little Thorpe. The young couple talked about everyday, mundane things, happy to simply enjoy the day, neither threatened nor intimidated with one another's company.

The farm and the few outbuildings seemed unusually quiet, hinted of abandonment, the dozen or so houses and cottages that paralleled the small road used by *Thorpe Farm* employees appeared deserted. The whole area was serene and peaceful apart from the distant, muted mechanical sounds lifting from the diary itself. A lone trio of interested cows, heads poking through the decrepit fence, faces steaming, vacant eyes following, watched the kids saunter through the place as they headed for the dene.

There was a tried and tested walkway that traversed the woods and reached the coastal colliery of Horden, could have followed it for maybe half an hour. Joe, like his teenage temptress beside him, had lofty things on his mind. Finally able to muster courage, the boy suggested they rest awhile. "That would be nice, Joe," said Miriam, words came out more like a whisper, "maybe," she suggested breathlessly and in a rush of emotion, "maybe we should go further into the woods, path is always busy with people?" Joe, shaking like a leaf on an autumn tree tried to act nonchalant and at ease with the developing situation, said, "Sure, Miriam, could find a place and sit awhile." Talking like a grown-up, insides shaking like jelly.

Miriam liked Joe Connelly, he didn't act like a normal eleven-year old. The only drawback was his lack of stature, awkward talking down to him the way she did. Still it was a minor problem. The good thing was Joe was a prospective boyfriend, her very first and she couldn't wait to tell Janice Longfellow the good news, push came to shove and she played her cards right, she might be able to persuade Joe to ask either Sammy McAndrew or Davy Duckworth to consider Janice Longfellow as a girlfriend, maybe hint she'd definitely let them play with her tits, *'All in good time,* she thought, *'first things first,'* she had to think of herself first and foremost.

They made their way slowly from the bridleway and into the wooded, quiet area. They presently came across a beautiful clearing, a vast carpet of green surrounded by a lush, dense canopy of trees and thick bushes. Miriam smiled and glanced awkwardly at her companion, "Nice here, Joe, you think?" decided to take matters into her own hands when Joe Connolly appeared to waver and dither. "Yes, we'll sit here, eh?" plonked herself on the warm thick sea of grass, eased back and lay spread-eagled and seemingly relaxed and waited for him to join her. The expanse of greenery was warm to the touch and Miriam Roche closed her eyes, felt the sun on her, heard the birds whistling and singing and ached for Joe Connolly's touch.

Children in the Garden of Eden.

Miriam sighed, said provocatively, "It's hot, Joe, might take off my cardigan."

Joe felt like a bull with his nose-ring being pulled, said, "Okay."

A short distance away, the stranger slowed then stopped. Didn't want to disturb the kids, anxious to observe their frolicking, perspiring profusely, head in a delightful frenzy. Heaven for Morris Buckingham, the village sleaze-bag, despised and shunned by most decent folk, tended to look further a field for liaisons, maybe take a bus ride to the nearby towns, Middlesbrough, Hartlepool, perhaps Sunderland, knew the places to visit, the side-streets, back-alleys, adventure playgrounds for the youngsters, a stranger there, face wasn't known, better than Easington district, too many could point a finger. He always carried money, change, jingle in his pocket, pulled the kids like he was the Pied Piper.

He knew the boy, seen him walking to the shop several times since the summer, hand in hand with his grandmother, Annie Goodrich. Went to school with Annie, *'Good for the goose,'* he thought, okay for her to find her pleasures whenever, not a second thought when she used to go behind the air-raid shelters at school, an eleven year old tycoon charging tenpence a time to have a squint down her knickers, first girl in the junior school to have pubic hairs. Devil she was, knew the power she possessed when she viewed the queue of the keen and the curious, all with money in hand, all wanting to see the strange and compelling sight. Morris fourth in line, didn't like what he saw, repulsive sight. All right for the likes of Annie Green, as she was known then, Micky's wayward younger sister, all right if folks said it was normal behaviour, little boys chasing little girls, nature's way, people would say, birds and bees.

Morris had always enjoyed boy's company, never could see the attraction with little girls. *'Boys without dicks,'* in Morris's personal opinion and what good was a boy without his little snake? Consequently he had been castigated, chastised and ridiculed all of his life because of his sexual preferences, shunned by so called decent folk. Made him angry, mad as a proverbial hatter, because he could name some local folk, big-fry, important fish in the community, whom he'd spend the occasional evening buggering. Open his mouth and he could rock a few so-called solid institutions, professional people, happily-married people, top of the proverbial pie people. Hypocrites, all of them! Lost his position at the colliery years ago, and him with an important job, Training-Officer no less. Couldn't understand the fuss, all because he enjoyed the company of young boys, law ought to change and allow folks to do whatever, so long as they weren't hurting anyone. Left the pit, worked at Broughs, the retailers in Peterlee, all fine and dandy until the manager got a big dose of conscience, married man, decided he couldn't afford to take risks any more. Didn't matter a jot that they'd been lovers for two years, made excuses and Morris had to seek pastures new. He eased through the thicket, carefully brushing aside branches and obstacles, needed to be closer to the cavorting youngsters, wanted a birds-eye view. Perspiration ran freely over his palpitating body. Loosening his clothing Morris began fondling himself.

Joe Connelly looked at the prostrate figure next to him, the gentle rhythm of her chest, the skirt, slightly crumpled and showing the briefest glimpse of naked thigh, wanted so much to touch Miriam, wanted to kiss her on the lips, didn't have the nerve.

Miriam knew what the trouble was, said innocently, "Still too hot, Joe," opened her eyes and squinted at the boy. Saw the discomfort, played an ace, said matter-of-fact, "Shall we sunbathe?" didn't wait for a reply as she fumbled out of her skirt. "Joe, I'm taking off my skirt, you've got to promise not to do anything to me, you know?"

Joe almost choked with anticipation, couldn't speak but managed an agonising nod, gaped with incredulity as the girl stood and removed her thin cotton dress and placed it carefully on the grass next to her discarded cardigan then sank slowly on to the garments.

Miriam said modestly, "The grass doesn't half prickle my skin, Joe!"

Joe Connelly felt giddy with a sensuous pleasure as he gloated at the pencil-thin body next to him; thin tee-shirt and not even a hint of breasts, blue cotton knickers tight across her flat stomach, white knee-length socks, wrinkled and at half-mast next to her ankles. He leaned across and toyed with her hair, too young to know he had full and unconditional approval to explore and enjoy. The girl, on the other hand, was ripe and ready for plucking, almost thirteen and literally on fire, waited a few impatient moments for Joe to stop playing with her hair and start some serious petting.

Miriam whispered, "If you want, Joe, you can take off my knickers." Thought she might help him along and gently and expertly arched her lithe body from the ground.

The faintest of groans fell from the boy's open mouth. With fingers shaking, Joe valiantly attempted to manipulate the flimsy garment. Miriam, grunting and snorting with pleasure, reached and grasped her pants and dragged them down her reed-like legs, kicked and flipped them out of sight.

"There!" she said enthusiastically, and rested, legs slightly open.

Joe was mesmerised by the grotesque, compelling sight of Miriam's budging pudenda. Started making soft gasps of delight mixed with a growing panic, gasps increased in volume when he saw Miriam's hand start to snake towards his midriff, as her long delicate fingers toyed and played with his trouser-buttons, lost his breath as his trousers were expertly opened. Miriam's fingers slipped inside his underpants, perspiration ran like a river over his entire body as the boy fought the growing sensation of panic, tried to relax, his eyes darting from Miriam's open legs to her grasping fingers, shaking with fear, wanting to ravish her, wanting to run from her.

Miriam hammered the nail on the head, slapped his diminishing ardour into touch when she asked, "Joe, what's the matter, don't you like me?"

Crack!

Excuse enough for the boy who whispered, "Someone is close by, Miriam, someone watching!"

Crack! Crunch!

Miriam heard it too, removed her hand from Joe's underpants and grabbed at her knickers, dressed in a flash, skirt fumbled into place, cardigan close to her chest, waiting, listening.

Morris Buckingham grunted with annoyance, so close to the youngsters, watched them glance around the clearing, looking anywhere and everywhere. Knew he was safe, stayed stiff as a statue, trousers down, erect and waiting, head burning with anticipation. "Come on boy," he whispered, "get on with it!" seen the female, skinny as a stick-insect, spread-eagled on the grass, naked apart from tee-shirt and socks, begging for a good time and the boy, hesitant and unsure. "Take off your clothes, boy, slide on to her, let me see your tight little arse!" His mind swimming with lurid thoughts, wanted the boy so bad, wondered if he should run at them, knew he couldn't, life wasn't worth it, too close to home, little beggars would tell on him. Temptation goading and torturing him, all he could see was the little boy, naked as the day he was born. He looked around for a stick, a piece of wood, moaned loudly as he saw the boy and the girl sprint away from the meadow. Morris Buckingham howled to the skies in frustration, screamed to the heavens with his soul demented with insatiable, unquenchable lust, wandered round and round the thicket, trousers still over his ankles, eyes opening and closing as the surreal images rocked him, could not stop masturbating.

"Thought you didn't like me, Joe," gasped the girl, struggling to keep up with her companion.

Joe said, "Course I do, Miriam." Only slowed when they reached the outskirts of the farm. "I heard him for ages, heard him coming closer and closer!"

"Why didn't you say anything!"

Joe said, "Thought it might have been an animal."

"Been one of those perverts, Joe," said Miriam, "who spy on people!" A sudden attack of guilt and conscience made the girl say, "Joe, do you think he'll tell anyone about us?"

"Nothing to tell."

"Joe, I was naked!"

"He'd just arrived, heard him when you took off your knickers."

Miriam, calmer now, still passionate said, "Should have told me Joe, pervert will have seen my fanny," glanced innocently at the boy, "only wanted you to see it, Joe."

A hint of a smile registered on the boy's mischievous face as he said, "I saw it Miriam!"

"Was it nice, Joe?"

"First one I've seen," he replied, added wryly, "apart from Ma's, but that doesn't count."

"You want to see it again, Joe?" teased Miriam, laughed. "If you want, Joe, we could go back to your house?"

**

CHAPTER ELEVEN

Adam Connelly pulled up midway along the long terrace, sat awhile trying to think of the right words to say to his wayward brother, George. Full of good intentions, mainly about himself, Adam finished a last cigarette and still hadn't decided on his lame excuses for travelling two hours into deepest Yorkshire to have a heart-to-heart with his kid brother. Looked again at the house, George's new home, shook his head at the thought of meeting Joyce, his pregnant girl-friend and her two kids, and wondered how long it would be before Joyce became the second Mrs Connelly.

Adam could never understand his brother. The man had it all, thirty one years old, three years younger than Adam, a cushy number at the colliery, a greaser underground, normally poorly-paid, day-work, only George's *so-so* spinal injury caused by a mishap at the coal-face boosted his pay so that he was on par with big-money hewers. Left it all; a lovely wife, colliery-house, two fine boys and his grease-gun, and ran away to another county and for what? There had always been a want in George, all his life, no matter what came his way, he wasn't satisfied, wanted more, especially women, like a fly to grease-paper. He couldn't resist the fun of the chase. Married twelve years to poor Vera Goodrich and he must have snared enough women in that short time to satisfy Rasputin. Stupid with it too, didn't have the sense to be discreet about his dalliances, caught most times with his trousers down and Vera, loyal Vera slapped him then forgave him. Never learned his lesson though but that was George Connelly, life of Riley but it wasn't enough for George. Insatiable could best describe his brother. Confided in his big brother one time, said, *'Can't ever have enough of the honey-trap, Adam, wake up to it, think about it every working minute of the day; go to sleep with it. I love sex more than food; it's the way I'm made.'* Didn't seem to care who he hurt on the way; George and his twisted psychology, *'Men marry to have sex, women have sex hoping they'll snare a husband.'*

Met Joyce on one of his thrice yearly excursions to Blackpool. Couldn't simply enjoy the fun weekend and return to Vera; wasn't George's style, took Joyce's address and telephone number and for the next few years detoured to Yorkshire, via Blackpool. Made the most of his long weekends: Friday he'd make whoopee at the holiday resort with his cronies; Saturday and Sunday he would be gallivanting in Pontefract enjoying the charms of Joyce Smedley, and when Yorkshire became too strong a magnet, George abused his membership with the Territorial Army so that he could play happy-families with his girl-friend, sometimes staying all week at Joyce's home, telling everyone, boasting and bragging like it was something to be proud of. He probably would have sickened himself and eventually returned to Vera full-time, but cute Vera Goodrich found a love-letter from lovesick Joyce, and no one had a temper like Vera, would have frightened Genghis Khan ... Vera empty-handed and Genghis with a sword, would have been a one-sided battle for the little Mongol. George Connelly felt the full wrath of his wife, waited until he returned from having a Friday-night skin-full and demolished her best crockery over his head, George kept overnight in Hartlepool General, *Accident and Emergency,* laughed about it later to his parents and his big brother, thought it was hilarious, said Vera never liked the Marks and Spencer dinner-service, any excuse to get rid of it! Then he was gone, did a bunk, and didn't tell a soul until he was safely away from the North-East.

Adam Connelly liked Vera, wanted to find out if George had put down permanent roots, didn't want any family squabbles, George undecided and Adam wouldn't approach Vera Goodrich, wouldn't even mention a thing. He wasn't that kind of person. Adam was a one-man woman, liked Vera for years, watched when the two of them were courting, thought his kid brother a lucky man, told himself if things ever changed he would tell her how he felt, wasn't bothered if Vera chased or chastised him, better to tell her about his feelings, at least she'd know.

He knocked on the door and waited an age, checked his watch, gone noon, knew it was too late in the day for sleeping, family must be shopping. Not George, however, George was old-fashioned, worked every day at the pit and that was his contribution to family life; cleaning, cooking, changing nappies was woman's work, take it or leave it, knew how to hold a pint of *Federation Best*, but a shopping-bag, wouldn't know which way was up. Knocked again loud enough for a door, two houses away to open and a squat woman, bespectacled, smoking, head full of curling-pins, leaned out and a toothless smile blossomed over her wrinkled face.

"Yer'll be wantin' our Joyce?" she barked phlegmatically, bronchial and raw, the cigarette staying hanging precariously from chomping lips, stared too long at his disfigurement.

Adam said, "George Connelly?"

Adam Connelly began subconsciously rubbing nicotine-stained fingers across his heavy moustache, pulling and smoothing until it hid the thick scar tissue. Borne with a cleft lip, the collier had camouflaged the disfigurement with whiskers since his teens. From a distance, especially when it was combed correctly overlapping his mouth, it was barely noticeable.

"Aye, man," said the female, "our Joyce is up the park with the bairns, George is livin' wi' her!"

Adam Connelly said, "It's George I want, love, he's my brother."

140

She looked him up and down, inspecting the stranger, "Aye why, yer look about the same, apart from the daft fuzz on thee face."

George would have retaliated with a mouth full of bile, dry as sand was his kid brother, would have reduced her to tears in an instant, if his fists were as quick as his tongue. George Connelly would have been heavyweight champion of the world, *'Say again love, this time with your teeth in!'* quick as a flash, maybe jibed her, *'I know you, you're Quasimodo's sister!'* Adam was the fighter, took a bomb to light his fuse but, once lit, you knew about it. George, on the other hand, couldn't fight butter but could hurt more with his sarcastic biting wit than his brother's fists could ever do.

Adam asked politely, "You wouldn't know where I could find him, pet?"

"Second home, love," she said dryly, "the bloody Club, where else?"

Adam Connelly was about to ask directions when the door clashed shut. Muttering obscenities under his breath he crossed the road and headed for the small corner shop.

The Workingman's Club was packed, the bar-counter dripping with thirsty, talkative miners; close by was the billiard-table surrounded by the younger clique. The place smelled of good cheer and camaraderie, could have been in any working-class pub in the country. Adam eased to the bar, nodding and greeting men as they eased aside and allowed him to order, knew eyes would focus on his harelip, on the thick, drooping moustache that almost hid it. He cared less, saw his rogue of a brother lounging at the opposite end of the counter, in deep conversation with a busty, middle-aged barmaid. Adam paid for his drink and sauntered towards his kid brother, nudged him and the intimate conversation immediately ceased. George grinned impishly, the woman went back to her duties.

"You'll never change," said a bemused Adam, shook hands warmly and was led to nearby seats.

George said, "How's tricks, Adam?" finished his drink like he'd been lost in the desert and found the oasis, stood, said, "same again?" Didn't wait for an answer as he strode back to the bar.

"Wine, women and song!" said Adam Connelly when his brother returned carrying drinks.

George laughed, said, "That's what it's all about. Only get one ride on the roundabout." Glancing at the billiard-table he shouted happily, "I'll play the winner!" He took another drink before he continued, "What d'yer think of Rosie, the barmaid… cracker eh? Worked on her for a week, cost me a fortune, girl can sup ale better than some men, but I'm on track, Adam, not be long before she's ready."

"You've not asked why I'm here?"

"Thought you'd called to see me," he said happily, then gave a quizzical look, "nothing wrong at home is there?"

"Ma's worried," said Adam, "Dad doesn't give a hoot!"

"Nothin' changes then?"

"Don't you want to know about Vera or the boys?"

"Rather not," he muttered, "it'll only chew me."

"She's still your wife, George!"

"Old news, Adam," retorted the brother. Sipped at the ale and said poignantly, "Life goes on, eh?"

"You know Vera called to see Ma?"

"That's Vera," muttered the collier, "never say die!"

"She mentioned the boys."

"Joe and Jack," George nodded, grimaced, "two good kids."

"Vera has a job," said Adam, "part-time. She's short of cash, mentioned that you hadn't sent anything for the boys."

George was becoming irritated with the line of questioning, said, "Hey, let's change the chat, Adam," gulped at his ale, added, "now why are you here, you worried about me, brother?"

"You've hardly ever phoned, Ma gets worried," shrugged broad shoulders, added reluctantly, "I'm worried, George."

"I'm fine, Jesus Christ, enjoyin' life, what more can I say."

"Not comin' back home then?"

"Made my bed, Adam and it's a hell of a lot softer these days. I'm stayin' here, new start. Listen, Vera asks, say it's over. She's got to get on with her life. Mentions money, tell her I've got three kids to support, well, almost three and it's a struggle for me. God, I hand over half of my pay to Joyce, that doesn't leave a lot of pocket-money." Grabbed the ale and said, "Cheers," finished the pint and stood, "same again, brother?"

**

Agnes Lincoln said, hesitantly, "When I said move in, Elmore, I thought maybe you'd be contributing. *Charnos Garments* isn't the best factory to work for, I only earn basic." She smiled hoping it would melt the icy atmosphere.

"This is embarrassing, Agnes," replied the man indignantly. He put down the coffee, "I did tell you the inquiry was ongoing and I'm suspended on half-pay."

"Thought you said full-pay?"

Elmore couldn't remember what he'd had for breakfast never mind the multitude of lies he'd concocted over the past months since his dismissal from the Hartlepool Authority. He continued digging holes for himself.

"That was a month ago, now I'm on half-pay!" Kept up the deceit, "Next month I'm on unemployment benefit,

Agnes. It's Hartlepool's way of tightening the screws, hoping I'll hand in my notice before the court-case!"

"But you told me you're innocent, Elmore," Agnes said, "surely you'll fight them?"

He nodded pathetically, looking for sympathy from the naïve woman, "It's dragged on so long, Agnes, don't know if I have the strength to fight it. It's been months!"

Agnes Lincoln moved towards him and sat on the edge of the sofa. Stroking his thick hair she said, "I do understand, Elmore, I know you're suffering!"

Pushing his luck he whispered dejectedly, "Can't go on fighting the department, Agnes," shook his head slowly, "I might look for another position. It's going to get ugly, lots of recriminations and accusations. Shit sticks, Agnes, people will start to label me if the case is publicised, no smoke without fire, you know? If I leave now I could obtain references, might be a better chance of employment elsewhere." Puppy-dog eyes focussed on the woman for a moment before they shifted to the floor, "I'm at the end of my tether," he whispered.

"Hey," said the female, nudging him fondly and taking the bait, "it's Saturday, let's have a decent night out and talk about our options tomorrow. We'll try it for an hour, if you still feel bad about it we'll come home, what do you say, Elmore?"

"Few months time and I'll be thirty," moaned Elmore. "You know what it feels like to be an abject failure? Can't seem to do anything right, story of my life, Agnes. I don't think celebrating will really do me good."

"I know it will," she answered resolutely, stood, reached for his hand, pulled Elmore Stoker to his feet and pushed him gently towards the door. "Have a long bath, shave, it'll make you feel better." She paused then added, "I'll do some shopping, pay a few bills. You have a nap, Elmore, put you in the mood for tonight."

The man smiled pathetically, sauntered slowly from the room and slowly climbed the staircase. Tried to work out the value of the Thorpe Road home, his mind on calculating mode: Agnes Lincoln, twenty nine years old, one year younger than him, mentally naive, the perpetual misguided teenager, twice married and twice divorced, Elmore's favourite kind of girl, lacking grey matter between her ears and left a valuable asset, a house by stupid parents who would rather end their working days in a colliery house and gift their beautiful home to their only daughter. Fools born every day, and rich pickings for Elmore, the Thorpe Road home worth thousands, wondered if he should propose quickly or wait awhile, maybe if he could persuade her to write a will? *'Agnes,'* he thought *'what's mine is yours. Everything I own, all of my possessions, I want you to have. It's my way of showing I care for you.'* Maybe leave it at that for a while and see if it pulls at her conscience, could even hint that he owned a share in Evelyn's shack in Stockton Road, *'It's always better to be prepared, Agnes. God forbid, what if I have a heart attack, get run down by a truck, I certainly wouldn't want my brother to inherit my estate. No, worst-case scenario I would want you to benefit, no one else in the whole world. I thought you might feel the same way.'* Yes, he quite liked the sound of that. A will was a distinct possibility, either that or marriage, piece of paper either way would give him half shares in Agnes's home, then if things didn't work out they could go their own separate ways with no grudges from Elmore Stoker.

He filled the bath with scalding water and slipped in gingerly, closed his eyes and relaxed. It had been an eventful week, caught a bitch early in the week, too much baggage though, a whore of a mother and two brats to support, pretty, but too clever by half, first time they met, subtle hints about Evelyn buying the drinks all night in the *Southside* pub. *'Elmore,'* whisper whisper, *'your brother*

145

has bought the last three rounds of drinks,' and then the humiliation, when Vera Connelly waltzed to the bar and purchased booze for the group! Still she was an attractive filly and he would have enjoyed a round in bed with her. Too much booze consumed that first night in her council house. Between them they drank a full bottle of Johnny Walker's finest malt. Evelyn wouldn't have minded though, he had plenty of spares, money coming out of his tiny ears, the little tightwad!

Thought of his half-brother, eyes closed and he still grimaced at the image of the stammering fool. Always the favourite with his parents, couldn't do any wrong, even when he fell at the final hurdle and his examination certificates weren't up to scratch, did they complain when the choice of universities became limited and his goals had to be amended. He remembered still, all of them in the big room and Evelyn broken-hearted with his mediocre results and his father reasoning with him, *'There's always pharmacy, Evelyn, or dentistry even. There are so many other opportunities and professions, doctor, dentist, chemist, all related professions, choose another, son, it's not the end of the world.'* Evelyn sniffling like a proverbial woman, *'You really think so father?'* turning to mother. *'What do you think, mother?* Elizabeth Stoker, cold, polite, always correct, shaking her head, *'You're asking my advice, Evelyn, listen to your father. Father always knows best, always a step ahead of everyone, isn't that right Simon?'*

Images that made him wince. All of his life, favouritism was at the forefront of his mind, no matter what, where, or when, Elmore felt second-best, surplus baggage, nothing too obvious, but always present, the distinct, insidious feeling that he wasn't really wanted, tolerated maybe, nothing ever directed at him. It was always Evelyn. Evelyn the star, Elmore the also-ran, made him so angry, made him purposely do things to see reaction from his parents. His step-father always indifferent, his mother occasionally embarrassed with his infantile behaviour. His matriculation results astounded him, eighteen years old and already showing signs of immature and aggressive antics that embroiled the whole family with tension and tantrums, rarely studied at school, partied and played and yet his examination results were superior to Evelyn's. There was no flag-waving or rejoicing at home, a grudging comment from Simon Stoker to his step-son, *'I can't believe the results, Elmore! Still, it's there in black and white, so it must be right. Maybe now you might start behaving in the manner expected. Are you thinking about university, you're not sure yet, well when you have made up your mind, let me know and we'll discuss the matter.'* No *'Well done, son'*, no celebrations or party to show the world how clever he was, not even from his own mother.

The bath water relaxed and soothed him. He thought of Agnes Lincoln and smiled. She was a lackey, a plaything, nothing more, to be used and discarded whenever the whim took him, a rather rich lackey who, thanks to his conniving and presence of mind, now possessed several fine pieces of jewellery, his late mother's finest which of course could be immediately retrieved if he ever left his new abode. Elmore had found the stash of goodies hidden in the top shelf of the bedroom cupboard, his late parent's jewellery wrapped in loose pages ripped from an ancient *Littlewoods* catalogue. Jewellery and old faded black and white photographs, had to focus for some moments on the prints before he recognised the young man, his step-father, Simon Stoker, dressed as an Arab sheik. Another showed him as a spiv, complete with fake moustache and trilby hat, another showed a man dressed like some biblical figure in long beard and garish robes, Simon Stoker the amateur dramatist, the actor-doctor, an embarrassing fool, like his son.

Something else caught Elmore's eye. Picking up the loose catalogue sheets he stared in disbelief. All the grubby, coloured prints depicted scantily-clad young men advertising underwear; probably half a dozen or more pages all showing male models. Made Elmore stop and think. Did his brother like men, were the catalogue pages pulled at random from the books or torn out deliberately, his brother's sexuality in doubt ... no, couldn't be, the collection of loose sheets must have been ripped indiscriminately from the annual. Wasn't diminutive Evelyn bedding the old whore, Annie Goodrich, for months? He threw the pictures in the waste-bin and pushed aside silly thoughts.

The cache of jewellery was substantive and worth a lot of money and Elmore knew he could change the hoard into cash by visiting one of Sunderland's pawn-broking firms. He decided to hold it for a rainy-day, chuckled again at the hiding-place used by his brother, Evelyn imagining the hoard quite safe under the pile of clothing. Silly man, silly short man! Tall Elmore didn't need a chair or stool to reach and search for the booty, the treasure-trove, his by right, his birthright, Elmore redressing the balance after years of neglect. His brother was out of the house pulling teeth, playing with dentures, and acting the professional so Elmore seized the opportunity and packed his suitcases, well, Evelyn's suitcases actually. It mattered little, he was leaving. Agnes was waiting outside in her car, an early finish from the factory, a Friday perk apparently, waiting to chauffeur him away. *'The television is yours, Elmore,'* she quizzed, *'and the record-player?'* Dizzy Agnes making three separate journeys with her vehicle crammed with household stuff, all his very own personal possessions assured Elmore.

Putting right the wrong, according to Elmore Stoker, and he was still many thousands out of pocket, still crocked of his fair share of the family gold, Evelyn feigning friendship and brotherly love, all an act, a sham to ease his guilty conscience. Words came easy to his fawning excuse of a brother, '*Let me buy you a drink, Elmore. Here, Elmore, take this money and have a decent night out. Come and stay a few weeks, brother, forget your troubles at Hartlepool, stay in my house.*' The stammering half-pint could pulverize his younger brother with biting sarcasm, a smile on his pudding face with seemingly innocent remarks. *His house! His house!* The house was not Evelyn's house; it belonged to both of them. A vindictive demented Simon Stoker, the step-father from hell, continued to play his evil games even after his death. Evelyn should have understood his brother's hurt, and acted like a real brother, and shared the property equally. Elmore hated his brother, always had and always would.

CHAPTER TWELVE

Saturday saw Delwin Mix mowing the lawns for the final time that year, the cold autumn weather slowing the growth and making the task less cumbersome. Early afternoon and the sun burned an iridescent bronze of false hope across the skies; a cold incessant breeze scattered and whirled leaves like confetti over the long drive and the vast garden. The man rested, the perspiration ran rivulets down his blotchy features as he looked back at the palatial home and grounds. They counted for nothing, such possessions meant not one iota to him, would have traded it all for happiness and contentment. He stood alone. His wife, Mildred was more in love with herself and her pretentious position at the library than to stoop so low as to share such menial tasks with her husband. *'Delwin,'* she scowled, *'hire some help if you can't manage!'* His selfish son, Albert, had made his usual excuses not to help, *'Dad, it's Saturday, I'm seeing my friends, can I cut the grass tomorrow?'* and cycled away with his two friends either side of him. *'Fickle friends,'* thought Del Mix, wondered how long the peace treaty would last. Albert being his usual clever-clogs, *'Dad, meet Sammy and Joe. Joe's mother works for you at the store,'* tried his best to describe the woman but couldn't resist the little dig at his old adversary. Delwin Mix saw the glint in Joe Connelly's eyes as the sarcasm registered, watched them drive off along Stockton Road and shook his head, Albert so like his mother it was frightening.

Saw his neighbour, shouted, "Evelyn, how are you?" wandered towards the man, handkerchief wiping away the heavy sweat, on a mission, couldn't miss such an opportunity.

"Hi!" shouted the neighbour, stopped scratching the lawns and hesitantly moved towards the dividing fence, garden-rake held straight like a flag-pole next to his diminutive frame.

"Nice day," said Delwin Mix, wanting the formalities over, wanting to show his disapproval.

"Del," greeted the neighbour, working around his speech impediment, "okay?"

Evelyn Stoker didn't like his neighbour, hadn't liked him for years, not since he found out about him, found out the truth about the arrogant, brash selfish man.

Delwin Mix grinned coldly at the man, "Partying over, Evelyn?" eyed him up and down, comparing and contrasting, thinking he was a Stoker through and through.

"Pardon m, me, me," stuttered the dentist, knew what was coming from the big, bombastic fellow.

"Quiet last night for a change," said Del, smirking. "You must have tied your brother up so he can't make music?"

"Gone," he answered and nodded approvingly.

"Miles away I hope, Evelyn," retorted the taller man, "damn nuisance he is!"

Evelyn Stoker shrugged his shoulders in sympathy, "He's had some ba, bad, bad, luck, Del."

The man said sympathetically, "Too soft, Evelyn, you've always been too soft with that nuisance of a brother. Why on earth did you allow him to lodge with you, I'll never know. He's nothing but a waste of space!" He paused, sucked in air, added grudgingly, "Tell you something for nothing, Evelyn, Mildred wanted me to call the police because of the racket. Only because I liked your parents, Evelyn, that I didn't take action. No one wants to be a spoil-sport, son, but week in, week out, bloody music loud enough for the entire street to hear, no way!" Shook his head from side to side to register disapproval, "And as for falling on hard times, your brother is his own worst enemy. Any excuse Evelyn, any excuse and Elmore is drowning his sorrows in drink. There comes a time, son, when you've got to let go, brother or no brother, you hear me?"

"Yes."

"Can I ask a question, son?"

"Yes."

"You frightened of him, younger brother and all?"

"No... no."

"Only some times I hear shouting, and I don't mean Elmore enjoying his floozies. I hear argument between ...."

Evelyn interjected, "No! We...we...we..."

"You don't, eh. I could beg to differ, Evelyn. I've seen it with my own eyes. Phone the police, you hear me, phone the police because that brother of yours is no damn good. This street is a quiet street son, maybe that kind of behaviour is okay for the council-houses but not for Stockton Road!"

"He's gone." Evelyn didn't stammer, felt at peace with the world for the first time in months. His brother had taken everything but the kitchen-sink and he didn't care.

"I hope you're right, son, although I very much doubt it. He'll always come back with his begging-bowl and you'll always be filling it!"

"Sorry, Del." The dentist easing, the stress lifting as he watched his neighbour turn to leave.

The older man started moving away from the perimeter fence. "Had to tell you, son," he called out, "it was getting to be more than a joke and some of us work for a living, need our sleep."

"Bye," said Evelyn Stoker. Closed his eyes and prayed that his brother would leave him alone, thought *Floozy* was an apt description of Agnes Lincoln.

Evelyn wandered aimlessly back to the kitchen, made coffee and sat in the spacious conservatory which, despite the chill of the day, felt pleasant and warm. He sipped at the drink and regurgitated his neighbour's words. Stunned by Mix's horrid remarks he looked morosely across the extensive gardens and saw the autumn sun coating trees and bushes in plush copper and gold. Evelyn started to relax, finished his coffee and eased back into the comfortable chair, closed his eyes and thought of better times ....

In his final year at dental school, his stammer almost conquered thanks to years of treatment, 'Sing your words,' said the therapist. 'Evelyn, try it, sing your words to me,' which he did and found a rhythm that lifted his blues and almost conquered his burden. He could still picture his younger brother, Elmore, still headstrong, at war with the world around him, buoyant, happy and somewhat surprised at his unexpected examination results, dumbfounded at the unbelievable prospect of university ahead, the happiest and proudest day of his life.

Evelyn wandered through the garden. He heard voices, quiet, hushed, urgent voices; adult voices, and recognised his mother. She sounded so different, her tone high and pitched with emotion, he listened with utter disbelief. 'Another lie, Delwin, another lie, how could you! You said it was over. After all this time you can still lie and manipulate. Why can't you leave us alone, I'm tired of it all, you hear, Delwin. Can't you make up your mind who you want, who you love? Your wife is pregnant! You must have some feeling for her or you wouldn't sleep with her. I was happy once, Del, can you understand, happy. Despite everything, Simon loves me and I love him. People make mistakes! Please let it go, please don't destroy two families!'

Evelyn, cringed with despair and embarrassment, listened to his mother who was gravely ill at the time, pleading with their neighbour. An approaching vehicle entered their driveway, a car-door slammed and quick staccato footsteps echoed on the concrete garden path. It was his father, Simon Stoker, diminutive, stocky, clever, a general practitioner, normally so placid and caring. Not this day as the accusations and name-calling reached

153

fever-pitch as tempers boiled and scalded and worlds collided. Evelyn crept away, walked along the tree-lined street. Then he was running wildly from the place, his mind so confused and hurt

His mother, Elizabeth Stoker, was ill with cancer. Months into chemotherapy and as brave as any mother would be, fighting the disease and refusing to weaken, her beautiful mane of hair a memory, replaced by a wig, telling folks she would beat the tumour. Everyone believed her but, a week after the arguments and confrontations with her neighbour, Elizabeth took a massive overdose. Everyone assumed she had committed suicide because of the invidious plague growing in her, that she had lost the will to live and wanted peace. Only Simon Stoker and his eldest son knew the truth and they never spoke about it.

Evelyn could still recall the fateful day as if it were yesterday. Alone in the large house, his younger brother away from home, his parents returning, voices raised in growing disagreement, thinking the home empty, free to attack and condemn. Evelyn, could only sit in his bedroom, his face covered with his hands as he listened to the horrid, gut-wrenching truth about the sham of a marriage. The accusations and counter-accusations were serrated and barbed, Simon Stoker trying to shore up the marriage again, 'I don't understand, you're leaving me, why on earth after all this time are you determined to destroy our marriage. You're ill, my dear, you're not thinking rationally, let me get you a drink. We can resolve this problem.' Then the shouting diminished and his mother spoke quietly and resolutely, so quiet that Evelyn could not comprehend the hushed tones and a horrid silence seemed to percolate through the house. His father, shaking with pent-up emotion and incredulity shouted, 'Dear God, don't you have any conscience and compassion! I know that anyone can make a mistake; I'm not a naïve fool to think it only happens to others. It happened to us but we mended it,

154

fixed our marriage once, we can do it again! It doesn't mean we should part. I don't want you to leave me, I know it won't happen again, I'll make sure it doesn't happen again. What did you say, I've never loved you for years? How can you say that, Elizabeth, when I've brought up both boys as if they were my own! Both boys, Evelyn and Elmore, you know how hard that's been for me? Have you thought of the damage it will cause if we separate. Elizabeth? I will not allow you to leave. Don't make up your mind today, you're not well! Please, darling, don't be hasty. This is not only about me, please spare a thought for the boys!'

The argument ceased. A door banged and Evelyn remembered seeing his father striding furiously out of the drive. The youth wandered to the top of the stairs and faced his mother, her eyes wild, crumpled wig in her fist, bald head sprouting dying clumps of wizened locks, glaring blankly into space, lost and abandoned. 'Dear God, Evelyn, you've heard everything,' crying now, her toupee a sad excuse for a handkerchief as she pawed at her tears. 'It's not your father's fault, Evelyn! You must understand, it's not your father's fault. Sometimes people have to make choices, son. Please try and understand why I have to leave. I can't live a lie any longer!'

He tried to tell her that if she wanted a life without them it was okay. Tried to explain that she should perhaps wait until she was able to leave, when she was strong enough, but his words came out gibberish. The stammering and faltering was so awful that the woman began crying again and ran wailing into her bedroom ....

Evelyn Stoker fell into a deep and troubled sleep, slept and thought again about his childhood. An image blossomed of an old man, his grandfather, pleading with an aloof, callous Elizabeth Stoker.

**

155

He walked the three miles north from Easington to the small village of Hawthorn, the day warm and pleasant for September. Could have used public transport but Morris Buckingham had all the time in the world, unemployable, on the early slide to an old-age pension. The hardest part of any day was filling the long, lonely hours. He decided on a steady stroll towards Easington and sauntered past the infant school. It was the weekend, the primary school closed and quiet, preferred midweek when he could enjoy the little lambs frolicking in the playground. He tended to shuffle past break-time or lunch-time, lean over the boundary wall and feed the innocent faces with assorted sweeties. Not his first choice, too young, preferred older, the *Double T* he called his favourites, teenagers or twenties, more adventurous more hardened to life, looking for a quick return, *quid pro quo* as they say, and Morris was happy to oblige.

The man continued on his way then turned right, left the main South Hetton road and headed for the old mill and the sprawling wilderness that would eventually lead to the hamlet of Hawthorn. He strolled towards the distant coastal route. Morris could see the incline, the high ground that was the outskirts of the village and, a little to the north, was the dog-track, the racing-stadium, open twice weekly, Wednesday and Saturday. He wondered if he should call that night.

Morris Buckingham thought about past lovers. Some he missed, one especially ....

Only time he had been cast aside for another man, made him cry bitter tears. Morris and his lover had cut an imposing pair, both well over six feet tall, both muscular and had always apportioned roles, shared so much happiness and joy. Then the stranger appeared on the scene, took up his surgery in the colliery and *Hey Presto* they met, doctor and patient, few months later and the diminutive

Doctor Dare had the strength, the audacity, to move house from Durham and plant himself next door to his ex-love.

Morris acknowledged it would never last. The stranger was too different, too high up the social ladder. He actually met him, wanted to see for himself so he feigned illness and visited the surgery. The man was quite beautiful, striking in fact. Morris found himself smitten in the presence of the medic. *'It's my chest, doctor,'* he'd said, wheezing, told the practitioner he rarely smoked, lied of course, forty a day minimum. The doctor sounded his chest, hands like silk, words soothing. *'Rarely smoke, Mr Buckingham?'* said the M.D. his eyes alive with laughter, the smile brazen. Married too, talking to Morris Buckingham, guiding and coaxing him into changing his smoking habits when the telephone sounded and the fellow began chatting to his wife. Made Morris realise that the liaison would be nothing more than a temporary affair. He was so right, a brief encounter, little over a year and the smitten practitioner had dumped Morris's ex-love. Weeks after the affair had ended he witnessed the glazed, miserable face as he shopped, made polite conversation and knew the bubble had burst and his love, like he, had been cast aside. He waited patiently for weeks and weeks and the expected reunion did not materialise. Morris finally made the first move, a careful hint as they passed one another on the High Street. The coaxing, the wheedling came to nothing. He was rebuffed. It was as if he had never existed. There was no response, no calls, nothing. His old partner seemed dejected and defeated.

He reached the coastal road, the section of roadway that dipped precariously midway between Easington to the south and Hawthorn to the north. In the incline between the dog-racing stadium on the hill, close to village and the abandoned R.A.F. prefabs close to the high ground and Hawthorn. Morris found the council seat and rested, pushed aside all thoughts from yesteryear and thought of his mother. Daisy Buckingham, eighty-three years old, widowed a lifetime and still happy-go-lucky, despite being house-bound. The woman wore a permanent smile that shamed all who visited. Morris called daily since her illness. His head-in-the-clouds sister, called birthdays and Christmas, couldn't change her selfish nature, ready-made excuses too, worked round the clock at the library, husband and new kid, no time to visit her mother, too busy living her life.

His mother stuck by him through good times and bad. Not like his sister, spoke when she had to speak, didn't like him, didn't like the shame he had brought to the family. There had been times when Morris wanted to tell his precious rose-between-her-legs sister the truth about her so-called loving husband, had so much dirt he could have started a battle. His mother, Daisy, out of her head with morphine, bravely adjusting her lifestyle around a colostomy-bag, had supplied the bullets when she told him in confidence, *'It's not his, Morris,'* she had mumbled, smiling serenely through the pain, *'the boy... it's not his! No one knows but me. Called one night, hysterical with worry, 'What'll I do, Daisy? I'm pregnant, he'll know!' Told her not to worry, not when the same man drinks himself into a stupor every night. Told her to wait till he's asleep and creep into his bed, next day let him wake up first... men are so stupid. Once, twice a week, especially after he's had a good session on the booze, share his bed, say nothing. Few weeks, leave him be and forget about it. When time comes and you can't hide it, don't be a shrinking violet. Attack him, ridicule him, tell him you want rid of it, put it all on to him, you hear?'*

The news pleased Morris Buckingham who knew his ex-love could never be intimate with his sister. Pushed and prised to discover the identity of the boy's father, hindsight, he wished he hadn't, because he uncovered a whole can of worms, it seemed a bizarre merry-go-round. Daisy on overdrive as she spilled the beans on the Stoker clan, all the muck from way back. Morris blamed the morphine for distorting her mind blacker than black. 'Ma, *you've heard it wrong, what you're saying can't be true.'* Made Morris realise why his ex-love crumbled years ago. Morris was too long in the tooth to believe in coincidences but he was gagged, tied hand and foot, and could only watch and wait and hope.

"Mother," said Morris knocking and entering the semi-bungalow, hearing the radio full-blast, feeling the rush of heat from the massive coal-fire, "only me... Morris!"

The stench stopped him, gasped at the foul air. Knew he'd have to be brave, show willing and help his mother with her daily task. *'Ma,'* he would chortle, *'it's nothing to worry about, only shit at the end of the day. Of course it doesn't bother me, you're my bloody mother, I know you'd do it for me, now shut up!'* Found he could breathe through his mouth and the smell eased enough to stop him gagging, made both of them strong enough to cope. *'Colostomy-bag, Ma,'* he'd say, *'not a problem for me.'* Arthritic hands and warped fingers were a drawback for Daisy, made her struggle with the mechanics, didn't stop her smiling. Mind as strong as an ox; her decrepit body was the let-down.

Morris saw her lying there and realised immediately his mother wasn't sleeping. Daisy Buckingham had finally thrown in the towel.

**

CHAPTER THIRTEEN

"Mum, please!"

Vera Connelly shook her head, smiling at the tots, trying unsuccessfully to dissuade them, knew she couldn't but made one last attempt, "Nana says you can play indoors if you're quiet. I'll only be an hour Jack!"

Alice Raine said sweetly, "Stay at mine, Jack, if you want?"

Jack shook his head, wanted to be with his mother, wanted Alice to accompany him to the colliery, anxious to show her the sights, never visited his old haunts since his mother took them to live with their grandmother.

Annie Goodrich loomed, cackled, toying with her spectacles, "Leave them Vera. Soon as you're out of sight they'll be on their trikes again," gestured at the small boy, full of sarcasm, and said, "either that or playing with Alice's skipping-ropes!"

The humour was lost on the toddlers. The small girl grabbed at Jack's hand and tried to pull him out of the open door, "Come on, Jack, Mum will be making tea soon, ice-cream and custard!"

"Ice-cream and custard?" wavered the boy, couldn't remember the last time he's tasted such luxury. Looked at Alice, glanced at his mother and said, "Ice-cream and custard, Ma?"

"Sounds lovely, Jack," she replied, "and I'll be back in an hour, what do you think?"

Alice Raine chirped in, "Mum has *monkey's blood* to go over the ice-cream if you don't like custard, Jack!"

"Think I'll play at Alice's house," Jack answered, a big grin on his cheeky face. "Come on, Alice, we'll take our bikes over," he bolted from the kitchen, dragging a hysterical girl after him.

Annie Goodrich said, whimsically, "Think I'll join them, Vera, it sounds lovely."

Vera Connelly slipped on her coat, said, "After I've been to Leith's shop I might take a bus to Horden, call in and see George's lot. I wasn't going to trail Jack and Alice there but now that they're busy... might as well see if there's any money on the table."

Annie snorted, "Silly bugger, you're wastin' your time, easier gettin' blood out of a stone."

Jeremiah Leith owned an electrical store situated in Seaside Lane, Easington Colliery, few shops down from Equi's Coffee Bar. The busy shop opened for business six days a week because old man Leith offered credit, few quid down and payment on the never-never, revolving credit, bill almost settled and Jeremiah or his son, Joseph, could usually persuade folks to buy more appliances.

Vera Connelly handed over her payment-card and the money, said perkily to the chunky figure of Joseph Leith, "One more, Joe, and I'm out of your net."

"Mrs Connelly," said the bald, brown-eyed man, rising from his stool and folding his copy of the *Telegraph* and using it as a pointer, "this I must show you, come." Shuffled from the small, cluttered office, stopped next to the plush cabinet, stooped and eased open the doors, "You'd like one for yourself, yes?"

The television was a beautiful, top-of-the-range Phillips.

"Too much for me," Vera answered. She caressed the mahogany. "What size, Joseph?"

Joseph Leith grinned like a wolf circulating the lamb, "Bigger than yours, am I right?"

Annie Goodrich's 10 inch was out of sight upstairs, been there since Vera had moved house and installed her own television, a huge Bush 14 inch, sadly on the blink with *B.B.C.* working and *Tyne Tees* permanently covered in snow and buzz.

"Not as big as that, Joe."

161

Joe Leith said, "Guaranteed one year, parts and labour, Mrs Connelly. Free installation and probably the biggest screen in the whole of Easington… a massive 21 inch!"

"Bloody hell!"

"It's yours, Mrs Connelly. No deposit, same weekly terms, you could be watching it on Monday!"

"Can I think about it?" said the vacillating woman. "I'm not living in the colliery anymore, Joseph, I'm at my mother's address at the village. Might have to have a quiet word with her."

"That's not a problem," soothed the part-owner. "Tell you what I'll do. Monday I'll have the engineer call with the television, he's working in the village anyway. If you still want it, he'll have it up and running in minutes, if you change your mind, he'll return it, no questions asked. You can't lose, can you, Mrs Connelly?"

"I'm not sure."

"Your mother's address, Mrs Connelly?" he asked, leading her back to the office. "It's no problem. Monday and you don't want it, chase the engineer, what could be better?"

The shop-door clanked open. A bell tinkled and the young woman strolled along the shop floor, eyeing up the merchandise. Almost reached Vera Connelly before she recognised her old rival.

Vera said, "Agnes!" too shocked to say anymore. Only a few days ago she was cursing the woman to her oldest son.

"Vera, bloody hell!" Agnes faked a smile. "Paying bills like me?"

"Buying a new television, Agnes," boasted the woman, wanted to stick one on her, shut her arrogant mouth. Gesturing at the electrical display, she said, "Phillips 21 inch, getting it Monday."

Vera Connelly knew all about Agnes Lincoln's loose reputation. Divorced two men before she was twenty-five which had to be some kind of record, especially when it was all down to her philandering ways. Morals of a tom-cat had Agnes Lincoln, anyone, anytime, anywhere. Two years ago she made a play for George Connelly, cheeky with it too, in the lounge of the Club, didn't give a hoot who she hurt, blamed the drink, blamed amorous George. Couldn't help it if men found her irresistible she said brashly. Changed her tune when Vera pushed her against the toilet-wall trying to choke the life out of her, *'Look at my man again,'* threatened an irascible Vera Connelly, *'and your life is over!'*

Felt a fool later when George caught a fast train out of the county.

"In the money, Vera?" said Agnes, trying to keep the peace.

"Working now," said Vera Connelly, "co-op at the village. You still at the factory?"

"The last place I want to be, but what can you do, can't rely on men any more." Realising her gaff she paled, closed her eyes involuntary and waited for the rebuke. When none came Agnes stammered awkwardly, "That wasn't meant the way you think, Vera! I'm sorry, I heard about you and George."

Vera smiled bravely, said, "Water off a duck, good riddance!"

Agnes Lincoln foolishly continued the conversation, should have stopped while she was ahead. "I'm courting again, Vera, have you heard. He's a professional, think I've landed on my feet for once."

Vera sugared her answer with a dollop of sarcasm. Said dryly, "Third time lucky," filled her gun with bullets anxious to demolish the whore, "has he a name?"

"You'll laugh," Agnes chortled to herself, a lamb to the slaughter.

"It's funny?"

"It's his name. Elmore, he works for the Social Services ....."

Vera interjected, feigning astonishment, "Hartlepool! Not Elmore Stoker?"

A surprised Agnes nodded, "You know him, Vera?"

"Know him?" smiled the bemused woman, "put it this way, same man asked me to help him to look for a house, wants to rent somewhere, and you know when we were supposed to do the rounds, Agnes?"

Agnes Lincoln could only gawk.

"Today, but I changed my mind!" Vera stared coldly at her old advisory, "Talks more bullshit than George Connelly ever did. As for working for Hartlepool Council, he was sacked. No doubt he'll have told you he was suspended?"

"Yes," whispered Agnes, crestfallen, "suspended."

"You want to hear the truth, Agnes, ask his brother, he lives ...."

"Stockon Road," interrupted Agnes, depression turning to anger. "I helped him move his belongings."

"He found a house on his own?" Vera Connelly loving the task, words hurting more than her fists.

"Mine," groaned Agnes, "he's moving into mine!"

"You're not serious, Agnes!" Vera gasped, "You haven't let him move in with you?" Stuck the knife in deep, twisted it enough to destroy organs, "Ask a personal question, Agnes?"

Agnes nodded sorrowfully, felt she was swimming in quicksand, wanted to run a thousand miles, knew she couldn't without first hearing the truth.

Vera asked bluntly, "How long?"

"How long ... what?"

"How long you been seeing Elmore?"

"Few months, why?"

"Agnes," sighed Vera Connelly morosely, as if she carried the whole world on her shoulders, "I'm sorry but

164

I'm going to have to tell you, better from me than someone else."

"I don't understand, Vera?"

"Elmore was with me Monday night, Tuesday night. He stayed all night Tuesday!" Shook her head, her features sullen and sour.

Agnes gasped, her tone incredulous with grief, "Honest, Vera," the woman more used to destroying lives than being destroyed, "he was at your house?"

"He's a bullshit artist, Agnes," said Vera Connelly, suddenly tasting the exquisite quality of retribution, "a bastard!"

Agnes Lincoln felt faint. The news too awful. Knew she couldn't go home, not today, couldn't face Elmore Stoker today. She would walk to her parent's colliery house in Boston Street, minutes away. They would understand. They always understood, talk to her father, maybe he could be persuaded, maybe he would visit Thorpe Road, tell Elmore to leave. That's what she'd do tomorrow, yes, persuade her dad to see Elmore, tell him Agnes didn't own the house. Yes, he could say Agnes was a liar and the Thorpe Road house was his, demand Elmore to leave and if he didn't then the police could be called. Always a way around a problem, took time, that's all.

"Agnes," asked Vera Connelly, "are you okay?"

Agnes Lincoln did not reply, turned and strode from the shop, her mind preoccupied, had to stay focussed, knowing she had to evict that lying no-account bastard!

**

The first time Evelyn had felt strange and not in control of a situation was when he attended Peterlee Technical College. Years later he could still remember the cataclysmic gut-wrenching explosion deep inside his skull, a pneumatic drill, twisting and burrowing and releasing passions and emotions never before experienced. Until that day he imagined himself a normal, healthy passionate youth, his impairment gradually losing ground as he gained confidence, shared discussions, found friends and eventually dated.

It was during a physical-education lesson at the college that Evelyn suddenly realised his sexual preferences. The whole class was watching the young teacher, a twenty-plus sports graduate, a beautifully-built Adonis, showing the eager pupils how to vault the wooden-horse, running and lifting and spreading his thighs, and Evelyn glimpsing the tutor's bulging genitalia as the shorts momentarily revealed all. A fire inside Evelyn exploded, his passions enveloped him with a sensuous delight and he became mesmerised, his eyes boring on that one delightful place. Knew it then, his heart pounding like a big drum, knew immediately and forever that he was gay and wanted to shout it from the rooftops.

He told no one, not a living soul, felt it was essentially wrong and hid the shame for years. Essentially a private introverted young man, Evelyn held his predilection in check, contented himself with his training and then his career. All through dental school, into his practice, and never once successfully recognising a like individual, only once did he transgress. Celebrating his final examinations with fellow students on a jaunt through the hot nightspots of Newcastle. Found he didn't have the strength or impudence to approach strangers, couldn't reciprocate when approached, fled from the place disillusioned and disheartened.

The obvious thefts from the house hurt him but didn't surprise him, nothing about his younger brother shocked Evelyn Stoker. Elmore seemed impervious to shame or guilt. Elmore took what he wanted, when he wanted and cared little about people's feelings or the possible consequences of his actions. He was unscrupulous, unethical and unprincipled. In other words, Elmore Stoker was essentially a scoundrel.

Saturday afternoon and, although cold and overcast, it was dry enough to take an invigorating walk across the village green to the co-operative store. Evelyn needed to purchase a television, hi-fi, and a record-player. Who but his brother would have had the audacity to load so much equipment from the house in broad daylight? The locksmith was coming Monday to change the back-door locks. Knew he'd be back, guaranteed to return as soon as money ran out, fortunate that the door could be bolted from the inside.

Evelyn Stoker hurried through the double-doors of the store and collided with the under-manager, both stumbling, holding one another as they struggled to keep their balance and the chemistry ignited and the electricity showered over the pair.

"I'm terribly sorry," spluttered a bewildered Alvin Brown, eyes wide with pleasure as he stared at the diminutive stranger, felt the power of his gentle touch ignite something inside his belly.

Evelyn smiled, knew instantly they were kindred souls, searched high and low and there before him the man of his dreams. "My fault," he said without a stammer or blemish, "I'm sorry too."

"Can I help," croaked Alvin, trying to mask his feelings from the stranger, "it's almost closing-time." Checked himself instantly, "I didn't mean you won't be served, I'm here until the last customer leaves," beaming at the fellow.

"My next-door neighbour, Delwin Mix, I do believe he works here?"

"Manager, yes," reached over and gently closed the doors, "he doesn't work on Saturday but I can help. I'm the under-manager, Alvin Brown, at your service."

"I wanted to buy a television," glanced around the food section, "but I think I've come to the wrong shop?"

"No, on the contrary," bleated the ever anxious Alvin Brown, "if you'll follow me, all the electrical and equipment is kept upstairs. Please," gestured at the wide staircase in front of them, touched the stranger's arm and felt a pulse of delightful pain, "this way, Mister...."

"Evelyn Stoker," replied the man, couldn't stop his tongue. Still not a hint of a stutter in his voice, felt blissfully happy and he didn't know why. He was touching heaven simply by being next to the charming, compassionate stranger. "I live in the village, Stockton Road? I work at Peterlee, have a dental practice."

They walked together up the imposing staircase, the under-manager seemingly spellbound, couldn't stop looking at the man.

Smitten Alvin Brown gushed, "Your name is delightful, first Evelyn I've ever met. Heard of Evelyn Waugh: *Decline and Fall, Brideshead Revisited.*"

Evelyn Stoker couldn't stop himself, he chortled, "*Vile Bodies*, yes?"

"Chance would be a fine thing," Alvin tittered as they reached the expansive landing then recovered enough to add, "I've never read that particular novel."

"Satire, you'd like it," returned Evelyn warmly. Took a gamble, couldn't help himself, "I have a copy, you can borrow it if you want?"

Alvin Brown said, "I live in the village."

"Never!"

"All my life, opposite the church," he announced proudly. "Hall Walk*?*"

"And I live on Stockton Road, other side of the church," talking fast now, excited, anxious to prolong the conversation, "all this time and we haven't met!"

"Unbelievable."

"Married?"

"Never… couldn't!" Smiled when he said it, "You understand?"

"Yes, I understand."

Alvin Brown spluttered, "And you, are you married?"

"What do you think?"

Silence fell as both men stopped talking and stared intently at one another. Not a pin dropped to break the spell.

"Fascinating," whispered Evelyn Stoker, "and frightening."

"No it's not," said the under-manager, the words whispered.

"You're so right," gasped Evelyn.

Alvin Brown felt strange. Thought he was dreaming, everything about him imaginary, surreal, his gaze locked on the stranger as if he'd known him all his life. He was not frightened by his presence, knew it was meant to be. His mouth was dry and devoid of speech. Myriad emotions exploded like a kaleidoscope in his brain, knew what was about to happen, knew and embraced the passion, felt the touch of the stranger's lips, welcomed the first kiss of love.

**

CHAPTER FOURTEEN

Dolly Connelly opened the door of the council semi in Wraith Road, Horden, her eyes rolling with surprise at the sight of her feisty daughter-in-law. She tried to smile a welcome but her wrinkled features portrayed an obvious grimace as she reluctantly retreated into the kitchen. Beckoned Vera inside.

"Hello Vera," said the older female, "how are you, how are the kids?"

Vera could not mask her anger, her reply cutting, "I'm still working part-time, almost lost my job at the store when I took a day off to see George!"

"You've been to Pontefract?" Dolly Connelly dutifully acting the part of a concerned mother-in-law, pretending ignorance even though her oldest son had spilled the beans on wayward, wanton, George.

"Last Monday," she replied brusquely, "didn't do any good though!"

Dolly moved to the sink, grabbed and started filling the kettle, said half-heartedly, "You'll have a cup of tea?"

Vera nodded, said tersely, "Did you know George had a brood of kids down Yorkshire?"

"Heard something," answered Dolly. Her head downcast, knew George was without scruples or morals, cloned from his no-account father. "Suspected as much," shook her head sorrowfully.

Vera grunted, "He has a son and a daughter and one on the way, a ready-made family!"

Dolly sucked in air and raised her eyebrows in genuine surprise. Her boy could lie to the Pope himself, and he brought up a good catholic, church every weekend, Saturday and Sunday. She made tea, handed a cup to her daughter-in-law and gestured towards the living-room.

Vera Connelly said matter-of-fact, "Jack's too young to understand, but Joe is embarrassed, never been on free school meals in his life. He's almost eleven. Next year he's at the secondary with all his old friends. Free school meals, Dolly, know how he feels about that, his bloody father cares so much about his first-born he doesn't send a penny-piece in maintenance?"

Dolly lied, she had little option, knew sparks were about to fly and had to throw water on the fire. "Adam drove down to see George, Vera, pet." Nodded valiantly, "We are all tryin' to resolve this, you know."

"Adam has gone to Pontefract?"

"We thought," Dolly stammered away from the mistruth, didn't have the gall or the stamina for confrontation, "actually Adam's idea. Thought if he had words with George he might come to his senses, George that is!"

Vera sipped at the tea, "Should have married Adam! Story of my life, I always pick the wrong one."

"Do a lot worse, Vera," replied Dolly, say black was white, up was down, anything to keep her daughter-in-law sweet.

"So Adam might be putting the job right?"

"Don't understand, Vera?"

"Well, either George comes back or he starts sending money for the boys?"

"I suppose," muttered Dolly anxiously.

The older woman supped noisily from the cup knowing fine well that George would never return to his volatile wife, not in a month of Sundays, and as for maintenance payments, Dolly couldn't visualise her youngest son having much left once his common-law and three kids raided his pockets, then there was his drink, fags and gambling. She thought of George, knew he always put himself first, imagined after booze, cigarettes and the horses, his common-law would be lucky to see much of his pay, and as for Vera, Vera Connelly would find more money growing on trees.

"When will Adam come back?" asked Vera.

Dolly said, "Straight away, least that was his plan."

"He was always nice, Adam," mused Vera. "Time George hit me, only married months, remember, Dolly? Adam kicked the shit out of him; I'll never forget that. He was really kind."

Adam had no damn business interfering, thought Dolly, wincing at the memory, especially since Adam knew his brother wasn't a fighter. Trouble was, her oldest carried a flame for the Easington girl, always had. The thought of Vera and Adam starting a relationship made her unconsciously wince.

**

Elmore dragged himself out of bed, checked the bedside clock, 6.30pm and cursed. Drugged with sleep and fatigue he struggled to the window and saw some middle-aged fellow striding away from the door. Elmore thought that Agnes must have had company and slamming the door or making a noise was her subtle way of waking him. *'Such a considerate bastard,'* groaned the man, pulled on pants and shirt and eased himself down the carpeted stairs, opened the door to the sitting-room, moaning loud enough for Agnes to hear. "I'll have a cup of tea, love, no sugar," he called, slumped on to the plush sofa and closed weary eyes. His hands pushed deep into trouser-pockets feeling the money, it was still there, all of it. He yawned noisily and wondered if Agnes had realised that he'd borrowed from her bulging purse earlier that day, obviously not or she'd have mentioned it, yawned again and thought, *God loves anyone who tries.* The woman had too much money and that was a fact and all he was doing was lightening the load.

Elmore stood and stretched. He moved towards the television, wanting noise, company, strolled towards the kitchen, fancied a bacon sandwich with his tea. Called for Agnes and was surprised when she didn't answer. She wasn't there, wasn't anywhere in the house. Elmore cursed her loud and long then reluctantly made himself a meal. An hour later he had changed, shaved and left the home, much as he liked the girl Elmore couldn't afford to waste valuable drinking time, checked his stolen loot and swore, enough for a couple of hours that was all. He decided to call on Evelyn. He would concoct some make-believe story about the missing gear, knew if he tried really hard, he could convince Evelyn any mortal thing. Mr Gullible was an apt name for his brother. He walked along Thorpe Road and juggled with several excuses. *Evelyn, did you get my note? I borrowed a few items, apparently Agnes was too embarrassed to admit she had no television, not even a wireless or record-player, told her you wouldn't mind if I borrowed them for a few days. Honest, Evelyn, couple of days, maybe a week, tops then I'll bring them back. I told Agnes you rarely watched the old box, preferred reading, you okay with that brother?* The explanation sounded plausible, all he had to do was keep a straight face, maybe a touch of depression when he spun the tale, apologise profusely about his earlier tantrums, hell he was going through hard times, anyone would be short-tempered and mouthy. Elmore tolerated his brother and he knew the feeling was more than reciprocated. All said and done, they were blood, had it been the other way around, with Evelyn down on his luck then he would have moved heaven and hell to help. *It's all about blood ties, there was nothing stronger,* mused Elmore, almost convinced himself it was true.

Elmore sauntered along the wide gravelled drive, sensors clicked and two large night lights shone over the yard area. He knocked more than once, knew Evelyn was home because his fancy motor was on the driveway. Cringed at the sight and immediately filled with a jealous rage, *Couldn't buy a normal car like everyone else! No, it had to be a big fat plum-coloured Jaguar, show people how clever he was, successful dentist! Fewer qualifications than Elmore, but daddy's boy nevertheless with a definite helping hand up the ladder. Nice when it happens,* thought Elmore Stoker, *wonder what it's like to have a helping hand. If I knew my father maybe I could make such a call!* Stared at the motor and scowled, could have parked in the garage but that was Evelyn all over, what he lacked in height and looks and personality he bought. It could be called a psychological boost, a kind of a materialistic lift to his flagging ego. Elmore contorted his face and mimicked his brother, *'Like m, m, my, my car, car?'* and laughed at the sick humour. He answered himself, *'Evelyn, look at me, do I need a car as a prop?'* The Jaguar was left on show for one reason only, to embarrass and humiliate him, Evelyn's way of sticking the knife in deep.

Elmore suddenly remembered he had the key. *Jesus,* he mused, *I'm losing the plot.* Fumbled and searched becoming more and more panic-stricken until he found it wrapped inside his handkerchief. Took a deep refreshing breath of autumn air and slotted home the key, turned it and heard the lock click, smiled benevolently as the image of Evelyn touched him. *Not a bad old stick,* thought Elmore, *hell, he could have left the bolt...* The door rattled in protest but stayed shut. He pushed the key into the keyhole, double-clicked it, locked and opened it, and distinctly heard the lock move. Evelyn had left the bolt in the door, barring him from his own home. Stepped away from the door, stood in the gravelled drive and called for his brother three times, each time louder than the last. 'Evelyn!' he shouted, 'Evelyn!'

"You want to wake the dead, Elmore?"

Elmore spun round in shock and saw the big wheezing neighbour, fancy-pants himself. He said mockingly, "What's it to you?"

He never liked the man. Parents hated him, told Elmore often enough, even when he was a kid, *'What's that, Elmore, the football has gone into next door's garden, and can you have permission to retrieve it. Not in a hundred years, Elmore! You leave that ball there! On no account do you speak to that man, you hear?'* Both of his parents detested the arrogant, obnoxious Delwin Mix. Only time his parents agreed on anything. His mother would nod her approval as his father laid down the law, *'I'll buy you another ball, Elmore,'* he would say, *'mother is right, you stay out of Mix's garden.'* His father would turn from calm to cantankerous in an instant, *'Elmore, go back in the house, play with your records, sing into your tape-recorder, anything, you hear, but stay away from that man!'*

Delwin Mix said cynically, "Getting used to the peace and quiet on a night, thought the partying was never going to stop. You thinking about practicing during the day, Elmore, maybe upset the birds for a change?"

"You got a problem, old man, this any of your business?"

"My business when we can't sleep on a night with you playing loud music, whole damn street is sick of your infantile behaviour!"

Elmore was sardonic, "Call the police," shrugged his shoulders.

"Told your brother this morning I'll call the police! He told me the problem was over, said you'd moved away." Delwin gasped for breath, "Is that right, or was Evelyn being diplomatic?"

Elmore grunted venomously, "Hey, it's none of your business!"

"Keep on with the noise and I'll make it my business, son!"

"I'm not your son," grunted Elmore. Took a deep breath and asked grudgingly, "I'm looking for Evelyn, okay?"

"Saw him leave few hours ago," replied the neighbour. "Looked to me he was out for a long walk."

Elmore nodded an acknowledgement, turned and walked along the driveway.

Delwin Mix shouted, "You want me to tell him you called, son?"

Elmore Stoker kept on walking. He muttered softly, 'I'm not your bloody son,' lifted an arm in the air, a lone finger raised defiantly.

**

Ten-o-clock and Elmore's sourness had lifted, his mood euphoric thanks to the speed and success of his dealings. He'd sold a few items of jewellery to greedy punters, made enough money to see him through until Monday, told himself he should have been a salesman, *'Don't worry yourself,'* he would say as the trinkets were displayed from table to table, played on their greed, *'this necklace cost hundreds, if you want I'll show the receipts tomorrow.'* Only one customer asked questions and Elmore played a blinder, walked away smiling and watched as the fellow followed. Earlier that evening he'd watched two women persuade their husbands to hurry home and find some cash, *'I'll wait ten minutes, tops, then I'm gone. Maybe call at the Half Moon, better clientele, know a bargain when they see one.'* It paid to show you didn't need them, that you weren't too bothered, the psychological shit working every time. Maybe he had enough shekels to take him to Tuesday and by then he'd have snared his brother. At the back of his mind he wondered about Agnes Lincoln, there was something not kosher, something amiss. He would check on her tomorrow. Tried to recall their chat before she shooed him to bed that very afternoon.

He sat on the small stage and took requests, kept looking for Evelyn, knew he liked the place because it was quaint and quiet, a perfect watering-hole for his nervous brother. Spoke earnestly to the audience, *'Pat Boone, sure I know Pat Boone, Texas boy, born and bred, same school ... same class as Roy Orbison. You didn't know that, not many people do, but it's a fact all the same. 'Love Letters in the Sand,' lovely song'* and smiled warmly at the punter, said tongue-in-cheek, *'make that a whiskey.'* Took a few minutes tinkering on the ivories, wanted the audience to sing along, played through the first verse, playing and smiling, realised the old whore, Annie Goodrich, was absent. Wondered what the hell was going on, Evelyn missing, Annie and her daughter out of sight. Took a deep breath, closed his eyes and started to sing.

Micky Green sat in one corner watching the antics of the man, understood why his niece Vera liked him, reminded him of George Connelly, couldn't point a finger and say it was this or that, something intangible, an inner quality. Elmore sparkled, more so when he was sodden with drink, made people around him happy, made them feel special, interesting. He glanced at Mary Jane, his obese spouse, years since she was able to find a chair wide enough to allow her to sit comfortably, preferred the benches that filled one section of the wall, tight-arse she definitely wasn't. Watched her gloating at the piano-man, beady eyes all aglow with lust for the man, butter in his hands, *'Hurry, Micky, run home and raid the piggy-bank, that diamond ring is for nothing! Hurry now before he changes his mind!'* Couldn't remember the last time he'd run anywhere, run to the toilet, run the cold-water tap, run a mile from Mary Jane's tongue, hell he could hardly walk without breaking into a sweat with his wheezing chest, fool he was scurrying home to buy some foolish second-hand engagement-ring.

"Oh, I do like those American singers," gushed an inebriated Mary Jane. Started singing softly with the folk around her, *'On a day like today, we'll pass the time of day, writing love letters.....'* kept glancing at the beautiful jewellery that she'd slotted on to her little finger, only one that fitted the delicate eternity-ring. "Still looks so... expensive, doesn't it, Micky?" gave him a smacker of a kiss for his generosity, felt the same way at closing-time and she'd let him play with her. Whispered the fact when she struggled and heaved her girth towards the small table, kissed him and promised Micky a good time, watched him blush with embarrassment. Good old Micky Green, broke the mould when they made him, turned her attention to Elmore Stoker, such a sweet voice and a gorgeous face, knew who would be on her mind when Micky was having his evil way with her, certainly wouldn't be her husband.

CHAPTER FIFTEEN

She was looking more at the moustache than his face, drawn to the thick weal of knotted scarring on the upper lip, Fontella Richards, seventy years old, husband, Wilbur, ex-collier, behind her in the wheelchair, staring vacantly into space, peaceful with dementia. It was a cool September morning, the whole village enveloped in damp clinging mist and the stranger was becoming agitated at the obvious scrutiny.

"Connelly," he said again, "used to live in the colliery?"

Fontella Richards removed the cigarette, twisted her stout frame and glanced at her silent partner, said, "What the hell I'm looking at you for I don't know, neither use nor ornament." Faced the stranger with the deformed face and said resignedly, "Senile dementia had Wilbur. Still, it has it's good points, the old bugger can't get up to much trouble this days!"

"Connelly, pet," he persevered, "Vera?"

"And she lives in Passield Square? I mean there's several squares. Next one is Stephenson Square, could try there?"

"Mother's name is Anne?"

"Not around here, love" she sighed, "lived here all my life. There's Annie Goodrich in the next cul-de-sac. Annie's been widowed years, got a son and a daughter, couldn't tell you how old they are, don't get out much these days. Barty Goodrich died of cancer years ago, only young, always thought Annie would have remarried. Always was a girl who knew how to enjoy herself was Annie. Still, life is full of surprises."

Took Adam Connelly seconds to reverse out of one cul-de-sac and into another, reminded himself to be on his best behaviour, knowing he had to impress Vera, the two boys and the sour mother. Second time lucky when he approached the house and saw the young mother gazing down at him from an upstairs window, waving and smiling at him before disappearing for moments before the front door opened. Vera beaming next to her shy son who appeared glued to her side.

"Adam," she said happily, glancing at her son. "Uncle Adam has come to see us, Jack."

Adam Connelly was ushered in to the council house. Annie subdued in his presence, eased into the kitchen to make refreshments, stepped over Joe who was busying himself, paraphernalia everywhere, preoccupied with the task and scowling at his grandmother's biting tongue. "Move yourself, Joe, sick of tidying up after you!" Annie didn't like Adam, found him guarded, aloof, and despite Geordie's faults she preferred Vera's wayward husband any day of the week. Man was always happy-go-lucky and comfortable to be with, made you feel good. Adam, in Annie Goodrich's opinion, should have been an undertaker, never smiled nor joked, always serious, doom and gloom, and an ugly bugger to boot. Adam, mid- thirties, unmarried, and too bothered about folks looking at his cleft-lip. She wanted to tell him that looks were only skin deep. Women weren't that shallow, a sense of humour went a long way, and a healthy bank account too, no good denying that, money made living a lot sweeter. Adam Connelly must have had a smidgen of Jewish blood in his veins or deep pockets because she couldn't recall the man being anything but stingy. Vera's wedding; he stood at the bar all night but never once offered to buy her a drink, despite subtle hints. What kind of person, eh? Another thing, the man was too interested in Vera, how sad was that?

Annie said, "Joe, don't be ignorant, we've got company!"

"Who is it, nana?" up in a flash, grinning, wrongly thinking his dad had made a surprise visit.

"Surprise," shooed him out of the kitchen, "maybe some news!"

"Uncle Adam," said Joe bounding into the living-room, bicycle inner-tube in one hand, puncture outfit gripped in the other, face glowing, "what's up?"

"Kid, how are you?" said his Uncle, returning the smile, "mother treatin' you okay?"

"Fine Uncle Adam," replied the boy, couldn't stop himself, "where's dad?"

The man, caught off-guard could only gawk.

"Shush," reprimanded Vera, "nothing to do with Uncle Adam!"

"Sorry kid," mumbled the man awkwardly.

Joe pouted then nodded resignedly. "It's okay," he answered.

"Put a smile on your face, Joe," said Vera, "things could be worse!"

Adam butted in, gestured at his sister-in-law and said, "Your Ma still greedy with pocket-money?"

"Adam Connelly!" exclaimed the woman.

"Poor on pocket-money, Uncle Adam, that's a fact!"

"Like his bloody dad, eh," said Adam, and fished out a handful of coins and passed them to an ecstatic nephew. Glancing at the younger boy still clinging to his mother's skirts, he nodded and winked. "Jack is it," he said softly, "the good-lookin' one?"

Jack acknowledged the complement, his face flushing with pleasure.

Vera spoke to Jack, "You can't remember can you, Jack, this is your dad's brother. Say something Jack."

Jack Connelly looked nervously at his mother, at his brother and finally at the man with the moustache. Bit his lip and waited.

"Want some money, Jack?" said his uncle. "Then you and your brother can go the shop for sweets?" he offered silver coins.

Hesitantly the boy put out his hand, palm up, pouting in anticipation, and watched in awe as the man filled his cupped hand.

"Thank you," he whispered gratefully. Looked at his mother, nudged her, and asked, "Can I spend it, Ma?"

Joe interjected, guffawed. "Let's go to the shop, Jack, come on!" and bolted from the living-room.

Jack Connolly whooped and scattered. Doors clattered and peace returned to the Goodrich home. Annie, bronze tea-tray filled to capacity, trundled into the room.

"Hello, Annie," said Adam Connelly. Determined to make a favourable impression on the old lady he added, "You're looking well, hair looks lovely."

First compliment ever from the collier, and Annie didn't know to respond. Clearly flustered she croaked acknowledgement, "Vera styled it, I wasn't too sure about it though."

Adam pushed, "Suits you, Annie, look years younger."

"You really think so, Adam?" she said and flushed slightly.

Still holding the tray she twirled like a teenager and glanced into the big mirror above the fireplace, pondered, smiled impishly at the reflection and saw them both nod approval. Looked again and tried to picture Jayne Mansfied wearing spectacles, wondered if Evelyn Stoker could see something she couldn't. Annie relented, thought maybe she'd been harsh in her opinion of the man. Responded to the sugar, thinking on reflection, *He's alright is Adam. Poor bugger, harelip that size never want to look in a mirror! Good worker too, thirty-five and never once married, must be worth a bloody fortune, like to see his bank account. Might see it if Vera plays her cards right, might look after his mother-in-law too!*

Vera glanced at Adam, asked, "Any news about George?"

Adam shrugged broad shoulders; there was no need for words.

Annie put down the tray, "Vera," she rebuked softly, "let Adam have a bite to eat. He must be worn-out with all of the travelling.

**

The headache was worse than ever. He dragged himself out of bed and hurried down the stairs, almost wrenched the door off its hinges so anxious to stop the incessant banging. Elmore recognised the girl, the big man next to her, spitting blood, was a stranger. Stepped aside to allow her entry, asked innocently, "Agnes, where have you been?" and watched them both troop past him neither looking nor speaking. He tried again, "Has something happened?" Closed the door and sheepishly followed, the garish pyjamas making Elmore feel decidedly uncomfortable.

"Want you out of my house, son!" said the tall, gaunt fellow, arms on hips showing his irritation. The prominent nose was bent alarmingly, a thin blue line of scar-tissue criss-crossed the damage.

Elmore looked passively at the girl and said calmly, "What's going on, Agnes?" Took a lungful of air trying to work up courage, "Thought you and I ….."

Agnes fumed with pent-up aggression. She barked, "You and I! You and I! Tell me where you were sleeping Tuesday, Elmore, or Monday? Where the hell were you Monday night?"

Knock him down with a stick but he still wouldn't be able to recall anything. Faltered badly as he struggled to recall, scratched his head and said naively, "Why, would that be a problem, Agnes?"

"Answer the question," said the tall thin man coldly.

"Who the hell are you?"

Agnes spat venomously, "He's my dad, and this is his house," which was a mistruth, a white lie to redress the imbalance of the situation.

Elmore shrugged shoulders pathetically, looked liked a schoolboy caught with his hand in the cookie-jar. Couldn't lie when he didn't know the truth, Monday, Tuesday, didn't have a clue… was it Sunday today?

Agnes said, "Vera Connolly?"

Annie Goodrich's daughter? A bell sounded inside Elmore's head and he struggled for excuses. "Ah, yes, I remember. My brother is seeing Vera's mother, I walked them home……"

"Stayed the night, Elmore!"

Elmore protested, "I didn't, honestly!"

Agnes Lincoln spat, "Rat!" and physically pushed at him.

"Steady on, Agnes," he whined, "that's rather harsh." Suddenly saw the cushy number going up in proverbial smoke, not to mention the house, the joint wills. He gasped at the reality of it all, colour drained from his face knowing he had to think of something, anything to stop the rot. Elmore, for once, was lost for words.

"Well?" said an incensed Agnes, stood with arms across her big chest, chin protruding defiantly, not giving an inch.

Elmore begged, "Agnes, I promise I'll do anything you say, but could we have a few minutes alone without your father looking as if he wants to hit me?"

She glanced at father, who gazed uncommitted. A stiff jerk of his shoulders was his only response.

Agnes mellowed, "Dad," she said, "you go home, I'll call."

"You sure, pet?"

Pet, mused Elmore, the stupor lifting and the sarcasm returning with a vengeance, *even her Daddy thinks she's a dog!*

Agnes nodded bravely, "I'm sure, Dad."

Thomas Lincoln, forty-eight years old, collier and ex-brawler turned silently and left the house, Elmore audibly sighed with relief, his mind racing as he fought to save the precarious situation from deteriorating further, glanced at the girl, still with arms tight around her chest, tears in her eyes.

"I'll make a cup of tea, Agnes."

"No!"

"Please, Agnes, let's kept this civilised," he begged.

"How could you, Elmore?"

"It's not what it seems, Agnes." Sensing a chink in her armour he pushed gently, "In fact the opposite happened!" *Think, Elmore, think!*

Agnes stammered, "What then?"

Elmore persevered, his mind racing, wondered if the two girls knew one another, maybe some rivalry between them, said succinctly, "Vera Connelly," left the conundrum open for scrutiny.

Agnes wept bitter tears, gasped, "I knew it, she's never forgiven me for ....," physically clamped her hands over mouth. Almost let the cat out of the bag.

Elmore punched home, "She's jealous of you, Agnes." Gauged her acknowledgment perfectly, "Told her I was seeing you and she was livid. That's when I left." He looked positively at her, full, unflinching eye-to-eye contact, "That's the truth Agnes, and as for sleeping overnight, well that's a downright lie." He closed on her, touched her shoulder and said humbly, "I should have told you, Agnes, I'm sorry," moved quickly away as she recoiled. "I'll make that tea."

Elmore had time to close his eyes in the kitchen and say a silent prayer. Wondered if he should wait a few days before mentioning wedding-bells or making wills, stopped in his tracks when he recalled Agnes's father statement, *'This is my house!'* Wondered if it was a simple ruse to

185

unhinge him, maybe he'd wait a day or two and casually ask Agnes the truth, but say it in such a way as not to make her suspect his ulterior motives. There was no point in proposing if she didn't own the damn house. Her parents could last for years before popping their clogs and that would never do!

He tried to think of the divorcee he met in the *Liberality Tavern* a month ago, seen her once or twice and knew she was definitely interested in him. He had to keep all options open, *Teresa,* he thought, *that was her name, Teresa McDonald.* Elmore's philosophy, *Look after Number One.* He was too long in the tooth to change his ways. *Agnes or Teresa,* he mused, *what could be easier?*

Agnes stood at the window, gazed blankly into the road, perceived the blur as vehicles passed and never heard a sound, her head aching with the jumble of conflicting images. Imagined she was a fool in love. Third time as a plaything, knew the idle gossip about her, the snide remarks, the wicked digs about her penchant for marriage. Sometimes the humiliation smacked at her face, no beating about the bush for some. Ryan for one, drunk at the time but the words still smarted and scratched even though she laughed along with his wicked observations. Ryan Jones's wedding-day, playing the funny bugger with his over-the-top speech, whining on about how marriage was for life. Pure baloney and bullshit of course but he was trying to impress his naïve bride-to-be, saw Agnes grinning at him, laughing at him, same man was seeing her few weeks before he tied the knot with Denise Bradley, *'I'm not going to be like Agnes, our very own Elizabeth Taylor, one time around for me and that's a fact!'* Agnes, caught off-guard, could only flush and cringe with embarrassment. Hours later, the reception going hell for leather and music blasting the rafters down, the happy couple approached Agnes. Ryan pensive next to his squat bride tried to mend the rift, *'Only a joke, Agnes, out of my head with nerves you understand.'* Chunky Denise nodding like a bulldog, never imagined their guest would retaliate, especially on their wedding-day. *'Can't remember you being nervous a month ago, Ryan. A little drunk I recall!'* Turned and faced the livid bride, *'Brewer's Droop, Denise. I had a very disappointing night with him!'* Turned away from the devastated newlyweds then decided on one last dig, *'I'd watch what he drinks tonight, Denise, can't have two of us disappointed!'*

My shitty life, thought Agnes, shoulders slumped and spirits dampened, *gets no better!*

Agnes thought of Vera Goodrich, Connelly, whatever her name was. She was catching up fast, not be too long before she had married again, too aggressive by half, tended to scare most men away and that included her husband, George. He was a devil, George, chased Agnes for months, out together in a foursome and George would hound her like a dog after a bone, and so reckless too, her second husband Jonty at the bar ordering drinks, Vera wandering half-sloshed towards the toilets, lights dimmed and George would start with the wandering hands, so arrogant and cool, like he was charmed. And then the journey back to their homes for a top-up and a dance after the club had called last-orders, the four of them easing through the doorway and George, always last, making his move and his wife, Vera, a breath away! George Connelly had some nerve, and so funny with it. She still missed him the little charmer, didn't miss the near-strangulation metered out by Vera when she found out about their occasional trysts.

And now another bombshell. Thought she had found the perfect partner in Elmore. Gorgeous, vivacious Elmore Stoker. He was like a superior version of Geordie Connelly. Only blight against him was the occasional disasters in the bedroom. Elmore blamed the booze for his lack of ardour. She wasn't too concerned, knew she only had to ration his drinks to make him function properly. Until a few days ago his sporadic bouts of impotence seemed the only drawback, Agnes bursting with hormones and aching for romance, Elmore would collapse on the bed and the night was over. That was the only cross against his name until Vera Connelly opened her big mouth and put everything on hold.

News of Elmore and Vera seemed odd. His explanation seemed plausible, even genuine. Something else bothered her, there was something about the manner in which Agnes had heard about the double-dealing. Something didn't quite gel about the confession from the scheming Vera Connelly. Why would she confide in her, Agnes was no friend, more a one-time rival for her ex-husband's affections? Maybe Vera was settling old scores, perhaps she had heard about the relationship with Elmore and wanted to put a spanner in the works and try for a fracture. There was nothing worse than a woman scorned.

She stood statuesque at the window, her mind in a quandary, *What the hell can I do,* she mused, *to put it right?*

**

CHAPTER SIXTEEN

The brothers reached the road fork close to the *Half Moon* pub, Joe, on a mission, took the right fork and reached the village graveyard, only way to get to the pool. The frogs and the fun was to hurry across the burial ground and climb the rickety fence situated at the southerly end. Joe had persuaded his kid brother to pool the monies from Uncle Adam, skip on the sweets and buy fireworks. Jack asked innocently, "Fireworks and frogs, Joe?" shrugging inexperienced shoulders as he hurried to keep up with his big brother. The morning mists had lifted and a September sun blazed surreal and cankerous through the leaden sky. Sunday morning with no one about; late breakfasts, newspapers to read as folks made a slow recovery from Saturday's excesses. Joe and Jack were alone in the small cemetery when the five-year old asked, "Aren't you scared, Joe?" glancing at the myriad gravestones, fresh mounds of clay, wreaths and flowers and messages to the departed, "in case someone has been buried alive, you know, fainted and put in a coffin then woke up under the ground, screamin' and scratchin' to get out!"

Joe said, "Don't be stupid! The doctor always checks them before they're put in the coffin, listens for a heart-beat. They're always dead!"

"What if it thunders and a bolt of lightning strikes him in the heart and it starts workin' and he's locked in the coffin and the screws are all fastened?"

Joe stopped, looked quizzically at his kid brother, then walked bristly and unafraid to a brand-new mound of muck and soil, clambered amidst the wreaths and flowers and starting jumping up and down frantically. "When you're dead you're dead, Jack," he shouted, "they can't feel a thing. The dead can't hurt you, understand? You don't got to be frightened," and gestured for his brother to join him, "come on!"

Jack stayed rigid on the lawned area, shook his head from side to side, said nervously, "Coulda woke him up, dancin' like that, Joe!"

Jack guffawed, "Dead as a doornail. Ma told me once when you die your soul goes straight to heaven. All that's left is a carcass and you can do what you want with it because it has no soul, see?"

Jack pondered, straight-faced said, "Like a Lemon Sole, Joe?"

"A Lemon Sole is a fish!"

"But it has a soul too, everyone has a soul haven't they? When you see the Lemon Sole in the *Trotter's* fish-shop it's dead isn't it?"

Joe grimaced, "Of course it's dead, stupid!"

"So why isn't it called a Lemon," asked a confused Jack, "if its soul has gone to heaven?"

Joe picked up a wreath and flung it at his cowering brother, started to run towards the decrepit wooden fence that led to the boundary space between the graveyard and the back gardens of the Stockton Road houses, no-man's land, with its festering pool of stagnant water and home to hundreds of frogs, toads and assorted rodents.

"Run, Jack" shrieked Joe Connelly. "Felt the earth shake under my feet, dead man scratchin' his way to the surface, run!"

Jack screaming at the top of his voice, "Wait for me! Wait for me!"

**

On the far side of the waste-land, past the second fence that led to the plush rear gardens of Stockton Road, more fireworks had started, but not the kind of explosives that could be bought in any shop. Minutes into the mayhem and Evelyn acquiesced and allowed the agitated and fuming brother into the family home. Elmore's stride faltered when

190

he observed the stranger in the enormous kitchen, so surprised at the sight, he could only gawk and splutter obscenities, "Who the hell?"

Evelyn interjected, calmly attempted to introduce his companion. "This is Alvin Brown," he said, gesturing at the small, slight fellow busy at the sink. "Alvin. My brother, Elmore," turned and faced the contorted, twisted features of Elmore. "Alvin works at the Co-Op store, I had to call there yesterday to replace the things you borrowed." Emphasised the word *borrowed* putting Elmore into a corner.

"So what's he doing here, Evelyn?" demanded Elmore. "Did he sleep here last night?" Like a snorting bull, arms on hips, head shaking incomprehensively from side to side, angry and confused with his brother. "Well?"

Evelyn said bravely, "It's really none of your business, Elmore!"

"You swapped sides, brother," sneered Elmore, "you queer?"

"What do you want, Elmore?"

Alvin Brown interrupted the family squabble, said, "I'll go, Evelyn, better if I leave you two to sort it out."

Evelyn Stoker somehow found the strength to face his obnoxious bully of a brother, moved in between them and said, "You're staying, Alvin," and blocked his route.

Years of pent-up emotion welled and burst like a dam from Elmore Stoker, shook his head, smirk so big as to sparkle, and grunted venomously, "Daddy would be so proud of you, Evelyn, his only son a bloody homosexual!"

"Whatever," said Evelyn, "you can't hurt me any more!"

"Please let me go," begged Alvin Brown, fearing for his life, knowing an escalation was imminent.

Evelyn was resolute, barked, "Stay, Alvin!"

Elmore mimicking his brother, "Stay lover-boy, Evelyn wants to give you a present!"

"I'd like you to leave, Elmore!"

191

Elmore muttered, "If your father could see you now."

"My father loved me," Evelyn spluttered defensively, "proud of me!"

"He was a spineless excuse for a father! Jesus Christ, his own wife was messing about and he allowed it to happen! He forgave her, how could he live with that?"

"He cared, Elmore!"

"My arse," whined the taller man, "he was pathetic!"

"My father was the best!"

"You have to say that, Evelyn. Man spoilt you rotten! Whatever Evelyn wanted Evelyn got, forgot he had another boy.... sorry, your father forgot his wife had another son in the same house!"

Evelyn retorted, "It must have been hard for him, Elmore, surely you understand that?"

"If seeing me obviously turned his stomach, why didn't he move out and start afresh? I was tortured by him!" Elmore pondered then added sourly, "Tell you something Evelyn, never told a living soul until today, my Granddad told me his son was a fool. Your father, Evelyn, a bloody fool! My Grandfather used to sit me on his knee and cuddle me and say nice things to me. I loved him better than my step-dad; you know that, told him once I wanted him to be my father! He wasn't angry. He cuddled me and said I had to be brave, said I was the sweetest thing alive. I asked him why no one seemed to care about me, wasn't only my step-dad, it was mother too, too occupied with her empty life. Parents from hell as far as I'm concerned. Granddad was a lovely man, only one who showed any interest in me. It was a blessed relief when he finally died. Missed him so much, he cared about me, un like your twisted, sick father!"

"Loved Grandfather so much you never visited him in the nursing-home!"

"How do you make conversation with a vegetable?" said Elmore, defensively, "didn't mean I didn't care about him! Anyway, you never visited."

"Mother didn't like him," said Evelyn. "When father used to visit, Mum refused to allow me to go."

"Mother didn't like anyone at the end!"

Evelyn barked, "Always hated Grandfather!"

Elmore whined, "She hated everyone before she died."

"Never hated Dad."

"Wrong again brother. They might have shared the same house but they never shared the same bed. I think they tolerated each other, but love? Never known affection between them."

"My mother loved my father," replied an indignant Evelyn, "and I loved my father."

"Your father was a cold, weak person, too frightened to leave the matrimonial home … despite the fact that his wife had another man's child…"

Evelyn intervened, said loudly, "I had a father! I could put a name to my father!"

The speed and strength of the slap sent Evelyn tumbling back into the trembling arms of Alvin Brown. Didn't cower as he had in the past. He faced his fear, resilient and strong as he struggled back to his feet and moved towards Elmore. Alvin Brown slunk back to the far wall of the room, intimidated and terrorised by it all, hands over his face, eyes closed with the coming calamity, weeping and sniffling and wanting so much to be far away from the stranger.

"Your father was a poor imitation of a man, Evelyn," snarled the younger brother. "Reminds me of you, matter of fact!"

Elmore grabbed at the shirt of his diminutive sibling and hoisted him off the ground, pulled him close enough to taste the stagnant stench of alcohol. Inches separated the pair, the aggressor crimson with rage, and the victim cadaverous and squirming to free himself, Elmore incensed with a lifetime of neglect suddenly spat a wad of phlegm into his brother's face, threw him to one side like some human rag doll and whined dementedly, "Maybe why mother found another, couldn't stand the cold uncaring doctor you call a father! You think I'm right, Evelyn, mother wanting some affection, sick of living the lie, covering her shambles of a marriage?" The fellow gasped for breath as his mood raged out of control, "So I don't know my father! My mother must have loved someone so much I was the result! I'm right, aren't I? That's why your dad hated me, couldn't bear to touch me, wasn't only because mum had an affair! Hell, she wouldn't have risked everything if it was a one-night stand, don't you see, Evelyn, don't you see?"

Evelyn was wiping away the spittle and slime, perspiration trickling lines over his pale face, resentment bubbling through his head, years in fermentation, couldn't stop himself if he tried. Driven forward by some unseen demon, unleashing the shackles of decency and maturity forever as he finally ended his silence, "Mother was a fool!" he said purposefully as he moved towards his exasperated brother, steeled with the armour of determination.

Elmore smashed a fist into the unprotected stomach and stared benignly as images bounced and jarred and reality faltered. Evelyn gasped for breath, squirming like a worm across the tiled floor as Elmore continued with his manic ranting, "Mother loved me!" reminiscing, remembering, "couldn't really show it that's all! Found it difficult!" Stepped over the convulsing torso of his brother and closed on the trembling figure of Alvin Brown. "Has he told you about me?" he grunted to the half-bent, whining man. "About the way I was treated, a mother so ashamed of her action that she pretended I didn't exist, a father who showed his true feeling for me every day of his life, resented me but because he loved my mother allowed me to take his name, allowed me bed and board." He prodded at the demented Alvin Brown, "You know he never touched me, don't mean he abused me, no, I mean he didn't physically touch like a father does… should. Never once held my hand, told me a story, bathed me or treated me like his son. You know what that feels like, everyday of my life, being ignored, shown I wasn't wanted, can you imagine how I felt?"

Evelyn struggled to his feet. Stood behind his brother and said calmly, "I know who your father is Elmore."

Everything stopped for Elmore Stoker. Couldn't hear anything except a buzzing inside his head, turned and faced his sibling, saw his mouth moving, watched in amazement as Evelyn started prodding at his chest, and couldn't feel any physical contact. Nothing was registering, he was inebriated without alcohol, high without a whiff of marijuana, last time he felt such weird and bizarre feelings was when his mother, loud, angry and drink-fuelled, was shouting at him. A lifetime ago, almost forgotten, a child then, and he could remember as if it were yesterday, "You were a mistake, Elmore! It was my way of destroying your father, my way of hurting him, and you know what, Elmore, I succeeded, I destroyed both of us!"

Elmore said to his brother, "It was mother's way of hurting him, don't you see, she didn't mean it when she told me she didn't love me." He shrugged his shoulders in resignation, "Didn't really mean it," he said, his voice a whisper, "I was never a mistake."

Evelyn said, "Your father lives next door. It's Delwin Mix."

Elmore could only stare as his brother regurgitated the bile from the past. Stood transfixed and mute, tears falling from bemused eyes as swirling mists enveloped him.

**

"I don't care if you hit me, Joe," said Jack resolutely, refusing to hand over the two docile, slimy frogs, "I won't let you do that to my frogs. Come any closer and I'll throw them back into the pond!" He lifted both arms ready for action, "I'll do it, mind, really will!"

"They're frogs," seethed Joe, knew he should not have handed over the prizes, "they can't feel anything! You've got to have brains to feel anything!"

"Yes they can," he snapped, remembering Mrs Wainwright's lessons, "we're all God's creatures!"

"Frogs, Jack!"

"They live together, even have babies Joe, they're just like us!"

"Did you hear them cry when I pulled some of their legs off?" asked Joe, "course not, they walked around in circles!"

Jack was adamant, "I'll tell mum that you tied fireworks to the frogs and exploded them!"

Joe barked, "It was fun!"

"You're nasty," whined the kid, "killing frogs and dancing on dead people!"

"All right, just give me one of your frogs then."

A door banged loudly in the distance and someone started shouting obscenities. Both boys stopped squabbling and turned their attention to the big houses situated on the far side of the trees. Joe said, "Put the frogs in your pocket for now, we'll decide what to do with them later, come on," and he hurried to the far side of the pond. Reaching the perimeter fence he squinted towards the noise, added, "Albert Mix lives somewhere over there, Jack," and gestured towards the detached homes.

"Which one?"

"Not sure, I went to the front door yesterday. They all look different from the back. We swapped bikes."

"Can you fight him, Joe?"

"Think so."

"Joe, are you the best fighter in the whole school?"

"Think so."

"Can't see, Joe, will you lift me up?"

Joe Connelly pointed to the old orange-box that he'd used as the sacrificial altar for his frogs. It was still covered in bloody gore, "Bring the box and stand on it!"

"You, Jack, please!"

The wooden-box was retrieved, turned upside-down to hide the evidence and propped against the rickety fence. Jack hoisted himself on to the container and nodded excitedly to his brother. "I can see now," he whispered, peering through the tree-line. Clearly confused he added, "What am I lookin' for Joe?"

"Shh!" hissed the older boy. Lifting himself to the top of the fence, "Somebody is havin' a row."

Jack asked, "Like Mum and Dad used to?"

"Yeah!"

"Joe, is our Dad comin' back?"

"No, shh!"

"Joe, will our Dad buy us some Christmas presents?"

"Yes, now be quiet!"

"How do you know he'll buy us presents, Joe?"

"Ma will kill him if he doesn't, shh!"

Joe was still looking intently through the foliage, muttered disappointingly, "Whatever it was, it's stopped," and started to lower himself from his vantage-point. He spotted the familiar figure striding from the road and into the nearest house. Slowly, surely, he edged back on to the fence and stared ahead.

"Has it started again, Joe?" asked the kid, pulling at his brother's trousers.

"It's that man who was horrible to me in the chippy!"

"Mr Trotter?"

"No, idiot! The man from the council who was seein' Ma! I told you Jack! God, you remember anything?"

**

197

Elmore Stoker knocked at the door then impatiently rattled and pulled at the handle, his mind spun with a myriad of thoughts, all pulling him in every emotional direction. He started to cry. The door creaked ajar and a boy's chunky head eased into view, "Yes," grunted Albert Mix, almost inaudibly, mouth so full of chocolate, "you want my Dad, Mum's out?" Elmore blurted out some muffled, muted plea and saw the jowly face gawk with astonishment before the door was slammed shut.

Delwin Mix appeared, newspaper still grasped in his podgy fingers, saw the look on the caller's face and frowned darkly, "Son, what on earth has happened, you'd think you had seen a ghost?"

With hindsight Delwin Mix would have altered his choice of introduction.

Elmore stammered, eyes filled with tears, "You had an affair with my mother!"

Delwin Mix visibly quaked at the accusation. Shook his head vehemently as the newspaper fell from his hand, both palms open in a show of submission towards the younger man, "What's going on, son, why the hell do you want to talk about such things? Someone been filling your head with nonsense?" He stepped hesitantly back into the lobby, his arms still raised, "I think you should leave."

Elmore's answer was to grab and jerk the older man out into the yard and pin him against the wall. Delwin Mix's pudding features crunched with terror as he tried to shield himself from possible blows. Elmore, wild eyes inches away, face as red as fire as he shook and pushed at the heavier man.

"Please, son," begged the victim, "don't hit me, I've a bad heart!"

"I didn't know!" seethed Elmore Stoker, dementia and disbelief the devil's syrup. "You hear me, I had no idea!"

Suddenly, the front door banged open and the terrified figure of Albert Mix tore from the house and ran from the

198

place, arms pumping frantically. The young voyeur, safely out of sight behind the tree-line, gaped with incredulity, "Albert's done a runner, Jack," whispered Joe, "probably gone for the police, what do you want to do, stay or go, think there's goin' to be a proper fight?" Jack was so frightened he couldn't reply. Awestruck with the growing situation before him, he lifted his arms skywards and grasped at his brother's hand for comfort, then watched with incredulity as the bizarre events unfolded.

"Tell me the truth, you bastard!" whined Elmore, his hands firmly on the throat of his struggling quarry. "Tell me or I'll kill you!"

Delwin Mix nodded frantically and felt the grip relax as Elmore stepped back. The old man slid slowly to the ground, beetroot-red, retching and gasping for breath.

"Tell me!" said Elmore, and he kicked at the unprotected legs of the fallen figure.

"I didn't have an affair with your mother," he croaked.

"Liar! My brother overheard you and mother in the garden a week before she took an overdose! My brother wouldn't lie about something like that! Mother told you to stay away, that it was over, said she loved Dad!"

The older man gasped, "Elmore please, I'm not well."

Elmore was seething with frustration, "Don't try and deny it, you leech! Evelyn was there, heard it all! He was there when father turned up! That's why he never spoke to you again! My brother knows all about you!" He began crying again, sniffling and wiping at his swollen eyes, "I know you're my real father!" he moaned.

You're my real father! Delwin Mix jerked suddenly; the accusation made him struggle valiantly to his knees and then heave his bulk upright, a look of incredulity over his round jowly features. He pushed at the young, more powerful man, as new-found strength surged through his revitalised body.

"You young fool!" he snapped, prodding at a perplexed Elmore. "You idiot, I wasn't seeing your mother!"

"Evelyn heard mother shouting at you to stay away!"

"Yes," shouted Delwin Mix, his features red with anger. "That's right, fool, your mother was shouting at me to stay away!"

Elmore reply was subdued, "I don't understand?"

Delwin Mix bawled frantically, "I was seeing your father!"

Elmore seemed to stumble as his body visibly buckled, he tried to speak but the words were jumbled and incoherent. Delwin Mix couldn't contain the lifetime's misery a moment longer, gripped at the coat-collars of his adversary and started shaking him wildly.

"Your father!" shrieked the older man, "You hear! I was seeing your father again!"

Elmore felt a terrible pain in his head, he shrieked and lashed out at the old man, who instead of retreating or even attempting to defend himself, clung on to the neighbour and began shouting back. Elmore slowly stopped protesting, his body slumped and Delwin Mix started telling the story...........

"Your father and I were lovers, you hear? Most of our lives, you understand! He loved me and I loved him, biggest mistake of my life not leaving with him, too scared I was. Scared of what people would say, thought I'd lose my job. Your grandfather threatened to ruin me, you hear, not your father. Your father didn't care what happened, you hear, Elmore. He had a young wife and child and he would have left them for me, begged me, when I said I couldn't, Simon confessed to your mother. That's when she retaliated, went out one night and had a bloody affair with God knows who! Made sure Simon heard about it though! Years afterwards she tortured him! I should have moved away but I couldn't bear the thought of not seeing him. I couldn't leave, didn't have the strength. My wife Mildred had no idea about us, still doesn't. After all these years she still has no idea.

"That day in the garden, when Evelyn overheard the argument, your mother was screaming because she found out we'd started seeing each other again! Been apart for years and Simon, your father, phoned out of the blue and said he missed me still. He was crying, I started crying and one thing led to another! Your mother found out and went crazy, saw me in the garden and attacked me, then your father returned suddenly and everything went up in the air. He phoned me days later, hysterical with grief, said Elizabeth, your mother, had finally confessed everything about her affair. He seemed tortured with the news. I begged him to tell me but he kept crying. Whatever the news was, it destroyed him. Weeks later your mother died, and your father never acknowledged me again."

Delwin Mix released his grip of his young foe and stared morosely at the broken figure. He grunted, "I'm not your father," and turned as if to return to his home.

Suddenly Elmore Stoker exploded in a manic fury and began attacking the unprotected figure. A flurry of blows rained mercilessly on Delwin Mix who vainly tried to reach the door. Elmore, demented with pain, kicked and shouting incoherently, and didn't stop the savage assault until the old man collapsed.

A short distance away the two boys stared with a mixture of bewilderment and growing panic.

Jack whimpered, "Let's go, Joe, I'm frightened of the man!"

Joe lifted from the stupor. He barked orders to his brother, "Off the box, Jack, run for home and tell Ma! Go!"

Jack mesmerised with fear stood transfixed and stiff, "Scared, Joe!" he whimpered.

Joe Connelly jumped to the ground, grabbed his brother and lifted him free. He pushed him into gear, "Run!" he ordered.

Jack bolted like a frightened hare, limbs flaying wildly as he reached the graveyard boundary, up and over the fence with the grace and ability of an athlete, panting as he glanced back through the railings, needing his brother. 'Come on, Joe," he wailed and watched as his big brother fumbled and pulled fireworks from his pockets. He slowed to a walking pace, "Please, Joe, now," he shouted lamely, then began running again knowing his brother could make up missing ground in seconds. He sprinted over the open expanse, dashed across graves as his fear moved to a higher level. Shouting for his mother, Jack reached the exit-gate and looked back and saw his brother the hero, lighting and pitching fireworks over the tops of trees in the direction of the fight. "Joe!" he yelled at the top of his voice, "come on, Joe!"

Elmore was demented, crazy in grief as the man's awful words plagued him. Kicked and battered at the protesting, desperate man, and heard his victim's cries subside into moans and gasps as Delwin Mix slipped into unconsciousness.

Bang! Boom! The deafening noise made the aggressor falter. The explosions stopped momentarily and Elmore Stoker looked around, stared in disbelief as he witnessed the tiny missiles rocketing from above the tree-line. Bang! *Bang!* A firework almost hit Elmore and he instinctively scrambled for safety. Heard the warning echoing in the distance, "Leave him alone! I've called the police!" Elmore stumbled towards the rear garden and watched as a further projectile whistled towards him. *Bang!* The firework detonated at his feet and made him lurch forward and lose his balance. A young boy's voice, loud and threatening, bawled ominously, "The police are on the way, mister!" Elmore plucked up strength and moved slowly towards the perimeter fence. He saw the youth run across the wasteland and scramble over the fence into the graveyard. The boy stopped, turned and stared, "Come on, mister," he shouted defiantly, "catch me if you can!"

Elmore Stoker was in a state of deep shock. He meandered back to the house. Delwin Mix was gone; the door was closed and locked. A defeated Elmore Stoker knocked limply at the door, "Father!" he whispered, "Father, let me in! I'm sorry; I didn't mean to hurt you!" Fell to his knees and covered his head with his hands, wanted his father so much it hurt. "All this time and you were next to me!" He lifted his head and stared at the house, "That's why you wouldn't leave," he gasped. "I understand, father, you couldn't leave me... watching me." His voice choked with emotion, "I understand now, I really understand."

**

CHAPTER SEVENTEEN

Christmas had come and gone, mild and wet with only the occasional half-hearted flurry of snow. Spring followed, a cool, damp and depressing squid of continuous showers and overcast skies. A bad time for Elmore Stoker, his emotions shredded and pulped with sordid revelations from the past. He withdrew from the world into a safer place, his anger and humiliation replaced by medicated peace and stoic serenity. A surreal time.

Evelyn Stoker and his good friend and constant companion, Alvin Brown, arrived early at Sedgefield's Winterton Hospital. It was the dentist's idea to visit his sick brother before the Sunday treat for the doting couple, Barnard Castle. A pleasant drive and a leisurely mooch around the beautiful market town, perhaps a meal if the mood took them. "I'll wait in the car, Evelyn, if you don't mind," said Alvin, still fearful of Elmore's temper tantrums, the assault still fresh in his head. "I'll be fine, Evelyn. Take your time, you've a lot to talk about, mend bridges," a gentle peck on his lover's cheek. "Love you, now go see him!"

Evelyn was told to report to the main office before entering the maze of wards, the warren of corridors that housed the unstable and the psychotic patients. He knocked and waited and listened to the occasional wailing and pleading that filtered from distant rooms. Shivering involuntarily and growing impatient made him rap loudly at the door. *Psychological bullshit,* he thought, *bloody power game making me wait,* checked his watch again, lifted a fist to strike at the door when it slowly opened. He stood, half-cocked with his hand in the air and felt duly embarrassed.

The woman was young, mid twenties perhaps, too young in Evelyn's opinion to be a qualified physician. Pretty, a taller version of Vera Connelly, taller and heavier.

Her name-badge said 'Dr. Williams' and she was smiling, beckoning him into the small cluttered room. "Call me Ruth," she said confidently, "you must be Elmore's brother?"

"Evelyn Stoker," he replied, "how, how is, is, is….."

She nodded serenely, ignoring the impediment. "Elmore is as well as can be expected," fumbled in her pockets, brought out cigarettes and a lighter and offered the man a cigarette. Evelyn refused and Ruth Williams lit and sucked heavily for some moments, "Please, sit down. You'll want to know about Elmore's progress?"

Evelyn asked, "Good news or, or, or bad?"

The doctor started to discuss the case, "As you know, Elmore arrived here from Ryhope's Psychiatric Unit. He was a patient there for almost a month, before that he had some time in Ward Nine in Hartlepool General," She paused, took another long pull of smoke from the cigarette while she studied the wad of notes on her desk and said casually, "Have you heard the term, 'Bipolar Disorder' Mr Stoker?"

Of course, young lady, mused Evelyn, *hasn't everyone a degree in medicine?* He shook his head and stared at her, *Trying to make me feel inadequate?*

"The term is all encompassing, from definite mood swings that can be noticed and recognised … to total shutdown."

Evelyn looked at the doctor with cynicism written over his face.

"Schizophrenia cannot be ruled out," the physician spoke without emotion.

Evelyn could not hold his tongue, gawking with incredulity he said weakly, "Schizophrenia!"

"Too early to make a proper diagnosis, Mr Stoker, but Elmore is showing definite signs that make me think along those lines. His thought processes are not normal, in fact, disorganised might be an under-statement."

"What, what do, do you mean?"

"Elmore is exhibiting abnormal behaviour." She nodded solemnly, added, "He's started pulling out his hair!"

Evelyn could only gulp and pout with incredulity.

"He's soiled his clothing and I don't think it was deliberate."

"What about drugs," muttered Evelyn, "wouldn't they help?"

"Mr Stoker," interjected the doctor, her features hardening, "I am a psychiatrist! I prescribe medication! You must not confuse me with a clinical psychologist!"

Evelyn raised his arms and stammered an apology. He had no idea about the terminology the doctor was using. *Psychiatrist, psychologist,* he thought, *what was the difference?*

"Your brother, Mr Stoker, appears to be regressing and I'm at a loss as to why. I have some notes as to the background. Elmore is your half-brother," she glanced again at the notes, "appears to think his next-door neighbour is his long-lost father?" Shook her head, her tone serious and whispered, "I've read the police reports about the assault on your person, the thefts from your home by your brother, his employment history. If you could help me, Mr Stoker, I'd be much obliged. The more information I have concerning your brother, the easier my task will be to discover the trigger that led to his breakdown."

Evelyn nodded agreeably, he would tell her as much as he could but no more, thinking that some things were better left unsaid. He'd mention the argument, the assault but not the garbage from Elmore after he'd returned. Some dirty washing couldn't be aired for the public to see. He could still see the absolute horror on his brother's face when he returned from the neighbour's house, the confrontation, the altercation with Delwin Mix had forever disturbed him. Elmore incoherent, ranting and raving ....

Evelyn was leaning over the sink being comforted and nursed by Alvin Brown. Suddenly the looming, distraught features of Elmore appeared at the door, eyes wide and haunted, head shaking from side to side in disbelief. "Not true, Evelyn," he whined, "really not true!"

Alvin could take no more confrontation, the stress too much to bear, mumbling excuses and apologies he hurried from the kitchen, through the living-room and found the front door and freedom, and ran from the place sobbing hysterically.

"Go away, Elmore," begged the bruised and defeated older brother.

"My father," said a sighing, weeping Elmore, "I've found my father! So close after all this time!" Stayed at the open door, his dazed head shaking furiously "Can't admit it... won't admit!"

Evelyn stood tall, still groggy with the beating, "It's true, Elmore," he said, wavering, "I've known for years!"

"No, Evelyn, you don't understand! My mother, my father, it's all their fault." Elmore looked pensively at the ceiling, seeming lost in his own private nightmare, whispering, "My father, my father can't be ...." His words dried up as he focussed on the ceiling-light.

Evelyn repeated his words, "Mr Mix is your father!"

Head arched, Elmore began to guffaw, "You don't understand, you'll never understand!"

The older brother slowly backed off, moved into the hallway and picked up the telephone ....

The psychiatrist, Dr. Williams prompted the stranger, "Mr Stoker, if you could tell me about your brother, Elmore?"

"Not a lot to tell you, Doctor," said Evelyn innocently. "We both had the same upbringing. Privileged, you could say. My father, our father, was a G.P. He was a lovely, generous man, and my mother ....

Some things, in Evelyn's opinion, were best left unsaid.

**

"Ma," insisted Vera, hardly through the door and her mother barracking her for news, "I wouldn't lie about such a thing!"

"It doesn't mean there's hanky panky between them?"

"Ma, Alvin practically told me they were living together, kept off the detail but said they were an item."

Vera Connelly pulled off her coat, slung it across the back of a kitchen-chair and walked into the living-room. Her mother followed, her face furrowed with a mix of sadness and annoyance. She still missed the little dentist, especially the freebies that were part and parcel of the man.

"Alvin Brown living with Evelyn Stoker!" Annie moaned. "A bloody shirt-lifter!"

"Alvin has always liked men, nothing wrong with that. Christ he wouldn't hurt a fly!"

"So when you were sixteen and dating him....?"

"Yes, I knew, and I wasn't dating him, Ma. We were good friends."

"And I thought Evelyn Stoker was a gentleman, he's nothing but a bloody homosexual! Nothing but a pervert," whined Annie Goodrich, "and to think I let him buy my drinks."

Vera said defensively, "Evelyn Stoker is a gentleman, don't be so narrow-minded, mother!"

"He's a bloody queer, all the same," retorted an inflamed Annie Goodrich, "neither use nor ornament!"

"Mother," persisted the younger woman, "before you found out about them, you said they were okay, you always had a good word for Evelyn Stoker, and you even tried to play matchmaker for Alvin and me!"

"Because I didn't know!"

"So you judge a person by his or her sexual preferences?"

"His or her!"

"You think it only applies to men, Ma?"

"That's disgusting, our Vera!"

Vera answered, "Ma, I don't know Evelyn Stoker too well, but I've known Alvin Brown all of my life and there's not a kinder, sweeter, more honest person in the whole world!"

"Vera, it's the thought of two men actually lying in bed together, you know?"

"Probably the same kind of picture you get when you see a man and a woman squirming together in a lover's embrace! Nice to talk about … love's sweet promise, cosy and cute, eh, Ma, but pull the blankets back and feast your eyes …."

Annie interjected angrily, "Stop it, Vera, it's private!"

"My point entirely, Ma," said the daughter, "forget about the intimacy and the images and it all comes out the same in the wash."

"Vera," questioned the mother, "you agree with all the hanky-panky?"

"Not particularly bothered, Ma," said Vera Connelly. "Honestly, it's not that important. Ought to take people as they are. Good and bad in all of us. I just think a person's sexual preferences are not that important. You want, I'll give you a long list of so-called *straight* people who are cruel, vindictive and horrible. The likes of Alvin and Evelyn are in a different class altogether. Truth is, Ma, the world would be a better place if there were more people like those two."

"Suppose," said a chastened Annie Goodrich.

"I know!"

Annie pondered awhile, added venomously, "Evelyn said I looked like Jayne Mansfield, ugh, him pretending to be straight!"

"It's wasn't Jayne Mansfield, Ma," said Vera whimsically, "wasn't even Jayne, it was Joan."

"Joan?"

"Joan Davis," said Vera, smiling sweetly.

"The actress," seethed the mother, "the bloody comedienne?" She glanced in the mirror. '*Could've sworn Evelyn said Jayne*,' smiled at her reflection,' *could be a lot worse I suppose*,' she thought.

"Life, Ma, no rhyme nor reason," she said, "Alvin is living in Evelyn's house, said he was never happier!"

Annie said, "And that poor brother mad as a hatter!"

"Ma, don't be dramatic. Elmore's had a breakdown, he'll soon be out and about and singing the blues in the *Southside*, no doubt."

Annie smirked, said sardonically, "Mind you, pet, if someone told me that Delwin Mix was my father, hell, I think I'd have a bloody breakdown!"

Vera ignored the sarcasm, said, "Alvin said he doesn't think Mr Mix will be returning to work. Reckons he'll be retiring, I mean, it's been months since he showed his face at the co-op."

Annie said, "Every cloud, eh?"

"Don't know what you mean, Ma?"

"Why, Alvin will be promoted from temporary manager to permanent, don't you think?"

"He's good" said Vera, "he deserves to be manager."

"You sayin' that because he's hinted you could be in line for under-manager, Vera?"

"Ma, don't be a gobshite! All the other girls are part-time, there's only Alvin and myself full-time."

"Of course, pet, I believe you, thousands wouldn't!"

Vera Connolly flashed an evil glance at her sarcastic mother but held her tongue.

"You out tonight, Vera?"

"It is Saturday night, Ma."

"Adam?" smiled when she mentioned Adam Connolly's name.

Vera pouted, folded her arms across her chest, said "Problem with that, Ma?"

Annie Goodrich shrugged her shoulders, "Not a thing. Maybe pleased that George only had one brother, you know, less to choose from?" The woman smiled broadly, "You reckon, our Vera?"

"Ma, the boys think the world of him, especially Jack."

"Kids are never a problem, Vera, buy them easily," said Annie derisively. Added casually, "Any plans for tonight then?"

"*Shoulder of Mutton*. Adam says there's a sing-along after nine."

"Elmore been straight in the head and he'd be singin' for his supper." She shook her head sorrowfully, "Never know what's round the corner, do you, Vera?" Annie grasped at the cigarettes and fished out two. "Wonder if Elmore can sing with a straight-jacket wrapped round him?" she said, snorting ironically.

Vera accepted the cigarette, said, "Ma, you're sick."

"Sick of bein' caged between four walls, Vera!"

"Why don't you ask to come out with us? Adam won't mind."

Annie sparkled like *Alka-Selsa*. "Why, Vera," she said, "if you're sure?"

**

Years ago and a frantic daughter-in-law begging Gilbert Stoker for help, wanting his advice and expertise. Temptation however, had got in the way of good intentions, a monumental lapse of control and everything collapsed and fell apart. On the surface, it looked as if nothing had changed and that Gilbert Stoker had again acted out the role of Good Samaritan, but the violation and the despoiling created undercurrents that lasted a generation. A chasm opened between the woman and the father-in-law. His son, Simon, had been shocked enough to forgo his wicked philandering and act the dutiful husband when Elizabeth had fallen pregnant and the man at the centre of the love triangle had taken a reluctant back-seat. He was sixty five years old, his working life almost over, still attempting a few hours of active duty most weeks, busying himself in the partnership when he received the fateful telephone call. It was Elizabeth and so conditioned to a lifetime of rejection and rebuffs, Gilbert Stoker handed the receiver to his wife, Simone.

Simone smiled benevolently and returned the phone. "She wants to speak to you," she said.

"Elizabeth," he answered falteringly, "how can I help?" Gilbert Stoker, hiding his fear, standing next to his wife, quaking and trembling with morbid trepidation, the distant past became the present as he waited for the usual barracking or sarcasm.

Her voice was almost a whisper, desperation overcoming pride as she asked Gilbert to visit her.

"If you insist, Elizabeth," answered Dr. Stoker calmly, masking the anxiety, wondering if his world was about to end.

Elizabeth said one word, "Now," and the telephone-line died.

Simone Stoker, wine-glass in hand, beautifully made-up and over-dressed as always, said, "Remember who is blood and who isn't! You're no longer a knight in shining armour, Gilbert dear, and that girl is married to your son!"

The man was waxen with fright, perspiring heavily and hardly listening to his inebriated, gin-sodden wife. Gilbert Stoker, Chief Psychiatrist, head of a private practice in Newcastle, a senior advisor to Her Majesty's Prison Service, Honour degree and a Ph.D. in Clinical Sciences, published several theses on his speciality, neurophysiology, paper published in the Lancet and in Life Magazine concerning Alzheimer's disease (his father suffered from the debilitating disease), three books published on the subject. Gilbert Stoker, a man of true status in the community, quaking in his boots at the mere thought of visiting his daughter-in-law.

Simone sipped at the drink then sniggered, "You're allowed to put down the phone dear," she said, musing. 'Gilbert, Man of La Mancha, my very own Don Quixote.'

"Pardon me, Simone," said the man in a state of torpor, "what did you say?"

"What on earth is the matter, Gilbert?"

The last thing Gilbert Stoker could say was the truth. He stammered, "Has to be bother, Simone, only time you hear from them is birthdays and holidays."

"That's not true, Gilbert," said the woman, finishing the drink, "we've seen them a lot more lately."

The man said sarcastically, "And you know why."

"Poor Elizabeth," uttered the spouse, "who would have thought?"

"You don't think," retorted Gilbert, rubbing his chin frantically, "you know old girl, that there might be bad news on the horizon?"

"The bad news has been and gone. Elizabeth is very ill but nothing would surprise me."

"How are you, Elizabeth?" he asked as he was ushered into the home.

"I'm fine, Gilbert."

"I thought perhaps your health…."

"I didn't ask you here to discuss my health", said Elizabeth brusquely.

Sweating profusely Gilbert Stoker took a deep breath to steady his nerves and said, "Spit it out, girl, tell me what's on your mind, no point in beating about the proverbial bush!"

213

Elizabeth lowered her voice to a whisper as she stammered, "I overheard Simon on the phone."

"I don't understand?"

The woman tensed and snapped, "Your son!"

"Yes?"

"He was talking to Delwin Mix!"

Gilbert Stoker left his seat, in a state of bewilderment, stood and gesticulated furiously at the woman. "I don't believe what I'm hearing, Elizabeth," he barked, "after all this time!" Shoving his hands deep into his pockets he started pacing up and down the large room.

Elizabeth ordered, "Sit down, Gilbert!"

"Damned if I will!" he replied defiantly.

Elizabeth stayed calm, almost serene as she spoke, "You once said you'd do anything to repair the damage, Gilbert, asked for forgiveness and said you'd do anything to help me!"

"Hell, Elizabeth, that was years ago!" he said. "Do you know how long it's been since…."

The woman interjected, "I can give you years, months and weeks, if that's what you want, Gilbert."

Gilbert Stoker stopped walking and folded his arms across his thin chest. Shook his head despondently and said, "If they're still meeting after all this time I really don't think we can stop them."

"Simon said Del Mix had phoned twice. First time in years." She stood and joined him. "Simon knows I'm ill. He's promised to ignore any further calls."

"Then I don't see a problem."

"I do."

"I can't, Elizabeth," he looked downcast, awkward, "I think two grown men who are that determined…."

"I'm not well, Gilbert," interrupted the woman, her tone desperate, "I don't want any more grief in this house. I need all of my strength to fight."

214

"But you're getting there, old girl," replied the old man chirpily. "You look really well, picture of health and all that."

Elizabeth Stoker removed her wig and watched her father-in-law gawk, blanch, then physically crumble at the image before him.

"Please, Gilbert, I want a few months of peace," begged Elizabeth. "It worked last time. Do it for me?"

The woman said matter-of-fact, "I've only known madness, Gilbert. Twenty three years of madness."

Gilbert had spent sleepless nights wondering how to tackle the dilemma, plucked up the courage one night and managed to walk to the Mix's home, stood and stared at the big house then panicked, made a hasty retreat and tried in vain to think of a solution. Then the fickle finger of fate intervened and brought the stranger to his consulting room. Introductions were made and for some moments the aged psychiatrist did not respond with the surname, his mind confused and befuddle. "Mix, never heard that name for years!" he beamed passionately, "Picture palaces! The Hippodrome! The Rialto!" he gushed, a peculiar look on his wizened features. "A few pennies and one was whisked away, Bronco Billy, Cheyenne Harry, and Mr Flamboyant himself, Tom Mix!' He grinned manically as the images swamped him. "I haven't heard that name in such a long time," he muttered. Then suddenly, abruptly, Gilbert Stoker came out of the stupor, glanced at the woman and flushed with embarrassment.

Mildred Mix fidgeted, her face clouding with apprehension and alarm, "Mr Stoker," she asked, "I have an appointment?"

A jolt went through the consultant as his mind cleared and his memory returned. He gasped audibly as he recognised the name of the patient. Gilbert Stoker saw the look of distain and knew he had to focus. Shaking her hand feebly, his greeting hesitant and wavering, the psychiatrist led her to the nearest chair. 'I do apologise," he muttered ruefully. "Please, Mrs Mix, if you will take a seat. I've had a very trying morning."

Mildred Mix was his first patient that day.

She was tall and rather regal, late forties and still attractive. Told the consultant she had worked in a local library for years and was chief librarian. Snooty and snobbish, Mrs Mix used disparaging terms to describe her sham of a marriage and casually mentioned her disappointment and annoyance at her husband's lack of motivation, his jaded outlook on life and his obvious disinterest in her. Gilbert immediately recognised the tell-tale signs of loneliness, isolation, and depression. He began unconsciously to gloat as his mind cranked into focus.

Mildred Mix seemed to shrink into the chair. "I need help, doctor, I feel so low, so helpless all of the time." Spoke hurriedly, mentioned her continuous visits to the local G.P. who had tried medication, rest, even suggested holidays to overcome the sadness that seemed poised to engulf her. "I've been seeing my local doctor for months, Mr Stoker. It was he who persuaded me to seek additional help." The woman paused and started at the consultant, "You can help me, can't you?"

Gilbert Stoker smiled and feigned benevolence. "Of course, Mrs Mix, that's why you have been referred to me."

She continued, "I should be happy, doctor. I've a new position at the local library, never imagined I'd ever achieve my goal. I'm finally in charge, I have people under me, it's something I've always wanted. I don't understand why I feel so miserable."

Gilbert Stoker smiled benignly, his mind jerking from Mildred Mix to Elizabeth Stoker, knowing he had the wherewithal to fulfil his promises. The physician spoke to her, comforted and sympathised, and all the while his head was plotting and planning. Told her not to worry; it was an awkward, sometimes turbulent age for a woman, especially one as pretty and obviously intelligent as Mildred Mix.

"Tell me about your husband, Mrs Mix, talk to me about your relationship. Please be candid and open. What you say to me will be in the strictest confidence, I'm a doctor, Mrs Mix, a psychiatrist, you can trust me."

"You want to know everything, doctor?" asked the woman, a blossoming mask of relief touching her stiff features.

"Everything, Mildred, you don't mind if I call you Mildred?" asked the physician, his tone as sooth as silk. He added softly, "My name is Gilbert, by the way."

"I don't know where to start, Gilbert."

"From the beginning," said the psychiatrist. "It's always best to start at the beginning." Gestured towards the couch situated in the far corner of the room, adding, "Would you feel more comfortable sitting on the sofa? If you wish, Mildred, you can stretch out and relax."

Mildred Mix moved comfortably to the sofa and stretched her body across the full width, said awkwardly, "Shall I close my eyes?"

He smiled compassionately and said, "Only if you feel more comfortable."

The patient closed her eyes and placed her arms protectively across her chest, "I'm ready, doctor."

The aging psychiatrist placed a chair close to the couch and said kindly, "Mildred, do you feel comfortable enough to talk to me?"

"Oh, yes, doctor," replied the patient, sighing and shrugging her shoulder., "There's so much to talk about."

"Right, Mildred," said Gilbert Stoker, his voice mellow and comforting, "tell me all about your husband………"

**

217

Delwin Mix had to get away from the house, couldn't bear the thought of another moment alone with her. He needed solitude in order to marshal his thoughts. Never felt so forlorn since he had abandoned Simon Stoker a lifetime ago. Elmore's ranting and raving brought it all back, all the misery of yesteryear, the heartache and the pain of loss. Elmore Stoker had screamed, insulted and then assaulted his neighbour. Elmore, wearing the mantle of clown, had insinuated Delwin Mix had a *liaison* with Elizabeth Stoker. Then his stammering imbecile of a brother, telling him outlandish tales about how he had overheard Elizabeth and himself discussing their affair.

The mayhem and torture that followed Elmore's furious assault made Delwin want to flee and hide until the pain eased. Months ago, his wife Mildred was absent from their home, socialising with friends and colleagues. His son, Albert, was present, albeit temporary, until the whiff of pending chaos caused him to forget they possessed a telephone and abandon his father and thus allowed the savage attack by the mindless neighbour. Mildred and Albert were two peas in a pod.

Months since the police knocked on his door and ripped his world apart with their uncanny knack of diplomatic blundering and lack of tact. "According to Mr Evelyn Stoker," said the plain-clothed detective, smirk as big as his pan face, "the present troubles stem from some years ago? Some kind of liaison between," the officer looked at his dour, chunky companion, coughed, feigning embarrassment then continued. "Well, if we are to believe Mr Evelyn Stoker," stole a quick glance at Del Mix who stood impassively close to the fireplace, arms behind his back, fingers gripped. He continued, "Some kind of relationship existed between Mrs Stoker, the late Mrs Elizabeth Stoker, and you, sir?" Paused momentarily then added dryly, "However, if we are to believe Mr Elmore Stoker, who is still volatile and extremely vocal," his eyes fixed firmly on Delwin Mix, "the relationship... perhaps a friendship, was between the late Mr Simon Stoker....Dr. Simon Stoker and yourself." Standing rigid and aloof next to her husband was a gaping, incredulous Mildred Mix who looked at the officers as if they were buffoons masquerading as policemen, shaking her head from side to side, glancing at the statuesque and silent Delwin Mix. "Del," she spluttered, "don't just stand there, say something!" What did Mildred want him to say? He was speechless, desperately searching for some logic explanation to clear his good name, bruised and aching from head to foot. Delwin Mix said meekly, "I really need to go to the hospital, I don't feel very well," couldn't think of anything else to say.

Week after week since the incident and the daily torture was unhindered and unabated as Mildred slowly ground the life out of him. "Well, tell me, was it him or her, Elizabeth or Simon Stoker? I have a right to know, there's no smoke without fire!" Mildred Mix as loud and as clear as a Dansette with a brand new needle, "Always struck me as odd the way everything turned topsy-turvy when Elmore was born, best neighbours in the world until then. One big happy family until that boy was born." He told her nothing, denied everything, no other way he was going to survive. Thought after months of unrelenting torture Mildred would ease back on the torment. Woman didn't stop for air, "Tell me the truth, damn you!"

Delwin Mix walked quickly along Stockton Road. He relished the isolation, even the incessant splashing rain could not take away the feeling of peace and calm. Reached the apex of the incline and felt the stiff battering breeze, cursed himself for forgetting his overcoat. Intended following the main road to Peterlee before circling back to Easington. He decided instead to snake left and wander down the abandoned minor road of *Andrew's Hill,* past the Maternity Hospital at Thorpe then return to the village. It was calmer and pleasant on the lee side. The wind struggled then turned into a whimper as the man strolled down the ancient single-line lane towards Little Thorpe.

Reaching the hospital gates he stuttered to a halt, his eyes reconnoitring the quiet, peaceful, undulating grounds of the Maternity Hospital. Years filtered and backtracked and he thought of the birth of his last borne, *'We'll call him Albert, after your father,'* she'd said, face flushed and oozing of weariness and wonder, oldest mother in the entire infirmary, so tired, so utterly exhausted Mildred fell asleep still holding the infant. Nurses lined up to congratulate him, proud as punch while the euphoria lasted, still in shock, almost as shocked as Mildred. All those years ago and she had barracked him daily. Out of her head, not only because she was pregnant but because of the embarrassment, "I'm too bloody old to have another, you old goat!" Snappy as a hippo having to share its mud-pool with too many others, blamed Delwin, cursed him night and day for destroying her life. "Ask me to sleep with you for a change, treat me like a wife again and this is how I'm repaid! You're nothing but a selfish bastard!"

He felt the same agonising isolation again, couldn't handle the situation, couldn't seem to overcome the pain. He sighed loudly and continued on his journey. Reached the Easington/Horden arterial road and pondered momentarily the direction he should take, right or left, then decided instead to cross over the highway and spend some time wandering the small hamlet of Little Thorpe. Years since he'd visited the place. There was little obvious activity, the distant growl of a tractor, the faint unremitting buzz of farm machinery lifting from the large byres, a small herd of meandering cows, listless and uncertain as they mooched and wandered aimlessly over the field. He reached the steel gate displaying the prominent sign, *'Close the gate after you,'* and decided to detour across the rough walkway towards the distant bulge of housing that was the *Waterworks.* Still needed the isolation, time to reflect, time to think.

A man approached, a tall, powerful-looking fellow with a shock of unruly white hair. He recognised the gait and the demeanour of the fellow, vacillated and wavered, unsure and nervous, then took a deep breath and strode towards the familiar face from the past. As he closed on the man Del Mix could see the anguish and apprehension spreading across the features of Morris Buckingham, his brother-in-law, his ex-lover, and felt a mixture of discomfort and trepidation. Knew the hurt still coated his one-time friend and understood the depths of his feeling.

Delwin smiled warily and stuck out his hand in greeting. "Hello, Morris," lost for words, struggling to converse, he added awkwardly, "I'm sorry about your mother," knowing he should have attended the funeral with his wife but the trauma in his life proved too great an obstacle to any social intercourse. It was all too much for him.

"Blessing really," answered Morris. He made small-talk and asked about Del's family, harmless chit-chat while he tried to think of inroads and detours that might rekindle more serious conversation. He asked innocently, "Have you retired, Del, I haven't seen you in the store for a while?" Morris was blissfully unaware of the calamitous episode in his ex-partner's life.

Delwin Mix took a lungful of air, "Been some trouble, Morris," he answered calmly, was unable to mask the obvious show of nerves. With face twitching and hands shaking, he continued bravely, "Personal stuff," he stammered and his voice trailed away, didn't know whether to confide or clamp. Despair and loneliness made him continue, "One of the neighbours has opened up a whole can of worms!"

"Neighbours?" inquired Morris, frowning, only one he knew by name, "Simon Stoker's family?"

"The youngest."

Morris Buckingham nodded and tried to remember the boy's names. Shook his head. It was all too long ago, "There were two boys?"

"Only the oldest was Simon's son," said Delwin Mix. "Name of Evelyn. He was short, like his father. He's a dentist."

He suddenly remembered. "Elmore!" he retorted. "Elizabeth's way of torturing Simon, her way of ending the relationship between you and Simon!" Smiled wryly as the memories returned.

"He wouldn't see me after Elmore was born," said Del, looking across the open fields. "He hurt me like I hurt you, Morris."

Morris said, "I understand, Del. I didn't at the time; I spoke out of order when you left me. I never meant the things I said. It was anger talking." He paused, reflected some then added poignantly, "All said in the heat of the moment."

Del Mix shrugged broad shoulders, "Past and gone, Morris."

Both were silent for some moments, reflecting, reminiscing, agonising about past and present.

"You mentioned the neighbours," ventured Morris. "Is there trouble?"

Del Mix started to relax, remembered all the good times before the break-up, before the accusations, the bile and squabbles from a distant time. Said simply, "Simon's youngest, Elmore, assaulted me. Accused me of being his father. Can you believe anything so ludicrous?"

Morris Buckingham was hesitant, could have told him so much, perhaps make the man realise about true friendship, true love, so close to telling tales about Del's wife, his wicked sister. Wondered if he should put the proverbial cat among the pigeons, maybe broadcast news about young Albert Mix, on the tip of his tongue to tell his old friend the awful truth.

Del asked, "Morris, are you okay?"

"I'm fine. Suppose I'm still in shock seeing you after so long."

Del said again, "Elmore Stoker said I was his father!"

Morris ignored the indirect approach, forgot the roundabout and the side-roads and said earnestly, "Are you his father?"

"Morris, don't talk like that," he replied wearily. Shrugged his shoulders and said, "You know where my preferences lie!"

"And Albert?" asked his companion sarcastically, "Albert was a mistake? You once told me you could never enjoy a woman's body, said it was repulsive?" His voice dipped then died.

Del's face reddened and he started to bluster.

"I understand, Delwin," interjected Morris, a twinkle in his eye. Chortling softly he said, "You don't have to explain to me."

First time in years Delwin Mix felt the tears spilling down his crimson features, couldn't remember the last time he'd wanted to confide in someone. He whispered desperately, "Walk with me, Morris, I need to talk to someone."

Morris Buckingham turned towards his old friend, his heart gladdened, hands stuck deep inside his coat-pockets, he said softly, "Link me, Del," felt the touch and the rush of emotion as his companion put his arm on him. "Talk to me."

"You don't mind, Morris, after all I've done?"

"I understood then," said the man honestly, "I understand now."

"You won't believe what's happened, Morris," said Del Mix, he was sniffling and fighting the tears, "there's so much."

Morris Buckingham squeezed the man's arm for comfort, pleased to be his confidante again, decided to wait until his old friend had finished speaking before putting the record straight.

**

They decided to decorate the second bedroom, Alvin Brown's suggestion really, left to Evelyn and the room would have been left well alone. The place was neat and always tidy although old-fashioned and somewhat dowdy, but Alvin relished his new role as housewife and ran a tight ship. Couldn't rest or feel comfortable if he got something on his mind, preferred spick and span ... and clean, had to be sparkling clean, adamant too, wasn't pushy or pouting, more determined when he offered, "I'm not asking you to help, Evelyn, love, and yes I know we share a double bed in the main bedroom, but I'd really like my own little bit of space. A bolthole for when we squabble, some place where I can relax. Early days, Evelyn, two bedrooms will stop our relations from talking!" The dentist sulked and carried a sour expression for a few short days then succumbed and crumbled to the pushy charms of his companion, spent the day in Newcastle buying the assorted paraphernalia to keep Alvin happy.

Second day of cleaning, late Sunday when Alvin Brown had reached the large, cluttered walk-in cupboard, took an hour before all the accumulated rubbish had been cleared and checked and bagged for disposal. He stood perspiring and staring, a tin of emulsion in one hand, large paint brush in the other, wondering whether to cover the cupboard carpet with newspaper, thinking it was pointless really, the remnant was being dumped anyway. Alvin sighed, knelt and was about to commence when he detected the faintest of obstacles under the thin carpet. Placed the tin of paint inches away, last thing he wanted was to spill paint, noticed the way the tin still looked skewed, said to himself, '*Like the Leaning Tower of Pisa*' and moved it fractionally. The paint-can still looked slanted. Alvin moved the tin, lifted the carpet and saw the thin booklet.

He frowned, his features twisted with wondrous awe as he started reading the diary. Alvin Brown forgot about the decorating. A while later he walked down the stairs, "Evelyn! Evelyn!" he called excitedly, "I've found your father's diary!"

Evelyn Stoker looked decidedly uncomfortable as he put aside the newspaper and was joined on the sofa by his friend, wanted isolation and space knowing the material could be personal. He said tersely, "Do you mind, Alvin, I'd really like to be alone?"

Alvin Brown understood, fondled his partner's thinning locks, "I'll be upstairs, Evelyn, call me when you're ready."

Evelyn opened the diary, flicked quickly through the yellowing pages that remained; leaves had been unceremoniously ripped from the binders leaving only a few handwritten pages. Some of the script was in ink, other pages in an almost illegible scrawl...........

August 10. ..... after so long, a virtual lifetime of refusing to name Elmore's father, Elizabeth had finally destroyed me. My own father! My own flesh and blood who has bullied and harangued me all of my life, ridiculed and tortured me about my sexuality, even threatened to expose and ruin me is nothing more than a charlatan, a scoundrel, a fraud!

My father is Elmore's father <u>and</u> grandfather? <u>I do not believe it.</u> My father, Mr High and Mighty Gilbert Stoker, is Elmore's father? Elmore is my brother? This is madness and I won't believe it! Elizabeth is lying, festering because I made contact. Elizabeth wants me to suffer. Is Elizabeth telling the truth? Has my wife slept with my father, is she capable of inflicting such pain? Is this her way, was this her way of seeking revenge? Could she be so cold and calculating towards me, is she without compassion, is there no depths she wouldn't trawl to destroy me?

I never meant to hurt her. Never. I was always truthful about my love, never disguised or hid my feelings. Elizabeth said it was a mad love, a tainted, sordid love. I thought it was beautiful. My only mistake was not following my heart. I should have left Elizabeth, then perhaps Delwin would have realised the depth of my love for him. I understood the fear because I felt it too. Two families would have been destroyed. I knew so well the calamitous effect our relationship would have caused. I really knew!

August 12. Awful row with Elizabeth. She brought it up again, thought it was some kind of bizarre joke, said it was tit for tat, wanted me to know the pain she'd suffered for a lifetime. I don't believe her, I'll never believe her! It's... I'm visiting father **TODAY.**

August 13. Mother said father was too busy to see me, disappeared on some pretext, waited until dark but he didn't show. Desperate to find out the truth I confided in mother. Simone was stoical, diffident .... left the room and never came back... even when I called and said I was leaving, she didn't acknowledge me. I went upstairs; mother had locked her bedroom-door. Please don't let it be true!

Afternoon. Delwin phoned again, desperate for news. I love him so much it hurts, but he is so selfish, always looking after himself, worrying as always, wondering if Elizabeth is finally going to tell his precious, pregnant wife, Mildred. What is the attraction... what does he see in that awful woman? <u>He lied.</u> Delwin Mix. Always swore he couldn't wouldn't sleep with her.... told me he couldn't love another, said I was the only one in his heart. Years ago and I believed him, I understood his worries ... if our liaison was made public. He had a wife, a boy and a girl ... couldn't find the strength to leave them for me. I really understood. When I said this to him, when I unburdened my soul to him he reminded me about Elmore.... screamed down the phone, called me a hypocrite for impregnating my wife...knows that's untrue. Elizabeth had an affair! My wife and I have never shared the same bed since Evelyn was born. Beautiful innocent Evelyn, my only son brought up in a household full of pain and regret, my only true love, so vulnerable.... so like his father, it's starting to show!

August 14. Do I tell Delwin that my wife slept with my father? How do I tell anyone about my sick father?... No one would believe me! It might not be true. It can't be true! I will visit father again.

August 15. Gilbert Stoker would not talk about it. He called Elizabeth deranged! I won't ever again call him my father. Mother refuses to leave her bedroom!

August 20. We talked, Elizabeth and I. Managed to persuade her to stay, told her we can get through this crisis. She appeared calmer today, wanted to talk... information was to be some kind of bargaining tool, wanted to know about my feelings for her... and Delwin. Had I been seeing him, had I ever contacted him since the birth of Elmore (gave my solemn vow at the time, told her I would never speak to Delwin Mix again), truth was I wanted to see him, wanted to speak to him but I kept my side of the bargain. Naturally I didn't tell Elizabeth I occasionally weakened over the years, sometimes phoned him so I could hear his voice. Nothing more, until the day I was in the bedroom doing nothing in particular, happened to see his horrid, abominable wife, Mildred, fawning over him. Delwin, seated in the deck-chair, reading a newspaper, guessed it would be the *Times,* only paper he read, bless his heart... Mildred acting like a schoolgirl as she pouted and played and acted like some macabre flirtatious child, touching him, caressing him, and Delwin throwing down the newspaper in disgust and storming into his house, leaving Mildred bemused and bewildered, arms on hips. I was so confused; known them all of my life and any open show of emotion between them was non-existent. I started to imagine all kinds of things. I phoned him and we started talking again, met a few times but nothing happened. It would have, he still cared for me. Then he told me Mildred was pregnant! <u>Pregnant!</u> How disgusting! I told him and he tried to deny it... said he was drunk most nights! <u>Liar! Liar! Liar!</u> Elizabeth must have overheard me on the telephone because I returned to the house and found Del and Elizabeth at each other's throats in the garden!

Elizabeth made me swear on the bible and I did. I had not started sleeping with Delwin Mix! She didn't ask if I wanted to!

Afternoon. Elizabeth seemed to calm after my bible bashing, made lunch, acted normal. I should have known something was amiss when she carried two large whiskeys into the lounge. I still remember her words, matter-of-fact, her voice so quiet, 'Are you ready for this, Simon .... . Your father is Elmore's father, he raped me. He was drunk. He'd confronted and threatened Delwin Mix. He raped me, Simon, and I would never have told a living soul ... would have taken it to my grave but something else happened. Something so despicable you'll not believe it. Gilbert Stoker, your evil perverted father seduced Mildred Mix. did you hear that, Simon? .... Impregnated Mildred Mix.' No! No! No!

August 21. <u>I have decided to kill my father.</u>

Evelyn snapped shut the diary and closed his eyes. His parents had lived a life of anguish. Simon, his father, had spent almost all of his adult life fraudulently loving someone so near yet so far, his adoration, his true passion barred from ever finding fruition or having any kind of contentment. His mother, poor Elizabeth, would have yearned for normalcy but shared the deceit and showed the outside world the sham that was her marriage. He could recall his father occasionally visiting Evelyn's ailing grandfather, always taking the journey alone to the nursing home. Could remember the rows and tension as he departed to call on Gilbert Stoker, and the bitter recriminations when he returned glum and depressed. *I have decided to kill my father!* Manic notes from a diary. Were they true? Did his father try and end grandfather's life? Did Simon Stoker react demonically to his wife's bating? Evelyn pictured his father fastening his overcoat, placing the trilby on his head, his mother's voice piercing and echoing, *'Guilty conscience, Simon!'* his mother's savage mocking tones as his father departed for the visit to the nursing home, *'Guilty conscience, Simon, can't do anything right can you? Can't finish anything you started!'* Evelyn opened his eyes and visibly jumped at the sight of Alvin.

"Let it go, Evelyn," his companion said earnestly.

"If you knew what was in the diary, Alvin," gasped Evelyn Stoker.

Alvin smiled benevolently, "I've read it, Evelyn," he stooped, grasped the booklet and walked to the fireplace, "time to let go."

"You've read it, Alvin?"

Alvin Brown sighed and nodded, said softly, "Read enough."

Evelyn slumped into the sanctuary of the sofa, his head shaking slowly from side to side, "My grandfather raped my mother!"

Alvin answered sympathetically, "I know, it's awful," and he joined his companion on the settee, grasped at Evelyn's hand and held it firm. "It's not your fault," he whispered.

Evelyn Stoker scratched his scalp nervously, "My grandfather...." His voice faltering as he tried to marshal

229

his thoughts, "My grandfather was acting on behalf of my mother, he was trying to dissuade Delwin Mix from seeing my father?"

"Elmore told you as much after his confrontation with Mr Mix."

"I didn't believe him, I didn't want to believe him."

"Your father was gay, Evelyn!"

"I didn't know," he whispered. "Why didn't I know, Alvin?"

Alvin Brown squeezed his lover's hand sympathetically, never spoke a word.

Evelyn Stoker said incredulously, "He loved Delwin Mix."

Alvin Brown said, "He loved your mother too."

"Mother said his love was a tainted love, a mad love."

"Your mother couldn't understand, Evelyn," answered Alvin Brown, his voice was steady and strong. "Your father was in an awful dilemma. He loved someone as much, if not more, than his wife. He loved you, Evelyn, loved you as a son and couldn't bear to leave you."

"You're being too kind," replied Evelyn. "Father said he was too frightened of the consequences, knew that the shame would destroy him. He was a moral coward, Alvin. He loved another but lacked the moral fibre to follow his heart. All those years, all those years together as a family. A farce, that's all it was, a farce!"

"It's over, Evelyn."

"It can never be over," said Evelyn Stoker. "How can it ever be over, my brother, my own brother has been destroyed. I told him what I honestly thought was true, that Delwin Mix was his father. Then Delwin Mix denies him, tells Elmore he's the result of a one-night stand. God, if Elmore ever found out that his grandfather was his father!"

"Leave it, Evelyn, you're simply destroying yourself! It's not important, Evelyn," said Alvin, "not now, not after all this time."

Evelyn Stoker was quiet, his face clouded, his features strained and troubled, "I remember something else. There was a furore when grandfather died and Mum and Dad attended the solicitors for the reading of the will."

Alvin Brown said, "I don't understand, Evelyn?" and moved closer towards his partner, still cradling the slim diary.

"Grandfather lived in Neville's Cross, in Durham, near to the college, opposite side of the road. It was a large detached house in about three acres of grounds. The house was next to the highway and most of the plot was hidden from the road."

"Okay," said Alvin, his features crunched with confusion, "but I don't see what that has to do ...."

Evelyn Stoker interrupted his companion, his voice slightly raised in frustration, "Something must have been mentioned when grandfather's will was read because both my parents were livid about the conditions of the will. Grandfather's house and land was sold but there was something else."

"You can't remember?"

"I wasn't really listening, wasn't bothered about family squabbles." Evelyn Stoker closed his eyes and concentrated. "They were disputing the fact that the will had provisos attached," he said, "Mother and father had received the bulk of the estate but some of grandfather's stocks and shares were to be held in trust, until ....." His voice trailed away.

"Until when, Evelyn?"

"I can't recall," retorted the dentist. "I can't remember, but it must concern Elmore and me. I know Mother was livid and demanding that father should dispute grandfather's will.

"It's funny nothing's been said since?"

"By whom?"

"The solicitor," replied Alvin Brown. "Or the executor, or whoever was in charge of the last will and testament of your grandfather."

Evelyn muttered, "Come to think about it, it is odd."

"What are you going to do?"

He grasped the diary, "I will destroy it, I promise, Alvin, but not yet. I'm not too concerned about the actual will. If and when I'm called to the reading then so be it. It's not as if I'm desperate for money, I couldn't spend what's in my bank!"

**

CHAPTER NINETEEN

The rain disturbed him and pulled him from sleep, head aching so much he wanted to cry. Elmore Stoker tossed and turned as the night grew wild and angry, windows rattled mercilessly as the wind buckled and thumped at the panes and made the heavy drapes flutter and dance to its manic tune. Imagined his eyes were playing tricks when shadows behind the windows jigged and groaned. Elmore had never felt as isolated or detached in the whole of his life, his mind like a sieve as it strained and sifted and separated images and pictures, groaned out loud as his head toyed and tantalised and pained as reality split and jarred and merged with a spectacular picture-show of surreal and grotesque slides from his past life. He was bombarded with imagery. Struggling from the bed he made his way hesitantly towards the window, pulled aside the curtains and saw nature's demented ballet in all its glory. Watched as the heavens showed a splendid, spectacular display of buffeting cloud formation, occasional thunderclaps and lightening bolts. Stood for an age fighting the inner demons that plagued him. Elmore Stoker was lost and alone, a frightened, abandoned recluse unable to concentrate or think rationally about anything or anyone.

Elmore had visions of performing to an audience. Was he a singer, an artiste? Was he a musician, did he play an instrument? He had no recollection of ever being on stage. Elmore bit his lips and tried in vain to concentrate, closed his eyes and centred on the pictures rolling around inside his head. He had no recollection of his own name or his age. Did he have parents, were they alive or dead, brothers or sisters?

A stuttering melody from yesteryear suddenly jarred through his aching skull and a brief smile touched his features as he recognized the song. Elmore opened his eyes and began miming the words. He knew the tune. Elmore

Stoker was awake, nodding manically, knowing he was a singer, a performer, convinced he could sing professionally. Yet why couldn't he recall anything about himself? He stared morosely out of the window, his mind full of expectation and hope as tunes inundated and overran his thoughts. Elmore's body slumped with the weight of despair, left the window and wandered about the darkened room, reached the door, tried and tested the handle then reluctantly stepped back towards his bed.

Why couldn't he remember anything apart from stupid, irrelevant songs? Why couldn't he recall anything about his past life? He closed his eyes and allowed himself to drift and dream, forced his mind to relax and unwind.........

It was time again and, although he felt exhausted, he knew the audience demanded his appearance, Elmore walked from the side-room and into the small ward, waved at the excited audience who looked anxious and spellbound by his arrival. The thought of performing seemed to push aside the nausea and bizarre pictures that floated around in his head, surreal images made him question his very sanity. He blamed the stress attributable to his fame, night after night, another town, another city, the lights, the audience, adulation. Checked again his attire, smiled at the impeccable taste, the long sleek white coat that almost touched the floor of the auditorium, the garish wrist-band, his trademark, even had his name displayed across it, security reasons, of course. His minders watched after him night and day. Good men. A few days ago there'd been trouble from the audience; some hecklers had rushed him and Bernie and Harry, his security guards had hoisted and carried him to safety. Troubled times but he always survived, always would.

"Ladies and gentlemen," he said clearly into the microphone, turned and looked for his back-up crew. There appeared to be a problem with the sound-system. "Hey,

guys," Elmore said, glancing back into his private dressing-room, "the mike isn't working properly, it's got a definite rattle," shook the apparatus again and the sound evaporated. He pulled at the rubber leads, "It's okay," he called, "it's fine."

The audience seemed to appreciate his appearance because they began, hesitantly at first, to close on him, mumbling with a mix of awe and appreciation. Stood so close to him and dressed so peculiarly, fancy-dress maybe and he tried to remember the gig. Was it some kind of charity affair? It had to be, looked back to see if Bernie or Harry were watching him, didn't want a repercussion of the other night, couldn't see them anywhere. Looked into the sea of smiling faces, the unmistakable presence of fans, he sighed, grinned, switched on the microphone and lifted an arm in appreciation.

"Ladies and gentlemen," he said in a deep mellow voice, "my name is...," He wavered, his head in turmoil because he could not recall his own name. Elmore waited patiently for the rapturous applause to ease when a small voice rattled through his skull, 'Tell the audience your nom de plume, you've forgotten again.' Lifting a pensive arm he waved at the selected band of worshipers, "My pseudonym is of course ...." but his mind was a blank and he stood stiff and uncomfortable. A cheer went up as someone in the crowd clapped and his anxiety immediately faded.

A member of the audience was a little close for comfort and purely for his own protection Elmore pushed the man away and watched as the fellow appeared to gasp and grab at those around him before he disappeared. Elmore Stoker looked anxiously for his minders. 'The price of fame,' he thought, 'the show must go on, with or without them!'

"Requests," he said, "this is after all a charity event." Smiled benignly at the gaping silent fans. He decided to push on, shouted, "I want you all to sing along."

He started the song then abruptly stopped. The orchestra was missing. Then he realised he'd hired a small band. Elmore cursed at his inattention, knew he should introduce the members, memory like a sieve these days. Turned and faced the drummer, "Ladies and gentlemen, a big round of applause for ....." His words dried up. The old man hogging the drumsticks seemed so familiar, so like his neighbour, Delwin Mix, made his head hurt so much. Couldn't fathom out why the drummer was so old and why he ached and sweated every time he saw him. He decided to dismiss him, not immediately, but soon, put him out to pasture and hire someone more able, more acceptable. Glanced at the decrepit female holding on to a guitar and then at the dwindling audience. He sighed knowing he had to get the show on the road before he lost them all, shouted enthusiastically, "Show your appreciation please, a guest appearance from ..." but he could not remember the woman's name. A sudden splash of recall blossomed before his weary eyes, and he stammered, "She used to be my mother." Elmore felt an excruciating pain cutting across his forehead, made him whimper out loud, took a deep breath and continued. "No, sorry, I'll say that again, my mother, my mother used to be ..." He was becoming more and more confused. Elmore wondered if it might be the cocaine making him so befuddled. He was taking more and more. The damn press had found out and were crucifying him, had to categorically deny taking any harmful substances. No one understood the stress he was under, the unmentionable and awful price of fame.

"Elmore," it was his personal physician, Ruth Williams, a trooper who was at his beck and call, "I think we should rest awhile."

The fellow shook. She had called him by name. He acted nonchalantly, didn't want to appear startled by the revelation.

"The audience, Ruth," he whispered desperately, wondered why was she calling him Elmore, then he realised, it was another of his fictitious names that cloaked his true identity. "I can't let them down, the show must go on, girl," Checked his watch, "Few hours and I'm at the Southside Social!"

"Intermission, Elmore," she soothed, "time for a break. Time for your medication," and led him slowly from the ward. "We'll call at the toilets first, Elmore, you've had a little accident."

"Accident?" he quizzed, and then he understood. Her way of helping him to break with the audience, she meant a short-cut, a ready-made escape hole in case the fans rioted again. Happened last night, bad last night, wrong venue, agitated crowd, the name-calling, the barracking, who could blame him for erupting and retaliating. So bad when he finally made it back to the dressing-room. Elmore started to appreciate the needle, the way he relaxed immediately, took away the bite and fire inside his head. He was working too hard, he knew that, finding fault with his loyal band members, hell they'd been with him for years. Del was more a father figure than a drummer and Elizabeth, damn she could cook a meal with that banjo on her back. "You brought the tablets, nurse?" he asked. Ruth liked being called nurse, or doctor. Funny too, he thought, maybe he would sign her to a permanent contract. Only person who unnerved him, caused him unease, was the road-manager, something odd about him. The fellow too nervous, all that stammering and jabbering, and he was short. Short people made him panicky and anxious. He confided in Ruth, "'Why does he always insist I need to recuperate? Why does he want to take me home with him? What's with the teeth talk, he disillusioned with being a road-manager?" Man would have to go; needed loyal folks around him. Last thing he wanted was disquiet and unrest,

237

teeth hurting so bad he should visit a dentist, not a problem.

He liked Ruth Williams, seemed to have an uncanny perception of his mood swings and knew all about the stresses and strains that dogged his life, had the power to pull the switch in his aching skull. Elmore thought he might wait awhile, check her out properly, give her the spiel, make his mark, maybe settle down with her, joint names on the house, write a will, all above board of course, look after number one. Joint names, Elmore thought, making a will, had a sense of déjà vu. A name tickled through his head so he said to Doctor Ruth, "Honey, you have another name, when you're away from the stage?"

"Whatever, Elmore,I can be anyone you want."

He glanced around the cold room, saw the glistening tiles, wash-basin and big bath. The woman taking advantage of his exhausted state,"Elmore, I'll take off your pyjamas, I want you to step into the shower, we need to wash you down, little accident again." He tried again, before the name in his head vanished, that was something else he had noticed, forgetting things, names, places, all to do with weariness, "Honey, your other name?" felt decidedly uncomfortable naked as a baby, and the smell, was that Ruth or himself? Whatever, the stench was overpowering,; maybe Ruth should be put on a back-burner until she cleaned up her act. "Hey, I asked a question? Is your name Agnes, Agnes Lincoln?"

The woman grinned, "You want me to be Agnes, I'll be Agnes!"

He didn't answer, something peculiar about Ruth Williams, kind of girl wants to pretend she's something she's not so he smiled and stepped submissively into the shower. 'Two can play at that game,' he thought, cunning like a fox, "You want to call me Elmore, I'll go along with that," felt so tired and wanted to sleep forever. Closed the shower-curtain forcibly, wanted to give off the right *signals, wasn't going to allow the woman to wash him ever again, knew her game, read her like a book.*

"Do you need a hand, Elmore?" she asked, voice loud enough to be heard above the din of the shower.

"I'm fine," he said with authority. "If I need you, I'll call, okay?" and smiled as he heard footsteps echoing as they disappeared across the tiled room. "Elmore, what kind of stupid name is that?" he said.

Elmore woke up with a start, words and names still jarring in his head. He tried to concentrate and attempted to link names with faces. Delwin Mix, Elizabeth Stoker, Evelyn Stoker. Ghostly images swamped him; faces and names jolted in disarray then submerge into his conscience. Delwin Mix and Elizabeth Stoker seemed familiar! Evelyn Stoker, yes, his brother and Elizabeth Stoker was his late mother! His memory was finally returning. He dragged his weary frame from the bed. *'Elmore Stoker'* he mused, *'that's my name!'* and smiled through the grey dawn of a new day.

"I'm Elmore Stoker!" he whispered, meandered towards the window, the drugs making him sloth-like and lethargic. Couldn't stop repeating the name, "Welcome to my world, Elmore, it's good you're back."

He heard the rhythmical tap-tap of approaching footsteps, knew enough to keep his good fortune to himself, hurried back to his bedside and slumped on the corner of the bed. The uniformed nurse entered carrying a laden tray, "Wide awake today, Elmore?" said the nurse, features crisp and alive and white teeth sparkling, "are you going to be a good boy and take your medicine?" Elmore Stoker smiled a reply and waved a greeting, *More than one way to catch a fly,* thought the fellow as he observed the tray placed on the bedside-cabinet. Saw all the pills and potions, the water, and the solitary cup of steaming tea. "Morning, nurse," he heard the words rattle like candy in a jar, didn't know if he were thinking or speaking his reply, *I'm supposed to take all those tablets?*

"Forecast is excellent, Mr Stoker," said the nurse and she started apportioning the medication on to one side of the tray, placing perhaps a dozen pills of all sizes and colours into one small plastic tumbler. "There we are, my love," she said cheerfully, "tablets first then a nice cup of tea, okay?"

Mr Stoker, he mused, ecstatically, *that is my name.*

"Could you open the curtains, nurse?" asked the seated figure politely. "If it's going to be sunny, I'd like to enjoy the day," grasped the tablets and the glass of water and watched as the young woman moved towards the window. A quick sleight of hand and the container of pills were tipped expertly into his pyjama breast-pocket, the empty tumbler noisily replaced on the cabinet and the water swallowed in anguished gulps. "Nurse," he questioned, "do I have to take so many tablets?" grasped the tea and sipped thankfully at the nectar.

"All for the best, Elmore, pet," answered the girl, still fussing with the drapes, turned and beamed a lovely smile at him. "You seem a lot better today, have you slept well?"

He nodded, full of beans, "What day is it today, nurse?" he asked.

"Sunday," she replied, returned and grasped the tray. "Any visitors today, love …. your brother, maybe?"

Neurons clicked and electricity spun through his brain as data registered. *'Brother, Evelyn. Mother and father, Simon Stoker and Elizabeth Stoker, both dead.'* A shearing pain enveloped his entire skull. *'His father wasn't his father!'* He remembered now and he winced as memories taunted.

"Mr Stoker," asked the nurse, leaning close to him, "are you feeling okay?"

"Headache," he replied, forcing a smile, "too many tablets."

"Breakfast in half an hour, Mr Stoker," said the nurse, moving away towards the door, "will you need a hand dressing?"

"I'll manage, nurse," said Elmore, and watched her disappear.

His head began to ache, the burden too much to assimilate. Elmore was desperate to talk to someone, anyone. Needed to take away the pain and forget the lurid past. Slowly he began to relax and drift as schemes and plans lifted him from the mire of reality. *Priority,* he mused, *first things first. I have to get out of here, find a way to slip the net and take a bus-ride home. It's time to put my house in order!*

**

"Bright and early?" quizzed Annie Goodrich as Adam Connelly bounced through the kitchen-door. "They're all in the living-room."

"Fancy a ride out then?" said the collier, big infectious grin over his moustachioed features.

Annie frowned, "Me?" she answered, wasn't used to surprises or kindness from folks. Annie's philosophy, *Look after yourself first, then family, and to hell with the rest.* It was a tried and tested formula guaranteed to keep her place in the race. "You're askin' me, Adam?"

She couldn't fathom out the man, still generous and kind-hearted after months of courting her daughter. Always imagined the initial sympathetic and humane manner was a ploy to win hearts and minds. Months later and the man was as compassionate as ever. One hell of a catch was Adam Connelly, head and shoulders bigger than his shifty no-account brother, George. Harelip or no harelip, he was a good man, big enough not to hide his feelings for her daughter, Vera.

"Sedgefield," said the man, moving away from the door.

"A day at the asylum," answered Annie ponderously, "what could be better, Adam?"

Adam Connelly laughed at the woman's warped sense of humour, "The car-boot fair," he said, "it's held at Sedgefield Racecourse, every Sunday. What do you think, Annie? It's sunny, it's a few hours out, maybe see a few bargains?"

Annie nodded excitedly, wished she were twenty years younger, would have had Adam Connelly safely down the aisle by now, not like her wavering dithering daughter, "Thanks, Adam," she said contentedly, "I'll enjoy that."

The man wandered into the next room, grinned at the sight of Vera, slumped back in the big arm-chair, *News of the World* crumpled over her thighs, snoozing. The two boys were busy, spread-eagled over the floor. Joe, practically-minded, miniature spanner in hand as he struggled with the logics of *Meccano,* Jack studiously watching, seeing the stranger, smiling and giving a little wave. "Building a crane, Uncle Adam," he said. Joe pausing, glancing and studying his mother's beau with trepidation, a quick nod of the head and back to the grind of make-believe construction.

A tremor shot through Vera's body as she drifted back to consciousness. Shaking her head, stroking her hair subconsciously she asked, "Adam, how long have you been standing there?" Folded the newspaper and struggled to her feet, "I'll make a cup of tea, love," she said.

Adam said warmly, "Your Ma's put the kettle on," moved to the sofa and sat on the arm. "Fancy a ride to a car-boot, Vera?"

"Why not," she said, "it's a lovely day."

She remembered marriage to George Connelly, Mr Routine himself. Sunday morning and it was always the Workingman's Club by eleven-o-clock, back at two, sodden and stupid with drink, big dinner and then a few hours in bed, '*Come on, Vera, give me a cuddle, helps me sleep,*' he would always say, quick shag, more like, and then up and out by seven-o-clock. Same every Sunday, set your clock by Geordie. Adam Connelly was so different, called every weekend, asked Vera what she wanted to do. Didn't tell her, asked her. He was such a lovely man.

"What's a car-boot, Uncle Adam?" asked Jack, leaving his brother's side and shuffling up to the man. He liked his uncle, he was always kind to him, always bought him nice things.

"It's like a fair, Jack," explained the man, ruffling the youngster's hair, "like a market. People selling stuff, it's good fun."

"What kind of stuff, Uncle Adam?"

"All kinds, Jack," chortled the man, "toys and games, and they're all cheap too!"

Jack asked anxiously, "Can we come, Uncle Jack, me and Joe?"

"Of course," Adam Connelly glancing at the industrious older brother who appeared lost in his endeavours. "Might even be some cheap bikes for sale. Joe," he called, "you fancy a look out?"

Joe Connelly shrugged his shoulders, "If you want, I'm not bothered either way."

Vera leaned forward and slapped at Joe unruly hair, "Cheeky pup talking like that when someone is trying to be nice to you! You ungrateful bugger!"

"Leave it, Vera!" said Adam forcibly, added diplomatically, "Joe's well stuck into his *Meccano* set. I always found it too complicated. We'll have a cuppa and see how the land lies."

"What time are you going, Adam?" asked Vera.

"Sooner rather than later," replied Adam. "Sooner we get there, the sooner we snaffle all the good bargains!"

Half an hour later and the big *Morris Oxford* was full to bursting, and trundling up the quiet back street, heading for Thorpe Road, the A19 and Sedgefield, Vera relaxing in the front passenger-seat, Jack and his grandmother lounging contentedly on the back seats. The woman was reading *Women's Own*, Problem Page naturally, Annie Goodrich spellbound with the caption, *Do men go through the menopause?* smiled whimsically at the image of her Barty. Shook her head, her lips answering the literature, *'Poor sod never reached that age, God rest his soul,'* never realising she was being observed by her daughter through the rear-view mirror. Vera glanced at her son and smiled. Jack was slumped comfortably against his grandmother with a cache of comics around him; *The Two-Gun Kid, The Wyoming Kid, Johnny Mack-Brown,* and two dated copies of *The Beano*. The youngster lost in a fantasy world.

"Uncle Adam?" asked the boy, lifting his head away from the comic-book.

"Jack?"

"Johnny Mack-Brown?"

"Yes?" said a smiling Adam.

"He a proper cowboy like the Wyoming Kid?"

"The Wyoming Kid is make-believe, Jack, never existed. Johnny Mack-Brown was a football star in America, he's a real person." He hesitated and tried to think of examples, "Like Tim Holt, real people who started acting, became so famous playing cowboys that comic-books used their proper names in their stories."

"Tim Holt is real," asked the bemused boy, "Johnny Mack- Brown is real?"

"Real as you and me, Jack."

"Never!" said the enthralled boy.

The car reached the apex of the village and headed southbound, "Look out for the Trimdon / Hartlepool turn-off, Vera," said Adam Connelly. "Miss that and we'll end up in Middlesbrough!"

Annie Goodrich said, "Barty used to always take the Wingate turn-off, Adam, and head for the Trimdons." Eyes never left the magazine, read the headline opposite the Problem Page: *Forget the good looks, read the truth about Hollywood's glamour boy, Rory Calhoun.* The side-heading drew her attention: *Calhoun was a Borstal Boy.*

Jack Connelly shouted, "Uncle Adam!"

"We'll be there in half an hour if we don't get lost, Jack," replied Adam, in anticipation of the question, glanced at Vera and smiled warmly.

"Uncle Adam," snorted the indignant lad, "not that!"

Adam Connelly asked, "What then?"

"If Johnny Mack-Brown and Tim Holt are real people," asked Jack, putting aside the comic-book, "what about Clark Kent?"

Annie Goodrich momentarily closed her *Women's Own* magazine, glanced darkly at the boy and then at his smiling mother. Shook her head slowly, "Stupid boy!" she muttered.

**

A mile from the car-boot fair was Sedgefield's *Winterton* Hospital. The huge site, a mix of pre and post-war buildings was fragmented. The hospital was dispersed over many acres of rolling, picturesque grounds disseminated with trees and flower-beds. Meandering walkways and a phalanx of seats could be found dotted here and there in a haphazard regiment of refuges and bays and used by both in-patients and visitors alike.

By eleven-o-clock Elmore had recovered enough to ignore the drone inside his head. He washed, shaved and strolled into the wide expanse of gardens. Sat next to an old couple who were attempting conversation with their non-responsive, introverted and sullen daughter. The girl, forlorn and muted, seemed only interested in the vastness of sparkling skies.

"Marlene, pet," said the dumpy, over-dressed father, patting an enormous handkerchief over his thinning locks, perspiration running freely over the thick skull and on to the bull-neck, "your mother asked you a question!"

Marlene Kenny, more *Olive Oyl* than Shelley Duvall, beanpole tall, eyes like a hawk, with long, thin nose and bulbous lips, ignored her parent and focused instead on a nearby tree infested with noisy rooks and crows.

Marlene's long-suffering mother, Minnie, head and shoulders taller than her under-sized husband, skinny and cadaverous with facial structure and the same desperate, haunting quality of someone in the final throes of anorexia nervosa, smiled pathetically. "Leave her, Oliver," she whispered, "she'll come out of it in a minute or two," and glanced nervously at the tall handsome stranger, nodded a greeting, then focussed again on her daughter, reached forwards and grasped the limp hand, squeezed and fondled it like some precious ornament.

Marlene Kenny closed her eyes and smiled a goofy smile that lit up her face. Sang softly, "Sing a song of sixpence, a pocketful of rye, four and twenty blackbirds baking in a pie ......"

"Shh!" said an embarrassed Oliver Kenny. Looked at Elmore and grimaced, "Sorry about this."

"Don't worry about it," sympathised Elmore Stoker, "I have a brother who is suffering too."

"Not a lot you can do," whispered the discomforted mother.

Devious Elmore asked casually, "Have you come far?"

"Murton Colliery," said the man, "about forty minutes drive."

"North of Peterlee," said Elmore Stoker, plotting and planning, could suddenly see an escape route from the place.

246

"Is that where you live?"

"Easington Village, next door to Peterlee," he retorted. Turned his body and faced the man, "I mentioned Peterlee because I had to use public transport this morning … bus from the village to the town, then another bus to Sedgefield. Bloody annoying when your car breaks down! Still, I had to see my brother, you know how it is, worry so much about them, don't you?"

"If you want, Mister," said Oliver Kenny, "we can give you a lift home. Easington is only minutes away from Murton." Glanced at his wife, "We could, couldn't we, pet?"

Marlene grinned and started singing, "One potato, two potato, three potato, four … five potato, six potato, seven potato … more."

CHAPTER TWENTY

The family had been gone for an hour when Joe Connelly realised he had to alter his plans. His Uncle Mick had stuck his nose in and mentioned he was about to mend the back fence for his sister and Joe was to act as labourer. "Back in a few minutes, Joe, need to visit the bog,"said Uncle Mick, time enough for Joseph Connelly to put on his thinking-hat, alter his plans, think of a new locality and scarper. The foursome: Davy Duckworth paired with buxom Janice Longfellow, Joe with lusty *Lolita*, Miriam Roche, the gang all ready to spend time in Joe's abode, Joe and Miriam booking the front bedroom, Day and Janice, relegated to the smaller back-bedroom, until Uncle Mick stuck his stubbled face through the open door and exclaimed, "Annie didn't tell you?" Bemused Mick Green, chortling to himself, nodding when he remembered he'd promised to fix the fence the day previous but a hangover had meant all plans were cancelled. Lay on the settee for most of the day with Mary Jane acting as the nurse from hell. "Still," his uncle said, "we've got all day, Joe."

As soon as his uncle had shuffled out of sight, Joe had called over the back fence for Miriam, told her to meet him at the top of the street. Minutes later, flushed with the exertions of bolting through several rear-gardens and then running non-stop, he finally reached Davison's shop. The two girls hurried to his side. "Thought you'd changed your mind again, Joe," said a teasing Miriam. Nudging her chunky companion she said, "Janice, this is Joe Connelly, my boy-friend I was telling you about," turned back to the lad and asked, "where's Davy Duckworth, Joe, you said he'd be here?"

"We can share him if you want, Miriam," said the diminutive ogre with the melon-sized breasts. Janice looked Joe up and down hungrily, "If you want?"

Joe spluttered, "His dad has the garage at the top of Stockton Road, he'll be walking down now. Come on, we'll meet him half-way."

"Where shall we go, Joe?" asked Miriam, sporting tee-shirt and shorts for a quick undress, "it's all houses up there!"

"Naw!" corrected Joe Connelly. "Top of Stockton Road, behind Davy's garage there's *Andrew's Hill*. It's always deserted."

"It is quiet, Miriam," agreed the bloated dwarf. "When Ma had our Edward at the Maternity I got sick of all the screaming kids so I went for a wander up the hill. There was nobody about."

Miriam Roche said, "Suppose we could try it."

"We could separate," offered Joe, glancing at Miriam's trim rump, "we could stay near the top of the hill and Janice and Davy could wander to the bottom. Meet in the middle later?"

"Later," laughed Miriam, "after what?"

"Joe! Joe!" shouted the approaching boy.

It was Davy Duckworth, grinning like the cat that found the cream, beady eyes feasting on his young woman, zooming on to the huge heaving breasts of the smiling pixie.

"How do," he said, "I'm Davy. My dad's got the garage at the top of the bank!"

Janice nodded, said, "Joe told me all about it."

"It's called *Banktop Garage*," said Davy proudly.

"Because it's at the top of the bank?" smirked the female sausage, quick as a flash.

"You taking the piss?" asked Davy Duckworth.

Janice frowned, spluttered indignantly, "I don't think so!"

Joe interrupted the spat, "Davy, what say we have a wander to Andrew's Hill?"

"Why?" asked his companion, not the brightest spark in the fire, "it's bloody dead up there!"

"Exactly, Davy, there's no one about!"

"Thought it was going to be a few hours in your house?"

"Change of plan, it's sort of occupied."

"If we have to?" said Davy Duckworth.

"We have to!"

Miriam said perkily, "It's a nice day, anyway!"

"Better outside than inside," retorted Janice Longfellow. "We can sun-bathe." Glanced slyly at her beau and felt a mite disappointed, would have preferred to share Joe Connelly. Joe who looked like a miniature Alan Ladd only with dark wavy locks, and a twinkle in his eye.

Davy offered, "Shall I buy some sweets?"

Janice gushed excitedly, "Sun-Pat nuts, Davy. I like them and a tube of Rollos, Dolly mixtures ...."

Miriam interrupted, "Some blackjacks, fruit salads. If they have any, Davy, sherbet lemons or maybe liquorice allsorts?"

Inside the poky interior of the corner-shop, Davy Duckworth was having second thoughts about the day.

"Joe," he said glumly, "that's a chunk out of my pocket-money. I don't know whether it's worth it or not?"

Joe Connelly bursting with hormonal fever said anxiously, "Shut your gob, I'll split the bill. You buy for Janice, I'll buy Miriam's!"

"And that's fair," croaked Davy Duckworth, "have you seen the size of Janice, it's like one for the price of two!"

"Miriam said she'd definitely let you play with her tits!"

"She did," gasped Davy hesitating at the counter. Whispered, "they're enormous!"

"Balloons!"

Davy Duckworth said, "In for a penny, in for a pound, eh, Joe?"

"Definitely get your monies worth!"

Davy spent all of his pocket-money at the shop.

**

A few minutes away, in Stockton Road, Elmore had reconnoitred his old home. Every door was locked and Evelyn was nowhere to be seen, unaware his older brother was spending the weekend in Scarborough with Alvin Brown. Decided to take his leave and make a call at Thorpe Road to see Agnes Lincoln or was it Ruth Williams, *'Does she work in one of the Peterlee factories,'* he pondered, *'or was she a doctor or nurse?'* The uncertainty bothered Elmore, so forgetful these days about major details in his life. He knew it was the accumulation of medication, wondered why he was initially installed in Sedgefield Hospital, what triggered his move to the institution? *'I remember arguing with Delwin Mix,'* he mused, *'and something about a firework display.'* Started walking away from the house when he noticed the upstairs window slightly open.

Elmore stood transfixed, a ten-year old again, the house empty, parents and favourite son away on some shopping trip, doors bolted and the single bedroom-window open. He gazed expertly at the spouting, the thick, cast-iron waste pipe that ran down the entire gable-end. Thought he might be able to shuffle a few metres up the pipe-work and then swing his frame on to the out-house roof and from the roof to the window, easy as pie. Elmore took off his jacket, turned up his shirt-sleeves, grasped at the waste-piping, deep breath and hoisted his frame against the down-comer. Monkey-fashion as he inched his way up the side of the house, sweating. Wheezing and aching, Elmore finally struggled onto the conservatory-roof and sat for some moments while he recovered his strength. Closed his eyes as the sun blazed over his crumpled body. The warmth of the orb soothed and seduced him into staying on the flat roof, felt at peace with the world, first time in an age that he felt so good. Never opened his eyes even when the boy called out his name and began haranguing him, imagined it was a dream, and the impertinent youth barracked and threw firecrackers at him. '*So real,*' thought Elmore, '*I can picture him.*'

Joe Connelly walked with his friends along the tree-lined Stockton Road, and glanced at the detached house next door to Albert Mix's home. Head in overdrive when he saw the prostrate figure squatting lethargically on the flat roof of the huge conservatory. He recalled the mayhem between Mr Stoker and Mr Mix, the savage assault that only ceased when Joe had intervened, knew his name, still fresh in his head, strange name too, never heard it before or since. Nobody had a good word for the man, not his Ma, or his grandmother, Annie, even Uncle Mick called him a loser. He was a drunkard, remembered he fancied himself as a singer. He was a liar too, told his Ma he worked for Easington Council.

Joe asked his friends, "Fancy a dare?" and saw the three heads bob in unison. "Might have to run all the way to Andrew's Hill?"

"Game if you are, Joe," said Davy Duckworth, full of youthful bravado and spiralling hormones.

"Hey, Elmore," Joe bellowed, "sing me a song!"

Elmore relaxed and concentrated, wanted the dream to move on a gear, tired of the barracking childish taunting, weary of the tirade of filth.

"He's dead," said Miriam, matter-of-fact, "come on, let's go!"

"You reckon?" asked Davy, shifting his hungry gaze from Janice Longfellow's stupendous breasts to the spread-eagled figure slumped on the roof. "Suppose we could call 999 and say a man was dead on a roof."

"They wouldn't believe us, Davy!" muttered Joe Connelly.

"Wouldn't believe you," chortled Davy Duckworth. Added sarcastically, "How may times you phoned this week, Joe?"

"Every night!"

Miriam, exacerbated, and feeling decidedly rampant, said hopefully, "Tell you what; let's leave the telephone until we come back. If he's still on the roof, I'll dial 999, okay?"

Davy said, "Fine by me!"

Joe said, "Man chanced to be dead drunk!"

"Let's go," begged Janice Longfellow, sucked in a lungful of air and tried to pull in her stomach, "day's almost over!"

The gang moved off along the winding road, the incline zoomed in the distance, apex of the hill and they would reach the lonely expanse of the rarely-used back-road. Hardly a word said as they struggled over the final hurdle, all deep in thought, all wondrous and waiting for the ecstasy to begin.

Elmore yawned, stretched and gazed at the road, listened as the occasionally car zoomed past. Recognised a Ford *Zephyr*, a Ford *Consul* and a smoking Hillman *Minx*. Loved the Hillman, two-tone, cream upper-body and crimson skirting, '*Cool colours,*' thought Elmore, remembered his neighbour, Del Mix had a *Minx*, dull brown which matched his personality. Years ago Elmore had a car, a yellow V.W. loved the beetle so much, hated having to ditch it. '*Don't drink and drive,*' he mused,'*don't drink and drive and smash into a police-car, not a good idea!*'

He stood and gingerly made his way to the open window, took seconds to hoist himself inside. Elmore closed the window behind him and started calling out for his brother, checked room after room, Evelyn had flown the nest, second piece of good fortune to fall at Elmore's feet that day; a free ride home and then an empty house with no nagging older brother trying to persuade him to return to the hospital. The fridge was bursting with food so he filled a dinner-plate with assorted goodies and made himself tea, wandered into the living-room and switched on the television, determined to enjoy the remainder of the day.

His head was beginning to clear and he made a mental note to refrain from touching any kind of medicine or medication ever again. Elmore thought about his stay in hospital, wondered if his nerves were the result of his fracas with his obnoxious neighbour. He smiled grimly, gratified and relieved that Delwin Mix was not his father. When Evelyn returned from his outing he would apologise for his behaviour and beg for leniency until he could sort out his troubled head, decided to blame the accumulation of stress for his dreadful outburst. Elmore was minded to contact Sedgefield Hospital, not today, maybe tomorrow, and talk to his doctor. He was sure her name was Ruth Williams. He'd think of a plausible story for his absence and beg a few days leave. The more he thought about his stay in Winterton the more he was convinced that his erratic behaviour was due to his daily grind of medication, took him to another place, weird and mysterious, made him hallucinate and act irrationally. Maybe he could demand more discussion and fewer tablets? Hell, his mind was like a kaleidoscope with the intake of poisons, made him think ludicrous thoughts, proof enough that the medicine was doing more harm than good! He relaxed; his mind made up, closed his eyes and slept.

**

"The garage is deserted, Davy," said Janice Longfellow.

254

"It's Sunday, dad doesn't work Sundays," replied the boy, eyeing the dilapidated single-story garage. "Dad tends to check it out in case there's been a break-in or vandalism. We always have a shuffty every Sunday, just in case."

"Anything worth stealing, Dave?" asked Joe.

"Of course," answered a sardonic Davy Duckworth, "I'm definitely going to steal from my own dad!"

"What about the petrol you nicked when we were raiding for bonfire," reminded Joe mockingly, "or your dad's big torch that you lost in the quarry?"

"That's different," said a defensive Davy, "they were just bits of shite!"

"Thought we might borrow a motor and drive down Andrew's Hill then take it back and your dad would never know?"

Bravado by the bucket-load from Joe Connelly, especially in front of the fawning females, never been behind the wheel of a car, clueless and cavalier with the thrill and passion of the females so close.

"Can you drive a car?" asked Miriam.

"Piece of cake," chortled Joe, glancing at Davy, praying he wouldn't give the game away, "three forward gears and one reverse!"

Davy intervened, "Lots of cars got four gears now, Joe," He smiled knowingly, "Dad's working on a Ford *Corsair* at the moment and it's got a gear-stick on the steering column!"

"Next to the steering-wheel?" spluttered Joe incredulously.

"Honest, Joe," replied Davy, "Dad reckons they're crap though, said they'll never catch on!"

They detoured around *Banktop Garage* and wandered idly down the gentle decline of the old roadway, minutes later they reached the first bend in the road as the single-track highway twisted, dipped and meandered towards the Maternity hospital and Little Thorpe. The vegetation was luscious either side of the tarmac, grasses and nettles wild and thigh high, trees and bushes followed the contour of the road with occasional tracks through the thicket to fields either side. The kids slowed as Joe Connelly took charge of the situation, "See you two in about an hour, eh?" he said with authority, looking directly at Davy Duckworth, "meet you here," gestured towards a rough path that skirted away from the road and led into a small patchwork of meadow and bush. Janice Longfellow, like a bitch on heat, grabbed her partner's arm and started down the hill, "Come on, Davy, we've only got an hour," and the pair sauntered away leaving Joe and Miriam alone.

"Give me a piggy-back, Joe?" said Miriam and gestured for the boy to turn away from her. He dutifully obliged and the lithe, slim poppet hoisted herself easily on to Joe's back, "Giddy-up!" she ordered, giggling like a child as they hurtled into the thicket, through the miniature meadow, past the first line of stunted trees and bushes and entered an opening into a vast corn-field.

"Okay here, Miriam?" asked Joe as he threw her to the grassy verge, squatted next to her writhing body and wondered how to start the game.

Miriam was smiling coyly, feigning modesty. "Let's talk first," she said. Didn't mean it, wanted her boyfriend to relax, didn't wish to appear too anxious to begin the foreplay, and certainly didn't want any repeat of the last sorry episode.

Joe's face stiffened as he heard the heavy thud of footsteps, "Shh!" he whispered, easing down on Miriam's welcoming body. "Shh!"

Miriam thought it was an act so she closed her eyes and whispered demurely, "Anything you say, Joe, you want me to pretend I'm asleep?"

"Listen," hissed Joe, alarmed, "there's someone on the road!"

Miriam twisted her face with obvious displeasure, thinking nerves had overtaken hormones in Joe Connelly's head. Sticking out her non-existent chest, she spat impatiently, "Of course! It's Janice and Davy looking for somewhere to sit!"

"Davy's wearing baseball-shoes, Janice was wearing sandals!"

The sound of footsteps grew louder and men's gruff voices echoed through the undergrowth. Miriam put her hand over her mouth and waited anxiously, her eyes wide and locked on the roadway.

"They've gone," whispered Joe, sighed and slumped next to the girl.

There was movement in the meadow as two tall figures made their way to the first line of trees, both were talking earnestly in hushed tones. Joe put a finger to his lips and glowered at the prostrate girl to keep still and not make a sound. Miriam clamped her eyes tightly shut and started praying, her heart banging like a big drum. Only yards separated the two sets of couples, a thick barbarous thicket of perimeter bushes the only barrier. The two men stopped, gazed about the place then, as one, squatted on the grass, leaned against a huge craggy oak tree, facing away from the line of hedgerow that hid the young couple.

Joe Connelly recognised both men. One was the old man who tried to accost him in the cinema months ago. He was talking loudly and there was something familiar about his voice, the tone was pitched and whining. Suddenly Joe recognised him, it was the pervert who had spied on them in the dene, recognised the voice when he and Miriam bolted from the clearing. He glanced at the girl and pointed through the tiny gap in the bushes, mimed, "That's the same man….!"

Miriam Roche nodded frantically; she too had recognised the fellow. Fearful now, silently nudging the boy, whispering, "Let's run!"

Joe shook his head, "Shh, listen."

Albert Mix's dad was talking now, loud enough for the boy to hear clearly. The man was conversing as if he were friends with the white-haired pervert. "Got to end this soon, Morris, we can't go on meeting like this." The other fellow, deep-voiced and determined was insistent about the friendship continuing, "Are we hurting anyone, Del? It's meant to be, you and me, can't you see that. After all those years apart we're still involved, we're still an item! Why stop a good thing?"

"Mildred will find out," barked the companion. "You know what's she's capable of, after all she's your damn sister!"

"Milly cares about no one but herself!"

"I'm not acting rationally anymore," insisted Delwin Mix, "It's Sunday, how many times can I pretend I need to walk and get my strength back? I've told her I'm not going back to work!"

"Forever?"

"Listen, Morris," blurted the fellow, clearly agitated, "this has to be the last time we meet. People are going to suspect. Those two kids we passed, did you see the weird looks we got?"

"All in your mind, Del," said Morris Buckingham wilfully. "Those youngsters were annoyed that someone was walking close to them. All they wanted was to be alone. They kept looking back at us, not because they saw two men walking together, but because they were disturbed!"

"I've my good name to protect," grunted Del Mix. "Got a wife and a child to consider!"

"They couldn't care less!"

"Don't say that, Morris, you're rubbishing your own sister," said Del Mix sternly." Albert," he said, "Albert needs me. I know we've had our disagreements but at the end of the day he's my son. And Mildred, well, she's stuck by me over the years, at least she's loyal! I simply can't turn my back on them now!"

"Idiot!"

Del Mix struggled to his feet, muttered, "There's no need to talk like that, Morris, no need at all!"

Morris Buckingham was adamant with his stinging reply. He growled, "You're an old fool!"

Del Mix started to walk back to the roadside, arms gesticulating, spitting blood at the continuous insulting remarks, said angrily, "I'm going, Morris!"

"Wait a moment," shouted Morris Buckingham, and he rose from the warm grass and followed the man. "I can tell you something about your precious wife that will change your mind about her!"

Behind the hedgerow, sighing buckets of relief, the two would-be lovers, watched the spectacle develop. Joe whispered, "Shall we stay or go, Miriam?"

"Stay?"

"Might hear something juicy, eh?"

"Yes," agreed the girl, parted a tuft of grass to get a clear view of the mounting disturbance. Nudged the boy and said, "Albert's dad a homo, or what?"

"The other one definitely is," said Joe in hushed tones. "But Albert's dad, well ... he's manager of the co-op store!"

"And he's married to a woman!" replied a confused Miriam Roche.

Joe nodded earnestly, said, "And he made Albert, don't forget!"

Miriam said, "I can't hear them, Joe."

Suddenly the two men started grappling with one another. Albert's stout, cumbersome father, suddenly found the vigour and the stamina to launch a two-fisted assault on his companion. Morris Buckingham, caught unawares, fell backwards under the onslaught, flaying arms and the manic fury of a revitalised Delwin Mix. The victim howled in pain as his nose burst like a geyser and he was punched and pulled to the ground. The pensioners landed in an untidy heap in the middle of the roadway, Del Mix the unlikely victor as he rolled off the prostrate wheezing, protesting figure of Morris.

"God," said Miriam with incredulity and wonder, "I wonder what he said to make Albert's Dad so mad?"

"Look," said Joe, "it's over!"

"Got no wind left!"

The two battling old-timers had stopped fighting, the hostilities over only seconds after starting. Sat next to one another on the ancient tarmac, heads lowered as they struggled for breath. Slowly, awkwardly they pulled themselves upright and stood facing each other.

"Do you think it's starting again, Joe?" asked Miriam, enjoying the novelty, the frolicking and passion forgotten about as she witnessed her first ever fist-fight.

"Jesus," gasped the boy, gaping open-mouthed with surprise through the gap in the hedge. "Look Miriam!"

Miriam gawked in astonishment as both men embraced and held one another in a lover's embrace, whispered, "Wait till I see Albert Mix!"

They watched as both men set off walking unsteadily towards the apex of Andrew's Hill. The taller of the two, Morris Buckingham, still bloodied, gesticulating and prodding the air with wild abandon, deep in conversation with the other man.

Someone whistled in the distance. Joe chuckled and said, "Davy's on the way back already!" stood tall, searching for his friend.

Miriam fumed with impatience and a new-found irritation, she growled, "He can bugger-off!"

"Let's see what he wants first, Miriam," said Joe and started waving at the two approaching figures chomping along by the hedgerow.

"Get rid of them, Joe!" grunted the frustrated girl.

Davy Duckworth reached them first, Janice, blowing like a bellows, face blotchy with perspiration, came in a close second.

"Are we off, Joe," asked Davy, a pained expression on his face. "Time to go home?"

"We've only got here," said Miriam, "what's the problem?" and looked at the friend.

Janice Longfellow shrugged her wide shoulders, pouted like a miserable lost soul, "Spat his dummy out didn't he!"

"Naw, I don't think so," replied her beau, arms welded on slim hips, spoiling for a battle. "It's all your fault, I've spent all that money on sweets for nothing!"

"It's your fault," insisted the dumpy diva, "you didn't have to tell me we're related!"

"What's that got to do with anything, Janice?" said Joe.

Miriam interjected, "What's going on, Janice?"

"We're cousins," said Janice, who tried in vain to cross her arms over her pendulous chest, gave up and fiddled with her fingers instead, "and you know what that means?"

"Oh, no," muttered Miriam Roche, "you're not related!"

Miriam had heard all about the dark and weird thoughts from her best friend, believed her implicitly. It was thanks to Janice's advice and guidance in such matters, Miriam had put an immediate stop to her brother Roy's evil ways. Bad enough having a baby when you were still at school, worse if you delivered a freak into the world. People who were related stayed away from each other. Janice told her it was in the bible, also told her she'd read an article in one of her mother's magazines that was hidden under the mattress and full of dirty pictures of couples *doing it* to each other in all kinds of kinky ways. Read it in black and white, brother and sister and even cousins should not *do it* or there'd be bad trouble with any baby that was born. Miriam didn't know for sure if Janice was exaggerating about kids being born with tusks or tails, wondered if she was trying to frighten her enough to keep her brother Roy's wandering willy from causing untold damage to her. Anyway she half-believed Janice Longfellow who hardly ever lied, well, not about things like that.

Davy muttered sarcastically, "My Auntie Beth is Janice's cousin, so, according to Godzilla here, we can't have a bit of fun or we might end up having three-legged, wall-eyed Cyclops!"

Janice was livid, "Godzilla! Me! How dare you call me names. That's awful!" She started to weep.

"Wouldn't even let me grope! After all the money I spent on her!" whined a frustrated Davy Duckworth. "I'm going home, are you coming Joe?"

"You're disgusting!" cried Janice, hiding her head in her hands.

"Wasn't disgusting when you asked to have a look at my Charlie," retorted the incensed boy. "Asked if you could rub it like a Genie's bottle and make it grow!"

"Shut up!" howled the embarrassed, crimson female.

"Wait will you, Davy," begged Joe Connelly, dejectedly. "Wait until those two men have gone."

Davy gazed along the meandering road and saw the men striding towards the A19 and the apex of Stockton Road. Nodded guardedly, he said, "I'll wait a minute, don't want to be caught by those two queers!"

"One was Albert Mix's dad!" said Joe, "and we've all been chased by the other freak!"

"Mucky Morris," retorted Davy Duckworth, "least that's what Ma calls him!"

"Albert Mix's dad bashed him!" said Joe. "Me and Miriam heard them talking. Albert's dad said he didn't want to see the other man again, ever!"

Miriam whined, "They're both homosexuals!"

"There's something strange going on between them," said Joe. "When I see Albert I'll tell him about his dad."

Miriam Roche approached her friend, wrapped an arm around the chunky frame, cuddled Janice, said sympathetically, "Stop crying, Janice, Davy didn't meant it."

"He did!"

Miriam glanced at Davy, "Say you're sorry, eh?"

Davy Duckworth had calmed enough to say, "Didn't mean it anyway, I was as horny as a toad! Would have been satisfied with a squint."

Janice Longfellow immediately sparkled, thinking, *Beggars can't be choosers.* She muttered quietly, "You could have had a look, Davy, I wouldn't have stopped you looking!"

Davy said, "Honest?"

"Of course!" replied Janice. It was only midday and there was still plenty of time to play games.

"What about after dinner," asked Davy. Checked his watch, it was almost noon and his mother was a stickler for mealtimes. "Say one-o-clock?"

Janice frowned, didn't want to wait another minute never mind an hour. Said reluctantly, "If you want."

Miriam looked at Joe, "Well?"

"I'm game," replied Joe Connelly, "One-o-clock it is. Meet at the form-seat in front of the church?"

The group agreed and started walking along the quiet road

Davy said, "Joe, do you think Albert's dad is a queer then?"

"Looked that way," Joe answered, "said they'd have to stop meeting in secret!"

Miriam said brusquely, "Tell Albert Mix about his sick dad, that'll shut his big gob shut. I can't stand Albert!"

Davy agreed, "Me too, he's nothing but a bully!"

Janice Longfellow interjected, "I wouldn't bother, I think Albert is a bit that way anyway. You watch him closely, always got his hand deep in his trouser-pockets.

263

Asked him one day, 'Albert what are you playing with?' Said he was jingling his change, 'More than money you're pulling,' I said."

Miriam asked, "What happened then?"

Janice pouted like a baboon, grunted, "He slapped me good and proper!"

"Typical of Albert," said Joe, "always picking on girls!"

Davy said, "Those men have gone," glanced at his pal. "Joe, come on, let's go for our dinner."

Joe Connelly nodded miserably, remembered, "Ma is out at the car-boot at Sedgefield."

"Come to mine," said Miriam, grinning widely, didn't want to lose sight of her boyfriend.

Joe took the bait, "Thanks, Miriam, I'll do that."

**

CHAPTER TWENTY ONE

Elmore awoke to the sound of argument. Struggling to his feet, he hurried up the long staircase, prised open the landing window and peered through the tree-line into his neighbour's home. The Mix family were barracking one another. Mildred, Delwin's obnoxious spouse, was prodding and pushing at her husband who stood, dishevelled, stone-faced and resolute. Elmore, voyeur extraordinaire, keen to hear the muck and gossip that for once wasn't directed at him or about him, stuck his head and shoulders out of the window and enjoyed the bedlam and mayhem of married life.

Mildred Mix bawled venomously, "How dare you insinuate such a thing!"

"I'm insinuating nothing," retorted the irate husband, arms arrogantly placed on hips, shirt torn open to the waist, pink tie adrift and a smudge of crimson covering his waxen features. Strong and resolute, he said loudly, "I'm telling the truth!"

"It's a blatant lie," shrieked Mildred, stomping her feet impatiently in temper on the concrete forecourt. "This is your way of getting out of a bloody hole." She pushed at him, "Last year the police said *you* were having a fling with that tramp next door! Either that or you were having a *homosexual* relationship with that pathetic excuse of a husband!"

Elmore Stoker's ears developed radar and he turned his head at right-angled to the fracas, wanting every morsel, every drop of tittle-tattle and scandal that related to his family.

"It's from the horse's mouth, Mildred!"

"Then tell me his name!"

Delwin Mix raised his voice to the rooftops, "All these years you had me convinced I'd slept with you! Carried the lie for a bloody lifetime! Conned me so well, Mildred! You are nothing but a scheming bitch!"

"I demand to know!"

"Demand to know what, the man who told me about you, or Albert's father?"

Suddenly the man lashed out and caught his wife flush in the face. The slap echoed to the skies, the sound barbaric and unreal as Mildred stumbled to the ground.

"There's one thing for sure," shouted the exasperated husband. "Albert comes from good stock! Mr Gilbert Stoker himself, the high and mighty psychiatrist!" Delwin Mix started gesturing towards the neighbour's home, howling to the heavens, "Same bloody stock as that lunatic Elmore!"

Elmore Stoker gasped with incredulity, eyes wide with disbelief.

"What are you saying?" stammered the quaking, beaten spouse.

"You didn't know, you really didn't know?" The man started walking round and round the fallen figure of his wife. Started cackling hysterically, "Thirty years ago," he bawled, "thirty one years ago," he corrected himself, "I was visited by Simon Stoker's father! Mr Gilbert Stoker himself, threatened me, said he would destroy me if I didn't stop seeing his precious son......"

Mildred interjected feebly, "So it was true!"

"Of course, you fool. You can't possibly think I loved you! The man threatened to expose and ruin me! And you know what! Do you want to know what happened, really want to know? Gilbert Stoker stood outside my door all those years ago and said he'd destroy me! You hear that, Mildred, destroy my life and reputation, said I'd never work in the area again! And then what does he do, he had a fling with Elizabeth Stoker! An affair with his own son's wife! Yes! Yes! Before you ask, Elmore was the result!"

Elmore's head went into orbit, pulled himself clear of the window and slumped to the floor of the landing. "My grandfather," he whispered hoarsely, "my grandfather!" shook his head trying to push away the weird images inside his head, didn't know if he was imagining the whole episode. He stood on trembling feet and made his way gingerly down the stairs towards the front door.

He turned slowly into the neighbour's driveway and stopped. The argument still raged but now appeared one-sided. Del Mix, like some demented soul, screamed and circled his broken wife, accusation after accusation as he shouted out of control. Never saw the young man as he started slapping at the woman's head.

"Your brother told me all about it!" shrieked Del Mix.

"Morris," moaned the woman, her head spinning as she tried to find excuses, "Morris told you, but how could he know …."

"Your mother told him!" interrupted the man. Spittle shot from his mouth as his temper spiralled out of control, "Had you forgotten? Remember Mildred, pregnant and running to your mother? Didn't know what to do! Think! Should have taken more care of your mother when she was ill and bedridden! No, too bloody preoccupied with your precious library as usual, left it all to Morris, didn't you? Well your mother never forgot your *kindness* all those years later when you were too busy to call on her, when she was ill!"

"My mum told Morris!" sobbed Mildred Mix. "How could she? My own mother!"

Delwin started mimicking his wife, pulled back the years as he re-lived the torture. *'I'm pregnant Daisy! Delwin will find out about Gilbert and me! My life is over!'* Walked manically around his stricken wife shrieking as he prolonged the side-show, "What did your mother tell you to do, Mildred? Shall I tell you what she said?" Started imitating Daisy Buckingham, *'Beggar is drunk every night you fool! Climb into his bed, the idiot will never know what he's done! He'll think it's his baby! Easy to outsmart a man, especially a drunkard!'* "

"I don't believe it," she sobbed, broken now, "my own mother!"

Footsteps echoed across the drive. Elmore, who had stood transfixed next to bushes, could not stay silent for a moment longer. The warring couple turned and faced him. Both wore expressions of horror as the young man approached.

"Hello, Mr Mix," said a morose Elmore Stoker, eyes wide with emotion, head surreally calm and collected. "Is it true?"

"Elmore," begged a worried Del Mix, glancing around for a possible getaway, "I don't want any trouble, please!"

"There will be no trouble," he retorted, "only want the truth. I've been listening for some time." Looked passionately at his unkempt, wheezing neighbour, "My grandfather was the only person who ever showed kindness to me, the only one who I thought loved me. If he is my father then I suppose I'll have peace of mind." He glanced at the bedraggled, squirming woman, "I have another brother too," he whispered, "it's so strange."

Delwin Mix sucked in air as he fought for control. Nodding warily he said, "You have a right to know, Elmore. Gilbert Stoker is your father. He had an affair with your mother and suffered the consequences. Blamed himself, always carried the burden of guilt until he died. As for Albert, my boy ... I think Elizabeth asked him to stop his son, Simon, from seeing me again." Glanced coldly at his wife and muttered, "I think that affair was pre-planned, and I think Albert was one way of destroying me in the eyes of your father. It worked. Your father, sorry, the man who you thought was your father, Simon Stoker, thought I was sleeping with my wife and never spoke to me again." He sighed loudly, miserably, "Until today I always

268

imagined Albert was my son. Always had my doubts because we, Milly and I, we were leading separate lives." He glanced coldly at his spouse, "Mildred fooled me and fooled everyone!"

The silence was earth-shattering as the trio stood perplexed and confused and uncertain as to what to do next.

Elmore stuck out his hand in a gesture of kindness, "I'm sorry we had to argue all those months ago," he whispered, "I wasn't myself."

Del Mix accepted the handshake but said nothing. Stood stiff with grief and watched Elmore Stoker slowly walk away. He glowered at his wife, passive and seated still.

"Listen to me," said Delwin Mix to his wife, his voice subdued and hoarse, "we can settle this amicably with no recriminations and no revelations." He paused for a brief moment before whispering, "Or we can destroy each other. The choice is yours."

"Albert is your son!" groaned Mildred half-heartedly, "I swear!"

"You've had your chance, Mildred," said a moribund Delwin, turned and started to walk back to the house.

"Wait, wait a moment, Delwin!" begged the woman. Her tone softened, her head lowered submissively, "Tell me your terms."

"Your mother's home in Hawthorn," said Delwin, "it's still up for sale. Take it off the market. I want to live there. You can remain here with Albert. I don't wish to see any of you ever again. The bank accounts, I want them splitting 70% and 30% in my favour, I'll open a new bank account in my name only. I have only a small pension and you are still working full-time. You have a wage, I don't. I choose what items of furniture I take. You can have the car. That's it, Mildred, no negotiation. You can tell people the marriage has broken down irrevocably. Tell them anything, I don't care."

"When are you leaving, Delwin?"

The man said, "I'll pack my bags now."

He turned and strode back to his home for the last time. Once inside he telephoned his brother-in-law, Morris Buckingham. Del Mix resolute and determined. From this day forward he would live his life to the full and damn the consequences.

**

Joe Connelly and his female companion turned into the cul-de-sac and observed the Morris *Oxford*. Joe muttered grudging, "Looks like I'll be eating at home!" Pulled his face knowing Uncle Mick would probably be still working on the fence in the back-garden, and be full of bile and piss.

Miriam asked hopefully, "It's still on for one-o-clock, isn't it, Joe, you promised?"

"Yeah, of course, wouldn't miss it for the world!"

They parted. Joe Connelly took a deep breath and walked towards his home knowing confrontation was high on the agenda.

Micky Green, Joe's uncle, sat comfortably on an old rickety chair in one corner of the small garden, hammer in one hand and a batch of long nails in the other. He smiled at the approaching boy.

"Well," he said stoically, "was it worth it?"

Joe acted dumb, "Don't know what you mean, Uncle Mick?" Remembered his lame excuse and said, "Davy Duckworth called just after you left. His dad had broken down, top of the village. Standard 10, flat battery, wanted a push-start."

Micky Green smirked. "Son," he chuckled, "you think I was never young? I saw you leaping over the garden fence just about the same time Miriam and her little friend hurried after you!"

Joe put his head down, chastised with guilt. "Sorry Uncle Mick," he muttered, "suppose Ma wants my guts for garters?"

"Not long back," he answered, aimed and whacked a nail expertly through the thin paling. Smiled infectiously, "I've not said a word about you," he said. "They're all in the house, dinner-time."

"Uncle Mick," said Joe enthusiastically, "you want to hear some gossip?"

"Makes the world go round, Joe," said the man, and threw the hammer and nails onto the grass. "Reckon that'll do until I've eaten."

Joe spent five minutes regurgitating the story and watched as his Uncle's mouth grew wider by the minute.

"Bloody hell," he said when Joe stopped. Rose from the rickety chair and muttered, "Wait till I tell Mary Jane!"

Joe said, "Shall I tell Ma?"

"You bet!" said the man as he ambled across the unkempt garden. "See you in a while, Joseph."

Jack appeared at the door, smiling at the sight of his big brother, "Joe, we got *Ludo, Chinese Chequers* and *Tiddly Winks!*"

Joe asked, "Did they get me anything, Jack?"

Jack glanced into the kitchen, at the boxes of goodies strewn across the table. "Three Airfix sets," he said, "a *Lancaster* bomber, a *Bentley* car and a ship, *The Victory.*"

Joe was ecstatic, wished now he'd gone to the Sedgefield car-boot, knew he could have persuaded Uncle Adam to part with more of his cash. He bounced in to the house, big grin over his freckled face.

Vera was bent over the sink, peeling potatoes; smiled at her oldest then continued with the task.

Joe said, "Where's Uncle Adam, Ma?" wanted to thank him for the presents. Touched and toyed with the Airfix sets, thought maybe he'd assemble the *Lancaster* first; show Jack how easy it was to construct.

"Popped to Horden, not be too long," said Vera. Started throwing thick carrots into the murky sink water, "Bought his mother a fireside-rug."

Joe offered, "He's okay Ma, isn't he."

"He's alright," replied the woman, her eyes lighting up.

"Ma," said Joe," when I was walking along Stockton Road ....."

"Thought you were helping Mick with the fencing?" interrupted Vera.

Joe repeated the lie, then added, "Saw that fella, Ma. Elmore something!"

"Elmore," said a surprised Vera, "must be feeling better."

"He's been ill, Ma?"

"You could say."

"He was on the conservatory roof of his house, looked fast asleep."

"Probably been working or repairing." She glanced at her mischievous son, "You haven't been cheeky to the man, have you, Joe. Elmore's been in the hospital you know!"

"Ma," continued Joe, "Albert Mix's dad is a queer!"

"Queer," said Vera, "you mean strange?"

"He was with Mucky Morris in Andrew's Hill! I think he's one of those homosexuals!"

Jack, agog with the gossip said, "What's a homosexual, Joe?"

"Shh!" reprimanded the brother.

Annie Goodrich appeared from the living-room, "Morris Buckingham?"

"What were you doing in Andrew's Hill, Joe?" asked Vera, stopped her work and started wiping her hands on a towel.

"Davy Duckworth's dad had broken down, Ma!" protested the boy. "We were pushing the car down the old road. Motor started and he drove down the hill leaving us to walk back to the garage on our own."

Vera Connelly said quizzically, "Delwin Mix was with Morris Buckingham?"

Annie Goodrich said, "They're related you know, our Vera. Del Mix married Morris's sister, Mildred, she runs the colliery library."

"Family business, maybe, Joe," offered Vera. Chuckled softly, "Can't see old Delwin changing allegiances, seems to me he's a rampant old Billy-goat. God he must have been fifty when Mildred got pregnant with Albert!"

Joe said, "Albert's dad said to the other man that they had to stop meeting in secret, said they'd be found out."

"Hell's teeth!" gasped Annie, "he actually said that?"

"Then they started fighting and Mr Mix bashed Mucky Morris then afterwards they cuddled each other and walked away!"

"Andrew's Hill, you say," muttered a curious Annie. "Mind it always was a meeting-place for young couples," she said. Pondered and reminisced for some moments before saying brusquely, "Aye, and there was always the odd bloody pervert hiding behind the bushes!"

Jack asked, "Nana, what's a pervert?"

"Shh!" said big brother.

"Barty and me done all of our courtin' around there. Either there or the dene at Little Thorpe.

Joe was one step ahead, "Ma, I was thinking about having a wander with Davy Duckworth after dinner. Might find out more information, eh?"

"Stay away from Andrew's Hill, my lad," warned the grandmother, "you might be grabbed!"

"Probably right, nana," said Joe craftily. "Might just play in Davy's house for a few hours."

**

273

Elmore awoke with the scrunch and bump of the back-door opening as the sound of voices invaded the interior of the house. His brother Evelyn had returned. They met in the kitchen, the same kitchen that was the scene of so much wilful wanton destruction months ago when the two brothers clashed. Evelyn and Alvin Brown were dumbfounded at the sight of the approaching Stoker, Alvin holding a clutch of unopened mail which he dropped like a pack of cards, his body quaking with anticipation and trepidation.

Elmore raised both arms in a submissive display, "Please let me talk, Evelyn! Please!"

Evelyn stood his ground, visibly trembling, the motley display of post like unwanted confetti about his feet. Visualising a repeat of the earlier incident Alvin Brown gawked and retreated behind his partner.

"What, what, what are you doing here, Elmore?" asked Evelyn, his stammer returning.

Elmore said softly, sincerely, "Evelyn, I needed a few days away from the hospital. The only place I could think of was here, our home. I'm going back to the hospital tomorrow, honest, Evelyn. I needed a few days peace."

"How long have you been here?"

"A few hours," said a contrite Elmore. "I've eaten and slept. I haven't mooched, I swear, Evelyn. Please let me stay until tomorrow. I've changed, I'm better now .... now that I know the truth about my parents."

The diary! Elmore has seen the diary! Evelyn wanted to run a mile, believing that his brother was feigning normality.

"You know the truth, Elmore?" asked Evelyn.

"I've been next door. Mr and Mrs Mix had a terrible row."

"I don't understand?"

"Delwin told me that my grandfather, Gilbert Stoker, had an affair with my mother. My grandfather is my father,

274

according to Mr Mix." He shook his head slowly from side to side. "Your father, Simon, apparently, was involved with Del Mix years ago. Grandfather warned and threatened him and then somehow ended up having a relationship with my mother. Oh, I almost forgot, twelve years ago my grandfather also had a fling with Mildred Mix, Del's wife. Young Albert was the result. Grandfather's way of ending the mayhem." He looked passively at his gaping brother, "Hard to believe, eh, Evelyn?"

Evelyn was lost for words.

"Delwin Mix is packing his bags," continued the younger brother, "he's leaving home." He suddenly realised that Evelyn was not showing surprise at the bizarre news. "You knew?"

"Few weeks ago," said Evelyn. "We, we, were decorating one of the smaller bedrooms, found, found, and found a diary. Well, well, the remains of a diary. I was going to destroy it because I thought, I thought...."

Elmore interjected, "You thought it would push me over the edge?"

Evelyn nodded but didn't reply.

"I feel better knowing the truth, Evelyn. My grandfather, my father loved me. Tried to show compassion as much as he was able. I honestly feel a weight has been lifted off my shoulders."

"You're in shock," said Evelyn carefully.

"No, just the opposite. All my life I wondered about my father, used to fantasize who it might be. Sometimes I'd be walking to school, going to college, and I'd see some tall chap, same hair colour, same built and I'd wonder if he were the one."

Evelyn turned and spoke to his partner, "Alvin, make a cup of tea for us all," glanced at his forlorn brother, said whimsically, "it's time to bury the past." He gestured to the sofa, "Shall we sit, Elmore?" picked up the handful of letters and followed his brother to the long settee.

Evelyn said, "I did call to see you at the hospital."

Elmore was incredulous; he had no recollection of any visits.

Evelyn said, "You didn't seem at all well."

"Medication!"

"You sang a lot," chortled Evelyn.

"I can remember singing but I thought I was hallucinating."

More laughter from Evelyn, "Could have been a professional."

"Mother seemed to think so, Evelyn."

Minutes past and both brothers fidgeted with discomfort. Then Alvin appeared carried in a large tray laden with tea and biscuits.

The trio made pleasant conversation, Evelyn especially felt as if a weight had been lifted off him. First time in an age that he had felt relaxed with his brother. As he talked Evelyn scanned the shoal of letters: gas bill, electricity bill, two brochures concerning dental products, a television licence reminder, and a letter addressed to Elmore Stoker.

"Elmore," said the brother, handing over the correspondence, "this is for, for, for you."

The letter was embossed with advertising highlighting the law practice of Jackman, Jackman and Steinman.

Elmore frowned as he accepted the mail. Said reluctantly, "Looks like my ship has come in and crashed on the rocks." Gazed for some moments before prizing open the envelope, "Probably the Hartlepool couple deciding to sue me." Studied the contents then said with grave resignation, "I have to call at their Easington branch tomorrow. Nine-o-clock prompt, I'm meeting Amos Steinman himself."

"Don't worry, Elmore, we'll sort it out between us."

Elmore sat quiet for a minute before folding the letter and pocketing it, "Evelyn," he asked cautiously, "could I see the diary?"

"I don't, don't, don't think you'll like it, Elmore," replied the brother. Glancing nervously at Alvin Brown, he added, "It's rather depressing. I don't think my, my, my father was well at the time. He wasn't writing rationally. Maybe another time, eh, give us all time to, to readjust?"

"I'd rather see it sooner than later," said Elmore, a determined look on his face. "Please, Evelyn?"

CHAPTER TWENTY TWO

"I can't see him," said Alice Raine, glancing with foreboding through the wide ancient fence that surrounded the graveyard.

"He might have climbed over the fence to see the frogs!"

"There's frogs in the graveyard, Jack?"

Jack Connelly pointed a grubby finger through the rickety fence, "See that other fence. Well, if we climb over that we'll see the big pond. Sometimes our Joe plays there. Last time we were here Joe tied fireworks to some frogs!"

"Why, Jack," whined the girl, "that's cruel!"

"Our Joe says frogs can't feel anything. He cut the front and back leg off a toad and watched it walk in a circle." Jack shook his head, "Said the toad would've screamed if it was hurt, but it didn't. It just walked round and round."

"Frogs can't talk," said the girl, "so how could it scream?"

"In frog language, maybe?"

"Your brother is awful!"

"Sometimes he's fun," said Jack, added poignantly, "but sometimes he's cruel."

They both stared through the fence; the place looked calm and pleasant. The sun bleached down over lush lawns, birds twittered and swooped and the graveyard didn't appear frightening at all.

"What shall we do, Jack?"

"Ma said Joe had gone to Davy's house, but no one answered the door. Thought they might be playing in the graveyard or the pond."

Alice Raine said hesitantly, "Aren't you frightened of graveyards, Jack. All those dead people buried under the ground?"

Jack answered lightly, "When you're dead, you're dead, Alice. Your lemon soul goes to heaven and that's the end of it!"

"Don't you mean *Heavenly Soul?*"

"I said *Heavenly Soul*, Alice!" clicked at the latch and the gate swung open, his face blushing with embarrassment. "Come on, we'll have a look about for Joe."

They ran across the grounds, reached the second perimeter fence and stared wondrously at the silent, stagnant pool. There was no one in the graveyard.

"Shall we read the words on the stones, Jack?" asked Alice, calm now that she was inside the place. Grasping the boy's hand she pulled him along the walkway of neat plots.

Some of the gravestones had photographs of the departed embedded on their fascias, which both fascinated and disturbed the girl. "Look, Jack," she gestured at one impressive black marble block showing a beautiful smiling woman, "she would have looked like that when she was alive."

"Wonder how she looks now?" inquired the boy.

Alice started counting on her fingers, "She'll look exactly the same as the picture, she's only been dead for five years!"

"When do they get horrible?"

"I think it's about a hundred years," said Alice knowingly.

A man strolled through the gate, arms held tightly to his chest holding some gift for a departed loved one. Smiling at the youngsters he began searching the myriad gravestones looking for a familiar name. Wandered aimlessly, eyes focussing, reading then moving along the green canopy until he came to a small neglected plot whose pots and jars were upturned and barren, whose grass was high, wild and forlorn. He stopped abruptly, stood transfixed and seemingly riveted to the spot and then stooped and touched the headstone delicately. The offering was placed upright against the headstone.

Alice watched from afar. She said, "His wife must have died!"

"Or his son or daughter!"

"I don't think he likes to come here, Jack."

"Why?"

"His wife's grave is all sad because no one ever visits."

"Might be scared of evil spirits! Maybe he thinks he can hear her calling to him from under the muck, '*Help me! Get me out!*' Things like that."

"Stop it Jack," said the girl, "you're frightening me!"

"Sorry, Alice."

She observed the stranger wiping at the accumulated filth on the headstone, "He's not frightened at all," she said, "he's cleaning up all the mess."

Jack asked, "Why bring a present to someone underneath the ground?"

The boy watched the antics of the man, half expecting a putrid, bony hand to emerge slowly from the earth. Normally fearful but on a summer's day like today with the sun scorching and not a cloud in the brilliant blue sky, birds singing and swifts darting and diving for the myriad of flies that drifted from the stench of the nearby pond into the wide expanse of the graveyard, the fear less real, the reality of the final resting-place less grim.

"It's a book," gasped Alice. "He's going to tell her a story so that she won't be lonely!"

"How can she hear, Alice?" said Jack, "she's dead."

"Shall we go over?" said the girl, mesmerised by the sight, gazing at the tall stranger now squatting comfortably next to the plot, the text in his hand. "He might let us listen to the story?"

"Might be a ghost story?"

"Shut up, Jack, you can stay if you want," said a determined Alice Raine, "I'm going!"

Alice led, Jack followed sheepishly.

"Hello," said the man, smiling kindly at the approaching urchins, "are you lost?"

Alice said, "We can't find Joe or Davy. We thought they'd be at the pond." She pointed in the direction of the rancid pool, "where the frogs and toads and tadpoles live."

"Joe and Davy?"

"My brother is Joe," answered the boy uncomfortably. "Davy Duckworth is his friend." Jack grinned at the man who seemed nice, not like some grown-ups who were nasty and were always shouting. "Sammy McAndrew and Ernie Bracken are Joe's other friends and they're called the *Top-Enders* because we live at the top of the village and they fight with the *Bottom-Enders* who ...."

"Let me guess," chortled the man, shifting his position and leaning on the side of the gravestone. "The *Bottom-Enders* and they live at the bottom of the village?"

Jack nodded enthusiastically.

"Your brother Joe has his own gang," enthused Elmore. He gestured to the pair to join him, the flat of his hand smoothing the grass. "Sit down the pair of you," he said. He mused whimsically, "I had a gang when I was small," and pointed away from the burial ground, his finger stabbing at the air, "Across the road. Between the houses and the back of the churches there's a small garth, a bridleway which leads to the Infant school? Our gang was called the *Garth Gang.*"

"Mister," interjected Alice, grinning, "that's our school too." Glanced at the boy who was sitting on the opposite side of the grave, "Isn't it, Jack?" she said, then plonked her small frame close to the man, and started subconsciously preening her skirt.

"Mrs Wainwright is our teacher," said Jack, "she's a woman and she's nice to us."

"Was Mrs Wainwright your teacher?" asked Alice. Started plucking daisies and dandelions and held them in her hand like some miniature bouquet.

"No," answered the fellow. He picked up the booklet that had been resting against the headstone, "My school was in Durham," he muttered, "a private school." He seemed preoccupied with the book, staring intently at the cover, turning it round and inspecting it more, lost in thought, forgetting about his young invited guests.

Alice asked, "Is your wife dead?"

"Shh!" reprimanded Jack.

The man's gaze wandered from the book to the gravestone, "It's my father," he whispered.

Jack and Alice looked at one another then back to the fellow who was now opening the text.

"Why have you got that book, Mister?" asked Jack Connelly, "does it belong to your dad, is that why you brought it"

"Is it a story-book?" asked Alice Raine.

The big man glanced from one to the other and smiled warmly. Moments past before he seemed to grasp their queries, "Story-book," he whispered, "I suppose it is a story-book."

Alice beamed, asked politely, "Can we listen?"

The man looked surprised, unable to comprehend, "Listen?"

"To the story," said the poppet. "When you tell your daddy a story can we listen?"

Elmore Stoker gawked at the girl then glanced affectionately at his father's headstone. All his adult life he had imagined Gilbert Stoker had been buried in Durham. His practice was based there; his palatial home was in Neville's Cross on the western boundary of the city, his last painful years in a nursing home in Belmont, close to the city centre. For years he had rested a stone's throw from his true son. *'He did it for me,'* mused Elmore, *'wanted to be close to me so that I would visit him. All these years and I imagined Durham.'* Elmore felt the deep discomfort of dishonour for not having attended the funeral of the only person who truly loved him. Whispered softly, "I'm sorry father, I'm truly sorry."

The fellow relaxed and spread out his long legs for comfort, an odd look spread over his face as he opened the booklet. Glanced at the children, open-mouthed with wonder, and looked at the first page, scanned it, flipped it over, then the next, his head shaking slowly from side to side with a morbid fascination as he deciphered and imagined. Saw the scrawl and scratch of the print and imagined the tortured state of the man who had composed it. Elmore Stoker looked again at the final entry in the diary, **August 21. I have decided to kill my father,** understood why his brother was reluctant to show him the grim, unpalatable truth. Simon Stoker, Evelyn's perverted father, had tried to kill Gilbert Stoker, his father, Elmore's father. Pushed him down a flight of stairs in an attempt to end his life. Evelyn had told him as much, Evelyn and his homosexual lover, sitting either side of Elmore, busy bees fitting the Stoker jigsaw mystery together, regurgitating ancient stories and half-truths, Evelyn lax and lenient when he spoke of the tragedy. *'Blood thicker than water,'* thought Elmore as he sat passively, assimilating all the information, Evelyn and Alvin, coy yet determined as they threaded a thin line between historic fact and conjured fantasy. Elmore between the sandwiched twosome, as they occasionally fed off one another, glancing and smiling as their stories matched, all the while thinking of them enjoined, together, as if it were right and proper. Imagined them fondling and kissing one another, Elmore's aching head awash with lurid thoughts. "Not normal," he said softly, "it's not normal behaviour."

"Mister," asked an impatient Alice, "are you all right?"

Elmore came out of the stupor, his mind wafting and waning gently, and smiled at the children, the captive audience, who sat, arms folded full of expectation and promise. He glanced at the diary and then at the infants.

Elmore said solemnly, "You want to listen to my story children; you really want to hear my story?"

Jack glanced at his companion. They nodded simultaneously.

Elmore Stoker took a deep breath of air, momentarily closed his eyes and witnessed the myriad images shunting before him, fairy-tale pictures with bold lettering glowing brightly from beneath the print. He opened his eyes and gasped, before him were illustrations, vivid and garish, a gaudy cinema-show illuminating and seducing him. Elmore rubbed his eyes in amazement: either side of the pictures sat the children, watching him, waiting for the enchantment to commence.

Elmore croaked, "Shall I begin, children?"

They nodded eagerly, their eyes filled with the expectation of magic.

"Once upon a time," said Elmore Stoker, "a long time ago ...."

Jack Connelly interjected exuberantly, "I love stories that start like that!"

"Shh!" hissed the girl, glanced and grinned approvingly at the stranger, nodding for him to continue.

The man smiled warmly and felt strangely at peace with the world. He was finally going to tell everyone about the trials and tribulations of the Stoker family. He nodded excitedly at the thought of dismantling the lifelong burden, glanced at the children, and decided he'd use a parable to explain his story.

"Once upon a time, a long time ago, in a land ruled by the good and courageous King Gilbert ...."

I've never heard of a king called Gilbert,n thought Jack. *King David, King John, King Kong!*

Alice Rained frowned and looked at Jack who sat cross-legged, head resting contentedly on hands, seemingly captivated by the soothing tones of the stranger. The girl folded her arms across her chest, full of expectation and promise and waited for the story to continue.

**

CHAPTER TWENTY THREE

Elmore felt refreshed and relaxed as he washed and dressed, pleased of his brother's generosity and good faith. The third bedroom, his old room, was as he had left it, even refilled the walk-in wardrobe courtesy of Agnes Lincoln who must have returned all of Elmore's personal stuff. He smiled as he recalled the girl, wondered if she had also returned the jewellery he had given her, chortled softly, bet his bottom dollar she had claimed the antique presents for her own, *A girl after my own heart,* he mused. Thought he might call on her when he was finally discharged from Winterton Hospital. He looked at his image in the mirror and knew he was on the road to recovery.

He crept past the main bedroom. It was early still and Elmore knew his older brother would be fast asleep. The bedroom-door was slightly open, peered inside and shook his head at the sight of his brother and his lover intertwined on the double bed. *A picture of paradise,* thought Elmore. Evelyn and Alvin wore matching crimson silk pyjamas, *Every picture tells a story!* He recalled a conversation the previous evening, Alvin acting all prudish and demure, "Early days, Elmore," he had said before retiring to bed. "Evelyn and I are still friends. If anything develops, so be it, but at the moment our relationship is purely platonic." Elmore didn't believe it last night and the proof was in front of him. *Live and let live,* he thought resignedly.

Evelyn had been so thoughtful allowing him to borrow the motor. Perhaps there was to be a long-term armistice between them with no more petty squabbles and spats. Elmore grabbed the car-keys and left the house, unlocked the *Jaguar* and climbed inside. Sat for minutes, relishing the luxury of the plush, pristine limousine, smelled the deep aroma of leather and money. Elmore thinking perhaps he had misjudged his brother.

He reversed into Stockton Road, drove carefully through the cut of the village green, slowed then braked when the chunky *lollipop* lady stuck her sign at him telling him to stop. Toyed with the radio as a posse of schoolchildren ambled and ran across the minor roadway, recognised the small boy hanging on to the coat of his older brother, little boy who he'd spoken to at the cemetery, couldn't recall his name but smiled and waved.

Jack Connelly returned the greeting, "Joe," he said to his brother, "that's the man who was talking to Alice and me yesterday."

"The man in the graveyard?" asked Joe as he recognised the driver.

The Council Man, thought Joe, *the drunk who was staying next to Sammy McAndrew's house in Thorpe Road? The same horrible man who tried to embarrass him in Trotter's fish-shop months ago, who bashed Albert Mix's dad, who was sun-bathing on a roof in Stockton road yesterday.*

"He had a storybook at the graveyard and was talking to his dead dad who had once been a king!"

"A king?"

Jack pouted, "If you don't believe me ask Alice Raine."

"What have I told you about talking to strangers, Jack?" harangued Joe Connelly, pushing at his perplexed brother. "You must never talk to strange men!"

Jack trembled and started to sniffle. He hated confrontation and stress, especially with his big brother. "I'm sorry, Joe," he stammered, "I was looking for you."

Joe Connelly immediately filled with remorse and guilt, knowing he had lied and deceived in order to make the rendezvous with the vixen, Miriam Roche. Sandwiched between his mother and grandmother at the time, coerced into looking after baby brother, and easing Jack into a false security, "I'll go for Davy Duckworth, Jack. You finish

287

your dinner and I'll be back in a flash. We'll play at the pond, I'll catch some newts for you and you can show them to the teacher tomorrow." A blatant mistruth so that he could steal away and enjoy some time with the luscious Lolita. Gone three long hours and his life was transformed forever. Couldn't get the images and the feelings out of his head, never slept a wink all night as he regurgitated and relived the ecstasy and the heavenly union with the wicked, wily Miriam Roche, his childhood and innocence gone in an instant and his life remoulded and reshaped, never to return.

Joe said, "My fault, Jack."

He was contrite and ashamed at abandoning his only brother but felt so weak and defenceless at the sensuous thoughts that bombarded his head. Wanted to explain to Jack but knew it was hopeless. He grimaced, torn between the feeling he held for his sibling and the powerful magical powers emanating from the young siren. Torn in two with the contrasting emotions of blood and family, self-satisfaction and lust.

The school-crossing patrol woman waved the stationary traffic forwards and the plum-coloured *Jaguar* zoomed silently away, the driver still eying the boys.

Joe looked towards the Norman church that dominated the high ground of the village. The big clock on the bell-tower read 8.45am, the graveyard was minutes away; troubled and curious enough to beg a favour from his naïve brother, he had to see the place

"Will you show me the grave, Jack?" asked the older brother, "we'll not be late for school."

"Why, Joe?"

"Come on," said Joe and darted towards the *Half Moon* junction and the old Durham road that led to the cemetery.

A solitary council employee was pushing at a noisy lawn-mower at the far edge of the graveyard, looked momentarily as the two boys entered the grounds then continued trimming the lawns. Jack led the way and Joe followed.

Jack stopped next to the plot, his features registering confusion, "That's the one, Joe, but it's different."

Joe shrugged his shoulders, "Different?"

"It was empty, Joe," said the small boy, and gazed uncomfortably at the mound of garish wreaths and garlands and flowers that littered the plot. "There wasn't one flower yesterday!"

Elmore Stoker had spent time the previous day collecting prize exhibits from nearby graves. There was nothing he wouldn't do for his father.

Joe Connelly looked at the headstone, said softly, "Gilbert Stoker, that must be his dad."

"That was the name of the king," said Jack, "King Gilbert." His eyes fell on the prize sticking out from beneath a beautiful garland of flowers, "Look, Joe, there's the book of fairy-tales."

Joe grabbed the ancient diary; a name embossed across the front cover, said, "It belonged to someone called Simon Stoker."

Jack became excitable and started tugging at this brother's coat. "Prince Simon was his evil son who could only make evil children," he said, his tone edged with emotion. "That's why the queen was sad when nasty Prince Evelyn was born and asked the old king to give her a proper baby!"

Joe Connelly was half-listening, turning the few pages, the diary entries incomprehensible to him, "Someone has torn most of the pages out!"

"Is it the fairy-story, Joe?"

"I can't understand it," said the older boy, then he read the very last sentence, said out loud, *'I have decided to kill my father.'*

Jack asked, "What do you mean, Joe?"

"The man who wrote this said he was going to kill his father!" Confused, Joe Connelly was about to close the booklet when he absently flipped over the final, blank page, didn't expect there to be any more writing. On the back cover of the diary someone had scrawled almost illegibly, the message simple and chilling, child - like and finger-dipped with a cherry-red paste:

Vengeance is mine

The prince will avenge the damage inflicted on the good king.

"Bloody hell!" gasped Joe as he read again the message.

"Joe," retorted Jack, "Ma finds out you're swearing again she'll belt you good and proper!"

Joe Connelly grabbed at his brother, "Come on Jack," he said, his voice pitched with emotion, "we got to go see Ma!"

"Joe, we'll be late for school, we'll get into trouble!"

"No we won't," replied Joe.

He pulled his brother from the cemetery, pushing him through the open gate, "In fact Ma will come with us to the school." There was no way Joe would face Mr Albright without the presence of his mother. Joe had a sneaky suspicion neither he nor his kid brother would have to attend school that day.

"Why Ma?"

"To show her the diary!"

"What's a diary, Joe?" said the confused mite, adding, "thought it was a book of fairy tales."

"A diary is used to write names and places you've seen."

"I don't understand, Joe?"

They stalled at the *Half Moon* junction while traffic buzzed past, Joe said, "If you kept a diary, a book, you'd write in today, *Monday, went to the graveyard with Joe, then went to school.*"

"That's stupid, Joe!" started mimicking, "*Dinner-time, had dinner then had a pee then played, then went to lessons!* Stupid, Joe!"

The traffic eased and the boys hurried across the road and past a middle-aged woman who nodded a greeting at the pair. Rosemary Bott, mid thirties and still unmarried, lived in Craig View, a few streets away from the boy's home in Passfied Square. Although several years older than the boy's mother, Rosie and Vera Goodrich had shared the same school and were on friendly terms. Rosemary liked Vera although never keen on her flirtatious, arrogant husband, George Connelly. A few years earlier, Rosie and her aged, infirm mother were on a rare night out socialising in the *Shoulder of Mutton* and George, safe out of Vera's radar, started making all kinds of snide and personal suggestions to her. Didn't like him then, didn't like him now, heard they had separated and she was genuinely pleased for Vera's sake. Nobody needed a cocksure, pathetic excuse like George Connelly for a husband.

Rosie wondered where the boys were going, certainly wasn't school, shrugged her shoulders and continued on her way. She used to work as a barmaid at the *Liberality Tavern,* opposite side of the road to the *Kings Head,* worked there until her widowed mother had her first stroke, gave up the evening work and started cleaning around the village. The money wasn't worth shouting about but she had her nights free and could look after her parent.

Rosie hurried along Stockton Road towards the Stoker house. She had cleaned there for the past two months, Monday and Friday mornings. Liked Evelyn Stoker, slipped her a few extra quid most weeks. The little dentist must have found a girlfriend judging by the recent decorating and the subtle changes to the big house, felt warmer these days, extra pictures on the walls, the occasional flower arrangement in the double bedroom, and the bulging fridge, once a barren and destitute place, now choc-a-block with food and drink. The quiet and reserved Evelyn never mentioned he was seeing anyone so Rosie played along with the charade, none of her business, only knew the change had lifted the man's spirits because he would talk freely to her, as if the stammer was irrelevant, laughing and jesting with her, like a man reborn was Evelyn, the speech impediment unimportant, acting like a man in love.

Using her key Rosie Bott unlocked the door and marched inside, three hours heavy work ahead and she thrived on it, entered the plush kitchen, into the pantry, now adapted for bric-a-brac and household appliances, grabbed the vacuum-clean, top-of-the-range *Electrolux* brand and carried it deftly to the staircase. Rosemary had a routine, believed everyone should have a routine, master-bedroom first, dusted then vacuumed, windows cleaned and polished, followed by the smaller bedrooms, which took a fraction of the time because they were rarely used, then it was the bathroom and the toilet, then the stairs. Top storey of the palatial home took approximately an hour; the rest of her time was spent downstairs. Routine! Routine!

Rosie walked briskly into the main bedroom then froze as she saw the horror. The vacuum-cleaner fell from her quaking hands and her head spun with the macabre sight before her. On the double-bed were two bloodied, naked men, quite dead, one on top of the other as if they were copulating. Evelyn's battered and bruised body lay under his companion, unseeing eyes focussed on Rosemary, legs wide apart, arms manipulated around his lover's back, wrists bound so that he was forever tied to Alvin Brown. The bodies coated with a copious sheen of smeared blood, the mattress soaked crimson with blood and excrement and urine. The stench was vile and overpowering.

Rosemary slowly, fitfully retreated from the room, only when she was clear of the repulsive, disgusting ghoulish sight did she finally scream and cry, running across the landing, down the stairs like some Olympian athlete, into the living-room, grabbing the telephone, wailing dementedly at the operator, "Help! Help me, please! There's been a horrible murder!"

"This had better be good, son!" barked Vera Connelly, her features grim with surprise at the return of her two sons.

The young mother was perspiring. Heavy clouds of sweat clung to her body as she worked, the small kitchen upside-down with untidiness, pyramid piles of washing scattered about the surface of the linoleum floor: sheets, whites, coloured, cottons, silks, all allocated their own special mound. Monday morning was washing-day and mayhem and irritation was guaranteed all day long. The *Hoover* twin-tub howled and whirled next to Annie Goodrich. The grandmother toiled over the ancient mangle, the second-hand *Acme* wringer, feeding the machine, heaving and twisting the protesting handle. Seeing Joe and Jack looming by the open door, she eased and straightened and waited for an explanation.

Joe handed over the diary belonging to the long-dead physician, Simon Stoker, passed it over and spoke quickly about the events of the morning, mentioned Jack's encounter at the graveyard as he tried to recall everything of relevance. The Hoover was switched off and Vera inspected the booklet, left the bedlam of the kitchen and wandered into the living-room. Annie Goodrich threw the fag-end into the garden and followed her daughter, gestured for the boys to follow, her face stiff and unbending. "This had better be good," she muttered as she fumbled in her skirt-pocket for the cigarettes and matches, "or woe-betide you two!"

Vera stood with her back to the belching, crackling coal-fire, one hand holding and reading the contents, the other hand hoisting her skirts so that the warm of the grate touched her thighs. Her eyes darting over the heart-rending confessions from a broken man, enthralled and bewitched by the script. Offered it to her mother, "Bloody hell, Ma," she gasped, "you've got to read this!"

Joe said sternly, "Ma, you haven't finished, turn to the back page!"

"There's only three pages altogether, Joe. I've read it all."

Joe insisted, "The back cover Ma!"

Vera let her skirt fall to her knees and opened the diary again, flipped the few remaining pages and inspected the back binder, blinked at the message, touched and caressed the surface of the book. Handed it to Annie Goodrich and said, "What do you make of that, Ma?" ran fingers over the rough ridged surface of the script.

Annie grimaced and read the grim warning from Elmore Stoker,

"'Vengeance is mine. The prince will avenge the damage on the good king,'" shook her head with obvious scepticism and started reading the contents of the diary.

"This was on a grave?" asked Vera.

Joe said impatiently, "Ma, I've told you about yesterday! Our Jack and Alice were in the graveyard looking for me when they saw that man you used to like … Elmore? He was sitting next to a grave and reading from that book. Ma, he told them a story!"

Jack offered his recollections, "Told me and Alice about the wicked Price Evelyn!"

Joe said, "Tell Ma about the good Prince Elmore!"

Annie gasped, looked horrified, muttered to her daughter, "Think you were mistaken about Elmore being released early from the hospital, Vera. I think he's escaped!"

Vera Connelly bit her lips, glanced at the mother and said, "Ma, that last entry, it's not like the rest. Touch it Ma, feel the writing, it's definitely not a pen that's been used!"

Annie Goodrich opened the diary, caressed the script, "Reminds me of finger-dipping at school, you know, Vera, using your fingers instead of a pen."

"It's blood, Ma," whispered Vera, "the message has been written in blood!"

Jack left his brother's side and snuggled up into his mother's skirts, his features ashen.

Vera stroked his head, "It's alright, Jack, there's nothing for you to worry about."

Joe asked, "Has someone been killed, Ma?"

Annie Goodrich grunted, "Don't be stupid. Elmore has lost his bloody marbles is all."

"You really think so, Ma?" asked Vera.

"Honey, this is Easington Village not Hollywood. Hell's fire, Walt Disney it isn't!"

Vera asked grimly, "What shall we do, Ma?"

Joe said, "Phone the police, Ma!"

**

A little after nine-thirty Amos Steinman, one of several partners of the law practice of Jackman, Jackman and Steinman, walked briskly to the large window that looked down into *Seaside Lane*, the main shopping street in Easington Colliery. His father, long departed to that great practice in the sky, was one of the original founders of the firm, which in a matter of ten short years had quadrupled in size, prestige and capital. A single decade had seen the partnership acquire firms in Durham, Sunderland and Newcastle as well as two colliery districts, Murton and Coxhoe, all thanks to the drive and the determination of the nephew of another of the co-founders and heir apparent, Nathanial Jackman.

Amos Steinman, seventy three years old and as fit as a proverbial fiddle, could have moved to a more prestigious office in one of the larger complexes, indeed was asked by Nat Jackman to head the Durham Branch but declined the generous offer. Too long in the tooth, Amos wanted a few more years of coasting before hanging up his ledgers to dry. Fresh out of law-school a lifetime ago, Amos had dealings with the Stoker family, indeed had worked for some time with Gilbert Stoker himself. He still recalled the bitterness when, as executor to the Stoker estate, he read the last will and testament of the old man, and remembered passionately the ructions and recriminations from his only son, Simon, and his most unpleasant wife, Elizabeth. The pair had caused an awful scene in this very office. Shook his old head as he recalled the distasteful and malicious accusations from the spiteful couple, looked down and smiled benignly at the street scene below.

Elmore Stoker, second son of Simon and Elizabeth Stoker stood awkward and stiff, the correspondence from Gilbert Stoker still gripped like a vice in his hand. Leaning against the *Jaguar* car, enthralled and captivated by his good fortune, Elmore stood and gawked at the letter from his father, his head in turmoil with the unexpected development. He had imagined that the request to attend the law offices would mean more humiliation and disgrace, thought Hartlepool Council, his ex-employer, was ordering him to face a court judgement against the abusing couple whose lies had already cost him his job as a social worker.

He glanced at the first-floor window of the law-office and saw the shadow of the solicitor standing behind the thin net curtains. He smiled and gave a wave, a grateful wave of thanks. Minutes earlier he had floundered like a fish out of water, shaking with disbelief at the shower of good fortune soaking him to the skin, listening as the lawyer, looking like a benevolent Methuselah with his long white hair and parchment skin, listed Elmore's newfound assets. Amos Steinman, features solemn, old eyes sparkling, informing Elmore of his inheritance, his just rewards: "Wimpey shares, ordinary and preference, amounting to £26, 000, Rank Xerox, cumulative preference, current value, £22, 500, Procter and Gamble, ordinary shares, £22, 000, British Leyland, cumulative preference shares, £7, 200. Furthermore there is in total, £99, 600 in Bearer Bonds and a named savings account with accrued interest annually compounded totalling £14, 800. All yours, Mr Stoker!"

Elmore gazed long and hard. It was difficult to grasp. He had made it, achieved his goal. He was rich, so rich he could hardly believe the change in his luck. His father, his sweet, blessed father had rescued him from oblivion in the gutter of life. Elmore grinned and watched the people hurry past, little people little lives; cars and buses hurtling by, busy, busy. The scene slowly changed before his eyes ... became a portrait, a landscape, and then a miniature picture as he focussed and fought the weariness. Struggled to focus and fit the key to the vehicle-door. He somehow managed to squeeze into the dinky-car and sat stunned and shocked as the world shrunk before his disbelieving eyes. Something was happening to him. He felt unsteady and desperately tired, closed his eyes and prayed for help.

He did not know how long he sat there, only that the sharp, painful tapping on the side-window startled and woke him. Elmore noticed the beautifully manicured, ancient hand, nails perfectly shaped and gleaming like pearls and contrasting with the dark blemishes that tattooed the back of the hand and he realised the fellow disturbing him was old. The thick, gnarled gold rings, on the man's index and small finger looked odd, eccentric even, especially on one so ancient. Looked at the features, registering alarm and confusion and saw the solicitor, Amos Steinman, speaking incoherently at him. Fellow looked what he was, a flamboyant, long-haired, intellectual who had seen it all and had come out smiling and better for the experience. Elmore gawked at the image before him, man so close yet so far away, knew the fellow was next to him and yet it was as if his mind was playing games because the solicitor looked a miniature caricature of himself. Rubbing his eyes with trepidation and disbelief, as if knowing the outcome, he slowly wound down the window and heard the man talking out of sync, voice booming yet low, reverberating and echoing through the vehicle, surreal and scary.

Elmore pushed open the door, knew he had to find some fresh air to lift the fatigue that seemed to resonate through his aching body. Frightened and alarmed at the way his brain was foxing him he pushed and struggled to free himself of the dilemma, "You're not making sense, man," he heard himself say, "is there something wrong?" Saw the minuscule, gesticulating Steinman drifting even further away from his vision. A crowd was starting to gather, close and yet distant, saw all the puzzled gaping faces as clear as day and yet they all seemed miles away. He panicked and shouted, "What's the problem, will you please tell me what you want?"

Amos Steinman appeared to grasp one of his arms, then a stranger, big and burly and wearing a ridiculous flat cap over oily locks, cigarette dangling perilously from one corner of his toothless mouth, grasped his other arm. Elmore started to panic, noticed that his coat and shirt were missing, standing there like some half-baked circus clown wearing only vest and trousers, panic replaced by dread and alarm because he had no recollection of removing his clothing. Horror descended on Elmore, torturing him because all he could perceive about him ...the people, shops, even the vehicles trundling past were minuscule and distant. In an act of desperation he pushed at the old man who disappeared in an untidy heap and back-handed the collier who quickly retreated.

Free of the confines and human shackles, Elmore stepped into the road. Knew he had to get away from the growing nightmare, heard people shouting and calling, horns blaring, all too much to assimilate, a multitude of alarmed voices rising in volume, the noises as traffic snarled and ground to a halt, whistles, calls, horns, folks shrieking out his name. *'Elmore! Come on, Elmore, you can do it one more time, please, Elmore.'* He suddenly realised what he had to do to ease the situation. Fool he was, should have known what to do, easy as falling off a tree, cleared his voice, spoke for a few moments to the audience and then began to sing. His first song, so special, for someone precious to him.

Oh mein papa,
To me he was so wonderful,
Oh mein papa,
To me he was so good ....

**

CHAPTER TWENTY FOUR

The rain splashed and sloshed against the window-pane and both boys closed on one another in the bed, back to back, Joe talking like a parrot, feeding Jack the gossip. Heavy blankets up to their nostrils, the chill of the big bedroom like the inside of a fridge, Joe Connelly, the proverbial yoyo, up and down the stairs for hours, eavesdropping behind the closed door, listening to the talk and chatter. Five minutes pretending he was a diminutive private-eye, the next five minutes snuggling up to his kid brother, telling tales, purposefully omitting the more gruesome titbits so as not to upset or unhinge Jack.

Jack quizzical, thinking his big brother was teasing and testing him, "Ma's friend is called Rosie Bott?"

"Swear to God, Jack," replied Joe, only his eyes above the heavy trawl of blankets, the night surprisingly chilly and uncomfortable, "she's called Rosie Bott."

"Why?"

"Haven't a clue, Jack," said Joe, shivering despite thick winter pyjamas, vest, underpants and woollen socks, middle of Summer felt like Winter, only thing missing was the snow. "Maybe her dad used to be a comedian! I don't know. Now, do you want to hear the chat or not?"

"Okay."

"The woman called Rosie used to clean at that man's house, you know, that man in the graveyard, called Elmore, remember? Well, he lived with his brother in Stockton Road. His brother was called Evelyn."

Jack snapped excitedly, "Prince Evelyn and Prince Elmore!"

"Sort of."

Confused, Jack asked, "So the story was pretend?"

"I think everything was pretend to Elmore," said Joe. "The last time I listened downstairs, I heard Adam say Elmore has a screw loose in his head!"

Jack said poignantly, "Ma said our Dad had a tile loose too!"

Joe answered firmly, no nonsense, "Ma was upset with Dad, didn't really mean the things she said about him."

"She didn't?"

"Of course not, Jack. That's why she went all the way to Yorkshire to see him!"

Jack started to think about the strange events of the previous day, Alice Raine and he spellbound as they listened to the surreal story, the fairytale regurgitating inside his head, remembered the strange word used by Elmore, the story-teller. He asked, "What's a momosexual, Joe?"

Joe corrected him, "You mean a homosexual?"

"Yeah, what's one of those?"

"Why?" asked Joe impatiently.

Jack retorted, "Because when that man in the graveyard told the story he said all nasty people turned into them!"

"Into what?"

"Homosexuals!" grunted an agitated Jack. "In the fairytale the Queen asked King Gilbert to make her a proper baby because her new husband, Prince Simon was *one* and when their first son was born, Prince Evelyn, he was *one!* Both of their bodies were full of homosexual blood, from their toes to their tongues! *That's* why the Queen begged for a proper baby from the old King. *That's* why Prince Elmore was made!" Jack sucked in a lungful of cool night air and repeated his query, "So what's a *homosexual,* Joe?"

Joe said, "Homosexuals like men more than woman."

"Honest, Joe?"

"Yes!"

The bedroom stayed silent for an age and Joe started imagining that his kid brother had finally succumbed to sleep, until Jack dug an elbow in his side.

"I must be a homosexual, Joe," whispered Jack sadly. "I like boys better than girls. I only like Alice Raine out of all the girls I know."

Joe persevered, "More than that, Jack. They want to marry each other."

There was seconds of stillness and peace as the younger Connelly struggled with the logic.

"Joe," he said eventually, awash with confusion, "you told me only girls have tits and slits?"

"I know that, stupid!"

"So why do ....."

Joe interrupted angrily, "I don't know why!"

"Why are you shouting, Joe? I only asked!"

"I'm sorry, Jack. I don't know why a man would want to live with another man."

"Joe, if they don't have slits, where do the babies come out of?"

"Christ! They can't have babies!"

"They just want to live together?"

"Yes!"

"And they don't want to hurt anyone?"

"Of course not!"

"Why don't people like homosexuals, Joe," asked Jack, "especially if they don't want to hurt anyone?"

It was Joe's turn to ponder, never had to think about it before, didn't really have an answer, "Don't know, Jack, only know it frightens some people enough to hate them."

Joe studied for a moment, trying to understand the relevance of Elmore's twisted tale, tried to fathom out the logic of the man. Nodded to himself and thought, *That's why he did what he did!*

Joe nudged his kid brother, "The man in the graveyard, the one called Elmore. He killed his brother and his friend but the police caught him and took him back to hospital."

"Joe, you once told me that if you killed someone then you had to be hanged or cooked in an electric-chair?"

"Hanged in this country, shot or electrocuted in America."

"So why don't they hang Elmore?"

"Because he's cuckoo, mad as a hatter, can't kill people like that!"

"Poor Elmore," said Jack, "he'll never be able to see his dad's grave again."

"I heard Ma talking downstairs. She was talking to Rosie Bott about Elmore being a millionaire."

"He'll have the finest rooms in the hospital, Joe, won't he, the biggest bed! All that money!"

Joe muttered, "Shut up, Jack, stupid"

**

Annie Goodrich, matriarch for the night as Vera took a back-seat and sat on the settee next to Adam Connelly, was holding council. Accepted her second cigarette from Adam, found the Swan Vestas and lit up, sucked greedily until she was sure the cigarette was smoking, "Thanks, Adam, pet, appreciated. All this business has got my head cabbaged and cut." Annie looked across the room, gestured to Rosie, "You want the matches, love?" The girl nodded and Annie flicked them expertly across the smoke-filled room. The old woman continued the casual, continuous interrogation, "So, you walked into the bedroom and Evelyn Stoker and Alvin Brown were naked, and one straddled the other?"

Rosie Bott took a deep swig of the *Double Maxim* stout, courtesy of Adam Connelly, man generous to a fault, bought a crate of beer for the others, himself included, and a bottle of *Gordon's* Gin and a small bottle of tonic water for Annie Goodrich.

"On my mother's life, Mrs Goodrich," replied the younger woman, toyed with the cigarette and glanced at the captivated woman. She was starting to enjoy the role of local celebrity, twice interviewed by the *Look North* news team, yesterday a ten minute slot on the *Home Service* programme. "Naked as the day they were born, poor Evelyn underneath, legs as wide as Wilma White's on a weekend (Wilma was the village prostitute, sixty if she was a day and still pulling in the punters, old and young) and holding on to Alvin like a man possessed, only his poor hands were tied with wire flex. Staring at me too! Honest to God, Evelyn looking right through me! I never knew, never had an inkling that Evelyn was, you know, queer. Alvin Brown always bought my groceries at the co-op. Never in a month of Sundays did I think he had turned that way. I mean, you really can't tell, can you?" Rosie took a long drink, wiped the wetness from her lips and shook her head morosely.

"Our Vera always knew," confided Annie, nodding diligently at her daughter, "had everybody fooled, didn't you?"

"Good friends Ma," replied Vera as she kicked off her slippers, eased herself on to the sofa and snuggled up to Adam.

Rosie said to Annie Goodrich, "Used to see Vera walking out with Alvin and I thought they made a perfect couple. Goes to show you never can tell with these devious beggars."

"Rosie," chided Vera, "Alvin never hid the fact from me. He was a lovely man and he didn't deserve what he got!"

Annie said whimsically, "And to think Evelyn used to flirt with me. Bought my drinks, compliments all night long." Glanced at the smiling, head-shaking Vera, "What, what have I said wrong?"

Adam said, "Jake Archer was comin' out of Equie's coffee-bar, next to the solicitors that day. On the way to work, day-shift, forgot his fags and called in Equie's because they sell ...."

Vera interjected, grinned, "Why beat round the bush, Adam, we've got all night. You want to tell us what Jake was wearing, what he had for breakfast ..."

"Cheeky bitch!" replied Adam Connelly, chortling softly. He scrunched fingers through her thick hair and continued, "Elmore was apparently standin' in the middle of the road. Stopped all the traffic, out of his head, singin' like his life depended on it. Even when the police grabbed him he kept on singin'. Jake said when the police-car drove away Elmore was still on a high!"

"Poor Elmore," said Vera. She leaned to the floor and grabbed her drink, "Always knew he'd had a hard paper-round."

"Doesn't justify what he done," replied Annie. She glanced again at Rosie Bott. "Bet there was blood by the bucketful, Rose?"

"Ma," interjected Vera, "you enjoying this?"

"No, not for a minute," she replied, annoyed that anyone, especially her own daughter, could think of such a thing. "Curious is all, our Vera!"

"Blood everywhere," said Rosie Bott, "floors walls, ceilings!" She glanced at all those present, "Used his fingers to write on the walls. Used blood instead of ink!"

"Like the diary, Ma!"

"What did he write, Rosie?"

"You wouldn't believe it," said Rosie, "because it didn't make sense. Above the bed he'd scrawled, *Oh Mein Papa*, you know, that trumpeter?"

Adam offered, "Eddie Calvert!"

Rosie continued, "Above the dressing-table he'd written, *No other love* ..."

Vera nodded, "Ronnie Hilton!"

"Next to the side window, Elmore wrote, *It's almost tomorrow*."

"That was an American group who sang that," offered, Adam, "I'm almost certain."

305

Annie Goodrich pouted, her hands clamped over her shocked features, "It's like something out of an Alfred Hitchcock film, our Vera!"

The room was silent as the group tried to find reason and logic behind the messages.

Vera Connelly started, "*Oh Mein Papa* has to be connected to his father. Maybe telling everyone he had killed for him?"

"The *Daily Mirror* said as much," answered Adam. "They quoted sources saying that Elmore's biological father was his grandfather, said the man who reared him, Evelyn's father, abused and neglected him!"

"Bloody hell!" said Annie as she poured herself a stiff gin. "I never read that?"

"Today's paper," replied Adam. "The *Mirror* is a good read."

Rosie Bott, amateur detective offered, "*No other love* could be Elmore highlighting Evelyn's dalliance with Alvin Brown?"

"Has to be," Annie sniggered, the alcohol relaxing her, "although *Forbidden Love* would have been a better title!"

"*It's almost tomorrow,*" asked Adam, "What do you think?"

Vera said matter-of-fact, "Elmore reminding himself that the game was almost up. Tomorrow he knew he'd be facing the consequences?"

"Aren't we the clever-clogs, regular Miss Marples," said Annie, wondered if she could persuade Adam to walk to the club and buy her another bottle. Smacked her lips loudly and said, "Can't beat Gordon's gin for taste, only trouble is the bottles." Smiled broadly and glanced too long at Adam Connelly, "They're far too small!"

**

Jack whispered, "I can't sleep, Joe,"

"Aren't you tired?"

"I'm frightened, Joe, all the talk about that man scares me."

Silence invaded the darkened and gloomy bedroom, each boy preoccupied with his own thoughts.

"Joe!"

"What now!"

Jack whispered, "I like Adam, do you?"

Joe said grudgingly, "He's okay, suppose."

"Why, do you think he likes us, Joe?"

"Who says he likes us?"

"He keeps buying us presents."

Joe said sarcastically, "Means nothing."

"But he needn't buy us anything."

Joe, wise beyond his years said, "There's a reason, Jack."

"Why for?"

"He likes Ma. Ma likes us. Adam buys us stuff and keeps on the good side of Ma."

"Joe."

"Go to sleep, will you!"

"Will Ma marry Adam; will Adam be our new Dad?"

"Hope not!"

"Why?"

"Because we've already got a Dad, that's why!"

"I don't think our Dad loves us any more, Joe."

Joe Connelly didn't answer, thought maybe his kid brother was right for once.

"Joe, will you tell me a story?"

"What kind of story?"

"From the pictures, Joe," begged the kid, "something from the pictures."

"Romans and slaves, okay?" *Spartacus* in mind, "or Norsemen and slaves," *The Vikings*.

Kirk the crew-cut Viking and Tony from the Bronx.

Midway and Jack was involved with the storyline, a little hazy with the complicated plot, he nevertheless was enthralled with the rallying call to loyalty. First Joe, *'I'm Spartacus,'* then Jack, *'I'm Spartacus!'* Twenty minutes later and Joe had almost finished the adventure story and was describing the awful climax to the tale of rebellion by the slave Spartacus with the hundreds of crucified bodies along the road to Rome.

"A lesson to be learned, Jack, never pick on someone who's bigger and stronger!'

Jack, drifting until crucifixion was mentioned, was now wide awake and much confused, "Thought only Jesus was put on the cross, Joe," remembered Good Friday, added quickly, "and one either side of him?"

"Naw, Jack, that's how everybody was killed in the olden days!"

Jack turned on his back, the bed warm and comfortable now, said, "Thought it was a special death for Jesus?"

"Naw, everybody," replied Joe, "Sometimes they stuck the cross in upside down!"

"By mistake, Joe?"

"On purpose."

Long studious seconds past before Jack asked, "But all the blood will go to your head?"

"Headache would be the last of their worries, Jack," said the older brother, knowledgeable in all gruesome activities. "Sometimes it took days or weeks to die!"

"Why, Joe? Don't they just go to sleep when the Lord comes down?"

"Daft sod!"

"So it hurts them?"

"Of course, stupid! Jesus was a fairy-tale, he would have been nailed on the cross for days, either bled to death, or gone mad because he had no water," Joe turned and looked at his baby brother whose eyes were tightly closed. He continued with the awful tales of destruction and death,

"But if you weren't crucified you could have been stoned or strung-up!"

"Nailed on the cross?" gasped Jack, eyes opened momentarily, "Jesus wasn't tied to the cross with a rope!"

"Big metal spikes through his ankles and wrists!"

Silence as the pair imaged the horror, only the rain battering at the window disturbed the silence.

Jack whispered, "I don't think I'll be able to sleep, Joe, think I'll have nightmares. Will you tell me another story, don't mind if it's a short story."

"I'm tired, Jack."

"Please!"

"No!"

"Please!"

"Have I told you the one where the three cowboys find a baby in the desert, after they robbed a bank?"

The Three Godfathers!

Jack asked, "Is it a happy story?"

"Of course it's a happy story. It's got John Wayne as one of the Three Wise Men, finds a baby and tries to get to Jerusalem!"

"You said it's a cowboy story?"

"It is, in the desert, in America, and he's like one of the Three Wise Men! Right?"

Seconds of silence as the younger boy struggled with the analogy, John Wayne on a camel or a donkey, carrying gifts, the image surreal and fantastic, made him want to go to sleep.

"What has John Wayne got to offer to baby Jesus," asked a curious Jack, fighting fatigue, "was it gold from Frank wrapped in fur?"

"What?"

Jack persevered and asked again, "The presents from the Three Wise Cowboys, what were they, and who played Frank with the golden fur?"

309

"That's it," muttered a weary Joe Connelly, "I'm going sleep!"

"Why, Joe?" asked the kid brother, "what have I said?"

**